To ou

Our best dinner
a long while, best
conversation & insights
Hope you enjoy!

Paula V.

MONEY MATTERS

THE NOVEL

PAULA M. VANDERHORST

Money Matters

© Paula M. Vanderhorst

Print ISBN: 978-1-09838-105-9

eBook ISBN: 978-1-09838-106-6

DEDICATION

This book is dedicated to the best dividends I have ever received: Benjamin, Jessie and Christopher

…and of course, my pilot, John

MONEY MATTERS

PROLOGUE: POWERLESS

Maggie scanned her phone a third time and, exasperated, reached into her bag for a credit card. *Great,* she thought, *now even my app isn't working.* Although she was late already, she had stopped to treat herself to a latte since there had been so many other minor irritations today—a missed delivery, delayed dry cleaning, a light drizzle. She told herself she deserved it. As she handed her card to the server she glanced at her watch and sighed again. Someone else was likely to be shown in ahead of her if she didn't hustle. The barista swiped her card, frowned, and tried again.

The young woman looked up with an apologetic smile and said, "It won't go through. Do you have another?"

Maggie breathed slowly, trying to hide the irritation which had inexplicably shadowed her all morning. She smiled and showed the barista the barcode in her app. She then tried to scan it, with no luck. Maggie's second and third credit cards also failed. Theatrically, she scraped the bottom of her Hermes bag looking for change she knew was not there. She smiled apologetically, shrugged to imply "out of luck" and turned to leave. This prompted the barista to generously call out to Maggie and hand her the order anyway. She said Maggie could make it up next time, which they both knew would never happen.

With just a head nod and the briefest of smiles, Maggie then slid out the back entrance. In a moment, she had already forgotten the kindness. She was frequently ceded these minor graces because she was well dressed, attractive, and lived in a world where wealth was subtly rewarded. She took them for granted. Checking her watch again, she almost ran down the street to her salon.

She was right; someone else had been let in ahead of her. This would mean at least a ten-minute wait until her brow touch-up. As she went to sit down with her coffee, the receptionist suggested she settle her tab prior to going in for the appointment. Maggie returned to the desk and without thinking, again handed over her credit card. When it was denied, Maggie was at a loss.

She knew better than to expect favors from this salon. Maggie apologized and excused herself to the receptionist saying she would be back in a moment, that she would get cash. She then headed to her bank's ATM. There she fed her cash card in, only to find the machine simply kept it. The display offered no explanation and after uselessly pushing a few buttons, Maggie stamped her foot and went into the bank to retrieve it. Her morning frustrations were multiplying.

A handsome young teller went to recover her card. When he returned, he asked her to take a seat, as the bank manager would need to speak with her. While Maggie waited, she tried to call her husband on the phone. Neal might know what was going on. He was supposed to have returned from a business trip last night, but it was not unusual for him to change his plans or be late getting home. In fact, he might have come home after she was in bed and then left before she got up. They had agreed he would use the guest room when he came in late, as she was a light sleeper. She had not thought to check before leaving the house.

She tried to remember when he had last called in—was it Tuesday night, and this was Thursday? Where did he say he was? They had been married so long and his trips were so frequent that she rarely paid attention anymore. Their calls were little more than a five-minute check in anyway. She didn't really understand what he was doing on these trips; she just knew that they paid very well. Investments for other people was the gist of it. She got his voicemail and left him an urgent message to call her as soon as he could.

Maggie hated when there were problems with her cards. It only happened occasionally, usually because Neal had lost one on a trip and failed to tell her he had cancelled it. He was very good with money and handled all their personal finances. After he had started his own successful investment firm, the money just flowed. She had quit paying attention after the mortgages were paid off, the kids finished their private educations, and the renovations were done. Money seemed unlimited to Maggie. She never gave it a thought.

As she waited for the bank manager, she realized she was a little embarrassed. She didn't know anything about the accounts, really. She only glanced at her balance once in a while. It was always in the thousands, so she really didn't even register how much there was. She rarely even went into the bank and only wrote the occasional check. She vaguely remembered that there were tellers and bank managers. She looked around and realized the bank was much smaller than she remembered. She only saw two desks and a single teller. *When had banks gotten so small?* she wondered.

Suddenly, a woman appeared. She smiled and held out her hand.

"Hello. I am Doris Leitner, the bank manager. Would you mind coming into my office so we can chat a little more privately?" Maggie rose and juggled her coffee to shake hands. She introduced herself and explained that her problem was actually more than just a card being swallowed by the machine.

"I am sure we can help. Right this way." Doris said, and they walked over to a small, glass cubicle with a view of the street beyond. "Have a seat, please. I have your card."

Maggie sat and sipped her coffee while the woman began to input numbers on her keyboard. Maggie watched her as she clearly passed through various screens. She then turned to Maggie, her mouth tight and her eyes questioning.

"May I have some ID please?" Maggie handed over her driver's license. The woman studied it, then gave it back. "I am afraid that account is overdrawn, Mrs. Mueller. There is no cash available."

"No cash? What do you mean?" Maggie asked, bewildered. "I know we have a variety of accounts with you."

"There is no overdraft protection on this particular account."

"Overdraft protection?" Maggie asked. The term rang a bell, but she was not sure what it meant.

"Overdraft protection is when you designate another account, usually a savings account, to draw money from if you accidently write a check or withdraw more money than the account has in it. This account is joint—that is, it has both your and your husband's names on it. I do not see any account in your name alone. There is no overdraft protection set up for the joint account using any of his accounts."

Doris continued, "I do see there is a monthly scheduled deposit of five thousand dollars that comes from one of your husband's accounts, but it has not posted for a while. There is simply no cash in the joint account at all. As I said, the balance is actually negative. What was the balance last time you checked?" She asked this while looking at Maggie with a peculiar interest.

Maggie did not want to admit she did not know. She was at a loss. She avoided the question and said, "There must be some sort of problem. I have tried to contact my husband but haven't had a chance to speak with him yet. He knows all of the bank details. We have been banking with you for years. We have multiple accounts. Is there any way I can get cash? I have an appointment I need to pay for."

She had a sudden inspiration and reached into her wallet. She pulled out the credit card that had the bank's logo on it. "Can I get a cash advance on this?" Maggie had done this in Mexico last winter, when her credit cards had not been accepted at a local cafe. She handed the card over to the woman, who took it gently and again entered some numbers. This time she looked a little more sympathetic as she said, "This card has been cancelled, I'm afraid. There is a negative balance on it as well. This is news to you?"

"Yes," Maggie said, not understanding what was going on. "My husband handles all our money. He has been travelling, and I have not been able to reach him. Clearly there is something wrong. I guess I will have to wait until I speak with him. Unless..." she said hopefully, "you can suggest anything else?"

"I can't really. All the accounts, except the joint bank account your cash card is associated with, are in your husband's name. Not yours. I am afraid I cannot discuss anything with you regarding them. The accounts are his and his alone, in both the eyes of the bank and the law." She hesitated a moment, then added gently, "I think it is very important, Mrs. Mueller, even urgent, that you have a discussion with your husband about this as soon as possible."

Something about Doris Leitner's tone frightened Maggie. She hesitated, then gathered her things, mumbled a thanks and—forgetting her coffee—left. Her morning's irritations had dissolved, and her appointment was forgotten. She headed for her Lexus, oblivious to the now sparkling sunshine the drizzle had left behind. Maggie hadn't realized all the bank accounts were *only* in Neal's name. It was odd, she had just never thought to check. It stuck her now that she was helpless, no *powerless*, when it came to their finances. That left her feeling uneasy, *very uneasy*.

The bank manager gently swiveled in her chair to watch Maggie make her way across the street. She shook her head. As she stepped out from around her desk to dispose of Maggie's unfinished coffee, a teller eagerly sidled up to her.

"Did you tell her?" he asked, hoping for gossip.

"No," the manager said, with a firm shake of her head. "She'll know soon enough. It always gets me. I will never, *ever* understand why women allow themselves to simply drift into these disasters."

TABLE OF CONTENTS

CHAPTER 1:
CREDIT IS NOT JUST ABOUT CARDS

Maggie's home was a cream-colored colonial set back on a private road. As soon as she was inside, she went up and checked the guest room. The made-up bed told her that Neal, who never made beds, had not come home after all. She was worried. She called his phone again and then his office, but both phones only rang.

If only Neal used the Find My Friends app which they had insisted the children use. Maggie remembered how he had stiffened when she asked him to turn his location on. His excuses for not doing so had always been weak but it had never occurred to Maggie to insist.

She went back downstairs, passing the bedrooms of her three grown children, still full of childish bits and pieces. Now that they were grown and on their own, the rooms always felt empty to her. She could not remember the last time they had all been at the house together. She texted each of them separately, asking if they had heard from Dad, but she knew it would be a while before she heard back. Regardless, she was not optimistic; Neal rarely contacted the kids on his own. Sadly, the children seemed to return Neal's disinterest. She had put this down to his general absence in their lives while they were growing up.

Maggie was at a loss. She went into Neal's home office to see if there was a calendar to check or something else to indicate where he was or where he was staying. She knew it was probably futile—he kept everything on his phone now, or the two computers he always traveled with. His desk drawers and file cabinets were locked due to client confidentiality. He would not even let the housekeeper clean his office. Maggie knew that his city office was his hub. This home office was only a minor satellite.

She doubted she would find anything that would help her. She moved around the large, mahogany desk with its embossed leather inset and sat in Neal's over-sized desk chair to think. Oddly, she noticed that the middle desk drawer was just slightly ajar. She pulled it open and was surprised to find it empty—totally empty. Not a pen, pencil, or even a loose paper clip. Everything had been cleared out.

Her uneasiness now progressed to anxiety. She went back upstairs and checked his walk-in closet. It was massive, almost a room of its own. It mirrored hers on the other side of their master bathroom. Everything was neatly displayed on matching hangers with custom shelves finished in a deep walnut. A granite-topped island at its center had drawers filled with neatly stacked shirts and sweaters. Custom shoe racks floated out at a touch of a button.

His things were there, which unexpectedly relieved her. On closer examination, though, she realized that there was quite a bit missing. Many of his better casual clothes were gone, as were a few pairs of shoes. All of his watches. Had he packed a larger suitcase than usual for this trip? She assumed she would have noticed. Neal always insisted the family travel with carry-on only. Had he put his luggage in his car before leaving so she wouldn't see it? What was going on?

She went to the luggage closet. *Yes*, she thought soberly, *something is going on*. Two of the larger bags were missing as were quite a few duffels. When had Neal packed all of these? How had she missed him carrying them out of the house? Could he have *left* her? She didn't dismiss it, but it was not Neal's usual style to do things under the radar.

She walked slowly back to the bedroom, sat on the bed and thought about who to call. Most of Neal's friends were from work—she generally did not socialize with any of them, really, and certainly didn't have contact information. Gone was the era of physical address books. Neal kept all his contacts on his phone. He had no family other than her and the kids.

She realized she would have to try to find Neal's business partners through the internet. She had only ever met a few of them on rare occasions. They were all so similar to Neal. Same expensive suits and shoes, same designer glasses, same expensive watches. They always seemed to talk blandly to her about "destination" vacations or new acquisitions. The women they brought along—their second or occasionally third wives—were uniform in their sleek, upscale trappings. Only their hairstyles and colors seemed to vary.

She wondered if this could all just wait until dinner time. She chided herself that she was just being an alarmist, and this was all overblown. There would be an explanation for the bank issues. Neal would just walk through the front door, expecting dinner, and laugh at her earlier predicament. She turned around and headed to the kitchen. She did not generally drink alone, but there was a half-finished bottle of wine in the fridge. She needed something to settle herself while she worked this out.

As she poured, she thought about this particular shortcoming of theirs. Neither she nor Neal had any close friends. Neal didn't have any additional family; Maggie's father had passed years ago, and her mother's awareness was so far gone she could not even speak anymore. There was simply no one for her to call in a situation like this.

She glanced at her wine glass and noticed it was cloudy. She returned to the breakfront and checked the other glasses. Soon she was pulling glasses out and preparing to hand wash them all, which quickly escalated into cleaning out the entire breakfront. It was mindless work that gave her time to think.

Maggie had two or three women she kept in touch with from college. It was lucky if she spoke to them once a year, and only when they called her. Over the years she had made no close friends through her children's school. She had never been good at forming adult friendships. Maybe she had just never learned how.

It wasn't for lack of trying. Maggie had tried to deepen friendships over the years, but she knew she lacked the gift of connecting with people. She had never been good at it, always landing in awkward, one-sided conversations about topics she wasn't interested in. She had always envied the women who travelled in packs and seemed to be closely involved in one another's lives, but she was simply too uncomfortable to share the details of her life with other people. Frankly, she could not see the point. Neal, too, shared that sentiment. He always laughingly referred to Maggie as his "best and only friend." Maggie often wondered if the fact they were both only children had something to do with their inability to connect with people.

When her children were small, she had actively tried to make more friends, mostly for their sake. Parents she had met through the children's private schools never interested Neal. He dismissed most of them as posers who had inherited and not worked for their money. The mothers that worked full time were the women who piqued Maggie's interest. They seemed to have more interesting lives. However, working also meant they had little time for other things, especially things that involved stay-at-home mothers. Or at least that was the impression they gave off as they hurried off to somewhere Maggie always assumed was more important.

Neal did make exceptions and sometimes attempted to make friends with people who had money to invest. If he was successful, these people were co-opted into Neal's client circle and the relationships were lost to Maggie. It was as if the couple and Neal were speaking a foreign language. Dinners with them were painful. Maggie tried to find something other than the children and their schools to talk about, but there were many awkward silences. Meals were always quickly wrapped up. No dessert.

Neal could not understand her difficulty with these sorts of conversations. "You were raised with money. Don't you have things in common with these people?" Neal wondered to her aloud.

He had grown up poor, as he frequently reminded her and the children. He seemed to believe that being wealthy gave an individual magic entry to certain circles. He thought Maggie should have the key. Before they were married, he had worked with Maggie's father at his private bank for a time. He had even met her mother before Maggie. He talked reverently about her mother's gift with people. Eventually, grudgingly, he accepted Maggie's inadequacy in this regard. His disappointment in Maggie's social skills was one of many things Maggie ignored in their relationship.

She finished the glassware and now found herself drinking alone in her perfectly appointed kitchen. She had nothing to do and nowhere to go. She had planned an early evening at the Museum of Fine Arts. She volunteered as a docent a couple days a week and got special access to members' reception. She enjoyed seeing the new exhibits before they opened to the general public; smaller crowds and more time to sit and take things in. But her brows had not been done and her nails were chipped and, honestly, she could not see the point. Something major was going on, she could feel it—and she needed to work out what it was.

She remembered the irritation that had been nagging her that morning. Had Neal said something when he left or when they talked on the phone that had somehow set her radar off? She made two more unanswered calls to his phone and then his office. She finally went to her laptop and began searching. She needed to find someone she could talk to who could help her figure this out.

She started with Ocean Capital's website, this was the name of Neal's company. She was surprised how little information the site actually had on it. There were stock photos that represented the types of companies and industries they invested in and a vague description of their business which fit with what she knew about the company. There were, of course, no names or details about specific clients. Maggie knew Neal's company guaranteed confidentiality and prided itself on its security. She and the children had been warned to never discuss Neal's trips or share any information about his deals with friends or schoolmates. Neal had explained that stock prices could soar or plunge, based on deals he was involved in.

Partners' photos were not shown nor were they even named on the site. Lower down on the page the site listed the regions Neal's firm was active in including countries in Eastern Europe, South America, and the Middle East. Under the contact details, however, there was nothing but the general number and an email. The email generated an automated response that someone from Ocean Capital would "get back to her" and the phone just rang. It was frustrating.

Neal did not have a personal assistant. All the partners at the firm seemed to manage on their own. She knew there was a pool of women there who helped out with schedules and a group of analysts, but no specific names. Neal frequently mentioned these people but always just their first names, and they were always changing. Nothing else to go on. She now wished she had taken more of an interest.

She then methodically scrolled through Facebook pages of people who shared the names of people she vaguely remembered meeting at functions, not sure if the spelling of the last names were correct or if these were even the right people. She searched photos and saw faces that could have been familiar but she was not good with faces either, so she was not sure. She could only see a fraction of what was on their sites due to privacy settings. One profile she checked had over a thousand "friends." Maggie rolled her eyes at the profile and at Facebook itself. She had never seen the point of so many empty connections. She tried LinkedIn, setting up a fake profile so she could access the site. She did not find Neal or any of the connections she recognized. The company was not even listed. Neal must not use it she decided. This surprised her because she thought it was a popular business networking tool.

Hours later, after many online distractions, Maggie was still without phone numbers or any answers. By the time she signed off, she had heard from all three of her children. All had checked in with short texts or emojis that meant they hadn't heard from Dad. Isobel had sent the longest response with a quick, "Love you, miss you, talk soon." Maggie knew that they would not actually "talk soon." She had a weekly FaceTime check-in with each of them on Sunday that rarely lasted more than five minutes. It was not unusual to skip a weekend or go a few weeks without hearing from one of them. She texted back a smiling emoji, the only one she ever used, and told them she loved them.

As she closed her laptop and thought about her kids, a sudden tsunami of despair caught her. She realized she really, really did love them, very deeply. Unexpected tears formed in her eyes, but the emotion that had come onto her unbidden passed as quickly as it had come. Within a minute, she was fine and in control. "What is going on with me?" she chastised herself. The kids were fine. Neal was fine. The situation would be fine. Breathing deeply, she willed herself to calm. Control was everything to Maggie.

Like counting beads on a rosary, she recapped the children's lives. Her oldest son, Ethan, was a senior analyst at a well-known investment firm and always seemed to be either working or at the gym. He had a wonderful, patient girlfriend, Hannah, who just smiled at his excesses and his chronic forgetfulness. Maggie hoped he didn't let her go. It would be nice to have a wedding to look forward to.

Her second child, Isobel or Izzy, was the family beauty and worked for a large consumer products firm. She wasn't paid well but her crazy, youth-targeted promotions meant lots of travel, entertainment events, and odd hours. She lived with a pack of roommates at the moment but was saving every penny, already looking at buying her first bit of real estate.

Her youngest, Charlotte, whom they all called Charlie, was more grounded than most adults Maggie knew. She was all about saving the world and had joined the Peace Corps right out of college. She was working now in Guatemala, using her gifts with languages and people. She was a gentle soul and always reminded Maggie of her mother. She seemed to be the happiest and most fulfilled of the three. Maggie surprised herself when she realized she envied Charlie's life the most.

Despite the fact they were all working, all three were perpetually short on cash. Their money management skills seemed lacking. She had always been generous with them, lending credit card numbers to clear up debts, and pay for unexpected repairs. She'd even donated huge sums for Charlie's many causes. She had the money and was happy to help. She supposed the kids had never questioned the flow of money in their parents' lives either.

She faltered in her happy recall. She looked at the texts from them on her phone and she wished she had a more personal connection with her kids. She would like to be able to call one of them and tell them she was worried. Talk about the missing suitcases, the cancelled cards. But this was not something Maggie could talk to her children about. Sometimes just their regular phone calls felt strained. She imagined breezily talking with them about who they were dating or how they liked their jobs. Or even asking whether they were happy in life, but all that felt too intrusive to her. Her actual conversations with her kids were frequently as flat as the ones she had with Neal.

Maggie checked the time and was startled to see it was now well after eight o'clock at night. There had been no Neal, no call, no contact. The house was as silent as usual, the only sound the hum of appliances and the occasional unspecified click or crack. It was a large house and the soft noises never worried her. She looked from her seat in the kitchen, through the large French doors, into the darkening backyard gardens. She had taken a Master Gardener course years ago when the children were small; twenty years of effort had resulted in a magnificent landscape. There were rose and meadow gardens, numerous vegetable beds, beehives, a small orchard, and even a formal garden—over an acre in total—broken up with sculptures from trips to international garden shows. Her favorite section was her white "night" garden that almost glowed as it became dark. She sighed at its beauty. Recently though, gardening had become stale to her. She still harvested bouquets for the kitchen table and her bedside, but mostly out of habit now. She rarely even changed the water before she simply threw them out.

She closed her computer and got up. The warm late summer night air beckoned her for a moment. Other nights, she might have taken a book out to her cozy reading nook in the white garden. A lounge sat under a moon flower arbor she planted every year. She loved to be out there this time of year, reading as the flowers unfolded and spread their intoxicating night perfume. She had lost many serene hours there, sometimes closing her eyes and drifting off to sleep before the chill woke her and sent her inside to bed. She considered the garden for a few moments but turned away.

She had not eaten but the wine seemed to be enough. She washed her glass and put it away, wiped down the already spotless counters, then headed up to bed.

If Neal was not back in the morning, she resolved to call the police and ask them what to do. They would surely have an idea on a way to contact him.

Her bedtime routine took time. She moisturized and then always set her shoulder-length hair in a few soft pin curls (looking a bit like a starlet from the forties, she always thought). She critically faced herself in her dressing room mirror.

Maggie carried a few more pounds than she used to, probably too many, but the extra weight had kept her skin mostly clear of wrinkles. Age spots had been handled by her dermatologist's hydroquinone cream. She had just turned fifty, but she knew she was still considered attractive, with her patrician features, unusual gray-green eyes, and full lips that would probably never need Botox injections.

She pursed her lips. But, then again…

She *had* consulted a plastic surgeon a few weeks ago about a couple of touch-ups she felt she was going to have to do—the chin tuck, the arm wattles, eventually the breast uplift. He'd called his plan the "Mommy Makeover." She resisted though, something felt off about it.

It was her mother's genes who had gifted her with her fairness—even now, in her eighties and bedridden, her mom was still beautiful. While she was grateful, Maggie worried she might also have inherited the more sinister genes related to Alzheimer's. It had devastated her mother's life. She had faded in her late fifties and was lost to Maggie and her father by her mid-sixties. Now, her heart continued to beat, despite a mind that had all but shut down.

As Maggie settled into bed, she tried one more call to Neal then pulled out a book from one of the numerous piles that lined her side of the bed. She started first with a new novel by one of her favorite authors. Dissatisfied, she tried a crime novel, then a biography. Finally, she got out of bed and returned with a tattered copy of *The Secret Garden*. It was a childhood favorite and like comfort food, it smoothed and distracted her.

After what seemed like moments, she realized she had again finished the book. She looked at her phone and realized it was now well after one. Her stomach growled as she turned off the light. She reached for her bedside pills. She rarely slept well naturally, even when she was bone tired, but with the pills she was soon in a deep, dreamless sleep.

She woke groggily to an insistently ringing doorbell. It was just barely past sunrise. She shook off sleep and slipped out of bed, pulling out pin curls as she went. She was at the top of the stairs when she was startled by crack of breaking wood. *The front door?* she wondered in panic. She stepped back, crouching behind the bannister. Below her, she saw armed men with FBI jackets swarming into the house. Her heart raced at the sight but at least they weren't armed thugs.

As her bedroom was down the hall, she could easily get back there unseen. Should she call out? Hide? Would they come upstairs? She decided she wanted to get dressed before meeting the FBI. She backed up, turned and slipped back to her bedroom and locked the door. She went into her en suite, throwing on the workout clothes hanging on the bathroom's back door. She took a cold face cloth across her face and pulled back her hair into a ponytail. She looked like she was heading out for a workout. That would do. As she returned to the bedroom, she looked at her phone—it was only 5:30 a.m. No wonder she was groggy.

She breathed deeply and opened the bedroom door. She was met with startled stares of two men. They called out to someone who was downstairs in Neal's office. He came out, facing her as she was escorted downstairs. His look made a quick assessment, and she knew he was holding his judgment about her. He reached out his hand as she came slowly down to meet him. He was a handsome, muscular man. He introduced himself as Supervisory Special Agent Judge Munoz.

"Judge?" She raised her eyebrows quizzically. "Easier for people than the Spanish name," he offered simply. She introduced herself and looked meaningfully at the broken lock on the front door. "Couldn't give a girl a chance to make herself presentable? I was fond of that door," Maggie said with a practiced smile.

Maggie instinctively knew that she would not get much help from this man if she was indignant or aggressive, and she needed to stall for time. The flirting was almost a reflex for her.

Agent Munoz looked a little sheepish. "We had reason to believe that evidence might be at risk. We did not expect there would be anyone in the house. I am sorry about the door."

"If you didn't think anyone was home, how was the evidence going to destroy itself?" she asked lightly. Munoz eyes narrowed a bit, it was a quick-witted retort. Maggie re-set and made her tone a little more neutral. "Do you mind telling me what is going on? Do you even have the right house? We are not exactly mafia, you know."

"Yes, ma'am. Again, sorry about the door, but we do know this is the right house. We have a warrant." He held out a set of folded papers. "We are actually interested in speaking with your husband. Is he home?"

Maggie's gut clenched; they were after Neal. She struggled to keep her tone light. "No, travelling. In fact, I have not been able to reach my husband for a couple days. Is he OK? Do you know where he is?"

"We would like to know the answers to those questions as well, ma'am. We are in the process of investigating his firm and have not been able to reach him. His former partners have said they have not worked with him for over two years. Do you know any of the principles at his current company? Do you have any information that could help us locate either them or your husband?"

Maggie considered her answer. This was all too much to process. Neal's firm was being investigated by the FBI? They knew Neal was missing and did not expect to find him at home? Perhaps that explained no one answering the phones at his office yesterday. It sounded serious. Wait, Neal's *former* partners? She could not think fast enough, still too groggy from last night's pill.

She replied carefully, "Not really sure. A lot of what you are saying is news to me. How about I get us both a cup of coffee and we can talk? I am afraid I am not very awake yet."

Munoz hesitated for a moment until he said, "Sure, sounds great."

He nodded to his men as if to say, "carry on," then closely followed her as she went into the kitchen. She opted to use the time-consuming espresso machine rather than the quick Nespresso she typically used. The ritual gave her time to settle herself and work things out in her mind. By the time she handed him his steamed coffee, she was composed and ready to answer questions. She decided she needed to be careful and give the shortest answers she could get away with. No extra information for them until she had a better handle on what was happening.

The agent pulled out a notebook and seemed to read a bit before he began to ask his questions.

"So, your husband is travelling?"

"Yes, he left early Monday morning."

"Where was he headed?"

"Not sure. Twenty years of weekly trips and I have learned there is little value in keeping track. His schedule can change daily. We only really care when he leaves and when he gets back. The 'where' just isn't as important."

"We?"

She sipped her coffee. "The kids and me. I mean when the kids were living at home."

Munoz did not follow up with any questions about the children, so Maggie relaxed a little. It appeared they were not going to be involved. Munoz then followed up with, "So, you have no idea where he is? When did you say you last saw him?"

"I said goodbye to him Monday morning. I was still in bed when he left, so it was very early. I think it was Tuesday night that I spoke to him on the phone; it was only a check-in really. I think he mentioned something about the weather being bad and that his flight was late. For some reason I think he was in Chicago, transiting, but I don't know that for a fact."

"Hmm." Munoz paused for a moment, and then said, "Mrs. Mueller, do you know what we are here for?"

"No clue."

"We are looking for paperwork related to his firm. Financial statements of any kind or any financial instruments. Is there a large amount of cash or any other major assets related to the firm kept here at the house? Is there a safe perhaps?"

"I think everything related to his company is kept in his office in the city. There is no safe in the house, and...what exactly are 'financial instruments?'"

"Financial instruments are real or virtual documents which serve as legal agreements involving any kind of monetary value. Things like securities, bonds, or deposit certificates. Bitcoin paperwork. We are also interested in any large sums of cash on hand, or even gold."

"Gosh, cash? We don't use cash, and the only gold I have is my jewelry. What are 'deposit certificates?'"

"Not to worry ma'am. Where are your personal bank statements, credit card receipts, and tax returns? They are specified in the warrant."

"Neal handles every aspect of our financial lives. I have never even seen a statement. I simply sign the tax returns once a year and that is about it." Maggie felt the sense of powerlessness from yesterday creep back. How could she be so clueless about their money? "All my receipts are there." She pointed to a small basket she kept in the kitchen. Neal collected these periodically and she had assumed they simply disappeared into files. She noticed the basket was empty.

"Mrs. Mueller, we have tried the files and desk drawers in the office. They are all empty. Surely you must keep paperwork somewhere. What about your personal documents? Your marriage certificates, life and auto insurance policies, birth certificates? Do you have safety deposit boxes?"

Maggie was visibly startled to hear that the file drawers were empty. She had dusted the Father Day's knickknacks he kept on top of his metal file cabinets just last Friday. She was sure she would have noticed if they had thudded on empty drawers. They must have been full just four days ago. She looked at Munoz and said, "Again, I have always assumed our personal paperwork was in the file drawers. We don't have a safety deposit box; that sounds very old fashioned for someone like my husband."

Agent Munoz eyed her appraisingly. She realized he was trying to determine whether she was acting or was actually oblivious about the paperwork. She subtly changed her body language. She cast her eyes down and arched her back slightly. She played with her wedding and engagement rings in an almost helpless gesture. Transitioning from her normal self to a "helpless female" mode, a trick that disarmed most men. She deliberately did not meet his eyes when she asked with a slight tremble to her voice, "Is Neal in trouble?"

Munoz hesitated and then seemed to make a decision. He sighed and, with a less aggressive tone, said, "Your husband is not being charged with anything; he is just a person of interest. We just need to speak with him. Is there any other office in the house or places where he may have kept documents? Does he have another office in the city, perhaps an apartment there?"

Maggie shook her head. "No other place in the city other than his office."

"Is his car here? Did he say or do anything out of the ordinary before this trip?"

"He took his car to the airport and I didn't notice anything unusual when he left." She told herself that it was the truth. She hadn't noticed anything unusual until last night, when she had discovered the missing bags. This was a detail she held back as she did not want to make it look as if Neal had planned anything at this point.

"Where do you keep your paperwork?" Munoz asked.

"I work here in the kitchen on my laptop. I don't really keep any paperwork, just use my laptop. There are some file drawers in the garden studio, where I paint, which hold drawings and sketches."

Munoz called over one of the men who was opening and closing cabinets in the kitchen. At the senior agent's direction, he went out into the garden. He returned shortly after and shook his head at Munoz. Maggie answered some additional questions about her recent activities, what she knew about Neal's business associates (at least the ones she used to know), and what Neal had been like before he left. Maggie told Munoz that there had been nothing out of the ordinary. He seemed satisfied with her answers and when an agent stuck his head through the kitchen door, he excused himself to go talk with him and with the rest of the agents. He came back a few minutes later and explained they would be leaving.

He made it clear to Maggie that he wanted to be informed if Neal contacted her in any way. He gave her his business card. She, in turn, asked him to call her and let her know if they found Neal or learned where he was. She explained she had considered contacting the police. She did her best to look just helpless and concerned, although her real emotions were closer to alarm. He said she should hold off contacting the police, as they would only direct her back to the FBI. She wanted to ask about the broken door before they left, if they would pay to fix it. She decided against it, as she did not want to seem petty or delay their departure. She decided she could secure it on her own and use the garage door to get in and out for now.

After they left, she was about to phone her handyman when it occurred to her that she would not be able to pay him. Normally she wrote a check, but if she was overdrawn that would be a problem. She went to the door and was relieved to see the dead bolt had not been engaged when they broke it. She turned it now and then wrestled the heavy dresser she used as an entry table against it the door. It was not a perfect solution, but the door would stay closed until she could get it fixed.

Although it was still early, she also thought to call her housekeeper and the landscaper, both of whom would also expect a check this week. She was grateful now that they always insisted on being paid the day they worked. She didn't owe them any back pay. She apologized to them, dodging her housekeeper's concerned questions but explained there was a bit of a family emergency. She told them they would have to hold off coming again until things settled down.

She checked her watch and had a second cup of coffee. She needed to work out how she was going to pay for the door to be fixed—or anything else, for that matter. In the kitchen, she pulled down the biscotti jar where she kept what she called the *kid's kitty*. The FBI had not disturbed it. This was cash that allowed her to hand a hundred dollars to her children on their way out the door in a hopeless attempt to encourage them to visit more frequently. She was grateful now to find over six hundred dollars there. She had never thought having cash in the house would be so useful. It would give her some breathing room. She wondered how much it would cost to fix the door.

She drove confidently to the bank, expecting the six hundred dollars to clear her overdraft and free up her account. She sat in her car and waited with a third cup of coffee until she saw the bank manager from the other day, Doris Leitner, head into work. She quickly followed her in, still in her workout gear. She was anxious to try and get her checkbook and credit cards working.

Maggie was in the seat in front of her before the woman could even put away her bag. If Doris was startled to see Maggie again so soon, she did not show it.

"Good morning, Mrs. Mueller. Did you speak to your husband?"

Maggie was not sure how much to tell her. She started haltingly. "Hmm, not yet. Neal is still travelling. I was wondering if you could check again about our bank accounts. I was going to write a check today and I was worried about what you said about being overdrawn. Perhaps the problem cleared up overnight?"

The woman, who Maggie now realized looked kindlier than she had remembered, sighed. She asked for Maggie's card and after signing in, again checked her screen. "No, the account is still overdrawn, and the credit card is still cancelled. There is no other money available to cover the overdraft."

Maggie's disappointment showed on her face.

"I have some cash," Maggie offered. "How much is the overdraft?"

"$2,380.62"

That much? Maggie's face drained. The six hundred dollars would not put a dent in the overdraft. If she did deposit the money, she would be without any money to live on. And she would *still* owe money. Suddenly, the tension broke. As tears glistened in her eyes, she found herself telling a perfect stranger about her early morning visit from the FBI, her missing husband and how his disappearance had left her without any access to cash. As Maggie finished, she softly asked rhetorically, "What do I do? I feel completely powerless."

The woman across from her softened. She had seen many wives like this before, totally clueless about the financial underpinning of their lives. She smiled at Maggie and said, "I know this must be a shock to you. Especially not having access to your money. Something similar happened to me. I lost my husband when I was a young mother. He died in a rush hour accident. I had let him handle everything and we were too young to bother with a will. It took me a while to get up to speed on the financial issues. It can be daunting at first, but you *will* manage."

"I'm sorry about your husband," Maggie murmured, dazed.

"Thank you." Doris knew the authorities would not let her tell Maggie what she had seen yesterday on her computer screen. Neal Mueller's accounts had been frozen and were part of an active FBI investigation. She knew they would tell Maggie when they thought it was appropriate.

Doris also was aware that huge sums of money had been withdrawn just a week before. The authorities were now watching all his accounts for any sign of activity. She could not let Maggie know that there were actually a few accounts left with substantial balances. Maggie was probably unaware of these accounts and would have no access regardless.

Maggie's current money worries might have been solved if she had simply insisted on joint accounts with her husband. Doris understood there was a place for individual accounts in a marriage. A small account for each partner, funded monthly with an agreed upon amount from a joint account. These individual discretionary accounts often stopped couples from bickering over minor self-indulgent expenditures. Doris, however, liked to see all the important accounts a couple held owned jointly. When one partner has *all* the financial control, it was often problematic. She had seen sudden money withdrawals like this in nasty divorces where one partner was trying to hide assets or hoarding money for a lover. She had also seen situations like her own, where one spouse died unexpectedly, and the grieving spouse found their assets locked until the appropriate documents were processed.

The fact it was the FBI who had frozen Maggie's husband's accounts, not simply the police, suggested to Doris that something more serious was going on. Years of experience with this type of thing told her Maggie was probably just an innocent victim.

She reached over and patted Maggie's hand. "Honey, let's just start at the beginning, shall we? First, do you have any emergency savings you can access? Or family or friends that can help you out in the short term?"

"No savings of my own. My children are just starting out themselves, so I wouldn't think of asking them, nor any friends for that matter," Maggie said a little stiffly.

"Do you have any accounts or credit cards separate from your husband, in your own name?" Doris asked.

"No. Maybe before I was married, but not since. I have never needed one. We share our credit cards."

"Well, let's start there then. Everyone should always have their own account, separate from the family finances. If you give me your driver's license, we can check your credit rating."

"Credit rating?" Maggie said with a frown, unzipping her purse. "I am not sure what that is exactly."

"Oh, you may have heard it referred to as your credit score. It is a number from 300 to 850. Three big agencies collect information about you and put together a score based on your history of paying back debt, like on a car loan or credit card. The bank likes to have customers with credit scores above 740. Of course, today, with all the information about everyone online, there are other companies that gather even more information on you to assess your creditworthiness. I tell everyone to be careful—you would be surprised who is making judgments about you based on what you put online."

"Does everyone have a credit score?" Maggie asked.

"Pretty much. Credit scores tell someone whether you are likely to pay back any money they loan you. It is like a report card on your financial responsibility. We may be able to open you your own, individual bank account. Then we get you your own credit card as a start. A person should start building credit in their own name as soon as they can."

Maggie couldn't remember hearing about credit scores. As Doris checked, Maggie smiled. She was wealthy, which she assumed would mean her score would be excellent.

A moment later, Doris was frowning, "Oh goodness, here's a problem. Your credit score is below 500. That is a pretty poor score. Fortunately, you are only an authorized user on our bank's credit card, not the *primary* so you will not be responsible for the balance owing on it. But there appear to be other credit cards where you were a *joint* holder – so when they weren't paid on time, your credit score suffered. More critically though, it appears you have co-signed on your mortgages. It looks like they have not been paid in quite a while. Do you have a home on the Cape?"

"Yes, our vacation home."

"I am afraid our bank did the financing, and it's in foreclosure. Did you know that?"

Maggie was stunned and shook her head in disbelief. "That is not possible. The mortgage is paid off. It has been paid off for years," she protested.

"No, you have two current mortgages. Perhaps they were paid off, and these are *second* mortgages. You are a co-signer on both. Once you co-sign on anything, it can affect your credit score. You are jointly responsible if the debt goes unpaid."

"Responsible? Not possible. I don't have *any* debts. There are no mortgages," Maggie insisted. "I know for a fact we paid off both mortgages over a decade ago. We took a trip to celebrate. There must be some kind of mistake. Is this poor credit score really a problem though?"

Doris hesitated. The foreclosures were a bigger deal, but maybe starting at credit scores was a better idea. Maggie's first order of business was getting money to live on, and a poor credit score would limit her ability to do this. She could worry about the houses once she had enough money to put dinner on the table.

"Well, a bad credit score means that the bank can't offer you a new credit card in your own name. It is doubtful you will get *any* type of credit card anytime soon. Signing up for a new credit card generally requires a good credit score. Do you have any cash? With cash, I may be able to open you a new bank account just in your name and I can get you a debit card to use."

Maggie was reluctant to hand over the little cash she had. "Is there another option?"

Doris thought for a moment. "We could get you a *secured* credit card. It is different from normal, unsecured credit cards and is actually more similar to a debit card, but helps you build credit. You deposit money with the credit card company, and then you can use the credit card as needed, replenishing the cash as you use the card. The credit card company often gives you a small credit limit, usually about $200, to practice having credit. If we open you a secured credit card, you have to be very good about paying your monthly bill promptly. The interest rates on unpaid credit balances are crazy, usually over twenty percent."

"That sounds like an option." Maggie said hesitantly, she was still reluctant to give up what little money she did have.

"It would help rebuild your credit. We recommend parents get one for their college kids, so they can start to build credit in their own name and don't go crazy on Mom and Dad's card. Parents usually just add children as authorized users on their cards, which does not help them build credit in their own name. Secured cards help them build credit in their own name. Normally, it can take as little as 6 months to start establishing your credit."

Doris continued, "With your current credit score, you will probably be unable to refinance the houses or finance a new one. Of course, there will be no car loans. Furthermore, lots of potential employers do not like poor credit scores. Or landlords, so you may find it difficult to rent. If you do find someone who will offer you credit, you will pay a much, much higher interest rate than people with good scores. A poor credit score can be a real handicap."

Maggie stared at Doris. "Why would I need to do any of those things? I have two houses and two cars already. My problem is that I need cash *now*."

Doris looked meaningfully at Maggie and said slowly, "I understand you need cash now. But you need to understand. Your credit score will matter. I can see on my computer, that *both* your homes are facing foreclosure. You and your husband may have paid them off at some time in the past, but both properties were used as collateral for new mortgages just over two years ago. You are a co-signer on both, whether you were aware of it or not. Your credit report tells me this, and I have double-checked in our system as well. Do you have any other asset with a cash value?"

"I-I don't know," Maggie sputtered, getting flustered. "Why?"

"Well, to be honest, it is probably too late for your vacation home...but unless you make up the missed mortgage and interest payments on your home here in Concord, you will lose it as well."

Maggie instantly forgot Neal's disappearance and the FBI visit. Her heart raced and she felt cold, a sense of panic rising. *She could lose her home?* Where would she live? She didn't even have a job; she hadn't worked since college. She had no income. Her inheritance from her father had gone into Neal's business as a personal loan. Neal's disappearance was becoming a full-blown nightmare. Who was their lawyer? Who could she turn to? Maggie silently cursed her own ignorance.

Doris could tell Maggie was shell-shocked. She waited patiently, pretending to click around on her computer screen to give Maggie space.

"I'm sorry," said Maggie slowly. "I can't think about credit ratings or opening an account or getting a credit card or anything else right now. I have six hundred dollars in cash which will hold me for a bit. How much is the monthly payment on the house here in Concord?"

Doris breathed deeply when she found the total. "Nine thousand eight hundred and fifty-six dollars. It is a variable rate mortgage. You are going to have to talk to our mortgage department about this very soon if you are going to be able to do anything about it. I have the number here." She scribbled on a sticky note. "Ask to speak to Tucker. I work with him a lot, and I will call to give him a heads-up."

Maggie took the telephone number. Numb, she slowly rose and thanked Doris for her help. She had come to the bank simply wanting to pay off the overdraft and get access to cash and her credit cards. She had wanted to resume her life until this thing with Neal resolved itself. Now she realized her money problems were a lot larger than Neal being in trouble with the law. Unless he arrived soon and pulled a rabbit stuffed with money out of his hat, she was going to be homeless. Poor credit was the least of her problems. As Maggie walked slowly back to her car, she realized that being powerless about her finances was no longer an option.

CHAPTER 2:
FACING FORECLOSURE

Maggie still felt shaken when she got home. Her breakfast had only been coffee, so she toasted a couple slices of bread and smeared peanut butter on them. Then she got out a pad of paper and sharpened a pencil. She tried to calm herself by focusing on the pencil. Starting with a sharp point had always given her a sense of control and authority.

She began a list. The first item was "Stop Foreclosures." The second was "Get Cash," the third "Establish Credit." After a moment she also grabbed a journal from drawer where she kept her drawing supplies. She labeled it: *Financial Insights*. She was not going to let herself be powerless about money anymore. She jotted down what she had learned from the bank manager about credit ratings and cards. It was a beginning.

Her lists did not have anything about Neal on them. Clearly, something was going on with him. She resolved she was not going to waste time worrying about his situation until she had a good explanation from him. She knew in her heart of hearts that she probably *had* signed the paperwork regarding the new mortgages—just like with taxes. He probably had just shown her a page and asked her to sign it. She never read anything she signed, never checked or even asked questions. She could not believe how simple-minded and naïve she had been. *Never again,* she vowed to herself. She pulled over her *Insights* journal and added that observation as well.

She grimly assumed that she was not hearing from Neal because he did not want to be heard from. She knew they had lost whatever romance had been in their marriage—their polite but superficial conversation and faded sex life was proof enough of that—but she always assumed he respected the partnership.

She knew they had not been connecting for the past few years. She had put it down to empty nesting. In retrospect, perhaps Neal had seemed a little more stressed lately. He had upped his travel and was spending later nights in the office, but otherwise he seemed normal. There was no indication of any problems. They ran errands on the weekends and occasionally even went to a movie or out to dinner with Ethan or Izzy. No drama, but not much else either. They had never fought. Given his travel, she had occasionally wondered if he had a mistress. She realized she was indifferent if he did. She just thought that most marriages were probably closer to platonic than passionate.

Maggie felt she might be responsible for the distance between them. The house was large, and a second home compounded the drag on her time. She had always had trouble finding and keeping service people who met her high standards. In the end, she did most of the property upkeep on her own. She had allowed herself to be absorbed by everyone else's needs. She had made doing for others a full-time job.

When Charlie had left for Guatemala, leaving her alone, she had thrown herself into learning new things, from home improvement skills to beekeeping. Lately though, her enthusiasm had waned for any kind of activity. She often felt exhausted, but when she tried to sleep her mind raced with lists of chores that needed to be done. Maggie had felt so out of kilter that she had even sought out a psychiatrist. The doctor had prescribed the anxiety pills. Maggie had given up going, though, when the doctor had made her cry one day.

Crying was not something Maggie Mueller did. She prided herself on her emotional control. Lately though, she had inexplicably felt on the verge of tears. Her solution, which she had honed as a teenager, was to return to reading a great deal as a distraction. She now finished at least two or three books a week. The fictional characters had become her only company. Her days were filled with solitude, but she would never have admitted that she was lonely.

Now, she could not shake the sense that she had simply been hibernating.

Maggie broke off from her rambling thoughts and returned to her lists. Looking at them, she realized she was feeling oddly energized. She had things that needed to be done and done urgently. It was a time for action, not reveries. She added sub-categories under each heading and broke the foreclosures into two headings, one for each house. Perhaps this *was* the time to sell the Cape house. It had been the family getaway, but they never went away as a family anymore. The money would probably help pay for the Concord house.

Foreclosure on Concord, of course, would be different. Their *lives* had been in this home for over twenty-five years. The thought of selling it was so daunting she had not even considered it when Charlie moved out three years ago.

Foreclosure? Being tossed out? That was different. Very different. It could not, *would* not, happen.

When she had a list of questions ready, she called Mrs. Leitner's friend, Tucker, in the bank's mortgage department. He answered on the first ring and she introduced herself.

"Hello, Mrs. Mueller. Doris spoke to me. It appears you were not aware of the foreclosure actions. What can I do to help?"

"Well, first you can help me understand why I don't know what is going on. If I signed this mortgage, how can I not have been told about the foreclosures?"

"Well, let's start with the basics. What is your contact information?" Maggie gave him her cell number and was surprised that the addresses he had on file for payment notices were post office boxes in the city. The only phone number the bank had was their old landline. Maggie remembered Neal had it disconnected over a year ago because they were not using it. They both preferred their cells for calls. She had never considered who might have had that landline number as a contact for her. She suddenly understood how contacting her might have been difficult.

Tucker was clearly unnerved that she had no idea the mortgages were in foreclosure. Maggie hoped that the bank's failure to notify her personally might mean leniency. After they had sorted out the contact information, she asked Tucker about the status of the foreclosures.

"Well, the house on the Cape is about to go to a foreclosure sale. We sent you a Notice of Default after the third missed monthly payment this spring. Normally, even borrowers who have been avoiding us will contact us at that point. We usually try to renegotiate the loan with them. We give them a chance to reinstate the loan, reduce the payment or lengthen the term. We work out some type of forbearance. Sometimes we agree that the borrower will only have to pay interest for a while until things get back to normal. It can stop the bankruptcy process altogether."

"Didn't you contact my husband?" Maggie asked, surprised that the foreclosure process had clearly been going on for months.

"We couldn't reach him either. Our records indicate both properties are investment properties and we understood that, if occupied, there were only renters there. His home was an address in the city. If we had reached him, we would probably have recommended a *short sale*. This is where we give you the chance to sell the property yourselves. A foreclosure by a bank really hurts your credit rating; it usually takes seven years to come off your credit report, so people generally can't get new credit cards or mortgages during that period."

Maggie's heart sank at the idea that it might be seven years until she was able to get a regular credit card again.

"Please understand," Tucker continued. "As a bank, we really do not like to own or sell houses. We would rather work with a borrower than go through the hassle of selling the house ourselves. We will work with clients who have legitimate payment problems, for example a job loss or health issue. We do, of course, still expect the client to return the full amount of the loan and interest eventually. We can choose, however, to give people time to sort out their financial situation. In your case, however, no one responded to any of our efforts to contact you after the Notice of Default. The bank even gave you three months after the Notice. As both houses are in legal trusts, it gives us the authority to list them for sale without consulting a judge, which sometimes delays the foreclosure process longer. If the homes had been in either your or your husband's name, it might have taken longer."

"I just can't believe this," Maggie muttered as the reality of the situation sank in.

"Honestly," Tucker continued after a moment. "I am sorry about all of this, Mrs. Mueller. As I said, we only had your names and very limited contact information. We just didn't know how to reach you, specifically. The notices were never acknowledged, so we decided to sell. Mind you, the Concord house went into default later than the one on the Cape. Payments for Concord were being made up until four months ago. As a result, the bank is further behind in the process for that property. Have you been to either property recently?"

"Well, I live in the Concord property. I'm here right now. But I have not been to the Cape in months. Neal told me it was rented for the summer."

Another of Neal's lies, she realized.

"Oh, we were not aware that Concord is owner-occupied. It is listed on the forms as an investment property. That could have helped you earlier on, but it probably makes little difference at this juncture. I know there are notices on the house on the Cape. You may want to go down and get your personal items if you have any there. It will go to foreclosure sale next Friday."

Next Friday?!" Maggie was again flabbergasted. This was real, and this was happening. Next Friday was only ten days away!

The shock was overwhelming, but practicality took hold. If the house was sold, her money worries would probably be over. She could head down to the Cape tomorrow and work out what needed to be moved. The house had come fully furnished, down to the linens and kitchen cutlery, and they could sell it like that. Maybe this was a lucky disaster. The proceeds from the Cape house could carry her for a bit. She could use the money to resume mortgage payments on the Concord house and take it out of foreclosure. It made sense.

"How soon after the sale could I get access to the cash?"

Tucker hesitated. "Um, well, the trusts would get any excess cash from the sale. Are you a trustee?"

Maggie did not know the answer to that, or even where to get that answer—then a nagging thought came to her. The kids had trusts but Neal was trustee on them. When they had set them up he always said Maggie was too much of a "soft touch" when it came to money, so he was the more logical choice. She had never questioned it. He probably would not have made her a trustee on the houses. The more she thought about it, the more certain she was.

"If I am not a trustee, then what happens?"

"Well, the money goes into the trust account and will sit there until the trustee directs us what to do with the cash."

"Can I use the trust money to pay the Concord mortgage?"

"No. Unless you are a trustee, you have no access to the trust's funds. Of course, the Concord mortgage is in another trust's name."

"But my name is on both mortgages. So, I am responsible for the debt but I don't get the cash if you sell the house? How can that be? I owe the money but get nothing if the house sells?"

Tucker sighed. People just didn't get this. "When the Cape house sells, the proceeds will pay off the mortgage and the expenses related to the sale. If there is a difference between the sale price of the house and the mortgage and expenses owed to the bank, the extra will go into the trust account. The cash then stays there until the trustee directs us what to do. Do you have any idea how the trusts are set up? Who the beneficiaries are?"

Of course, Maggie didn't. She also had no idea who Neal used as a lawyer. "No, I don't. Is there a lawyer's name on any of the documents that I could contact to find out?"

"I cannot help you there," replied Tucker. "As you are not a trustee, we cannot disclose anything to you. I *can* tell you it looks like the bank attorney handled most of the paperwork, I will ask him for the name of the trustees if he has access to it. Please be aware—regardless of the trust, if the sale price does not exceed the mortgage you owe, then you *personally* will have to pay the balance, not the trust. That is called a 'deficiency judgment.' You and your husband are personally responsible for paying any shortfall created by the sale."

"Even more debt?" she repeated, stunned.

He hesitated before continuing, "Mrs. Mueller, I am not sure if you know this, but the current mortgages are for 90% of the assessed value of the houses. Since Mr. Mueller wanted to re-finance with only a 10% down payment, he accepted that he would have a higher interest rate. We also required him to pay for mortgage insurance. This added another 1% of the loan value to the payment. Avoiding the high cost of mortgage insurance is why we like new homeowners to have 20% for a down payment. However, Mr. Mueller insisted on the 90% funding level. This means that in addition to the mortgage payment and interest, there are also mortgage insurance fees to pay back."

Maggie gasped. "It sounds like you are saying there *will* be a shortfall. That after I lose the house, I may *still* owe the bank money?"

Tucker sighed. "As you probably know, Mrs. Mueller, in 2017 there were changes in the tax law. They call it the SaLT issue, an abbreviation for State and Local Tax. People are no longer able to deduct state and local property taxes from their Federal taxes. Mortgage expenses beyond ten thousand dollars are also not deductible. This new tax law has meant a steady erosion in the value of larger properties and second homes here in Massachusetts. Plus, foreclosures are priced to sell quickly, to get enough to pay off the bank, not to make money for the owners. It is quite possible you will have a deficiency and will owe us money. The property may be *underwater*. This term means more is owed to the bank than the property is actually worth."

Maggie's heart sank. The foreclosure of the Cape Cod house was not going to help her financial situation. In fact, there was a real chance it could make it worse. And her Concord home was still at risk. Her frustration with Neal was now transforming into something much sharper. She realized it was the strongest feeling she had felt about him in a very long while.

"Can I delay the sale? I only just heard about this and my husband is missing. I need to contact a lawyer and work out what to do."

Doris had filled Tucker in on Maggie's situation, and he felt sympathetic. This missing husband was an issue, but it was not the bank's issue. "Look, I doubt there is anything that can be done about the Cape house; that is set in stone at this point. But contacting me changes things for Concord. Can you put together an income stream estimate for you and your husband? Have one of you lost a job recently, or had a health issue? Maybe we can work something out there. I can definitely put things on hold until after the Cape sale. Let's see how that goes first, and whether you have a deficiency. That will let us know what additional payments we may have to factor in."

Maggie did not want to tell him there was no income stream for her, or for Neal at this point, that she knew about. "Okay. I appreciate you holding off for a bit."

"Happy to help. I understand that you are in a difficult position. I know banks get a bad reputation, but often people just don't like to hear bad news. When we try and talk about options, things go south from there. The bank would like to help you, especially if your husband is not in the picture. "

Maggie felt deflated but thanked Tucker for his time. Tucker closed the conversation by telling her that he would be in touch with her after the Cape sale.

Maggie got off the phone and breathed deeply. She pushed aside the sense of despair that threatened and realized she had work to do. She had ten days to handle the Concord foreclosure. She had six hundred dollars. She was going to get out of the hole she was in so she could save the house. She was not going to let the situation break her. She headed upstairs she felt stupid for not paying attention, for letting Neal take full responsibility and control of their finances. Her lack of interest in how her life was funded was coming back to bite her. At the end of the day, she only had herself to blame.

She went into her bedroom and quickly packed a small overnight bag. She left a note for Neal on the minor chance he actually came home. "Call me. Urgent!" it said. She then added she'd gone to the Cape house. That will worry him she thought smugly. She wondered about the FBI as she prepared to text him. She realized they could be tapping his phone, so she was careful with what she sent. She did not want to trigger any suspicions about her involvement in his situation. She simply said she was heading to the Cape for a break and asked him to call when he had a chance. She happily imagined his alarm if he was able to read the text, realizing she was onto his lie about the renters. *Would that prompt a call from him?*

She suspected now that Neal was in a great deal of trouble. She had decided she wouldn't worry about him until her money situation was solved. Putting her husband's struggles out of her mind was not the "loyal wife" move, maybe, but then, what loyal husband wipes out their bank account, puts their home into foreclosure, and then disappears without even giving her or the children a heads-up? No, loyalty was clearly out the window.

Maggie had to stop en route to buy gas. She shelled out over sixty of her precious dollars to fill the car. It startled her. She had never paid attention to the cost of gas when she simply slid the plastic into the machine. She realized she would have to fill it again when she headed home. Gas would take a big chunk out of her cash reserves. She was going to have to figure out how to raise more money soon. Her immediate options seemed limited.

Pulling into the Cape house was another shock on this day filled with earthquakes. The lawn was overgrown, the garden beds overrun with weeds. The front door had notices stuck all over it, including the original foreclosure notice. There were stacks of local papers on the stoop. If there had been renters at some point, they had not been there for months.

As she let herself in, the next shock hit her. The house was empty, right down to the appliances. The great room was bare. The dirty, oversized windows let in a warm late afternoon light where dust motes danced, disturbed by the gust of air she had let in. The large TV and its related electronics were gone, as was the mount itself. The enormous leather sectional and the rug that had defined the room were gone, leaving behind a lighter section of floor. To her right, her open-plan, gourmet kitchen was stripped of its Sub Zeros and her Wolf stove. There was nothing here. She moved from room to room. There were no beds or bookcases, no paintings on the walls and no toilet paper in the bathrooms. It was bare to the bones. Even the shelving in the garage was gone. There had been five furnished bedrooms, six baths, a gym, a game room, and all the family living areas. Now there was not even a lone hanger in the closets. She wondered, wryly, why the people who had cleared it had left behind the light fixtures.

She walked out onto the slate patio that edged the rolling back lawn. It swept down to a salt marsh with a long, elevated dock. The view was wonderful. The pool, however, was a pond. It was deep green and full of debris. The pool house had no towels, no chairs, no floaties. Even the outdoor kitchen was stripped of its pots and pans, dishes and cutlery. There was nothing. She did not see the pool cover or any chemicals which might have stymied the pool's stagnation. No wonder there had been no renters. The house's condition would not maximize its sale value.

In the kitchen, she found a few business cards from a local estate seller fanned out on the counter. It was her only clue. She called the number, and a cheerful young woman answered. When she explained the situation, the woman hesitated, unwilling to give out any specific information. She clearly knew something. Maggie asked to speak to the owner. He came to the phone quickly and said he recognized the name and encouraged her to stop by, the office being a ten minute drive from the house. Maggie took another, final turn around the property and realized that it already felt like someone else owned it. With a final look out the back windows to the wide salt marsh, and a final photo to remember it by, she simply closed the door and headed into town.

The estate sale office, Bartlett's, was co-located with a real estate agency.

"The wife handles the property sales and I do the estates," the owner, Patrick, explained as he jovially welcomed her. He told her he was an auctioneer, too, and he did estate valuations as well. Maggie introduced herself again and explained she was coming about her property at 34 Nipmuc Road. He sat her down in his office, arranged her a coffee, and offered her some delicious looking scones. She welcomed the afternoon tea, realizing she had not yet eaten today.

As she sat down, she was startled to notice a large watercolor depicting the exact same salt marsh view she had just left, hanging behind his desk. She was further surprised to realize it was *her* painting. It was the largest one she had ever done. She had been terribly pleased with how she caught the mist coming off the marsh as the sun rose one still morning. She finished the same day she started in a fit of creativity. She knew it was one of her best works, and the first she had thought about framing. She had forgotten about it until now.

"I am glad to see you like the scene," she said indicating the painting with a nod. "It was the first painting I completed in one sitting," she explained with a quiet pride.

He beamed. "That's yours? You painted it? You are quite the talent. It is lovely. I grew up fishing on that marsh and it just called to me." He then looked a little guilty, "It did not sell with the other items. Normally we donate the artwork, but the location had a sentimental attachment for me, and it wasn't framed, so I indulged myself. You are the MM in the corner, I take it."

"I am glad it ended up on display. And the driftwood frame you selected is wonderful. I am interested, however, in what happened to the rest of my things."

Mr. Bartlett looked surprised. "Why, the rest went with the estate sale. Mr. Mueller was adamant that everything had to go. We even sold the appliances which is a bit unusual for a 'living estate sale.' My wife had been renting it by the week, quite successfully I might add, so we were surprised and disappointed when the request came through. But Mr. Mueller said you were relocating overseas, so we understood. We thought it was to prepare for a sale, so we were very disappointed when we saw the foreclosure notices."

"Me too," Maggie muttered under her breath.

"My wife would have been happy to try to sell it for you. But when she looked the property up, she understood. That refinancing you did was at the top of the market. A short sale usually involves selling at hefty discount, and the market has cooled considerably since the SaLT deductions have disappeared. We did a final sweep at the beginning of last month when we saw the foreclosure notices go up. I like to think we did maximize your returns on the furnishings, at least.'"

"Well unfortunately, Mr. Bartlett, my husband's plan to sell the furnishings did not involve me." As soon as she said it, Maggie fought the tears that tried to appear. "I was not aware of the sale of the house's contents and when I heard about the foreclosure I had hoped to collect some personal items"

Patrick Bartlett blanched. "The property is in a trust and Mr. Mueller the trustee, so we just assumed that the personal effects were his to dispose of. I had no idea that you had not been consulted, Mrs. Mueller. I am so sorry. I do have an inventory document and a record of where most of the items ended up, if you would like to try to recover them." He shuffled around in some files, then asked in a lower voice, "Is there a divorce proceeding going on?"

"No divorce, just a missing husband and quite a few people looking for him." Maggie smiled a little sadly, then reassured him, "None of this is your fault; I would have assumed the same as you did. It is just disappointing. I am happy to see my painting there, though." She gazed at the painting wistfully. "Our three children and I spent most of our summers there. Lots of wonderful memories. I'd thank you for those inventory documents. There may be some things the children would like to have that I can recover."

It surprised her how resigned she had already become to the disappointment of not finding anything at the house. It was probably easier on her; she doubted she could have emptied the house on such short notice, anyway. She did wonder just how much she missed out on from a money perspective. Could she have taken some things and sold them herself? Would that have been stealing from the trust? Likely it would have been, she told herself, not that she would have cared at this point. It seemed like every possible solution she thought she had found only led to a dead end.

Patrick Bartlett pulled out a folder and called his assistant in to make copies while Maggie ate two scones, realizing she was more than hungry—she was ravenous. They talked about painting and shared memories of their favorite local places to eat or swim. At one point, he jumped up and returned with a large, familiar portfolio folder, filled with older paintings of hers. They were more amateurish, clearly her practicing color schemes and brush strokes. He happily turned these over to her, as they also carried her stylized initials.

Maggie did not know why she felt so open with Patrick Bartlett. He was older, maybe a bit like her father. He clearly returned the feeling. Maggie knew he did not have to give her a copy of the inventory, it was a kindness. And she was grateful. They chatted like old friends and Maggie relaxed a little for the first time in days.

When his assistant finally returned, he handed Maggie the paperwork. "I don't know whether giving you a copy of the inventory and the sale results is strictly kosher. I would appreciate it if we keep it between ourselves."

"Of course, I am only looking for personal items that we may have left behind. My husband is not the type that pays attention to that sort of thing."

She flipped through the document scanning quickly, and nothing jumped out at her. Then she got to the last page of the document and she shuddered. The sale of the furniture and fixtures had raised well over $100,000, and just in the past month. She could have paid the mortgage on the Concord property for *months* with that amount. Where had that money gone?

As she got up to leave, Mr. Bartlett cleared his throat and awkwardly reached into his desk, pulling out a checkbook. "I need to pay you for your painting," he insisted. Without asking her for a price, he wrote out a check and handed it to her. She glanced at it and went to hand it back.

"It is too much," she said.

"Not at all." He smiled. "It represents a memory for me. And remember, as an estate auctioneer, I know the value of things. Believe me. I am doing well by this, Mrs. Mueller."

She hesitated a moment longer before she tucked the check for five hundred dollars in her bag. She had just about doubled her cash reserves. She thanked him, took her portfolio, and headed back to her Lexus.

Maggie realized that the check was the first money she had earned since her marriage. Now, she calculated, she just needed to paint and sell about twenty perfect paintings a month, every month. Then she might be able to save her home. She smiled, knowing it was unlikely she could do even one painting a month as good as the one Patrick Bartlett just purchased. Painting was not going to be a living. It was only a hobby, perhaps a paying side gig. It occurred to her that she might need to start thinking about getting a job sometime soon.

As she drove home, Maggie considered how she was going to tell the children about the sale of the Cape house and Neal's disappearance. It wasn't necessary to tell them that the house had been foreclosed, nor that Concord house was also under threat. Neal's disappearance would not register as anything unusual yet. He had once been gone for three months, putting together a deal in Australia. She knew if she told them more, there might be fireworks and she saw no reason to upset them until she herself knew more. Ethan and Neal did not get along as it was, so any hint of an issue with him would set Ethan off. All three would welcome the Cape sale - both girls had suggested it years ago. They hated to see the extra work it created for her. Ethan had used it once or twice with Hannah but they both preferred more active weekends when they got time off. It was off all the children's radar. Neal could explain things to them when he got back. After he explained them to her, of course.

On her long ride home, Maggie became resigned to the loss of the Cape house. As she drove, watching the sun set, she felt a chapter in her life closing. The inventory sitting in the passenger seat beside her, however, highlighted a lost opportunity. It got her thinking about her next steps. She had lost one house, and its contents, today. Her second foreclosure was going to be an entirely different story.

CHAPTER 3:
CASH IS KING

Maggie returned home drained. For a moment, she imagined opening the door and finding Neal catching up on some Netflix series, all smiles and apologies for the mix-ups. But the house was dark when she arrived. It fit her mood.

She turned the lights on in the kitchen and dropped her bag. Out of habit she looked in the fridge and then closed the door. There was nothing there, and she was not really hungry anyway. She considered ordering take-out for herself for dinner, as she frequently did, but rejected the idea when she realized pizza involved cash. She opened the cupboard and settled on almonds and crackers for dinner.

Maggie made a cup of black tea and pulled out her wallet. She went through it methodically, pulling out the credit cards she knew did not work and laying out the cash. She found a number of forgotten store credits from Bloomingdales, Bed Bath and Beyond, and Lowes. These obviously came from some returns she had made when she did not have the receipt. She had no idea how much they were worth, or if she could access the cash they represented. She would check with the stores. She began another list titled "cash."

She went again to the kids' biscotti jar and this time poured out the contents. Loose change and a few more small bills formed a pitiful pile. Suddenly, she jumped up and fumbled in the utility closet. There, on a low shelf pushed to the back, was the coin sorter the kids had bought her years ago. Behind it were stacks of neatly wrapped coins she had accumulated over the years. She had occasionally taken a roll of quarters for parking meters, back when meters still took coins, but the bulk of rolls were still there. In the past, when she finished a coin roll, she had simply added them to the stack.

Now as she pulled out roll after roll, she was surprised to find they were stacked two, sometimes three, deep. There were twenty-eight rolls of quarters, forty of dimes, and fifty-two of nickels. At first, she ignored the penny rolls, but then she realized they were the bulk of the stash—there were over eighty slim, red rolls. She added it up in her mind as she went, and it came to $624. With the change and loose bills on the table, it surely totaled to more than $650. She was thrilled.

Beneath the stacked rolls was another find: her coin collection. Maggie vividly remembered exchanging her wrinkled dollar bills at the local bank for coin rolls that she would carry home. She had always sorted through them excitedly, treasure hunting. She was happy when she found the odd "S" coin or a zinc penny to fill an empty slot in her collection. Here were seven trifold blue books that she had pressed her findings into. Her parents always included three or four rare coins in her Christmas stocking. This collection could be valuable. She remembered she had tried to interest her children in collecting but they were unimpressed. She had tucked the books away years ago and forgotten they even existed.

She had begun the day with 600 dollars, and now she had almost three times that amount. She might have substantially more, with her coin collection. It was not going to equal the proceeds from selling the contents of the Cape house, but it was a start. She pulled the blue books out and excitedly went to her laptop to do some research and find a coin dealer.

She searched for the estimated value on a few of the rarer coins. She was pleased to find many were worth well over one hundred dollars. She found the name of the nearest coin dealer and planned a visit in the morning. It would be a good way to start the day. She was surprised she was so energized by the decision. Despite an overwhelming sense of panic just below the surface, she was not giving into it. She had surprised herself, finding a resolve she had not known was there.

Yes, she told herself, *this is a crisis. But the situation has to be managed, so I will manage it.* She could rely on herself.

Maggie was grateful that this would be her problem and not the children's. They were out on their own. She shuddered to think how this might have changed their lives ten years ago when they all lived at home.

It suddenly occurred to Maggie that she would probably not be able to be their emergency fund anymore. That would be an adjustment for them. She felt like she would be letting them down but hoped it might be good for them in the long run.

Given her conversation with Doris Leitner, Maggie realized she was going to have to get smarter about money, fast. Not having plastic meant she needed to understand how to manage actual cash. Purchasing things was going to be relatively straightforward but what about the utility bills? The lights were on and her phone worked, but how were the bills being paid? She checked the computer and realized she did not even know which utility companies to call. She added "Find out who is responsible for the lights" to her to-do list. After the coin dealer tomorrow, she would call each utility and work out which ones serviced her house. She worried how much she might owe them, and then wondered how to pay the bill without a credit card or check. Would paying in cash even be possible?

Maggie knew then that even with the sale of the coin collection, she would need more cash. She had no idea how much she would need to live on, but it was clear with the mortgage alone it was likely to be more than she could raise in the short term—and this thing with Neal no longer felt like a short-term problem. It was not a maybe, some type of employment was definitely in her future. Surprisingly, the prospect of work did not daunt her as much as she expected. If she was honest with herself, she imagined it might be nice getting up each morning with a specific purpose to each day.

She went online and looked for books about returning to the workforce and found one that looked short and sweet. She went to order it and found Amazon did not let her—the credit card attached to the account was not working. Here it was then, her first reality check. No books? She tried to set up a new account, but again it required a credit card, so she signed off. The credit card issue was going to temporarily stop her online shopping life, that was pretty clear.

Maggie thought that perhaps it was time to try the secured credit card the woman at the bank had suggested. With the cash she had and the check she had gotten for her painting, she should have enough now to get one, she figured.

She also realized she was going to need a new bank account. While she was grateful to the bank manager, Maggie worried that if she went back to her, the manager would probably want some of her money to go paying off her overdraft. Maggie planned on paying it back but did not have enough money to spare yet. Walking around with all her cash, especially the coin rolls, was simply not practical. She was not a keep-cash-in-the-mattress person. She added *new bank* on her to-do list, then yawning and needing a good night's sleep for the next busy day, headed up to bed.

The next morning, Maggie went well-armed to a coin dealer in Boston. She knew approximate values for the coins and sold her entire collection for more than

$5400. The coins her parents bought had appreciated substantially and she was thrilled. She was well over halfway to a mortgage payment. Maybe she could negotiate an interest-only mortgage payment, like Tucker had explained. She might even be able to hang on until she got a job and her first paycheck.

It had been a surprising tug, selling the collection. It was one of the clearest memories of her childhood. Maggie had been naturally drawn to coins, as she was numeric and excelled at math from an early age. She could quickly calculate the value of any pile of coins, even the foreign coins her father brought home to stump her. Math was once her favorite subject.

Unfortunately, her math skills had been scuttled in middle school by a problematic algebra teacher named Mr. Harris. Her math class had been the most advanced one offered at her school. There were only two girls. Mr. Harris had generally ignored her whenever he saw her eager hand waving. Finally, one day he said, with clear exasperation, "Miss Gagnon, pretty blonde girls like you do not need math." With a grin, he added, "You should focus on the important things," and gestured vaguely in the direction of her chest. The boys in class all laughed at the innuendo. Maggie shamefully pulled her hand down.

Most adults would have dismissed Mr. Harris's comment as little more than misogynistic attempt at humor. Unfortunately, to children, seemingly minor things frequently have outsized impacts, particularly in middle school. Mr. Harris's comment stayed with Maggie and took root.

As the year went on, Maggie became the first girl in her class who wore a bra. Mr. Harris started bumping into her when passing back her papers, frequently brushing against her hands, legs, or even her top when he could. His touch made her uncomfortable, but she was too young and sheltered to really understand why. After his comment, she sat at the back of the class and nursed a growing dislike for both the teacher and subject.

As the year progressed, boys noticed her chest expanding. Then, more importantly to Maggie, the popular girls noticed the boys noticing. Suddenly, she was not the math geek on the sidelines but in the center of the most popular group of girls. All of her new friends took the lower levels of math and gossiped about how creepy Mr. Harris was. Late spring of that same year, Maggie dropped her advanced math class. She told the guidance counselor and her parents it was "too hard," despite her perfect grades. Maggie harbored a secret hope that someone would challenge her request, but the adults in her life were indifferent.

As Maggie moved onto high school, she still got A's in her English and history classes, but she let her math and science courses slide. The only praise her father had for her was about her looks, and her mother only talked to Maggie about boys and her appearance. Neither parent took the slightest interest in her academic prowess.

Maggie knew she could have done better in her math and science courses. She understood everything easily. When she craved attention she would ask, with a honeyed voice, for some handsome boy to explain something to her. Ironically, she could have done a better job explaining to him. Maggie did her homework well enough to get by but played helpless in class and labs. As a result, she was pretty, popular, and, later, prom queen.

Only her younger brother, Will, used to look at her funny when she said something that sounded vapid or dumb. He knew she bested him in chess and almost any other game they played. This said a lot, as Will himself was at the top of his class—as his parents proudly boasted to their friends. He knew Maggie demolished crosswords and taught herself bits of Russian and Chinese from library books just for fun. They argued about science fiction heroes and watched Star Trek together. They were as close as two siblings could be. In the afternoons and evenings, away from the gossip and school dramas, Maggie was free to be a pure geek with Will. They reveled in each other's company.

There was a downside to Maggie's intense closeness to her brother. In his junior year, while Maggie was a senior, Will was killed in a skiing accident while on a school trip. Maggie was devastated to the point of desolation. She had been scheduled to go on the trip as well but had stayed home to work on college essays. She blamed herself, imagining if she had been with him it would not have happened. She retreated from everything and everyone.

After Will's death, their parents seemed to visibly shrink away from her. It was as if they were afraid of the pain of possibly losing her, too. Her father, whom she had been very close to, pulled away entirely. Maybe, she told herself, they wished she had been the child they lost. With her guilt and their silence, her home life became solemn and stilted. She simply accepted the first college offer she got, not caring where she went as long as there would be some distance between her and her home.

Maggie didn't understand it at the time, but Will's death broke something in her. He was the only person who really understood her and admired her raw intelligence. In the months that followed his death, she gave up completely on academics. She didn't crave any accolades. People, including her friends, avoided her. She dropped her high school boyfriend and kept to herself. She made plans for a quiet college life in Boston. She did not ever really recover from Will's death as much as she walled it off. Maggie's solution was to just try and forget Will.

Oddly, as she drove home from the coin dealer, she found herself keenly missing him. Her childhood played vividly in her mind. She was flooded with memories she had rarely let surface over the past decades. She saw Will helping her sort coins as she taught him what to look for. She remembered Will's wit and enthusiasm for life, his pride in her and her joy in his company. They had always shared a secret celebration when she completed a coin book in her collection. She remembered the mock toasts they had, illicitly drinking soda from her parents' crystal champagne glasses. Her eyes were wet as she pulled into her driveway. Letting the coins go was bittersweet for her. She felt drained.

As she entered the house, she breathed deeply. *Focus,* she told herself. She made Will recede from her thoughts.

Now, she asked herself, *what else can I raise money on*? If the contents of the Cape house netted over one hundred thousand dollars, then the Concord house furnishings must be worth many times that. The Cape house had nice things, but it was "rental ready." The furnishings were Pottery Barn, not the mahogany antiques that filled every room here. She also had three sets of bone china, silver sets from her grandmother, and any number of valuable paintings and rugs, most of which had come from her parents' home. She just wasn't sure how to value or to sell things, but she would. She reasoned she would have to downsize sometime. Why not now? She rarely went into half the rooms of the house. She could clear the extra rooms and live comfortably on the proceeds until she got a job.

Remembering Mr. Bartlett from her day on the Cape, Maggie called him first. She asked if he knew anyone in her area who did estate sales, or partial estate sales, explaining that she was going to downsize. She told him she had inherited a lot of her parents' furniture and antiques. She had china and silver to sell. Mr. Bartlett asked how much, and she explained there was an entire formal dining room with two full breakfronts, as well as a formal living room with a baby grand piano. There were multiple bedrooms' worth of furniture and an entire storeroom in the basement filled with items from her parents' home that she had yet to sort through, including oil paintings, oriental carpets, and figurines her mother collected.

Mr. Bartlett was intrigued. He said he had someone he might recommend, but he wanted to come up and take a look himself. "It might be worth my time to manage it. Could I perhaps bring my wife up as well? We might make a day of it on Sunday. Would that work?"

Maggie readily agreed. She liked Patrick Bartlett, and she guessed she would like his wife. She told him she would use the rest of the day to try to get together an inventory for him like the one he had given her. They agreed on 11 a.m. on Sunday.

Keeping to her plan, Maggie then spent the next hour sorting out the utilities. She found all the bills paid up, which was a pleasant surprise. When she tried to discuss how to pay them going forward, she was frustrated to find the customer representatives would not give her the balance due or send her copies of the bills. They suggested she access the information online, which she could not do without an account number. The trust was listed as the contact, so they would not give her information on the phone. Maggie called back, getting another representative and said she was the trustee and wanted a paper copy of the bill sent to property itself. That did the trick. She would figure out how to pay them once she got a paper copy of the bill.

Afterward, Maggie took her laptop around the house and began the inventory spreadsheet. For each room, she made a list of sellable contents and her estimate of what each item might be worth. She worked in Excel, which she had learned while working with the Parent Teacher Council at school. Everyone at the school had complimented her on the clarity and simplicity of her spreadsheets. It had always pleased her inordinately.

She decided to label pieces either 1, 2, or 3, and mark them accordingly with a colored sticky note. If it was marked with a yellow "1," it could be sold immediately—it was little more than clutter. A pink "2" meant to sell if the price was right. A green "3" meant to hang on for now, because it was either necessary or had sentimental value. It took the rest of the day to do all the rooms, leaving off the basement storeroom.

Maggie's parents' belongings had been in the basement storeroom since her father's death over ten years ago. She was still not prepared to go through them, despite everything that was going on. Maggie decided she would let Mr. Bartlett poke around and tell her what might have value in there. She was still uncomfortable with the memories her parents' things stirred. If the coin collection had her in tears, the storeroom would be a disaster.

As she reviewed her inventory, she was surprised how few items she had marked with a "3." How could these things, which she had spent years with, really mean so little to her? Even most of the children's furniture and the things she had grown up with seemed inconsequential. When had she stopped caring about her life's souvenirs? Were there just too many of them? She was amazed that she had mentally let go of so many things that anchored her to her old life—and without even realizing it.

Shaking off the melancholy, she went back to the dining room. She took photos with her phone of a few items marked with a "1." She was planning to try a few on the online sites to see what she could sell herself. When she tallied up the estimated value for all the inventoried items, she was excited by the sum. She could easily live off half that total for quite some time.

Maggie sat again at her computer and began to look at similar items on the well-known sites. She quickly lost her enthusiasm. She had scanned every resale site she could think of. Her antique wool and silk Orientals with their high knot count and wonderful patterns were worth a couple of thousand at best, not the tens of thousands she and Neal had paid for them. The twenty-year-old baby grand piano was probably worth less than five thousand. Her china sets were popular patterns, but they sold for more on a per-plate basis. There was no apparent market for a full, twelve-piece china dinner set, complete with servers. People simply wanted to replace a broken item here and there. Desks or tables similar to her antique furniture were selling at prices that were little more than giveaways. Her traditional style had been superseded by clean modern designs.

Maggie was disappointed that the Pottery Barn furniture in the Cape house would have been in higher demand than her solid Henredon desks and sideboards. What had been the height of fashion twenty-five years ago was simply not in style anymore. No wonder her children did not want anything. She knew the estimated values on her inventory would have to come down considerably. Trying to keep herself motivated, she gave up looking for similar pieces and instead just began to scan the sites to try and understand what items moved.

The items that commanded the best prices and seemed to be in highest demand were electronic devices, sports equipment, and tools. She could find those—there were extra TVs in the house and the garage was stocked. She also saw a lot of cars being advertised, which immediately piqued her interest. Her car used too much gas, and she no longer toted children and their gear. Sedans were cheap on the site, while her Lexus SUV—which was new last year—appeared to be in high demand.

Selling her Lexus would be a quick way to raise money and put the mortgage back on track. She rarely paid any attention to what type of car she drove. She really only needed reliable transportation. She could use the kids' car for that. It was a seven-year-old Toyota they had paid cash for. It sat, barely used, in the garage. A little more research and she planned her Sunday: after the Bartletts left, she would head to the dealer with her Lexus and see what she could do. Again, Maggie went to bed and slept surprising well.

On Sunday, she got up early and scrubbed the Lexus clean, clearing out her personal items. The glove box appeared to have all the paperwork. She then baked for the Bartletts' visit, mixing up some muffins from the canned pumpkin and raisins she had on hand. They arrived exactly on time and appreciated her inventory and her baking. They were both in awe of her gardens and they took their coffee and muffins outside to enjoy the beautiful late summer day.

Patrick was kind and enthusiastic about everything he saw. He was grateful she had done her research. As she suspected, he determined that while she had wonderful things, they were not worth as much as she thought. She learned that he, and any other estate-sale coordinator, would charge, on average, 35% of the market value on goods—less on high-ticket items, but up to 60% on smaller goods. If Patrick took goods on consignment—he co-owned a shop on the Cape—he could charge people more than if the item sold at auction. However, he explained that she would have to pay to transport the goods and then she might have to wait months for a sale. He looked at her preliminary evaluation and gently told her to halve it, and that was before paying any fees to sell things.

Sensing her disappointment, he also recommended that she try to sell some things herself. Some people had real success with this, he said. He advised limiting sales to people who were local and always insisting to be paid in cash. He suggested posting photos of items at local businesses and perhaps local websites, or even trying the weekly community paper. It was old fashioned, he said, but the older people who might be interested in her things still did shop that way.

He warned her to keep buyers out of the house if possible. When possible, she should show things for sale in the garage and arrange to meet at a local coffee shop for smaller things she could carry, like electronics. He told her to be prepared for buyers to arrive "short" of what was agreed upon. It was a common ploy for a buyer to hold out what they had in cash, sometimes half of what had been agreed to, to try to get an even better deal. Buyers knew that sellers were often desperate for cash and would take any offer. Maggie should know in advance if she was willing to accept less.

Maggie thanked him for the advice. She knew he was trying to help. Patrick went on to say that there was enough value in the house for him to run a sale for her, or to even try and auction some pieces or take things on consignment.

"But," he added, "if it isn't urgent, time is your friend. You may be able to sell quite a bit on your own. People who live in your area might have similar tastes, so selling locally might yield some good results."

Maggie was again surprised at how comfortable she felt with the Bartletts. They were both a little older and practically strangers, but they felt familiar to her—maybe because they knew about the drama with the Cape house foreclosure. This was an intimacy she would never have shared with anyone normally. She now admitted to them that she might have time constraints. "There is a pending foreclosure on the Concord house as well," she admitted. She held back letting them know about the FBI issue. She simply said her husband's business was in trouble. She explained she was working to keep the house.

At this point, Patrick's wife, Gina, interrupted. She was gentle with Maggie. She asked about the house and Maggie explained that it, too, was in the foreclosure process, but she was going to try to renegotiate the payments. She was hoping to get an interest-only payment on the mortgage until she got back on her feet and sorted things with her husband.

Gina frowned. "Your husband refinanced just three years ago?"

"I'm not really sure, but probably about then."

"Did you know that the bulk of the payment you make this early in the life of a thirty-year loan is mostly interest, not principle?" Gina asked. "If you ask for an 'interest-only' payment at this stage, you would still be paying about seventy-five percent of the current payment, probably more. Unless the bank can offer another plan, an interest-only payment will not reduce your mortgage payment by much."

Maggie was alarmed. She had not been aware of that math. As she thought about it, it was logical that the early payments on a mortgage would be mostly interest, as the loan is largest at the beginning of a repayment plan. As the balance owed on the loan shrinks over time, a person would pay less interest and more principle.

If Gina was right, a monthly payment of interest-only would be about seventy-five percent of her current mortgage payment, that meant it would be about seven thousand dollars, instead of the entire current payment of $9,856. It would not help her much.

Gina suggested Maggie contact the bank and see if there was some other temporary reduction in mortgage payments she could look at, like some type of forbearance or deferment. Maggie thanked her for the advice and took their tea pitcher inside to refill. As she reached for the handle on the glass French doors, Maggie saw in the reflection, Gina shake her head sadly at her husband. Clearly Gina did not hold out much hope for Maggie talking the bank into a better deal.

The Bartletts left by early afternoon and Maggie headed immediately down to the Lexus dealer. She walked in and asked about selling her car back to the dealership. A salesman magically appeared at her elbow.

"Come and sit with me and we will see what it is worth." He smiled widely as he led her into a glass-fronted office. "Of course, it will be worth more as a trade-in, if you are interested." Maggie shook her head and they made small talk as he entered her license plate.

He looked up, clearly disappointed, and said, "Uh, your car is leased. You knew that, right?" Maggie did not. "Great rate, about $540 a month. But..." he looked up over her head and through the glass. "Excuse me a moment, please." He left the office and flagged down an older gentleman, who soon dismissed the younger man. He had a grim expression on his face as he headed into the office.

He was a very heavy man but impeccably well-dressed. He did not bother to introduce himself before asking Maggie where her husband was. Maggie, a little taken-aback, explained that he was travelling. Before she could say more, the older man said, "You know, your husband? Not my favorite customer. Yours is one of three cars we have leased to him, and all are well behind on their payments. I am afraid I am going to have to ask for your keys."

Maggie began to protest, but the man would have none of it. She explained she had no way to get home, and he simply called out to the receptionist to arrange a ride for her. He held out his hand with a frown on his face and she gave him the keys. At least she had had a chance to clean it out. He told her to tell her husband not to expect any slack when it came to the other two vehicles. He muttered something about Neal "...not being man enough to deal with his own shit" on his way out. Maggie was a bit dazed by the abruptness of it all.

Maggie felt humiliated. She pretended she was busy with her phone as she went back to the receptionist. In the back of her mind, she wondered briefly about the third car. She and Neal were the only family members with a Lexus. Where was this third car? None of the children owned a car. Another Neal mystery to add to her list.

The young woman at reception gave Maggie a wave. She was on the phone and simply indicated to Maggie that there was a car outside. Maggie recognized the elderly man behind the wheel as the gentleman who had dropped her home on many occasions when her car was being serviced. He was a retired insurance salesman, if she remembered correctly. She rode silently with him this time and he did not make small talk, only glanced at her occasionally in the rearview mirror. She collected herself and again busied herself with her phone to hide her shaking.

When she got home, she rallied herself. *The car is gone, get over it,* she told herself sternly. She still had the Corolla, and it was *definitely* paid for. She could listen to the radio again rather than use her iPhone port. She liked NPR. The Lexus's leather seats were too hot in the summer, anyway. The real disappointment was that there would be no cash from a sale. Another dead end.

She went to the computer and she pulled up an online mortgage calculator. Gina Bartlett was right—since they were in the third year of a thirty-year mortgage, over seventy-five percent of her payment was interest. She understood, now, why paying off the mortgage in the early years made such a difference. Making a separate payment earmarked to be applied to principle would mean the interest on the lower balance was less. This meant that, from then on, more of the monthly mortgage payment could go toward principle every month. It was a winning strategy, to pre-pay a mortgage.

Maggie learned that for the first years of a fixed rate, thirty-year mortgage, she was basically paying the bank interest to live in the house. She knew she would not have any way to pre-pay her mortgage. Furthermore, the more she put off making payments—or just getting behind, like she had been—the more interest would accrue on the loan. No wonder banks liked mortgage lending so much.

Everything she had seen online said she should not pay more than a third to a half of her salary to housing. If she had to pay over seven thousand a month, after tax, to simply live in her house, she estimated she would need at least twelve thousand a month in income—and that was without knowing specifically what utilities cost or what taxes she would have to pay. This meant an annual salary of well over $144,000, just to be able to stay in the house.

She had done cursory job searches on the internet and knew right away that making over $100,000 a year was much more that she could realistically expect to make. She had not worked for twenty years. She would be lucky to initially make $50,000 a year, and that was only because she lived in a part of the country where salaries were relatively high. In fact, being realistic about it, it might be a while until she actually found a company that would hire her.

She sat back. She was going to be lucky if the whole contents of the house earned her $200,000, net selling expenses. This was going to be her nest egg until Neal resurfaced. She had no idea how long that might be. If she didn't get a well-paying job soon, the mortgage would eat up the nest egg quickly. In a year, she could be right back where she was now, with nothing left to sell, being foreclosed. It was not an attractive option.

Suddenly, it was clear. Unless Neal showed up in the next nine days with a big bag of cash, she was going to have to move out of this house. In just a few days, she had learned what people living paycheck-to-paycheck always knew in their bones: cash is everything.

Maggie froze for a moment as the realization hit her: she simply could not afford the life she was used to. This change in circumstances was not going to be a temporary situation. She felt almost faint. She got up and numbly walked out to the garden. Another beautiful day. The smells were intoxicating, the sun warm, and her bees were busy on the drift of purple asters just coming into bloom.

Her idyllic life was coming to an end. She lay down on the reading lounge and closed her eyes. Breathing deeply, she said to herself, *No more drifting through life.* As the afternoon wore on, she resigned herself to the reality of selling the house and letting go of the memories it held—her gardens, her former life. She did not move for hours. As the evening came and the air began to chill, she got up and went inside. She pulled out the *Financial Insights* journal she had started and wrote in bold, bitter letters *"If you can't afford something don't buy or live in it!"* She then slammed the journal closed and threw it back on the counter.

Maggie knew she was going to have to start to build another life. In this new life, she realized, cash was going to be king for quite some time.

As she slowly climbed the stairs up to bed, the refrain from an old Joni Mitchell song played in her mind: "Don't it always seem to go, you don't know what you got until it's gone." It wasn't just the house that she would have to give up. What was gone was her life as she had known it. What was ahead, was any-one's guess.

CHAPTER 4:
LIQUIDITY IS NOT ABOUT WATER

Maggie woke up the next morning with the sensation of breaking through the surface of a sparkling pool. It was an odd feeling, but she could not connect it to anything she had been dreaming. As she swung out of bed, she placed it. Water and *liquidity*. It was a term she had heard Neal use. He had talked about having a *liquidity event* when he sold a company. Now, Maggie was working on a liquidity event as well, only she would be selling the things that had populated her life.

Currently her assets—that is, the house's furnishings and her personal belongings—were valuable but not *liquid*. To become liquid, she had to convert them to cash. Letting go of them would have been hard in ordinary times. Trying to empty the house with foreclosure bearing down on her was going to be even harder. *No time for sentimentality,* she reminded herself. She needed money.

Patrick Bartlett had told her that if she turned the sale of everything over to him, she would be handing him 35% of her potential cash. She needed every penny she could find, so she was determined to do what she could on her own. It was going to be work, but she knew she was ready for it. She was not sure when she had crossed the line from feeling overwhelmed by Neal's betrayal to being energized by it, but she had.

Occasionally, she would hear a small voice in her head that told her she was rushing things. She should wait until Neal resurfaced. What if this was all explainable, and she ended up selling the house out from under them? Her more practical side reminded her that the FBI raid was not a sign of good things to come. The condition of the Cape house made clear how quickly things could change. If she wanted something to show for her twenty-seven years with Neal, her instincts told her she had better hustle. She had a nagging fear that if he owed money, the house's furnishings and her personal items might get caught up in his debts. She needed to make sure she got what she could, while she could, before he or the law returned.

She started that morning, listing furniture on Craigslist. It took her a couple hours to really master the posting process. She had to have photos, measurements and descriptions, which was a hassle, but regardless she had twenty listings up by noon. She got a number of phony-looking responses on the more expensive items, all talking about money being wired. Patrick had warned her about that, so she sent back, "Cash only. No shipping." She *was* willing to ship, but she wanted to sell what she could as quickly as possible and for her that meant in person transactions. The requests for money being wired in advance stopped.

By midafternoon, she had a few texts going between her and some interested local buyers who appeared genuine. Two would come by tomorrow to look at the dining room set and a coffee table. Other texts that had looked promising just dropped away. No bites on the rugs, piano, or any of the paintings. As the day progressed, she added more posts, but began to get a little confused as the texts between her and potential buyers kept coming. She stopped posting, deciding to wait until she could delete some posts on items that she sold before she added more.

For a break, she went up to her closet and pulled out her jewelry box. She knew her collection, while not large, was probably worth a fair bit. The "1, 2, 3" system she had put in place for the furnishings was a lot harder to implement when it came to her jewelry, though.

She did not have any costume jewelry, since anything except pure gold made her skin itch. The first thing to catch her eye were the few "statement pieces" by newer designers, which had never been to her taste; Neal had gifted these pieces to her simply to have Maggie wear them for client dinners. He wanted her to look more like the other wives. They would be the first to go.

There was a pile of her own pieces she rarely wore and didn't really like which were easy to say goodbye to, but that pile was small. Next were pieces she had selected while on trips or to mark special occasions. They were her mementos. Most of these she liked, and she wore all of them occasionally. They, too, were gold and she was reluctant to let any of them go as most triggered happy memories. She decided she would wait and see what they were worth, and then decide on a piece-by-piece basis.

What was left was the bulk of her collection. These were old vintage pieces her mother had owned, many of which may have come from her grandmothers, or maybe even her great-grandmothers. Her mother had told her stories about each piece, but she had not paid attention at the time. Now her mother's mind was gone.

The stories were lost. She regretted assuming that there would always be time for her mother's memories. She wished she had written some things down.

She examined one of the delicate gold bracelets that looked Victorian and wondered who had worn it and what it meant to them. There were gold bangles and art deco pieces, her mother's charm bracelet, gold chains, and a couple of what she thought may have been engagement rings. Everything appeared of very good quality. Some even had Tiffany marks. Many had the fine filigree work she had always admired. They were old family heirlooms, she supposed. She hesitated; shouldn't she save them for the girls, as her mother had done for her?

Unable to work out what to do, she decided just to take the entire box to her local jeweler and see if they could give her an estimate on what things might be worth. It would help her decide. She checked the time and realized she could just make it before they closed. She repacked the box and went to find the keys to the kids' car.

The tan Corolla turned over easily, despite her being unable to remember when it had last been out of the garage. Gratefully, she saw the tank was full.

When she got to the jeweler, Maggie was surprised to learn there would be a fee for the appraisals. Just glancing at the box, however, the owner told her he would be interested in buying quite a few of her pieces. Assuming that the appraisal would fund itself, Maggie turned the box over to him. He had a helper write out a couple pages of detailed receipts for every piece. The young woman, a good twenty-five years younger than Maggie, complimented her on a number of her bulky "statement pieces." Maggie was again reminded that her tastes were probably behind the times.

The appraisal would cost one hundred dollars per hour. Maggie looked surprised. The owner also warned Maggie that many pieces would simply be weighed for their gold value and then assigned a subjective value for their decorative characteristics. He held up one of her hollow gold bangles, weighed it, and looked at his computer screen.

"This," he said, "is worth less than one hundred dollars for the actual gold and perhaps another hundred for the detailed decoration and age. It will take less than four minutes to properly assess." He then picked up a large, three-stone engagement ring, "This, on the other hand, will take considerably more time. Each stone will need to be cleaned, graded, weighed, and categorized individually."

Maggie grimaced. One hundred dollars per hour could really rack up.

"Do you have the paperwork on any of these pieces?" the jeweler asked.

"Paperwork?"

He explained that higher-end jewelry pieces generally came with an appraisal that listed the value based on grading of the stones and the weight of the metal used to make it. It was generally used for insurance purposes. If that was available, appraisals were quicker as the grading work on the stones was already done. It made resale more profitable, as well.

Maggie did not know what paperwork Neal might have on the more recent items. With the file cabinets empty, she would not find anything anyways. Her mother's things would have had appraisals, but they were probably buried in the storeroom somewhere. Maggie knew she didn't have the time to look for them. She told the owner he would have to start from scratch.

The jeweler estimated that it would take about four hours to fully value the entire collection. He said he would call her when the work was done. Four hundred dollars seemed like a lot of money, but Maggie needed to know what each piece might be worth to help her decide what to keep and what to let go. As she was turning to leave, she hesitated, then she pulled off her engagement and wedding rings and tossed them in with the rest of the pieces. The young store clerk looked at the owner meaningfully, but neither said anything as the woman wrote out one last receipt and handed it to Maggie.

As she left the store, Maggie texted both her daughters. "Reviewing my jewelry box. Never too early for you to let me know what you want. Thoughts?" The girls had played with the jewelry when dressing up, so Maggie thought they may remember a piece or two. If they had strong views, she would keep anything they wanted.

To her surprise, both came back to her within the hour with specifics. They reminded her that neither wore yellow gold, preferring silver and other colored metals. Apparently, though, someone had listened to their grandmother's stories. Charlie wanted a diamond and sapphire ring set in white gold that had been her great-grandmother's engagement ring. She also requested a white gold bracelet with delicate filigree and a gold chain that Charlie said came from Maggie's great-great-grandmother. Izzy wanted art deco pieces she said belonged to her great-grandmother, who she called "the Flapper Gran." Maggie could not remember ever hearing the word "flapper" associated with anyone in her family. She would have to ask Izzy what her grandmother had told her.

Charlie thoughtfully suggested Maggie asks Ethan about the jewelry. He might want an engagement ring for someone someday, or something for daughters. She reminded Maggie that Hannah, Ethan's girlfriend, appreciated antique jewelry. Maggie said she would send them photos of everything, and they could let her know what they wanted.

After she returned home, Maggie spent the rest of the evening moving things to the garage bay that used to house her Lexus. She appreciated Patrick's advice to try and keep people out of the house proper. As she looked around, she realized the garage was full of things she could potentially sell. Dusty bikes, skis, tools, and a range of sports equipment. She set up an area to take photos in, cleaned off the dust, and made things look their best before their close-up. She made sure to take a photo of the model numbers or any maker's mark, as everyone seemed to ask for this. She went back inside and added another twelve listings to her Craigslist account.

The next day she was up early and pulled the Corolla out of the garage. She swept the entire garage clean and started to stage it. If people were coming to buy, she reasoned, why not show them what she had to sell? She found small post-it notes and put prices on everything she could.

Her first buyer was a local, older woman Maggie recognized but could not place. She loved the sample dining chair Maggie had brought out into the garage. Maggie then took her into the house to check out the table, which had been too heavy to move, and the rest of the chairs. The woman complimented the set and said she would take it. Maggie mentioned she was also selling the matching side tables and breakfronts as well, all part of her downsizing. The woman looked at them carefully, clearly interested, but said she'd think about it and get back to her.

Maggie's first sale gave her three thousand dollars, all in hundred-dollar bills, exactly what Maggie had asked for the dining set. Maggie had never seen that much cash at once. The woman said she would come back that evening to pick up the set.

Maggie was elated. It was going to be easier than she thought. She added price tags to the rest of the dining room set in case the woman was in the mood for more shopping when she came back. She also grabbed a place setting from each of the china sets and set up a card table in the garage with them. She priced the entire twelve-piece dinner settings and all the related serving pieces at one price.

Looking around, she considered running a garage sale. She would need help for that. Her best bet was asking Ethan and Izzy to help. Was it time to tell them? Maggie decided to wait until the weekly Sunday call to make that decision and kept working. She was not in a hurry to let the children know what was going on. Maggie was afraid of the questions that would probably follow and, if she was honest with herself, a little ashamed that she was in this position in the first place. It was like admitting she had failed somehow to keep her life together.

Maggie spent the day staging and dealing with the five buyers who had arranged to stop in. She sold the items they had come to see, sometimes settling for a little less just to move the items. She talked some of them into buying additional items, like sports equipment, and even sold one of the full china sets to a young mother. Late in the day, her initial customer returned with a rented truck. She had an adult son and her husband with her. They quickly maneuvered the table and chairs out, but to Maggie's disappointment, she did not buy any of the matching pieces.

After they left, she closed up the garage, sat down with a microwave dinner, and counted the day's takings: $5,625 in cash. She also had the coin rolls and a check from the coin dealer, as well as Patrick Bartlett's painting payment. Over ten thousand dollars in cash. It was an excellent start.

Having so much money in actual dollars and coins made her uncomfortable. Normally she would have just deposited the cash into her bank account, but now she was cautious about this. She knew that $2,381 would have to go to cover her overdraft. She wasn't ready to sacrifice this amount yet. She also wondered if the bank could somehow take the balance of what she deposited to automatically settle her credit card debts or, even worse, Neal's debts. She realized if she didn't want to keep all this cash on hand, she urgently needed to find a new bank and set up a new account.

Once again, she sunk into research and finally decided on an online bank called Ally, rather than one with physical offices. The benefit to this was that the online banks were offering accounts with no fees or minimum balance requirements. She could use a variety of bank ATMs for free and there were ways to link it to PayPal, an online payment service. If she tied a bank account to PayPal, she could buy online again. Almost all online banks were paying higher interest on accounts than the traditional banks. They could afford to, Maggie realized. They weren't paying for bank branches everywhere.

Maggie originally worried that an online bank might be a scam, but as she did more research, she became confident that online banking was simply the way banking was evolving. Ally called itself a *digital financial service company* and offered a range of accounts and services. Many of their "product" offerings Maggie did not understand—all that was important to her was that money she deposited would be insured by the Federal government. Ally promoted itself as an FDIC, a Federal Deposit Insurance Corporation, member which (Maggie learned) meant any deposits of up to one hundred thousand dollars were guaranteed by the government if the bank went out of business. Even better, Ally's interest on savings accounts was over two percent. That was a considerably higher interest rate than her old bank was offering.

Through Ally, Maggie could also set up access to a phone app called Venmo, which she could use to pay people, assuming the person had a means to accept it. There was no need to even have checks. It was a whole new world for her. *Not your father's banking*, she thought wryly. Little wonder Doris Leitner's bank office had gotten so much smaller.

The downside to Maggie's decision to move online was that there was no way to deposit cash through a computer. She learned she could convert her cash into something called a "cashier's check." This was a physical check that a bank wrote and guaranteed, made out to cash for whatever amount she gave them. It would cost her about ten dollars to get a cashier's check, but there was no limit on what it could be made out for. She could then use this check to set up a new account at Ally. She considered buying a money order, which was another way to send cash. A money order was cheaper, but they were generally used for amounts of less than one thousand dollars. Given her current cash position, they were not going to work for her.

Maggie decided to go to her bank first thing in the morning and see Doris to get a cashier's check. She was excited; it had been a successful day. As she went upstairs, she passed the dining room without its table and felt a tug. How many Christmas and Thanksgiving dinners had that table seen? Would the kids miss it?

She turned away and headed back upstairs knowing that, on balance, her selling the dining set was better than the alternative of someone else doing it for her.

The next morning, Maggie felt a little silly going into her old bank carrying a canvas bag full of rolled coins and cash. Lifting the bag took two hands. She set it down on the teller's window and explained what she wanted. He looked into the bag and frowned.

"We don't accept coin rolls."

Maggie started. "You don't accept money?"

"Well, not coin rolls," he repeated sheepishly.

Maggie looked around and saw Doris Leitner busy with another customer. She excused herself and went to sit down and wait until she was free.

Doris came up to Maggie after escorting her other customer to the door. She smiled, Maggie was becoming a bit more than just a customer to her. Maggie explained her situation, incredulous that the bank would not accept the rolls of coins that she remembered so fondly from childhood.

Doris laughed. "We don't have a coin counting machine here. A lot of banks don't anymore. The rolls are heavy, inconvenient, and take a lot of time, so we do not have to accept them. If a bank chooses to accept coins, it is usually limited to an amount under two hundred dollars. Most people just use the large coin counting machines, like Coinstar. You can find them at supermarkets. Mind you, Coinstar takes a fee of over ten percent." Sensing Maggie's disappointment, Doris continued with a twinkle in her eye. "You, however, are a customer, and we can make an exception for you. Let's get this sorted out."

Doris and Maggie returned to the teller and he counted out the coins, accepting the rolls at their face value. When everything, including her paper money, was finally counted, the total was $11,678. Doris raised her eyes a little at the amount. Maggie sheepishly admitted she had sold a coin collection and some things she had around the house. Maggie then held her breath, half expecting Doris to suggest she put the money into her account to cancel the overdraft. Instead, Doris authorized the teller to make out a cashier's check for the full amount, and even waived the fee.

"You and your husband are still premier customers, and premier customers get free cashier's checks," she explained. Maggie was grateful; every penny counted at this point.

Maggie suddenly had a spark of inspiration. "Ms. Leitner, I don't have online access to my bank account or my credit card. The bank does have that, doesn't it? Could we set that up now?" She lowered her voice and added softly, "I will get the overdrafts paid back—promise."

Doris smiled. "Please, call me Doris." Maggie beamed and said, "I'm Maggie." They walked together back to her cubicle. She set Maggie up with an ID and password so she could see both her accounts for the first time. She, of course, would have no visibility on Neal's accounts or the trust accounts, but this was a start. As Doris worked, Maggie explained about the foreclosure on the Cape, what it had taught her, and how she was learning to master Craigslist. She even sheepishly admitted she was going to open an account with an online bank.

Doris told her quietly that, considering her current financial situation, an online bank was probably the way to go. A full-service bank like hers was better suited to larger clients with a wider range of needs. She also whispered to Maggie that both her sons had Ally accounts. They also wanted to avoid bank fees and get better interest. For basic banking, online banking was the way to go, Doris admitted.

When everything was set up, Doris allowed Maggie to sign in on her computer to make sure it worked. When Maggie was finally online, it was not surprising to her that both balances were still negative. Maggie was just happy to have access to the accounts.

She planned on going home and looking at it in more detail. That way, she could get a feel for how online banking sites worked and what she could do. She knew that the Ally site would probably be different, but she assumed the more familiar she became with any online banking, the better. She knew that actually using the site, like she had with Craigslist, was the best way for her to learn. She would just click on things and see where they took her.

Doris walked Maggie to the door. As she walked out of the bank, Doris called, "Good luck!" to Maggie as she headed to her car. Doris noticed it was not the Lexus. Maggie waved back with a small smile.

As Maggie fastened her seatbelt, she felt pleased with herself. She knew the money she had raised so far was a good start, but she had a very long way to go. The more she thought about it, however, the more her good mood faded. There was still an overwhelming amount to do. As she started the car, she sighed and thought that her *liquidation* was going to be a lot more work than she had imagined it would be.

As Doris turned to go back inside, she realized her mood had been brightened by Maggie. *No moss growing on that rolling stone*, she thought. She had seen a lot of pampered women suddenly find themselves financially adrift. They usually relied on friends or family, living in spare rooms and basements. They frequently denied, even to themselves, their change in circumstance.

If these women didn't move on to another husband, they generally slid into a gentle poverty, often finding themselves working retail at some boutique they used to frequent. They usually ended up bitter or depressed. Doris could not remember ever seeing any of her pampered clients go from gob smacked to driven so quickly and effectively. The amount of cash Maggie had come in with and how she had raised it was admirable. Doris even chuckled about the coins. Maggie, she thought, was going to be someone to watch. Adversity just might be the making of her.

CHAPTER 5:
NET WORTH IS ONLY A NUMBER

Maggie set up her Ally online bank account with her cashier's check. After working for a while on Ally's site and her old bank's website, she began to feel confident about navigating around both and managing her accounts online. Both sites allowed her to set up electronic bill paying for her utilities so she would not need checks. She could track her account activity, including any interest she might eventually earn. There also were a variety of tools and investing advice available through both banks. She made a point of looking at one new thing every time she had to use one of the sites. She was determined to start educating herself.

When not in front of the computer, Maggie focused on raising cash to add to her Ally account. She worked diligently over the next ten days, selling the sports equipment and tools quickly, the furniture less so. She sold the TVs and loose electronic equipment, even tablets and old phones she found in drawers. Her antique items did not even get a single inquiry. She was mildly irritated when most of her Craigslist items expired after a week, requiring her to reactivate them. Then again, she reminded herself, the service was free so what was she complaining about? She also tried a few other vending sites to sell things, including Amazon for the old electronic equipment. She found there were quite a few ways to sell things online.

The jeweler called her late in the second week to give her the good news: her jewelry was appraised for over $120,000 in total. She was thrilled.

"The quality of the stones was excellent," he said warmly.

Surprisingly, a good portion of the value was due to the quality of her diamond engagement ring. She asked him to forward her an electronic copy of the appraisals so she might work out which items to let go. She had a target of raising at least thirty thousand dollars.

She took a break on Friday morning to go to the jeweler, excited and ready with a list of what her children wanted to keep and what she would part with. Maggie was, however, disappointed to learn that the appraisal value meant little in terms of liquidity. The cash value was, at best, sixty percent of the appraised value.

Maggie was crushed. The jeweler explained that appraised values were generally used for insurance purposes. When it came to selling a piece of jewelry, it was what a buyer was willing to pay for a piece. He explained that his customers usually expected a discount well below the appraised value.

Adding to her frustration was the fact that the jeweler was unwilling to take most pieces as is. He offered to take them if she was willing to be paid only for the value of the gold each was made of. He explained he would be melting down the pieces, as they were unlikely to sell in his store as is. He explained she might have more luck with a jeweler who specialized in antique jewelry. Sensing her frustration, he said he was willing to buy all of the newer "statement pieces." He explained they were still in style and he could probably sell them but, again, he was only willing to give her half the value they were appraised at. If he paid full price, he explained, there was no room for his profit margin and the discount he generally offered to entice buyers. Furthermore, he said there were *holding costs* as he might have to display the items for a long time before they actually sold.

In the end, Maggie kept her engagement ring, her mother's charm bracelet, and the items the girls wanted. She also took a good number of old pieces she just could not bear to see destroyed. She took photos of the pieces she reluctantly let go of. In the end, she got a check for $22,600, net the appraisal fee. Not only was the amount disappointing, but she knew she would regret selling her mother's pieces for a long time to come. *Like with the coin collection,* she told herself, *you just have to be tough.*

As she drove home, she fumed over the difference between the appraised or expected value of things and what their actual cash value was. She was finding the same to be true with all her other personal items. On paper, she looked like she was rich; the value of her jewelry, the antiques, the artwork, and other personal effects was substantial, but turning those assets into cash meant realizing her value on paper was not necessarily the same as cash on hand.

Neal had always told her that their *net worth* was in the millions. She had assumed that meant their houses and investments and personal effects, when all added up, were worth that. Now she realized that net worth was frequently more of a guesstimate than a real number. This was especially true if someone owned non-liquid assets like antiques, jewelry, or even houses. The amount someone was worth was not so clear anymore. Houses could be mortgaged, appraisals could be inflated, and heirlooms could be worthless. It was possible to *look rich* and still be a deadbeat.

She knew by the end of this selling process that her net worth would be just the cash she raised, plus or minus a few personal items she would try to keep. She was looking forward to the simple honesty of measuring her net worth through the cash she had. It would be a real number, not an imagined or implied bragging point.

Late Friday afternoon, in the second week of her downsizing, Tucker from the bank called her. The sale of the Cape Cod house had been a success and there would be no deficiency on the mortgage, he said. Maggie almost cried in relief. She had been afraid the poor condition of the property would mean they would get less than they owed on the mortgage. Tucker assured her the bank did well enough that even their fees would be paid. The location had been key, he told her.

Tucker did not, *could* not, let her know that the trust had realized a solid profit. Maggie would see none of that. It would sit in the trust account until the authorized trustee, probably Neal, directed the bank what to do with the money.

Maggie let Tucker know, matter-of-factly, she had decided she was going to leave the house in Concord.

"I realized it was too big for me alone, so I'm not fighting its foreclosure. I would consider a short sale, but I suppose I wouldn't get any money from the sale," she said. She did not want to admit the truth to Tucker, that she could not afford to stay.

He told her she was right, a short sale would only benefit the trust. He then said he would get back to her with a date for the sale. Tucker did not seem like he was going to rush her, but Maggie felt some urgency now that she had told him. She, and whatever she had left, would need to be out of the house by the sale date. While that date was still in the air, Maggie mentally gave herself another two weeks to get cleared out.

Maggie had accepted the foreclosure defeat. She also realized she would have to call Patrick Bartlett and get his help with the rest of the house, particularly the antiques and her parents' things. She realized antiques would probably do better at an auction than at a garage sale. It was also time to call the children and let them know what was happening. She had not heard from Neal or the FBI over the past two weeks, so she accepted there was not going to be any cavalry riding in to save her.

She planned to make each call individually rather than a group call. She would do it on Sunday, during the time for her normal check-in call. She had deliberately skipped these calls with them for the last two Sundays to avoid having to share what was going on in her life. They had, of course, traded text messages, but not talking made it easy to avoid telling them what was going on.

This Sunday, though, she was going to explain that Neal was going to be unreachable for a time. A business-related matter. She would reassure them that she was not worried. She didn't think of it as lying, she simply did not want to upset them until she knew exactly what was going on. She also did not want to tarnish their opinion of Neal. Like her, they had always assumed that his absences were a result of his success. She did not feel it was fair for her to share her frustration with Neal at this stage or let them worry about her financial situation. She wanted to protect them as long as she could.

She had decided not to tell them the houses had been foreclosed or that the FBI was looking for their father. She would simply tell them the Cape house had been sold and she was now preparing Concord for sale as well. For the time being, she would imply that Neal had agreed to all this. Maggie did not feel guilty about the omissions. When Neal resurfaced, they could decide together what to tell them.

To help distract the kids from probing questions, she planned to ask each one what they wanted to keep from the house. That was a safe topic. She even thought about asking for their help clearing their rooms, which would be a novelty. She had conditioned herself to never ask for help from anyone, particularly from her children. Her request for help would be a first.

The calls were surprising. The girls simply sounded excited; they had been teasing her about downsizing for years. They knew how much upkeep the house and gardens required. Selling both houses sounded like a good thing to them. Neither of them questioned the abrupt timeframe nor seemed particularly sentimental about losing their childhood home. Maggie assumed they needed time for the magnitude of the changes to really sink in. Or maybe they had just successfully moved on with their lives.

Izzy assumed her parents would move into the city, to an apartment, to be closer to her and Ethan. Both girls were so used to Neal's absences they were not overly concerned when Maggie mentioned she was handling the downsizing on her own. They knew their mother frequently took on large projects like this and seemed to enjoy them. Their father rarely involved himself in household matters and generally made himself scarce until the worst was over. As to Neal's absence, since leaving home both girls had sometimes gone weeks without hearing from him. Since Maggie passed his absence off as a minor inconvenience, they seemed to accept it without question.

Only Ethan, her last call, seemed to sense something was amiss. He suspected the house sales were somehow related to Neal's absence. He seemed to hesitate for a moment on the cusp of a question but did not ask. It was an awkward moment that neither managed well until Maggie redirected the conversation. She asked for Ethan's help with clearing out the house. Ethan was clearly surprised by the request. He knew his mother rarely asked for anyone's help, and certainly never his.

"Well," Maggie said proudly, "I have mastered Craigslist. I even sold some furniture this week. I just need you kids to come home and let me know what you might want to keep. Take what you can, and then we can arrange to move the rest. Especially the things in your bedrooms."

"Mom, why aren't you using an estate agent for all this? You can't be moving furniture on your own, and I don't like the thought of you letting strangers into the house. Dad should be there to help. So typical that he bailed on you." Ethan was clearly angry. He went on, "Dad was never around for any of those renovations you managed. I can't believe you are having to handle this all on your own."

"Not to worry," Maggie soothed him. "I had an estate agent for the Cape house, and it went well. The agent is helping out here too. I just wanted to see if I could do some of it on my own."

She was a little hurt to hear Ethan so bitter about his father's absence but not surprised. Ethan and Neal had never clicked. They had spent most of his high school years on a slow simmer with one another. Neal took no interest in things that Ethan enjoyed, rarely played with him as a child, and dismissed his dyslexia as laziness. When Ethan developed a passion for planes at a very early age, Neal's only acknowledgement was to complain about them being left around the house.

Later on, Neal outright refused to let him take an introductory flying lesson which Ethan had painstakingly earned the money for. It was something Ethan had never let go of. Maggie thought of it as the tipping point that had permanently soured their relationship.

In college, Ethan had worked hard to overcome his dyslexia and focused on math and computer modelling. When Ethan started as an analyst at a prestigious investment bank out of college, Maggie briefly hoped father and son would finally have something in common. Neal, however, refused to talk to Ethan about his work. Unless Ethan was at the house, they never even spoke. Neal's absence and (in Ethan's words) abandonment of Maggie and the family. Maggie suspected that a close relationship was unlikely to develop.

At the end of each call, Maggie had let them know that she thought Dad's business was having issues, and perhaps that had something to do with his extended absence. She said casually that he was not contacting her much, and that she was a little cross with him lately. She finished each call with a request that they let her know if Neal contacted them.

She felt relieved having the calls behind her. Izzy and Ethan had both agreed to come to Concord and take a look at what remained in their old rooms. They would take out what they wanted. Charlie asked if most of her things could just be held until she got home, ignoring the fact there would be no home to come to. Hearing Charlie's dilemma, Ethan graciously offered to pay for a storage unit for all of them in case there were things they wanted to keep that they currently did not have room for.

Fortunately, not one of the kids thought to ask specifically about where she and Neal were going to live. Children like hers, who had grown up never having to worry about money, simply assumed their parents had everything under control. She did not mention that there was a possibility that she and Neal would not be living together, or that she might need to get a job to support herself. Maggie figured that the houses being sold and Neal being AWOL was enough for the kids to absorb at this point.

Maggie would let them know her next steps when everything was worked out. Where she would go, though, *was* beginning to worry her. She was not surprised that neither Ethan, Izzy nor Charlie had fully worked out that Neal's disappearance might be straining her financial resources. How many children realized how financially precarious their parents' later life might be? Did they just assume there would be money for retirement? Or that their parents could work forever? She suspected she was not alone in her rising concern about her future. She was grateful that she was luckier than many of her peers; she had no college loans for her children, healthcare issues or mortgages to worry about. She could focus on building assets, not paying off debts. She suspected she was ahead of many other parents in that regard.

Maggie felt it was time to reassess her financial situation as a whole. Again, the good news was that she had no major debts, no loans, and due to the foreclosures, no mortgages to worry about. She didn't know what other debts Neal may have subjected her to by having her co-sign on the other credit cards, but she would worry about those when, and if, the debts surfaced.

So far, her account at Ally Bank had grown to over fifty thousand dollars. She knew it was now time to deal with the overdrawn checking account and the credit card balance. She was responsible for them as they were her accounts, after all. The overdrawn bank account was at -$2,380.62. She now had the money to pay that, so she went online and made a payment from Ally to her old bank. Since the overdraft was paid, she realized that the account was probably available to her to use again if she put money into it. It was a win.

The credit card was a bigger problem, there, she owed over eight thousand. More importantly, looking at her statement online for the first time, she had realized she was being charged over two hundred dollars of interest on the unpaid balance every month. She had checked it to make sure it was not a mistake. In the fine print, she saw that the interest on her balance was twenty-six percent. She knew paying this balance off was critical, to avoid the massive two-hundred-dollar monthly interest fee. If she did not settle this credit card debt, in twelve months, she would end up paying $2,400 in interest on a debt of just eight thousand dollars. That was just crazy. Credit card debt was the worst, she decided. It felt like she was paying a loan shark. She knew when she got her credit card back, she would be diligent about paying on time, each month, so she could avoid interest charges. She would never keep a "balance" on a credit card again—it was just another name for a debt, and expensive debt at that.

Having online access to her credit card statement was a win for her. After she paid off the bank account overdraft, she finally had the courage to look at her credit card statement. She realized that a number of items she had charged were sitting unused in her closet or kitchen. She checked and found most still had the tags on them. First thing the following morning, she returned everything she could, reducing the balance to $3,400. She paid off this new balance immediately using the Ally account. It was a weight off her shoulders.

She called Doris and found she was now settled up, in the bank's view. Doris even offered to reissue her credit card and Maggie, reluctantly, agreed. She vowed to herself that she would not use it except for emergencies.

She accepted that she needed help with the household items that were not selling. She called Patrick and said she wanted his help to liquidate the house. She was going to keep up with Craigslist and eBay, both of which she was having success with, but there was simply too much left. Patrick agreed to return, and they would work out the timing. He suggested, however, that she first contact Aiko Hayashi, a young woman he occasionally worked with on sales like Maggie's. She was a personal organizer who helped people clean up their lives, get organized, and make money while doing so. She would help clear "soft goods," as Patrick called them.

Patrick explained, "Aiko calls herself a *closet Indiana Jones*. In her purges, she often finds things of value that most people overlook. I remember she once found a truly ugly leather jacket in a client's closet. Garish by all accounts, but from a well-known designer who was still in demand. Aiko sold it for the client for two thousand dollars!"

They settled on a time for Patrick to come back up to house and Maggie took Ms. Hayashi's number. She called her immediately. Maggie smiled when she heard a bright recorded voice say, "Aiko here. If you are overwhelmed with your things, I can help turn your Temple of Doom into a palace. Leave your number and we'll talk!" A crack of a whip sound effect finished the message. When Aiko called back, Maggie liked her immediately. She outlined what she needed, and Aiko explained to Maggie that she charged twenty-five dollars an hour to organize. She would help Maggie tag items and evaluate what to charge for things. She would also help her decide what to throw out.

"That's what most people need my help with, whether they realize it or not," Aiko said. "Permission to let things go."

Aiko said she would even post items Maggie wanted to sell on a variety of online sites and then manage the posts if Maggie wanted her to.

Maggie explained that she was short on cash. Aiko immediately changed gears, "I can work on commission instead, taking ten percent of anything I sell. My focus, then, would be on selling rather than organizing."

Maggie calculated that if Aiko worked an eight-hour day and she was paid twenty-five dollars an hour, Maggie would owe her two hundred dollars. Alternatively, she would have to find and sell over two thousand dollars-worth of goods to have her earn the same amount on commission. Maggie found it hard to believe that hiring Aiko would result in her finding two thousand dollars-worth of goods that Maggie had overlooked but why not give it a try? Maggie knew that with her limited knowledge about what types of things sold, she could very easily throw away something valuable.

"Well, let's work on the ten percent commission to start," Maggie offered. Using Aiko was definitely cheaper than using Patrick, with his thirty-five percent commission. "Can you come by the house tomorrow?"

"Bright and early! See you at seven!" was the chirpy reply.

Maggie hung up and realized she was looking forward to having someone else in the house. The downsizing had been lonely.

Seven a.m. was early for Maggie, especially because she got up even earlier than was strictly necessary to make muffins. They were hot when Aiko arrived, exactly on time. Aiko looked Eurasian, tall, her long hair streaked purple and pulled into high pigtails. She wore a mix of layers over black tights with combat boots. Maggie thought she looked more like an anime character than an estate agent.

During coffee and muffins, Maggie discovered Aiko lived in town and had gone to the local public school. Her mother taught chemistry there. Aiko told funny stories about her effort to avoid her in the halls, with no success as her mother always hunted her down. Aiko quickly finished two muffins as they talked and looked longingly at the muffin basket. Maggie insisted she have as many muffins as she liked, and Aiko happily apologized for taking a third muffin and tucking it into her bag. She excitedly explained she had never had home baked goods before. Maggie smiled at her enthusiasm.

She asked to start with Maggie's closet, which surprised Maggie. They went up to her master walk-in. If the size of the closet surprised Aiko, she did not show it. She immediately went to the bags lined up in a wall of cubbies and began to pull them out. Maggie inhaled sharply; she had not thought about the bags. They were pricey, very pricey. They had always been a satisfying purchase for her because she found as she got older buying clothes had become less appealing. She had spent many satisfying days accumulating her bag collection.

Aiko turned to Maggie, cocked her head charmingly, and asked, "How many can I sell?"

Maggie realized it was an easy question. "All of them."

"And priced to sell?" Aiko now asked enthusiastically.

"Sure. Make yourself at home. Choose anything you want. Go crazy. Please just leave me something to wear. And," Maggie grinned as she grabbed one of her favorite bags, "Not this one. I need to have something left over to put all the money in."

"What about the closet on the other side?"

Maggie was not ready for the question. *Neal's clothes?* Of course, he was going to want them. Maybe she could stuff them in the kids' new storage container. But then again...his suits alone were worth thousands and thousands of dollars.

"Leave it for now; it's my husband's stuff and I think he is still undecided on what he is going to do. We can revisit it later on. But there is a luggage closet just off the bedroom that might have some things you could add to the list."

Aiko pulled out bags and artfully displayed them on the closet's granite island to snap a series of photos. Maggie left her and went to the computer to check her messages and the posts. A couple more buyers were supposed to come by that morning, so she shifted more of the smaller bits of furniture, side tables, and chairs to the garage.

By this point, Maggie had sold most of the sports equipment and all the old cameras and video gear. Hardest to let go of were her collection of garden tools. Her small John Deere tractor sold for more than she had paid for it new. She left herself a handful of her best hand tools and a favorite spade, the new lawnmower, a leaf blower, and a rake. She justified it by telling herself she had to keep the house looking tidy up until the foreclosure sale. She would decide what to do with them when she knew where she was going to be.

Aiko came down around 11 a.m. with a grin on her face. "Quite a collection. You have over thirty bags up there, and a lot of them are vintage. Some look new. Great condition. There were a few great pieces in the luggage closet as well. I put all the scarves online, and a few jackets, but I left most of the clothes."

Maggie realized this was probably not because she was being left things to wear, but because Aiko didn't think her clothes had enough resale value. "What do you think I might get?" she asked.

"All up I think you are looking at well over forty thousand dollars."

Maggie just gaped at her. It sounded too good to be true. Was this like the jewelry, high retail estimate but less in cash? "Do you mean that they are worth forty thousand or that I *get* forty thousand?"

"Get. Well, minus my ten percent commission, of course," Aiko said with a grin.

She then went on to explain that bags and scarves like those in Maggie's collection, made by designers like Louis Vuitton and Hermes, held their value pretty well. Sometimes they even went up in value, like Maggie's Birkin bag. Vintage was hot and that could really hike the value up. Aiko generally got at least sixty to seventy percent of their original purchase price, well above the cash value of jewelry.

Maggie was astounded. She knew many of the bags she had purchased for thousands of dollars, but resale had never occurred to her. Aiko's next step was to ask if her children's electronic toys or game consoles were around. Maggie went with her to the basement, which was where the kids had always gathered with their friends. Aiko began to dig through drawers and happily found discarded Game Boys, loads of game cartridges, and stacks of video games. There were also a variety of old game consoles, another thing Maggie would have assumed had little or no value. Aiko quickly began to separate the drawer's contents, creating a pile of electronics to sell and putting things aside that she said were so outdated had little or no value. Maggie would have the children look at these before she sold or tossed them.

Aiko again began to photograph and post items to a variety of sites. She explained to Maggie that she was a "trusted vendor" on many of these sites, so when she posted things they tended to go quickly, particularly if the price was right. Maggie realized now why Aiko had been eager to work on ten percent commission. It was money well spent, though, as she would probably have donated or even thrown out most of these goods, never knowing how valuable they were.

Aiko continued going through various closets for the rest of the day, putting aside some things. Other things she bluntly told Maggie to donate or throw away, as they were not worth the trouble of trying to sell them. She said china, crystal, and silver were not her thing.

Aiko waved her hand and said, "Mr. Bartlett handles the *old-timey* things."

After a quick lunch, Maggie finally worked up the nerve to tackle the basement storage room. She pushed aside the boxes of personal effects which she knew would lead to tears and instead concentrated on the furniture, paintings, and knick-knacks. There was little of interest to Aiko in here, which Maggie was grateful for—she wasn't too eager to let any of her parents' things go, despite her circumstances.

At some point she noticed that one box was marked "Will," her dead brother. She realized it was going to be one of the last things she would go through. It would be too painful. She asked Aiko to move the boxes to the back of the room, so they were out of sight.

Patrick came by the next day and was very impressed with Maggie's progress.

"Well, you set the standard for me, Patrick. I don't think you left a crumb for a mouse in our Cape house. And I had Aiko here yesterday, and she does indeed crack a whip. I think she winnowed out a third of my life before she left yesterday. And we are both better off for it."

He laughed at her experience with Aiko.

"She is going to be a very wealthy woman someday," he observed.

They agreed to try a living estate sale at the house, like he had done in the Cape property. They would then auction the larger pieces that were left afterward. Maggie had prepared the inventory in Excel for him. She had suggested prices for each item, marking those she had already managed to sell and at what price. Patrick was impressed with how much she had already sold.

Maggie had bought brightly colored stickers and they walked through each room of the house, tagging all items. The price Patrick recommended was often well below what Maggie had hoped the item was worth. They finished up in the early afternoon and decided the sale would be in ten days. That way, Patrick would have a chance to advertise and Maggie's children could clear their rooms of personal items.

"You are moving very fast," Patrick said. "Where are you planning to go?"

"I haven't decided yet, though my daughter Izzy wants me to move into the city. A lot depends on how much money I raise with all this. And I am going to be getting a job. I suppose I will want to live close to where I work. I would love to walk to work, rather than have a long commute. I used to commute for an hour to my first job after college, and I hated it."

"What did you do then?"

"I was a 'case team assistant' at a consulting firm. I thought I was going to be doing analysis for them. In reality, I was just a secretary for a bunch of male, Ivy League graduates who didn't have a clue how to use me. I just ended up filing, getting coffee and copying a lot, that kind of thing. The job description sounded better than the work actually was."

Patrick laughed. "It sounds like they just wanted a secretary, but you had bigger plans."

"I was ambitious," Maggie said with a smile. "My third month there, I prepared a really complicated Lotus123 spreadsheet to organize the raw data they were working with. I was pretty proud of it—and yes, I admit, I had a crush on the guy I did it for. I wanted to show him I could do more than just file. He was really excited about my work and from then on asked me to stay back at night to check his work and do other models. He was always promising me a chance to eventually join the team in meetings, to travel with him to do client visits. He would flirt with me and give me back massages as I worked at the computer late at night."

Maggie paused and then said, "One day, I overheard him being complimented on *his* model by our boss. When I confronted him about it, he just told me I was being difficult. He had the gall to tell me I had only *proofed* his work, I hadn't originated it. He lied to my face and expected me to believe him. Then of course, he had me moved to another team, giving me a bad review and complaining about my 'attitude' so I wouldn't make trouble for him. I didn't dare complain, I knew they would believe him not a case team assistant. I felt like an idiot for trusting him, for liking him. I was branded a problem after that." She laughed, a little bitterly. "I don't have really positive memories of being in the workforce."

"Well, now I understand why the inventory you prepared for me is so complete! I even noticed you have prettied up the format quite a bit. Must be the artist in you. If you don't mind, I'd love to use it as a template for my clients going forward. It is much better than the one I have been using."

"Oh, of course! I'd be flattered."

"Given what we got done today, and my *new* template, I am only going to charge you twenty-five percent of what we raise at the estate sale. You have done a big chunk of the work we normally have to do prior to a sale. We are pretty much ready to go, except for the advertising."

"Sounds great!"

"On the day before and day of, I will have at least five helpers here. The house is large, and we are going to have to move all the 'carry goods' to one central location."

"What will the helpers do?"

"They'll take cash and help bundle the goods out. Think of them as high-pressure salespeople who double as furniture movers. They keep an eye out for the people who try to get the 'five finger discount'—that is, people who pocket something and try to walk off without paying. They also negotiate prices; most people will ask for a discount, and the helper then suggests a 'bundle' of items to make sure things move. If we left it to customers to make up their own minds, we would only clear half of what we need to sell."

Things moved quickly over the next ten days. Maggie steeled herself and called Agent Munoz at the FBI, but he did not offer any additional information. He assured her that if there was any possibility something had happened to Neal, they would likely know about it. Maggie took this as a good sign. She then explained that she was moving. Agent Munoz was interested that she was selling the house. "Where are you headed?" he asked.

"I honestly don't know yet, but you will be the first person I call. After the kids of course."

After she hung up, she realized that the longer Neal was gone, the more she felt it was natural for him to be gone. She realized she had not really missed him at all during this whole process, which surprised her. She had been pretty indifferent about Neal for these last few years, but she was disappointed to realize the only emotion she could muster was a minor concern for his well-being. And, of course, a deep anger and frustration with him for leaving her in the lurch like this. A lifetime with someone and he generated less emotion in her than a stranger might. It was sad, really.

Izzy and Ethan came by early morning three days before the sale. Izzy was a tall and well-polished brunette who came in work jeans and a tee-shirt. She hugged her mother and Maggie noticed her dark brown eyes glistening as she took in the cleared rooms and tags on things. Clearly, it was now really sinking in for her. Izzy rallied though, not wanting to make it harder on Maggie than she suspected it was. Despite the fact Maggie had again baked muffins, the banana ones the kids preferred, Izzy declined coffee and headed upstairs to her room. She would have a cry on her own.

Ethan followed her in looking like a handsome surfer in a tightly tailored dark grey suit.

"Not clothes to work in," Maggie noted with a motherly sigh.

"Need to go into the office later. I have a change of clothes if I need them." He held up his gym bag to demonstrate.

Maggie noticed his blond hair was a bit too long and his suit too tight around his biceps. Ethan was tall and classically handsome. He had deep set eyes that matched Maggie's and a full generous mouth that always seemed to find something amusing in life. He accepted her offer of muffins and, with coffee in hand, walked with Maggie through the downstairs, taking a few small items for his apartment. Some bookends, a vase or two. A painting. Maggie was surprised by the sentimentality of his choices.

Both children ended up taking more than she expected. An hour into it, Ethan called his office to say he would not make it in and changed into his gym clothes. Together they cleared Neal's closet for her, moving his clothes into boxes Patrick had supplied. They tagged items from their rooms that they were willing to sell. Sticky notes marked "Keep" went onto bookcases, boxes of mementos, and childhood books. They also marked dressers and some other items in the house which they said they would want when they eventually moved into larger places. They put everything they could into Ethan's room and Maggie locked the door.

Izzy helped her mother clean out the kitchen. She took the odd item—a juicer, a grater, and other things she said she remembered as part of her child-hood—but she said she did not want any china, crystal, or silver. Ethan and she split glassware and the everyday china and flatware. At the last minute, she reversed course and packed up Maggie's favorite china set and a few silver table accessories that had been passed down to Maggie and marked it for storage.

"For family Thanksgivings," she explained sheepishly. Maggie smiled and felt tears coming on which she quickly fought back.

Ethan came in to finish the muffins and claimed a few additional items for his kitchen. Old cutting boards, some Italian Majorca. They ordered take-out and had one last dinner outside in the garden. They all looked around wistfully but kept the talk small, offering work anecdotes and vacation plans. They all avoided talk of Neal or the move.

Ethan and some of his buddies came the Friday before the sale with a rented truck and moved his, Neal's and Charlie's things into a self-storage unit. His girlfriend, Hannah, came along to help and took some of Maggie's favorite vases. All of Charlie's room went into the unit for her to go through later.

Ethan and Hannah also offered to come help with the estate sale the next day. Maggie declined their offer, and later Izzy's, too. Watching the sale was going to be sad enough for her, and she preferred the children remember the house as full and happy.

Aiko came by and collected most of the remaining bags and all the games the kids had released for sale. She had already sold the bulk of Maggie's inventories, and once the bags were shipped, she said she would give Maggie a final check. The amount was almost at the promised forty thousand, with more to come.

The estate sale was a whirlwind. People came in waves. Maggie watched the nightmare she had been having the past two weeks become reality. People swarmed the house, even asking about fixtures. She sold a chandelier she had brought from her mother's home, the buyer expertly removing it. Her house was disassembled, and people carted it away. Finally seeing it, she realized it was more than just goods being sold. Her old life was being carted away. It was more of a gut punch than she had expected. She often excused herself throughout the day to hide her brimming tears.

Patrick's helpers hustled. They raced around their assigned areas, introducing themselves to browsers and highlighting the quality of everything. She saw them filling gaps as soon as things sold. She heard them hard sell many items offering them for almost nothing. She had to stop herself from intervening and grabbing things away from them.

After the estate sale was done, they still had the baby grand, the kids' pool table, the dining room breakfronts, various pieces of furniture, and a number of paintings and rugs that she would send to auction. Most of her books remained but Patrick said he would take them to sell. She had kept the things she wanted locked in her bedroom, including kitchen things, her coffee maker and a micro- wave, along with other odds and ends. She had pulled a couple more things during the sale, like a favorite antique lamp which she caught a helper offering for less than five dollars. She only realized during the sale that she was going to have to furnish a new place and all she had kept were a bedroom set, a desk and some kitchen things. She would surely need a sofa, for instance, and, at some point, a replacement dining table. How much would that all cost? Maggie hoped she would not regret selling everything.

The next day, Maggie paid to have the remaining large items—especially the piano and pool table—carted off to be auctioned or sold on commission. The house, now, was basically empty. The bank had given her a date, and she had another week until she had to leave.

When everything settled, the estate sale's final number was $204,000, net fees. With her other cash and the money Aiko still owed her, she had just over $286,000. She would probably get a bit more after the auction. The Corolla was probably worth an additional $12,000. If the house sale covered the mortgage and there was no deficiency, Maggie's net worth would be just over $300,000 she esti- mated. That was what she had to show for twenty-seven years of marriage. She knew it was more than most Americans her age had saved for retirement, but it looked paltry to her. She couldn't live on just this for the rest of her life. She imag- ined she had at least thirty years ahead of her, which meant less than ten thousand dollars a year to live on. It would simply not be enough.

It was, however, enough to carry her through the next phase, getting her settled into her new life. She would have to get a job and find someplace to live. With the house empty and the selling over, she was ready for a new beginning. While her net worth was only a number, today it was a good number. One she was sure she could build on.

CHAPTER 6:
A BUDGET THAT FITS

Maggie's search for a place to live started as most things did for her these days: online. She toyed with the idea of buying a small apartment with her nest egg, somewhere on the outskirts of the city where she could afford to buy a place outright. Gina Bartlett had told her she would get a better price if she could pay cash. That would be the only option for her with her current credit rating. Getting a mortgage was not an option.

She daydreamed about finding a place she could fix up and then "flip" like they did on television. She was pretty handy now, and she enjoyed the work. She knew she had a good eye, but she also knew something like that was a gamble. It was more likely that there would be unexpected problems with the place that could exceed her renovation budget. With her life where it was at the moment, everything would have to fall into place exactly. If she was younger and working, she might have taken that gamble, but not now.

The thought of renting made her crazy. She would be paying money to someone in exchange for a place to live. It would drain her cash. If she was using her money, she wanted it to be building something for herself, not for her landlord.

She looked online at the apartments that had gourmet kitchens and spa bathrooms like the ones she had taken for granted for years. She knew that they were well out of her reach. The places she thought she could afford looked like the ones she had lived in directly out of college. Was she going to have to go back to that? It was depressing.

Even thinking about renting was a problem. First, she needed to know how much she was earning before she knew how much she could actually afford for an apartment. Most landlords would ask about her income when they checked her references. Her poor credit rating might also be a problem. It seemed that some landlords also checked that out.

Maggie was committed to follow the financial advice she had heard, to keep her housing costs to only one third of whatever her take-home pay was going to be. That would leave two thirds of her salary to live on and save with. She would keep to that even if meant she had to take a room in someone's house. She was determined that she was not going to tap into her nest egg to live.

When Aiko came by with a final check for Maggie, she invited her in for coffee. While they chatted, Maggie asked Aiko her advice about living options. Aiko surprised her by saying she did not know the rental market at all. She had simply returned home after college three years ago and was still living there. She did not pay anything for rent.

Aiko explained she liked living with her parents. They had dinner ready for her every night, cleaned the house, did her laundry and took care of the yard. They even paid her phone bill and the utilities. She had finally gotten the pug she had always wanted as her parents were there to take care of him whenever she needed them to. She giggled a little and said, "Living with my parents is like having an old-fashioned wife. They take care of all the silly, day-to-day details."

"But there are downsides!" Aiko exclaimed. "My parents always want to know when I am coming home and where I am going. They do not like my friends coming over and staying late. They still treat me like a child."

Maggie hid an ironic smile behind her cup. Aiko wanted to be treated like an adult yet let her parents still handle all the mundane chores and costs associated with running a home. That did not exactly define Aiko as an independent, fully functioning adult. She was surprised Aiko did not see the irony.

"Why not get a place on your own then?" Maggie asked.

"Oh no! The best thing about being at home is that I can save just about everything I earn. I have a nice car, but I save the rest of my money. When I have enough for a proper down payment on a place, then I will move. I want to buy a place, not rent. I can't move until then."

Maggie suddenly realized that once the house sold, none of her children would ever be able to return home to live if they wanted to save for a place. What would Charlie do when she got back if Maggie didn't have a room for her? Live with a sibling? Maggie realized she may end up needing an even larger apartment than she had originally planned on - meaning more money. She shuddered.

Aiko did not notice. "My biggest frustration with living at home is that when I turn 26 this year, my parents say I have to pay for my own health insurance! Legally, I am going to be dropped from their policy." She pouted, clearly frustrated,

"Health insurance is ridiculously expensive. I told them I was not going to get it. After all, I am healthy and young and just don't need it. They say it was either buy health insurance or pay rent. They said they would use my rent money to pay for my health insurance."

Maggie found it amusing that Aiko was almost indignant that she was expected to pay for her own health insurance. If she was Aiko's parents, she would have insisted she have it as well. A healthcare crisis could bankrupt anyone, especially someone without insurance. If there was a problem, a parent would probably step in to help. That could pull them down the financial drain. Health care insurance for Aiko was insurance for her parents in some ways.

Then Maggie groaned to herself. She had not thought about her own health insurance. She hadn't received any notices about discontinuation. Was she still covered? She would have to check. And get herself a policy if she was not. Another expense. She pulled over her pad of lists and made a note of it on the page marked "Budget" while they talked.

Maggie had already moved her phone to a new, less expensive carrier last week to make sure her service was not interrupted. There had been a balance due on the old service, which had included her internet. She paid up to the end of the month and closed the account. She planned on using the free Wi-Fi at the library for her job search if she was not settled by then. She had not tackled other necessary expenses yet. There was so much she didn't know yet. She had been making notes about preparing a budget spreadsheet, but these new expenses just kept cropping up.

Realizing Aiko knew nothing about the rental market, Maggie switched gears and asked if she had any experience with Airbnb. "I have heard a lot about it from my children. They use it for their weekends away. I understand I can rent a single room in someone's house until I find a place. I was thinking I could take a room and then store some of my things until I work out my living arrangement."

"I do use Airbnb," Aiko said nodding her head. "It is very good, and I am picky. Generally, I only use the highest ranked sites, and they have all been great. I don't know about longer term rentals, though there are plenty offered on the site. Be careful about storage, though, it can be very expensive. Hundreds of dollars a month. The cost of renting a storage unit versus just getting rid of things is why I have so many clients. Why pay to store things when they can make you money, instead?" Aiko suddenly snapped her fingers. "Hey, do you want to live with some-one your age?"

Maggie smiled. "I am just getting out of a marriage, Aiko," she said, suddenly realizing the truth of this. "I think it's a little early to be looking for a new husband."

"No, no. I mean a *lady* your age. I have been working for her on and off this year, clearing out her things. She has a huge house with lots of rooms she does not use. She asked if I wanted to move in with her. She has two dogs and travels a lot, so she wants someone to live with her to take care of them when she leaves. She thinks they are happier in the house than in a kennel. She offered me the rooms at the back of her house. The area is really huge, with a big bathroom and even its own TV room. Separate door and a garage for your car. I could ask her for you."

Maggie's initial reaction was to say no, thank you. Then she thought about it. Would she do it? How would it be different from an Airbnb? It might be a good fit, at least until she got a job sorted out, which would influence both what she could afford and where she would live. Neal had never allowed any pets in the house; they were too much work. Maggie, however, had always liked dogs. How much work could it really be?

"Thank you for the offer, Aiko. You weren't even interested? What's this woman like?" Maggie asked.

"My dog doesn't like other dogs, and besides, I am happy at home. The lady, though, has lots of money. Her clothes closets are three full rooms, a separate one for just boots and shoes! They are in glass cases, all lit up. Beautiful. She only asks me to sell things because she needs room for new things."

Aiko didn't really answer her question about the woman herself. She was probably avoiding specifics, just to be polite. "Well, mention to her that I am look-ing for a place. If she is interested, she and I can get together and see what we think."

They finished their coffee. As she was leaving, Maggie gave Aiko a large terracotta pot containing the tubers from one of her favorite peony plants. She also gave her a painting of them she had done a few years ago as a thank you for all of her help. Aiko had admired this specific painting when they had discussed selling the better ones in her portfolio. They both thought the paintings would need to be framed to interest buyers. After Maggie looked into the expense to frame them, she thought it would cost more than the paintings themselves could be sold for.

Aiko was thrilled with the painting; it was her first *real* artwork. As to the peony, her mother was a gardener so she would give it a good home. She hugged Maggie on the way out and wished her luck.

Within a few days, Maggie got a call from a woman with a broad cockney accent who introduced herself as Olivia Mundt. She literally giggled about Aiko, saying, "A real matchmaker, that girl." After a few minutes of polite back and forth while they felt each other out, she invited Maggie for coffee at her house and Maggie agreed.

The address was just the next town over. Maggie had some trouble finding it until she realized it meant driving down a long unmarked road. The "house" she expected was actually a large estate. It was an old, two-story fieldstone building with a slate roof. The building and grounds looked a little tired, though. Maybe it was just that they were moving into fall, Maggie thought. When she rang the bell, it was answered by an extraordinarily stylish woman.

Maggie realized that Aiko might have been off on the age difference. Olivia was older, perhaps even into her seventies, but had clearly had some very good work done so it was difficult to work out her age exactly. Her hair was fashionably ironed and bleached an unnatural white that suited her perfectly. Her clothes and jewelry impressed Maggie, especially the enormous diamond on her hand and her matching earrings, which sparkled wonderfully. Her oversized but tailored sweater was a soft, warm cashmere and her knee-high leather boots were spectacular. Maggie knew she could never pull off this outfit. Everything was perfectly proportioned to Olivia's trim, athletic build. Maggie guessed she was currently wearing tens—or, given the diamonds, maybe even hundreds—of thousands of dollars.

Olivia smiled a perfect and clearly genuine smile. She held a graying Cavalier King Charles Spaniel under one arm while another, clearly younger, danced around her feet.

"Come in, come in! I have the coffee ready for us. I have the most wonderful tea cake. I have it sent over from Harrods."

Maggie was shown into what could easily have been an English country house, all chintz and overstuffed chairs. The woodwork was gleaming and the details impeccable. Olivia chatted happily while she poured from a china coffee pot into proper cups with matching saucers. She handed Maggie a cup with a coffee spoon neatly balanced on its side. She then sliced the tea cake, serving herself a generous slice and placing a smaller one on a plate with a tiny fork in front of Maggie.

"So, Aiko told you about the dogs needing a babysitter? I am in the UK a lot; my little brother has been diagnosed with cancer and doesn't have a wife or anybody else to care for him. I need someone to look after my little ones while I'm away. I am afraid Bunny here is getting on—deaf, we think, and pretty blind. Of course, Buster is still frisky. He is almost seven years younger and I think he bullies poor Bunny these days."

"Well, I have never had dogs," Maggie admitted. "But I like them." The younger dog wagged appreciatively as she patted his head. "What's involved in taking care of Buster and Bunny?"

"Well, Bunny is a bit of work. Her meds and all—injections, unfortunately. Both need to go out twice a day, but Buster especially needs a true walk outdoors. I have a stroller I use for Bunny when I am walking them. Not far really, just around the house and gardens. Bunny will mess occasionally. She has her old lady pills, but they don't stop the piddles entirely." Maggie noted Olivia's broad, lower class accent did not match the tasteful surroundings.

They talked more about the dogs and the house. Then Olivia asked Maggie about her family and her background. Maggie outlined the basics, three children and a lifetime of taking care of them. Olivia then asked, "Would you be interested in moving in?"

Maggie took a deep breath and said, "I think the dogs and I can get along. I would be comfortable giving Bunny her injections, but I would need to see it done a couple times. I need, however, to be honest here. Just so you understand, I am in a somewhat odd situation. My house has been foreclosed, and I have to be out in a week or so. I will need to find work; I don't have a job yet. I am not sure what work I am going to find, because I haven't had a paying position for over twenty-five years. If we both agree to go ahead, I don't know for how long it would be. I see it as a bit of a stop gap, really, a low-cost place to live until I can figure out my situation."

Olivia looked meaningfully at Maggie's engagement and wedding rings. "Husband?"

"AWOL." Olivia looked a little confused by the term. "Absent Without Leave. Not in the picture," Maggie clarified.

"Hmm. Been there, done that," Olivia sipped her coffee. After a moment, she said. "I think you are missing the point. I do not expect rent. Or for you to pay for utilities. You will be doing me a favor by house sitting, overseeing the housekeepers who come in twice a week and the landscape people. Of course, taking care of the dogs when I am away is the most important thing. I should probably be paying you, but I am too tight for that."

"Oh!" Maggie thought for a moment. That made things much more interesting. "Well," she smiled, "that means we won't be arguing about rent."

After they finished their coffees, Olivia took Maggie through a large, wonderfully appointed and modern kitchen to a narrow staircase that led to the back wing of the house. She opened a closed door that opened up to a musty set of rooms that could have been a second house. There was a large old bathroom with a recently glassed-in shower. The black and white tiles that lined the room were probably from the twenties. Maggie was excited to also see a large, antique, clawfoot bath.

The next room down was a small library with shelves that were only half filled, then another dusty room set up like a sitting room. On the opposite side of these rooms were a number of large double closets, one filled with garment bags. At the end, the corridor opened up into an enormous, sunny bedroom with an office area set up opposite a narrow bed. Most of the furnishings in this wing of the house were old and tired, dating from at least thirty years ago, but there was a lot of space—much more than a typical apartment in the Boston area.

"There used to be a full-time staff here in the house. The maids lived in the attic, but this was where the housekeeper and grounds man lived—they were married. This was all before my time, though. My husband always wanted servants in-house, but I prefer people that come in. Oh yes, there is a staircase behind that door that leads to the back garage. It was used by the grounds man to keep the landscaping equipment, tractors and such. It could be your garage, if you like. There's plenty of room to store things."

Maggie looked around. The rooms all needed a major cleaning, maybe some paint if she was here long enough. This part of the house had not seen the care that the main house had. There was, however, room to spare for the things she had not been able, or wanted, to sell. It would certainly work until she knew what she was doing.

"Would you mind if I moved some of my things in? I have sold most of my furnishings, but I've kept my bedroom set and some other pieces. And I have a lot of books."

"Not at all! The garage below us is empty, three bays. I use the other garage by the front of the house. Feel free to move whatever you want in there or up here, or vice versa, just as long as it goes when you do. Aiko just got it sorted and cleaned out a couple months ago. That garage had an Austin-Martin in it I didn't even know about!" She chuckled in a private joke to herself, then continued, "Be aware though, I like it quiet. No parties. But you are more than welcome to have your children here—you have three, you said? I miss young people, but truth be told I was delighted when Aiko said you were my age. Sometimes young people are difficult company. It is like they speak another language."

Maggie smiled at Olivia's comment about the two of them being the same age. Olivia was probably old enough to be her mother.

"You are welcome to fix the place up to your heart's content. It needs a paint job anyway, and I will pay for my painter to come in to do it, your choice of color."

After a few more minutes of talk about the rooms and Maggie's timing, Olivia showed Maggie out, saying she would love Maggie to consider moving in. Maggie said she would be in touch soon with an answer. She wanted to think about it - it all seemed too good to be true

Maggie pulled into her driveway and found herself getting a little excited. Maggie imagined moving the narrow bed into the sitting room so Charlie, or one of the other children, might have a place to stay on a visit. With her curtains, her bed linens, and a new color, the rooms would be fresh enough. She would also call Patrick and see if he had sold her books yet. There was room in the little library for most of them, and she was not going to get any real money for them anyway. With the reading chair from her bedroom, she would be very cozy in there.

She opened the door into her now almost empty house. It startled her to hear an echo as she walked in. She made herself another cup of coffee and pulled out her computer. Ready to finally create a budget. She had started it on paper but had decided to move it to a digital spreadsheet so she could change things more easily. She felt she needed to have a financial framework for herself. She needed a picture of what money she needed and how she would spend it. She had looked at some budget templates online and she now worked to transfer what she had learned onto into a spreadsheet. She knew a budget would help keep her honest about her spending.

For now, the values in her budget spreadsheet were just educated guesses. She did not know her income. She decided to estimate her expenses and then work backwards to figure out how much she needed to earn to support herself. She knew that once she got a job, she could start filling in real numbers.

First, she had listed her "fixed" monthly expenses, consisting of those things that were essential: rent, utilities, car, health, perhaps household insurance, and then her phone and internet bills. She was only absolutely sure of her phone expenses at this stage but she had estimated the others by checking on various websites. For the time being she put a figure of $1200 a month for rent. It was the lower end of the range she had seen for a very basic one-bedroom apartment in one of the towns a little closer to the city. The rest of the costs she guessed at.

Maggie realized she was lucky that there were not going to be any childcare or educational expenses for her to include in this section. They used to be a major fixed cost for her and Neal. Even without them, though, she had estimated she would probably need about three thousand dollars a month to cover her fixed expenses if she got health insurance.

Then she looked at what she called "variable" expenses. These were expenses she could control to some degree. She knew she could be very economical and keep these to a minimum, but she had to eat and keep her car running. Her variable expenses included: food, personal care expenses (like clothes and haircuts), car expenses (gas and routine maintenance), household supplies (like home office things and cleaning materials), subscriptions (like Netflix which was a luxury she wondered if she could keep) and other minor items. She added a "General/Miscellaneous" category for things she knew she was forgetting. Even assuming she scrimped, her variable expenses were almost seven hundred dollars per month.

She had put lines in her budget for building an emergency fund and adding to her retirement savings. When she had first come up with these expenses, she put them in her variable section. As she had thought about it though she remembered the numerous unexpected expenses that had regularly popped up with the kids and the house over the years. The fender benders, the broken appliances, the occasional emergency room visit. She realized that building an emergency fund, for that matter saving in general, should be as important as paying rent. She had moved both lines into the fixed expenses section. How much she could afford to save would depend on how much she could earn. She planned to scrimp wherever she could to fund her savings. She figured it would be good for her diet if she could learn to eat less, anyway.

Her budget looked like this:

ESTIMATED ANNUAL BUDGET

NEEDED INCOME TO COVER EXPENSES	*Monthly*	*Annual*
Monthly Salary (based on expense estimate):	3500	42000
Other income (painting?):	0	
EXPENSES		
Fixed		
Rent (include condo fees) - 1/3 salary	1200	14400
Utilities (electric, gas, etc.)	200	2400
Cell Phone/Internet	100	1200
Insurances		
Car	80	960
Health	900	10800
Household	20	240
Savings	150	1800
Emergency Fund	200	2400
Variable		
Food	300	3600
Car expenses (eg., gas routine maintenance)	70	840
Subscriptions (eg., Netflix)	30	360
Personal Care	120	1440
Household supplies (eg., cleaning, office)	100	1200
Miscellaneous	30	360
TOTAL	**3500**	**42000**

After Aiko had reminded her about health insurance, Maggie had called two different insurance agents in addition to her current one. The estimate for health insurance at her age was about nine hundred dollars a month. She had been shocked. Looking at her budget now, it changed it from being tight to being impossible. Her health insurance ate up the money she planned on using for most other things. It was no wonder so many people had to choose between having health insurance or keeping a roof over their heads. With healthcare insurance included in her current estimated budget it showed she would need about thirty-five hundred dollars a month to live on, which meant a salary of $42,000 a year.

To reach that amount, Maggie calculated she needed to make at least twenty dollars per hour. Minimum wage in Massachusetts was only currently $12.75. There were very few jobs that she was qualified for that paid twenty dollars per hour. In her searches, she had resigned herself to perhaps taking a receptionist job. That was the type of job that matched her almost nonexistent skill level and job experience. She reminded herself that it would only be a starting salary, and she assumed she would be able to use it to get to a higher paying job with experience. Or she would simply look for a second job. It was not clear her college degree helped her at all in her search. She was depressed just thinking about the job search.

Olivia's offer eliminated the need for rent and utilities. That represented a huge saving for Maggie. It would give her time to get herself settled and adjust to her new circumstances. She could even afford health insurance while she was doing it.

Maggie thought that living rent free initially would be a gift. Looking at her budget, Maggie realized that it would be, in fact, a life saver. She immediately called Olivia and told her she was going to have a roommate. Olivia literally yelled, "Hoorah!" They worked out the timing details and Maggie hung up relieved. Everything considered, Maggie finally felt like she was moving forward. She had a direction. Budgeting had forced her to deal with the reality of her situation.

It took Maggie a week to move. First, she spent three days cleaning Olivia's place, already breaking her budget with cleaning supplies and new curtain rods for the windows. She then went to Patrick's to retrieve most of her books. Olivia and Maggie agreed on a single color for the hallway and the rooms: a soft, modern grey. In the library, though, Maggie managed to convince Olivia to have the battered pine shelves painted a glossy white and the walls a warm blue-grey. All the yellowed moldings were also freshened up to a bright, clean white. Everything looked new and almost trendy when it was done. Olivia was happy to pay the painters. She was very pleased with the refresh and told Maggie she had a wonderful eye for color.

While cleaning the windows, Maggie had been excited to see formal gardens behind the house. They were overgrown, and since there had been an early frost that week, they looked dead and derelict. But they were gardens, nonetheless. Maggie immediately found Olivia and asked about them.

Olivia knew her gardens had gotten out of hand. The landscapers only really focused on the lawns and shrubs. Olivia shrugged and said she was, *a poor excuse of an Englishwoman*, and said she simply lacked a green thumb. Maggie thought it was more likely Olivia preferred hers to remain manicured. When Maggie explained her love for gardening, Olivia insisted she take charge and even suggested Maggie bring over whatever plants she liked from her old garden. Olivia admitted that she had never been able to tell the gardeners what to do beyond keeping things clipped back, she was happy to cede command to Maggie.

Feeling lucky, Maggie then asked about moving her beehives to the property. She assured Olivia that they would help increase the flowering of both the trees and shrubs and there would be honey. Olivia skeptically agreed with the understanding that if the bees did not "get along" with the dogs, it was the bees who would be asked to leave.

By the time of the foreclosure sale, Maggie had moved completely into Olivia's. The bank's assessment of her house at the time of the refinancing had been too low. It did not take into account the draw of the gardens and how Maggie's studio had charmed the potential buyers. The house easily sold for well beyond the outstanding mortgage. If she had owned the house, it would have been a windfall. Sadly, the surplus from the sale, like that from the Cape house, just disappeared into yet another invisible trust controlled by Neal. Any financial benefit Maggie might have realized from her twenty plus years of work both shaping and maintaining the house and gardens would have to await Neal's return.

Losing the house was heartbreaking in many ways. The only positive was that not having a financial *deficiency* meant she was finally clear of all the potential liabilities from the houses which had threatened her. It was a weight off her shoulders.

Ethan helped her move, renting a truck again. Two of his friends came by to help with the larger items. He whistled when they pulled up to her "new" place. Maggie had explained that the house had sold quicker than she had expected, and the new owners were anxious to move in. She explained this living arrangement was going to be a stopgap until she found a new place to live.

Olivia came out with the dogs to "supervise" the move and flirted shamelessly with Ethan every time he passed by her, carrying Maggie's things in. He played along and Maggie rolled her eyes at him, laughing at how brazen Olivia was. She kiddingly whispered to Maggie that he was a heart-stoppingly handsome boy and that if she was ten years younger, she would not have hesitated to ask him out. Maggie realized Olivia was going to be fun to live with.

After multiple trips with the truck, Ethan's friends headed home. They dropped him back, though, as he wanted to help Maggie set things up. Olivia insisted he stay for dinner and ordered them all steak and lobster from the most expensive steak house around. Ethan surreptitiously shared his dinner with the spaniels. The dogs, and Olivia who expressed mock horror at catching him with a morsel of steak for Bunny, fell happily in love with him.

A lot of the things Maggie had left over from the estate sale at her house were put in the garage. Feeling both sentimental and strong, Maggie asked Ethan to take the five boxes from her father's house (that had sat in the storeroom for years) upstairs to her little library. She told herself she was going to get through them before Christmas. Ethan helped her set up her printer and her own internet connection in the office space she had set up for herself in her bedroom.

Olivia had the internet, but rarely used it. She had never had a reason to set up Wi-Fi. Ethan had brought all the devices needed from the old house and had Maggie up and running in an hour or so. Maggie insisted on paying for a high-speed hook-up and gave Olivia a first payment of fifty dollars. This, Maggie said, would cover the higher charges each month. Maggie justified the expense as the internet was proving essential to her job search and expanding financial education.

Ethan stayed late and became Maggie's first overnight guest. He slept in her newly appointed little "guest room" on the daybed from Maggie's old bedroom. He left in the morning by Uber, letting Maggie settle in.

She realized, after Ethan left, that she could use a small fridge and perhaps an electric kettle in her guest room. That way she could have milk for coffee and breakfast for herself and guests without disturbing Olivia. She put them on her wish list, though—no more purchases until she was working, and no more dipping into her savings.

Maggie had taken as much as she felt was fair out of her gardens. Most were rare plants that needed dividing anyway, peonies that had been gifts to her from Neal and the kids, and her favorite golden raspberry plants. Altogether, fifty or so plants moved with her. They were now in pots in the unheated garage, but she was going to try and get some in the ground to winter over and then decide where to plant them in the spring.

Maggie had had two beehives in her garden, but both were now empty. The bees had absconded at some point during the dismantling of the house. Maggie had been disappointed when she realized they were gone. This had happened to her before—she had lost so many hives in the past few years she almost expected it. Still, the hives themselves were still full of honey and very heavy. She had Ethan move them into Olivia's garage and she sealed them from mice. She was planning to buy new bees in the spring, if she could afford them, and she would keep some of the honey as food for them. The rest she would harvest around Christmas to make gifts for people.

She made one last trip back to the house after the move and slowly filmed the entire place on her phone, especially the gardens. She had taken photos of many objects as they left her home, but she wished she had taken photos of the kid's rooms as they had been, or even hers and Neal's. It was hard to say goodbye to so much of her history, particularly as the future was still so murky.

It had all been so sudden. It was like Neal had died rather than just disappeared. Leaving the house that last time, she paused holding the car's handle and turned back to look at the house. She leaned against the car. Her heart was racing. She thought about the enormity of the changes in her life over the past eight weeks. It just didn't seem real.

After ten minutes or so, she breathed deeply and calmed herself. She reminded herself of all she had accomplished already, and the people who had come into her life and helped her. Her life was clearly changing, there would be no more hibernating. She finally opened the car door, slid in and buckled her seat belt. Then she put the car in gear and drove away for the last time.

CHAPTER 7:
THE GOVERNMENT'S CUT

Maggie's job search was not proving as easy as finding a new home had been. Prior to Neal's disappearance, she had toyed with the idea of some kind of job to fill her time, something beyond volunteer work. Unfortunately, the careers she thought might interest her involved more education. She just couldn't see herself going back to school. Now she no longer had the luxury of either time or money to pursue an advanced degree.

Maggie had pulled together a one-page resume using a template she found on a job search site. She had widened the margins to help the page look fuller, but it had not really helped. She spent a lot of time wording her profile to make it clear that she was a quick learner and hard worker, but the experience gap was too large to fill meaningfully.

Maggie felt guilty that she exaggerated her volunteer experience, but there was really nothing else to fill the page with. She did list all her skills, especially that she knew Excel and Word. After days of revisions, she knew it was done but she was not happy with it.

She had then put her search on hold while she concentrated on the sale of the house's contents. It was an easy activity to avoid.

Her first week at Olivia's, she made the job search her fulltime project. She first called her college's "career resource center" for leads, since they had helped her find her first job. They did have services for alumnae but needed her to be more specific as to what she was looking for. This intimidated her a little, as she had no real idea what she was looking for, beyond a decent paycheck. She redirected her efforts and surprised herself by calling two of her old friends—she could not remember when she had last called them. One woman she had met while in college, the second at her first job. She wanted to see what they thought her options might be.

Both women had always had full time jobs outside the home. They were helpful and excited for her, but they also wanted her to be more specific. Neither asked about why she suddenly was looking for work and Maggie did not offer an explanation. One friend suggested she hire a career coach to help her narrow down what she wanted to do. The other suggested a number of online sites to test her aptitude and interests.

Both women teased Maggie that her calls were the first time she had reached out to them in years. They both sounded happy to hear from her and upbeat about her eventual success. They encouraged her to keep in touch and let them know her progress. Maggie was surprised to hear herself promise to do so. She realized that she would look forward to more calls with each of them, that it felt good to have someone to share with. She got off the phone feeling more optimistic, despite the lack of specific progress. For the last ten years, she had not talked with them about anything beyond her life with the children and Neal. She realized she was looking forward to having some work news of her own to share with them next time they spoke.

She broke her search routine every day for lunch and frequently found Olivia in the kitchen waiting for her with a sandwich or a salad. Maggie had been surprised to hear Olivia had worked for years before she married, never having gone to college. Olivia's careers had been in what she called the entertainment and hospitality industries.

"I bee-lined for the strip in Vegas after I left my first husband in the UK. I had worked as a dancer in Manchester. We girls always considered Vegas our Hollywood. It only took me a year or two until I moved into working as a concierge of sorts at a casino there. That's where I met my second husband. Another poor choice I might add."

Her experiences did not offer any insights for Maggie's job search in Massachusetts, but her ribald stories were a welcome distraction. She had led a very colorful life and their lunches together frequently had Maggie in stitches. She realized she had not laughed so much in a very long time.

Maggie tried both her professional friends' suggestions. The online career assessments—at least, the free ones—were interesting, but too vague to really help her. The career coaches, meanwhile, were simply too expensive, although they all sounded like they might have helped.

Finally, she just began to send in cover letters and resumes for jobs that looked like a fit for her. She was aware she lacked the required years of experience, but she sent the resumes anyway. By the end of the week, she had written dozens of cover letters and sent in many more resumes, but she only got automated replies that went nowhere.

She was frustrated that her college degree did not seem to be making any difference. Low-skill jobs like work in restaurants, landscaping, and cleaning were in high demand, some paying over fifteen dollars an hour, but generally only offered part-time positions, under thirty hours per week. She gave herself one month more to find something that required a college degree before she turned to this option.

Ethan came out the third weekend Maggie had been at Olivia's to help her with her fussy printer. She casually told him she was looking for a job. She said she wanted to "get out of the house" and she was bored with all the volunteer work. She was worried he might be ashamed of her having to work, but as he helped recon-figure her printer, he surprised her by saying he was glad she wanted a job. He said it would keep her mind active, as if her brain was somehow about to sputter out. She had to suppress a smile. Ethan was worried about mental decline? Being over fifty, she must seem ancient to her children. Regardless, she took advantage of the opening and asked what he thought she might do.

Ethan replied, "Well, avoid part-time jobs. Companies don't have to offer benefits, like health insurance or retirement plans. My work benefits even include access to legal advice and a gym membership. There are a lot of great benefits that the bigger employers are offering these days."

This caught Maggie's attention; she had forgotten that she might get health insurance paid for by an employer. Maggie wanted to ask him more about work benefits but didn't want to appear too eager.

As if a sudden inspiration caught him, Ethan said, "Hey, why not try the local hospital for job openings? Healthcare positions seem to pay well and there would be ready access to doctors. Someone from work just took a job at Mass General recently and it paid more than I am getting. It was a real surprise to us all." Maggie was sure he was also thinking access to healthcare would be yet another benefit to his antediluvian mother.

After he left, she thought more about getting a job in a hospital. The local one would be convenient and perhaps a good starting point. They were part of a large network and Boston had all sorts of healthcare facilities. She checked, but her local facility did not seem to be advertising any positions online. At first, she was disappointed but then she considered going in person to see someone there, maybe she just needed a new approach. The online application process was turning into a depressing rejection mill.

Monday morning, Maggie got up early and took some resumes and went directly to the hospital. She was directed by the receptionist to Human Resources. Once there, Maggie was asked to fill out a number of forms and then asked to wait. Maggie had not expected to have an interview of any kind today but was grateful she had dressed in an outfit she thought was professional looking. She waited, uncertain as to what was coming next.

In about ten minutes, a smiling middle-aged woman came out. She was dressed in a simple navy suit and wore only a watch as an accessory. Her make-up was a simple light colored lipstick – everything about her seemed direct and to the point. She reached out her hand and said, "Hello, Marie Wright. I'm the Director of Human Resources. Do you have a minute to talk?"

"Of course," Maggie said as confidently as she could, and followed her to a spacious office.

As Marie sat down, she asked for Maggie's resume. After a quick glance, she put it down and said, "Tell me about your work and expectations."

Maggie was nervous. She had not expected any sort of interview and hadn't prepared for one. If she had known, she would have looked online to learn more about the hospital and their network. Maybe even checked LinkedIn for information about Marie Wright herself. She knew it was important to prepare for interviews. She pushed back her nerves, however, and talked about her first job and then her volunteer work. She emphasized the skills she had. She avoided the expectation question as she would have felt silly saying it was simply to get a decent paying job.

Marie said, "I see that you have gaps in your resume."

Maggie replied honestly, "I did not work while raising my children and really had not expected to be looking for a job at this stage of my life. But my circumstances have recently changed. I know I have limited formal work experience but I'm very quick to learn. I taught myself beekeeping and can fix drywall and even do some basic plumbing." As an afterthought, she said, "I am also very good with numbers. I actually thought about becoming an accountant when I was in college."

Marie paused. She noticed the rings on Maggie's finger and wondered briefly what her "change in circumstances" might be. Being a professional recruiter, Marie knew she could not ask. Maggie's timing was good. Marie had recently started looking for women exactly like Maggie. Although their work experience was minor, a couple of her recent newer-to-the-workforce hires were working out exceptionally well. Women who ran households and raised children rarely appreciated all the useful skills they developed - they were excellent multitaskers, managed change exceptionally well and worked effectively in teams.

The number of people applying for jobs throughout the hospital had dropped dramatically with the improving economy. There were now more job openings than people to fill them. Back-office healthcare work did not seem to attract young people. Marie preferred the older hires anyway, as they generally dressed more appropriately and were more punctual and courteous. Furthermore, in Marie's hiring experience, no woman ever said she was *good at numbers*, unless they were in fact exceptional. Marie wondered if she should gamble a little on Maggie.

"Do you have any knowledge of medical terminology?"

"No more than you get watching a medical show, I suppose," Maggie replied truthfully.

"Well, the hospital has a chronic shortage of something called medical coders. Someone has to assign a specific code to the medical procedures that are done here. It is how insurance companies know what to pay us. It is not hard work, but you have to be good with numbers, know the medical jargon, and make some judgment calls. Obviously, getting the coding correct is a critical function for the hospital."

"How would I learn this?"

"Well, there is a degree called a Certified Professional Coder, a CPC, which we require for full-time positions. We could put you in the Medical Records office as a receptionist to start with. The woman we hired last year just left for maternity leave. If you like the office and can get up to speed fast, we will pay to train you to become a CPC. It is a two- to four-month online course with a certification exam at the end."

Maggie hesitated for a moment and then awkwardly asked, "Well, how much can a medical coder make?"

Marie smiled. She wished more women asked this basic question. Men rarely hesitated to ask about salary. "Well, a coder in a medical office starts at about eighteen dollars an hour, but it goes up to thirty for experienced hospital-based coders, especially good ones. The real plus for many people is that the hours can be flexible. We measure your success more by output than by hours worked. There is always a backlog of reports needing coding, and we pay time and a half for overtime. Coders here can pretty much set their own hours and make as much as they are prepared to work for."

"So," Maggie asked, "This is a part-time job then?"

"No. We don't do part-time for these types of jobs. It will be at least a forty-hour workweek; it will just be flexible. You can work whatever forty hours you and the department see fit—not just nine-to-five. Medical Records has to be staffed twenty-four hours a day, after all. Insofar as benefits, we always offer our employees full medical coverage. You can even become eligible for a 401k. "

Maggie was not sure if she would like the work; it sounded dry. At this stage, though, she just wanted to get started at something. She told the woman she would welcome a chance to try.

Marie then asked for references, which caught Maggie by surprise. She gave the name of the Museum volunteer coordinator and a woman she worked with on a parent/teacher committee at Ethan's private school. This mother was a well-known lawyer and one of the few parents Maggie had been comfortable with. She would have to call them first though to make sure they were comfortable acting as references.

"I am afraid I don't have their numbers on hand," Maggie explained. "I left my phone in the car as I don't like being interrupted by it when talking with people. I will call you with them as soon as I can."

As it turned out, this little courtesy endeared Maggie to Marie and tipped the scale in her favor. It was a pet peeve of Marie's when phones rang during job interviews. She was very frustrated by hires that seemed to have their phones permanently attached. She had frequent complaints about people spending too much time on their phones and, after warnings, had even had to let a few people go. Assuming Maggie's references checked out, she was going to give her a chance.

At the end of the week, Marie called Maggie and told her that she had the job. She would be the equivalent to a receptionist while she shadowed the coders to see how she felt about what they did. If things worked out, she could start the online coding course by the end of a two-month trial. She could then move to coding full-time sometime in the new year. The starting pay was eighteen dollars an hour plus health care benefits. Marie made clear to Maggie that the hospital self-insured their employees within their system, so she may have to change her healthcare providers.

"Could you perhaps start on Monday?" Marie asked.

Maggie excitedly said yes. She had a job!

Although, she really did not know whether this coding position was something she really wanted to do, she realized finding a job she loved on her first try was unlikely. As it was, this job was not part-time, it offered healthcare insurance, and it gave her some needed experience. It could be a good start. If it didn't work out, there would always be another job. The health insurance meant she could drop the coverage from her old insurer, saving her nine hundred dollars a month. This would be worth it, even if she did have to change her general practitioner, a woman she had known for over twenty years.

Maggie did a quick calculation. If she was paid eighteen dollars an hour and worked a forty-hour week, she figured she was going to be earning about $37,440 a year. That was $3,120 a month. Not having to pay for medical insurance meant she would be able to get her emergency fund going *and* put fifteen percent aside for her nest egg, which was the target she had set for herself. Between free rent and a job with health insurance, she could shift to a focus on saving money rather than just using it for living expenses. Given how well it was going with Olivia, Maggie felt no urgency to get a place on her own. Having this job would be a major, positive change in her financial outlook.

Marie said she would email a copy of her offer. She said it would have attachments that Maggie should print and fill out. They agreed Maggie would stop by the Human Resources office at 7 a.m. the following Monday to complete some additional paperwork and organize her ID. When that was done, she would be introduced to the Medical Records Department. As a receptionist, her shift would be 7 a.m. to 3 p.m.

Maggie was thrilled. As a celebration for herself, she did some shopping. Now that she had experience with Craigslist, she quickly found a cheap bar fridge with a tiny freezer and small microwave. She bought both for fifty dollars from a college student who had moved back home but lived nearby. She also went to Bed Bath and Beyond and used her store credit to get an electric kettle and, happily, a little cash back for the card's balance.

As she was shopping, she realized she had not included any provision for fun in her budget. She had thought about entertainment like an occasional movie out which she had put in her miscellaneous bucket but bigger, infrequent expenses such as special occasions or splurge purchases had not been part of her thinking. She realized by not budgeting for them, she might find herself blowing her budget or even be tempted to reach into her emergency savings for non-emergencies.

She decided to put aside some *fun money* each week. If she put it in her budget, she knew she would be more thoughtful with her choices and make better trade-offs. Given her salary she decided to revise her budget and put aside two hundred dollars a month for extras. It could be used for extravagances like dinners out, spa treatments or a trip to a nursery. Without giving herself permission to enjoy or pamper herself once and awhile, she risked a splurge purchase that could throw her off track.

Olivia was elated that night when she heard about Maggie's job. She made it clear to Maggie that she should not even consider moving out, even though she was now employed. It had become clear to Maggie that Olivia welcomed her company in the house. The feeling was mutual. Maggie assured her that she would stay indefinitely, and that her new schedule would still allow her to handle the dogs' late afternoon walk.

To acknowledge her accomplishment, Olivia insisted on opening a bottle of very nice champagne to celebrate. As they moved onto their second bottle, as a toast, Olivia said, "To my dear new friend Maggie. I wish you the best of luck in your new endeavor. Just have to say, though, hospital patients are probably a little less lively than my old patrons. But then again," Olivia paused for a dramatic effect. "At our age, stripping for a living probably isn't an option."

Maggie choked on her champagne. "Stripping? I thought you were a dancer!"

"Well, I was a dancer. Just an exotic one," Olivia replied almost primly.

Maggie laughed. At this point in their relationship, this revelation did not surprise Maggie in the least. Olivia had yet to explain the transition to her current lifestyle to Maggie. As the champagne flowed, however, so did Olivia's ever more explicit stories of suitors and other strippers, paid vacations to exotic locations and extravagant debauched parties with famous people. The life she led in her early decades sounded fascinating and exhausting. By the time Maggie went up to bed, she felt like she had really missed out on life.

Maggie got to the hospital early, caffeinated and nervous. Her commute was less than twenty minutes. Her photo ID made her look ancient. The forms she had filled out at home were all correct, but she was asked to fill out even more.

Marie then led Maggie down to the Medical Records department in the basement of the hospital. There were no windows, but it was well lit. A small half wall and reception desk separated the door from a group of six desks. Surrounding these desks were stacks and stacks of institutional gray metal shelving holding thick manila folders with rainbow stripes. There appeared to be more stacks of files than books at any library she had ever seen.

She was a little surprised to see so many physical records. She assumed patient records would be digital and living on the Cloud somewhere, as everything else seemed to be. These must be records from before the era of electronic everything.

There were only three women in the room; they all looked up when she arrived. A pretty, slim black woman rose and held out her hand. She introduced herself as Tamar Withers, the manager of the department. Marie left Maggie with Tamar to begin her orientation.

Tamar said to call her Tammy. She introduced the other women, then showed Maggie to their break area, well hidden behind the stacks. There was a table there with three chairs, a nice coffee machine, tea things, and mugs. There was also a plate of homemade cookies. Tammy made Maggie and herself coffee, with real milk from a thermos. The phone rang twice while they chatted, answered by one of the other women in the room. Tammy told Maggie that it would be her job to answer the phone going forward.

The most common type of call Maggie would get, Tammy explained, was a request for a medical record from someone in the hospital. It would be her job to pull the chart, which would either be in the stacks, in the record room down the hall, or she would have to call offsite to request it. The calls came in day and night due to people coming into the emergency room. There were also lots of calls from insurers and, of course, the hospital's Finance Department.

When Maggie asked, Tammy explained that electronic records were generally just used as an administrative tool, for billing and data purposes. Handwritten medical records were still the gold standard for patient care. Paper and electronic records overlapped, but not completely. Maggie was going to have to become proficient in reading and understanding both. Maggie wondered how much this dual reporting system added to the cost of care; it seemed to be the first of many things she was going to find inefficient when it came to record-keeping in hospitals.

Tammy spent all day teaching, and Maggie kept up. It was three o'clock before she knew it. As the other two women waved goodbye, a man in his thirties arrived and took up another desk, joined later by another woman.

"Afternoon shift," Tammy explained she introduced them and then she packed up for the day too.

Maggie was relieved that she had found her new work interesting. By the end of the week, Maggie was not missing a single phone call. She pulled files as needed and hand-delivered a couple urgent ones. She was shocked to learn the stacks only held about fifteen percent of all the hospital's files; they often had to call to the offsite warehouse to retrieve files. She learned about ICD-10 codes, the numbers which categorized procedures and that were used to determine reimbursement. She learned to review a record for completeness before she sent it anywhere, and to make sure it was tidy. She also learned a great deal of medical terms and filed a lot.

The doctors' handwriting were as bad as people always said it was. Some days, it took an hour to decode a single page. She got better as she learned what she was looking for. Her days went quickly, the staff was generally easy to get along with, and she found she was looking forward to going to work. Maggie realized she was never going to love the job, but it was good enough for now. It gave her a chance to settle into a new life.

Maggie's first paycheck was a major disappointment; it was for far less than she expected.

The summary attached to the check helped her understand the problem. Her gross pay that first two-week period was over $1,440, but her net pay, the amount the check was made out for, was closer to $1100. The hospital had calculated how much to deduct for taxes based on the W-4 form she had filled out when she started. Her federal and state tax deductions, which she had expected, were just over $170. That was not so bad a bite.

What she had not expected was the Social Security and Medicare taxes. The Federal Insurance Contribution Act, or FICA, took out as much as her federal and state income taxes. She understood she would get the money back someday in the form of Social Security checks or Medicare payments, but she had not known they came out of her pay *in addition to* her taxes. Together, taxes and FICA took about twenty percent from her paycheck. The government's total cut of her paycheck was much larger than she had imagined. Her budget was going to have to be reworked.

The pay she took home, when everything was said and done, was about $2,300 per month not the $3,500 she had hoped for. Maggie found she had to rework her budget, sometimes weekly, but regardless of what she did, she still came up short. She frequently had no money for extras and at the end of the month learned to like rice and beans. She was frustrated at times, but she accepted the reality of it. Money was tight despite living for free, mostly because she refused to let her savings schedule slip. She was amazed at people who paid rent and raised families on even less than she was making. She learned to stretch every dollar she could, using coupons and finding sales.

Fortunately, work was going well. Tammy was smart and ran the department with a practiced hand; all problem cases were bumped to her and she resolved them smoothly and quickly. Before Maggie's one-month probationary period was even up, Tammy had recommended Maggie for the CPC training course. She was the quickest learner Tammy had ever seen. She always came early, stayed late, and offered to do the jobs no one else wanted to do. She was happy to work overtime. Maggie did the course in her free time rather than when she was at work. She got her CPC certificate quickly. In less than three months on the job she had moved from being a receptionist to a coder. As a result, her pay went up by another five dollars per hour. She breathed a little easier with the raise.

Maggie adjusted to her new life. She made her lunch daily. The hospital cafeteria was expensive, relative to what it cost her to make a sandwich at home. She brought muffins to work every other week, because homemade baked items appeared regularly from other department staff. She depended on them for breakfast and wanted to make sure she chipped in. Her dinners were generally soups or stews, which she made in bulk on Sundays.

Her diet was not as healthy as it had been. Meat and fish were expensive and most fresh fruits and vegetables cost more than fast food. She simply could not afford what she now thought of as her former *wealthy people's* diet. One Saturday, as she was shopping the produce section that offered older, bruised fruits and vegetables at a reduced price, she realized that if she had raised her children with her current budget restrictions, they would probably have gone hungry sometimes. It chilled her.

In contrast to Maggie's economies, Olivia seemed to only eat take-out. The refrigerator was regularly cluttered with old restaurant containers that the house cleaner cleared weekly. Olivia also went out multiple nights every week, but never explained where. One Sunday, as Maggie was preparing her weekly soup, she offered to cook for both of them one or two nights a week. Olivia, who did not like to cook, was embarrassingly grateful for the offer. She asked Maggie to provide a shopping list. From then on, the housekeeper stocked the fridge with gourmet ingredients like good cheeses or wild salmon. Maggie and Olivia had regular dinner dates every week and Maggie always made extra so Olivia could have leftovers when she was home alone for lunch. Maggie guessed that somehow in her wild youth, Olivia had missed acquiring any culinary talents. Cooking for them both was another bonus for Maggie, her diet improved and her food budget halved.

Maggie's life moved along. Maggie found herself really liking Olivia. Her stories about her former husbands, all three of them, were ribald. Maggie realized her life with Neal had been pretty dull in comparison. There were no naughty rendezvous in museum bathrooms or Swiss gondolas to talk about.

One night, the kids joined her and Olivia for dinner. As they were leaving, Izzy asked about Neal and Maggie waved off the question, saying she had simply not heard from him. The kids looked at each other meaningfully but neither said anything more. As she came back in from seeing them off, Olivia was waiting for her at the kitchen table with a newly opened bottle of wine.

"Wonderful kids. You must be proud. But, come on, Maggie. This thing with your AWOL husband. I mean, avoiding the question with me is understandable. But not answering their questions? They look pretty miserable about it. How can it be that bad? What is going on with you two that you don't want to tell them?

Has he left you and set himself up with another woman, or maybe another *man*? It floors me that you are so secretive about his disappearance. Is he a fugitive? A felon? I mean have you buried him in a garden somewhere and just don't want the kids to know?"

Maggie stared at Olivia. She had made a point of avoiding even thinking about Neal these past few months. She dutifully called Agent Munoz every few weeks, but beyond that she had let his disappearance fade from her life. She had simply not let herself think about how the kids felt.

But Olivia looked very determined. Maggie knew she could not brush her off. Suddenly, Maggie felt very resigned. She poured herself a wine and rather than sit down, she paced as she began. "Life with Neal was dull, Olivia. Capital D. He was a grossly inattentive husband and father. It was all about his work and his clients. The kids gave up complaining about it in grade school, I don't think he made a single parent/teacher night or student production. He would occasionally show up for one of Ethan's games, but he spent so much time talking to the other parents. He rarely even knew the score at the end. I never complained about it, though. Truth be told, I was not much of a wife, either. We just really were just two people who shared living space. There was not any emotional intimacy. Or physical for that matter for years. Since the kids left, I think I just drifted into depression, really. I wasn't enjoying my life. I really didn't feel anything about anything. After the kids left, I was almost a hermit."

Maggie paused for a while, finished her glass and poured another. Then she began again, "Then Neal just disappeared. More critically, though, so did the money. And there had been *a lot* of money."

"Oh," said Olivia, something clicked for her.

"Yeah. I mean, Neal disappearing was *not* the major issue. It was the money being gone that finally woke me up. My credit cards stopped working; bank accounts were frozen. I found that our houses were being foreclosed and I was going to lose a place to live. I had to start selling things just to pay for gas."

As she said it, tears began to glisten in Maggie's eyes. Olivia just listened. Maggie finally sat and then began again.

"Now, looking back, I realize I was probably furious then. Angry at Neal, angry at the situation and how powerless I was. But I didn't really understand I was angry, I just thought I had a lot of energy. I directed that energy into scrambling out of the hole Neal had left me in. And I did. If he comes back, I think we're done. Not because of the mess he made, but because our relationship was so pointless. I think I avoid talking about it with the kids, and they don't push, because we are all afraid that talking about it means acknowledging that our family is broken. Permanently broken. I just don't think any of us want to admit that."

"Would that be so bad for them? It doesn't really sound like it Neal was ever a big part of it anyway. Is it really any worse than not knowing where their dad is? Seeing you so indifferent?" Olivia asked gently.

"The girls will eventually accept us splitting up. I think they kind of see it. But I imagine it will permanently break Ethan's relationship with Neal. They have been on thin ice for years. The problem is, Olivia, that I really don't know where Neal is, but I suspect it is something illegal relating to his business. I don't want the possibility that their dad is a crook to come on top of the divorce news. I think I want to take things in order—first have Neal back and his issues out there, and then break the divorce news."

Olivia said, "Well, I think from talking with Izzy, she would just like to understand what is going on. She is worried about you and her Dad. I don't know your Charlie, but she seems a peacemaker from what you have said. It is likely she would want you and Neal to be happy in the end, no matter the outcome. As to Ethan, I am not surprised he would struggle with it more. Boys identify with their fathers. Neal's not exactly setting the example Ethan thinks he should. Ethan is, in effect, defending you. He may not say so specifically, but he knows Neal has turned your world upside down; that his dad has hurt his mother. You can expect that he is going to be angry with his father for a long time. It is pretty clear to me that Ethan is your biggest supporter."

Maggie's tears finally began to fall. Soon she was choking back sobs. It was her first real cry since the whole thing had begun. Olivia got up and hugged her and they moved into the living room. There they both talked into the night about marriage, Maggie's life, and Neal. Then how, and maybe when, to tell the children about Maggie's decision. Olivia was supportive and hugged Maggie deeply before she headed up to bed, drained and sad. Maggie finally was seeing the last few months for what they had been, an exercise in practiced avoidance.

Maggie was subdued the next day at work after this cathartic night of confessions. She came home and napped and when she finally came down to see about dinner she was surprised to find Olivia's last husband setting the table for a feast of take-out. Maggie knew Olivia had thrown him out four years ago for an affair with his forty-something secretary. She had *not* mentioned that they were still friends.

Graham Mundt had just turned eighty, but Maggie would not have guessed it if she hadn't known. He had a beautiful, thick head of gray-peppered hair. He was handsome, trim and well dressed in jeans, a crisp white shirt, and beautiful Italian shoes. Graham and Olivia looked like a matched pair. According to Olivia, throughout their tempestuous marriage, Olivia and Graham agreed they had been perfect for one another. It had been her longest and happiest marriage. Unfortunately for both of them, Olivia could not, *would* not, tolerate infidelity. It had broken both their hearts.

Over dinner, which they had insisted she join, Graham found every opportunity to touch Olivia. He held her hand and stroked her arm every chance he had. Maggie even caught them playing footsie under the table. He hung on Olivia's every word and they bantered like an old-fashioned movie couple. Maggie was confused. She knew he had married his secretary after the divorce.

After he left, as Olivia and Maggie cleaned up, she admitted to Maggie they saw each other at least a few nights a week, sneaking around behind his new wife's back. "Graham has his own apartment in the city," she explained. "His *wife* lives alone in a penthouse Graham bought after they married. He lived there about a week, couldn't take it after he realized she had conned him. Serves her right, us seeing one another," Olivia spat out. "Taste of her own medicine."

Olivia also admitted that Graham was still supporting her. In the divorce he had agreed to a very generous monthly alimony check and still paid for all her credit cards—again, without the new wife's knowledge. Despite their ages, Maggie had seen at dinner that they both clearly enjoyed a physical relationship with one another. They acted like a young couple in love. Maggie felt she was not in a position to judge this relationship. Graham and Olivia were old enough to know what they were doing.

As the year drew to a close, Maggie realized she was modestly content with her new life. She gauged this in part on the fact she no longer refilled her anxiety medicine. Her pills had been misplaced in the chaos of the move but when they had resurfaced, she happily realized she had slept soundly without them. Her job was not exciting or challenging, but she did it well. Her children were settled, and her living situation better than she could have imagined. She had new, good friends. She was even looking forward to the challenge of Olivia's garden in the spring. Her only concern was that she just did not earn enough. She toyed with the idea of a second job.

Her money worries were justified. Her mother had only been about five years older than Maggie was now when her forgetfulness became noticeable to her husband. This fear of the disease was one of the few worries Maggie still carried from her old life. Fortunately, her mother was the beneficiary of a Trust set up for her by Maggie's father. Maggie knew if she fell victim, she would probably have to fund her own care. It was frightening

She had not thought about the Trust in a while. She knew that any remainder in it was supposed to be a second inheritance for Maggie. Neal, who was of course the trustee, had once told her that it was unlikely that anything would be leftover. Her mother had outlived everyone's expectations, and the cost of her care had only risen over the years. Neal had suggested, on more than one occasion, that they may have to supplement the cost for her care one day soon. Maggie knew she should check on this now that Neal had vanished.

Ever since Maggie had found out the cost of health insurance, she realized she did not have anywhere near the amount of money necessary to set up a similar trust for her own care. She did not want to be a burden to anyone. Unlike many people, when Maggie thought of the money she needed for retirement, it was not to fund an easy life on a beach somewhere. For her, she needed a large amount of cash to pay for an extended stay in a nursing home.

She had recently heard about something called an HSA, a health savings account, that let her put money aside to be used for future healthcare expenses. What she contributed she could then deduct from her taxes and the money in the account would grow tax free. She made notes in her financial journal to check it out. Any legal way she could find to defer taxes was priority for Maggie.

One day just before the Christmas holidays, Maggie complained to Tammy about the taxes coming out of her paycheck. She was having to get inventive about the gifts she would give this year. Tammy laughed. She had been impressed with how quickly Maggie had learned coding. When it came to understanding and managing money, however, Tammy thought Maggie knew less than her own sons.

Maggie's talk about her life before she started working were not relatable to Tammy, who had worked and saved her entire life. Her two children, unlike Maggie's three, had no expectations that their parents would be able to pay for college. If they did not get scholarships, they were prepared to go to a less expensive, state school. In any case, they knew that they would be working all four years and they also accepted the fact that they were likely to have large debts afterward. Her teenage sons were already working and putting money into their college funds. Saving for college was a goal the whole family worked toward.

Tammy knew Maggie was struggling with stretching her income. Maggie had explained it was mostly because she was setting some ambitious savings targets for herself. Tammy, though, could not understand how she was having problems. Maggie was only taking care of herself, not raising two kids and saving for college.

Tammy shook her head and told Maggie, "Well, given that you started working so late in the year, you should get a full refund on all that federal and state tax you have paid so far."

"Refund?" Maggie had heard about tax refunds, but assumed they were for other people. Neal was always complaining he never got refunds like his other partners did.

"Yes," Tammy explained. "The tax taken out of your paycheck is based on how much you earn for the whole year, not per paycheck. Your annual standard deduction is $12,000 per person, per year. There are additional deductions for things like children, living at home, and childcare. If you make less than $12,000 in a year—and you will, because you will have only worked three months or so this year—the government gives back the tax you paid. When you get your W-2, it will tell you how much in tax you paid for the year, so you will know how much you will get back."

"What is a W-2?"

"A W-2 is the year-end statement of earnings that the hospital will send to you. Another copy goes to the state and federal governments, so they know how much you made, too. You attach your W-2s to your tax returns when you send them in. The hospital is fast; my W-2 usually comes about two weeks after the year's end on December 31st. I always file my taxes right away. I depend on that refund; it's like my emergency fund."

Maggie did not want to let on to Tammy how excited she was about a potential tax refund. It could be over a thousand dollars and it would probably top up her emergency fund or solve her Christmas gift dilemma.

After she left work, she went up to payroll. They agreed to give her the W-2 rather than mail it when it became available. She did not want any delay in getting it. She then looked up the office of one of the large national tax-preparing chains. She had heard them advertise on her car radio and wanted to speak to a tax preparer.

She was shown to the desk of a young man, who introduced himself as Robbie Stevens. He looked like he was still in high school. She showed him a pay slip and explained she was hopeful she could file the first week of January to get her refund.

He stopped entering her data when he learned this was her first job and that she had only been working a few months with no other income. He said, "You know, you can do this yourself. It is pretty simple. You file online for free with the IRS and Massachusetts Department of Revenue, rather than pay us to do it. We aren't able to charge a lot for simple filings like this, anyway. We just want you back if things become a little more complicated."

Maggie was confused. Neal's and her taxes had always been at least an inch thick. She did not see how she could possibly handle preparing them. When she explained her concern, the young man laughed.

"There are only a few reasons tax returns are thick like that; either you have a lot of investments, you run a company, or you are in real estate. When a tax return is an inch thick it basically means you are rich and probably *do* need a preparer." Tucker smiled, then continued, "Now, if you show me someone with over a *foot* of paper in tax returns. Then hires tax lawyers on top of his preparers, and I'll show you someone who is probably a tax cheat."

Maggie's eyes widened. Did Neal have issues with the IRS? Was that what was going on? Would she be pulled into it since she also signed their joint return? She tamped down her fear. She should just focus on doing her taxes, this year, for herself alone. She closed her eyes for a moment and repeated to herself, *Neal's issues are his issues, not mine.* She began again, "How am I supposed to learn to do my taxes on my own?"

Robbie showed her two forms, each just one page long. One was a labeled 1040, the other a 1040EZ. He also gave her a one-page form for Massachusetts, to use when paying her state tax.

"These are the tax forms everyone is so afraid of. I know the writing is a little small, but if you follow the instructions in the booklet it comes with, it is pretty straightforward. Most people only ever have to fill one of these pages, front and back, and nothing more. Then you attach or scan your W-2, sign it and wait for the refund check. For all the stress, Federal taxes are generally a single, double-sided page for most people. State tax is pretty much the same thing." He gave her a tax booklet, which was slim and unintimidating. "This booklet answers most questions. It also has the tax tables, which show exactly how much you owe for how much you earn. It is pretty easy, just try. Most of the information you need comes on the W-2. Plus, if you use the 1040EZ, it is even simpler. I taught my mom to fill out her EZ in an hour. She did it manually with paper and a calculator."

"Wow. Just an hour?"

"If you are okay with computers, you can even file online. You just enter the numbers and it does the calculations for you. Pretty simple. I hate to see you wasting money on me. Come back when you win the lottery or become a real estate tycoon."

Maggie thanked him but went home doubtful she could actually handle the taxes on her own. On his advice, though, she sat down with the 1040EZ. In a few minutes, she realized it actually *was* pretty easy, just like Robbie had promised.

She went online to the government site and entered the values she thought her W-2 would have on it. She checked out the likely refund she was going to have. She signed off before she sent anything. She was excited, the refund would be enough to top up the emergency fund she had created. Her target was to have four- to six-months of take-home pay in the fund, ready for the unexpected.

Christmas came. Olivia loved everything about Christmas and had hired landscapers to deck the house with lights, even if very few people ever ventured up the drive to see them. She went overboard with greens and Christmas baubles everywhere. Maggie did not even get a tree, because Olivia had a twelve-foot one in the living room. The house smelled wonderful, with the scent of pine and Christmas cookies in the air. Olivia insisted that Maggie have Ethan and Izzy stay for the holidays, using her guest rooms. She was going to be in London for an extended period.

Prior to Christmas, Maggie realized she had more people she wanted to give presents to than she had ever had. Fortunately, rather than worry about money she simply raided her beehives and made jars of honey for people as gifts. It cost Maggie nothing more than the cost of canning jars and everyone raved. Tammy loved her jar, as well as the smaller individual jars for each of her boys. When Maggie presented Olivia with the honey, after a single taste she completely changed her hesitation on having bees in the garden, wondering if they should have multiple hives.

Maggie had also attempted a painting of the dogs for Olivia, who had trouble keeping a straight face when she saw it. Maggie had tried to make the dogs look stately, but their expressions looked fierce. They both looked more like Chinese New Year dragons rather than the sweet spaniels they were. Not quite the reaction Maggie had been hoping for, but Olivia insisted she would have it framed to go up in her bedroom.

The holiday was bittersweet. Charlie stayed in Guatemala. She directed a wonderful Christmas video as a gift to the family. She enlisted a group of the children she was working with to help. It was a hilarious re-telling of Dr. Suess's *How the Grinch Stole Christmas,* complete with a dog with antlers. No one needed Spanish to follow the story. She dedicated the video to Maggie's parents, who had always encouraged the children's theatrical productions. When the kids were small her parents used to come for Christmas every year. They would help write, direct and act in a short Christmas pantomime which the children put on Christmas Eve. It had always been a highlight for Maggie and Neal. Now she regretted that she had never even thought to record them.

Charlie let Maggie watch it before Christmas so she could be sure Maggie understood how to access it on YouTube. She told Maggie had to save *the reveal* for Izzy and Ethan on Christmas Eve. No one discussed the reason Charlie was staying in Guatemala. Maggie had told her there was simply no money this year for a ticket home. If Charlie had been shocked by this change in her parents' financial circumstances, she hid it well. She insisted she needed to stay anyway. It pained Maggie deeply that she could not afford this, for Charlie or herself.

Izzy and Ethan arrived on the Saturday before Christmas. They had both had the week off. Maggie, with Olivia's encouragement, planned to share an abridged version of what she knew about Neal before Christmas Day. Neal had missed more than a few Christmas's, but he had always called. If he did not contact them this year, she wanted them to understand why.

Sunday night they called Charlie on Skype. Maggie told the kids what she knew, omitting details like the raid on the house or the financial issues. She said she had contacted the authorities shortly after Neal's disappearance and that the FBI was involved. She relayed what Agent Munoz had told her the week before, that he was certain that Neal was out of the country but not sure where. She told them the agent had assured her that there had been enough recent sightings to be confident Neal was well.

Maggie then soberly said, "I assume your dad is under some type of investigation. It may have something to do with taxes or maybe Dad's business. The FBI just wants to speak to him about it—there were no charges pending. I have not talked with Dad since he left. I am sure he would contact us if he could. He is probably just trying to make sure none of us are involved in this, whatever it is. I think he is trying to protect us all."

The kids were grateful they finally had the full story. They asked a lot of questions that Maggie couldn't answer. They admitted they had assumed his absence had just been about their parents' relationship. Somehow, it being about Neal's work made it easier for them. Before they probed too much about Maggie's feelings, Maggie was called into the kitchen. She had quietly set a twenty-minute timer before calling Charlie. She gave them time to talk among themselves and Ethan and Izzy joined her ten minutes later, saying Charlie had signed off. Maggie immediately put them to work decorating cookies for Christmas morning, and the family put aside the Neal issue for the time being.

On Christmas morning, they again Skyped Charlie so they could open presents as a family. She had the ones Maggie had mailed her in early November. The presents were modest, but thoughtful. Maggie gave the girls the family jewelry they had asked for. Ethan finally got his flying lesson. She promised she would go along and sit in the back seat. Izzy and Charlie gave Maggie a joint gift, replenishing her favorite face creams and giving her a book of manicures. Both were luxuries she had given up. Ethan gave her a prepaid credit card for a check-up at the local garage. He had heard the Corolla struggling the last time Maggie had taken him home. The siblings' gifts to each other were funny or useful. She got a little choked up realizing the kids had noticed the changes in her life but had not made her self-conscious about them. This, plus all the gifts exchanges and remembrances she had gotten from new friends, made this Christmas more meaningful than any of her recent ones had been.

In late January, an IRS letter came in the mail. Expecting her refund, Maggie eagerly tore it open. It was not a check.

It looked like a formal letter but sounded very specific to her situation. It said her returns were under audit and that there were irregularities with the prior year returns. There was likely to be *tax owing* and *penalties* involved. She was urged to contact the IRS immediately. There was a phone number. The letter, she noted, was directed to both her and Neal. They had always filed jointly.

Her call to the IRS the next day was exasperating. She explained repeatedly that she did not have copies of prior returns and could not answer any of their questions regarding earlier returns. She made it clear that her husband had handled all the tax information, and that he had been missing since late summer. The tax preparer's name, the man who had signed the forms, was completely unknown to her and she had no idea how to contact him.

Finally, in an effort to convince the IRS agent, she told him to contact Special Agent Judge Munoz, the FBI agent overseeing the investigation into the disappearance of her husband and their documents. The IRS agent fell silent.

"Do you have the agent's phone number?" he finally asked. Maggie gave him the number. His final question was whether Maggie was still married to her husband, given that she had filed as "married, filing separately." He told her people that used that designation often used it when a divorce was pending.

Maggie sighed. "No divorce pending, we're still married. Until I find him, I can't divorce him, can I?"

"Right," the agent said quietly. He then suggested she come by the office in Boston and pick up a copy of the returns. He said he would call her about setting up a time, after he spoke to the FBI.

After Maggie hung up, she realized she was shaking. Who knew how much she might owe from all the prior years? It could be substantial. She had a sudden fear that it might wipe out her nest egg and everything else she had fought for. The tax taken out of her paycheck had been bad enough, but *back* taxes and penalties? Just when she had thought herself free of debts and other liabilities, it sounded as if the government was looking for an even bigger cut.

CHAPTER 8:
TAKING STOCK

Maggie put the IRS on the back burner. She was very good at not thinking about things she did not want to. She told herself there was no sense worrying until she understood what exactly she had to worry about. She was deeply disappointed she was not going to get her refund, but if that was all she ended up losing, she could live with that. She added another angry grievance to her what she called mental *Neal's Damage* list.

Maggie had worked Christmas week despite the kids coming to stay at Olivia's. She did not feel bad about this. Her kids rarely got up before noon, so she generally got home in time to watch them have breakfast. Despite the holiday, or maybe because of it, the hospital was bustling. After Christmas, the kids left to join friends and Maggie took double shifts and some days worked even longer. She worked through New Year's. In return, she asked Tammy for a week off late January as a present to herself. Olivia was due home, and Maggie wanted a bit of time to herself.

The first morning she had off, she got up early and pulled out the long-neglected boxes from her parents' house. This was her New Year's resolution, to finally clear the boxes. She made herself a luxurious coffee tinged with sweet cocoa powder and pulled the first box onto her bed.

Maggie's mother had been formally diagnosed with Alzheimer's in her early sixties. Just three years later, her father, who was five years older than his wife, could not handle her any longer by himself. They then moved together to the Residences at Whitehall, a luxury retirement facility in Connecticut.

Two years later, her father was still active and alert, but her mother was suffering even more. He then moved her into the euphemistically named "Memory Wellness" wing. Maggie's mother's life was narrowed down to a single room on a locked floor. It depressed Maggie to visit her there. Her mother was confused and often angry. Over the years, her mother's condition worsened, and she moved from a walker to a wheelchair and now, finally, to her bed.

Fortunately for both her parents, money had never been a problem. Her father had been a very successful banker and he had planned their retirement well. He set up the Gagnon Family Trust, or the GFT, once his wife's dementia took hold and moved half their estate into it. He designated this trust to be used exclusively for the care of Maggie's mother. He told Maggie she would never have to worry about paying for her mother's care. He also made it clear to Maggie that she was designated as the *subsequent beneficiary* of the GFT and would therefore inherit the remainder after her mother passed.

Her dad had lived well on his half of their estate. He made himself busy with other residents and the many enrichment programs at the facility. He drove to visit old friends and was even taking cruises and other travel tours that her parents had always planned for their retirement. He really seemed to experience the golden years promoted by the television commercials.

Unexpectedly though, at a healthy seventy-eight, he caught an acute flu that progressed aggressively. He called Maggie from the hospital telling her he was fine on a Wednesday, that he didn't need a visit. He died before the weekend was out. Her mother, the "fragile" one, was still living and now in her late eighties. She had spent the last fifteen of her golden years oblivious to the identities of family or friends, in a slow mental and physical decline. Maggie knew better than most that there were no guarantees in life.

Maggie had originally found the boxes when she cleaned her father's apartment after his death. They were tagged with sticky notes marked, *For Maggie*. She had scanned a couple at the time and found them full of papers and photos. The box with her brother's name she could not even open. They had all sat in her basement, untouched, since she had brought them home after her father's death.

Her inheritance from her father was quickly whisked away by Neal into his firm for "investment" purposes. She knew it had been a substantial amount but had never seen the actual figure. Shortly after her father's death, the Residences Director, Kevin Kingsley, had asked to meet with her and Neal. He said it was to review her mother's ongoing care plan.

Maggie realized the meeting was not so much about the *how* of her mother's care, but the *cost* of that care. Mr. Kingsley assured them he understood her mother's Trust was well funded. He told them that her father had insisted no cost be spared, and that there were a variety of "memory services" they had incorporated into her care plan. He had also reminded them that while her mother was receiving Medicare benefits, the Trust paid for her supplemental health insurance and the extra services the home offered, it also had to pay for additional costs like dental and hearing. He noted that even her co-pays for prescriptions and medical transport costs were substantial. He just wanted to make sure that Maggie and Neal understood that there were major costs involved in the care for a medically-dependent parent. Furthermore, he pointed out that the longer she lived, which he assured them would be years, the more it would cost.

While the rest of the details of the meeting were lost to time, one figure still stood out for Maggie. He said her mother's care cost an average of $80,000 per year, about the same amount they were paying for a year of just one of their children's colleges. It had been a small fortune, even to Maggie's financially-deaf ears.

Maggie knew the lawyer handling her mother's Trust was the same one who had managed probate for her father's will. He was someone Maggie vaguely remembered as a family friend. At the close of the meeting, they had thanked Mr. Kingsley and said they would defer to his and the lawyer's combined expertise regarding her mother's care.

After that meeting, Maggie had dropped in to visit her mother before leaving. She found her in her room, seated in a large recliner, watching a cartoon. Her father's death had not registered to her mother at all, although they had brought her to the service. She was oblivious to Maggie's presence. Her cloudy eyes stared vacantly at the television. Maggie left in tears, believing that in the future visits were going to be about her need to see her mom rather than her mother's need to see her. She hoped her mother was not aware of what her life had been reduced to.

In the intervening ten years, Maggie's visits to the home had trickled to only two or three times a year. As her mother's mobility had decreased, her care needs increased. Maggie's children generally found excuses not to visit - they had loved their grandmother and hated to see her as she was now. After she had lost the ability to even speak, Maggie did not push them. Neal just refused to go—it depressed him too much, he said. Maggie watched her mother gradually decline into a bedridden, virtually comatose state. She now had twenty-four-hour nursing care. Maggie had not been to see her since Neal had left. She realized it was yet another reality she had pushed away, and guiltily decided she would go this week.

As she started in on the first box, the guilt was chased away a bit by a series of happy family photos taken on a long-forgotten vacation. Suddenly, she was glad she had waited to open them. Somehow, time had made the photos of her family more sentimental and less sad. There were both her parents' high school and college yearbooks, their wedding invitations, and a wonderful advice book for "The Bride to Be." There were lots of news clippings of her father and even some of her mother. His were of the young businessman serving pancakes at Kiwanis, or a stock photo of him as he rose in his career. Her mother's photos, far fewer, were as a volunteer at the local hospital or on a local literacy campaign.

There were certificates of all sorts from professional organizations or volunteer groups. Small silver knick-knacks with names and dates engraved. Awards and letters. Her parents' wedding album, full of beautiful black and white photos. She separated one she particularly liked with plans to frame it. There was even a very old family Bible from the 1800s.

There were marriage and death certificates going back many generations. There were dozens of photos of her grandparents, perhaps their parents, and lots of children she did not know in places she did not recognize. Some of the photos were labeled, but most were not. There were a lot of unfamiliar names. Maggie regretted that she would probably never know who these people were.

She did find a photo of her maternal great-grandmother. She did indeed look like quite the glamorous flapper. Izzy was clearly better informed about her family than Maggie was, perhaps because she had listened to her mother's stories. Maggie put the photo aside for her, then decided to pull out all the photos for the kids to go through. Perhaps they would remember other stories the photos might inspire.

There were a couple of diaries. One was little more than an accounting of the costs of her parents' first home, but another set of diaries outlined her mother's activities day to day. This included funny little notes here and there about friends, Maggie's father, or even about Maggie and Will. She dusted these off and put them on her bedside table to go though in more detail later.

One box was clearly all about Maggie. There were old report cards and school photos, neatly kept in envelopes, as well as a couple of old diaries from her childhood, unlocked, which she remembered keeping religiously. Reading bits from the younger versions of herself made her roll her eyes. She would never have guessed she was so melodramatic as a child, or so preoccupied with boys and how she looked. There were also letters she had written her parents from summer camp and from a college trip overseas. She remembered her baby book with its faded pink satin cover and, a major bonus, her original birth certificate. All her copies had been in Neal's files.

At the bottom of the box, amid other scraps, was a paycheck stub from her first job at a local dry cleaner/tailor shop. It stopped her breath.

She had a sudden, visceral memory of kneeling, at fifteen, and reaching between older men's legs to tighten the seam. Her knees had hurt, and she had tried to look away. It had made her queasy. The elder tailor had looked on and excitedly urged her to, "Make it tighter, tighter," exchanging looks with men standing around her as she worked. She could smell the wool, the dust, the tailor's chalk, and could see the men's grinning reflections in the three-way mirror like something out of a house of horror. She also remembered the day her father told her she was not working there anymore. He had found out from a friend that Maggie was being asked to "check the inseam" of pants that simply needed hemming.

Queasy now, as if she was there again, Maggie angrily realized that those men would probably be arrested today—or maybe even then, if she had had the courage to say anything. In those days young girls were generally kept very sheltered and they were conditioned to not challenge adults, men in particular. She began to put the box aside, to go back to it later, but without thinking she suddenly reached back in and tore the pay stub viciously apart. It surprised her, how angry the memory had made her and how crystal clear it was all these years later.

Maggie now realized why she had always carried a revulsion of kneeling in front of anyone. She had once struck Neal, brutally, in his balls when he had playfully surprised her, half dressed, as she had kneeled to retrieve an earring from under their bedroom dresser. She had never been able to explain it to him and he never forgave her. Would the men back then have done differently if they had understood the way it would permanently stain Maggie's life? *Probably not,* she thought. Men who treated girls and women recklessly, or as simple objects, were generally not thoughtful human beings. They were certainly not men of character like her father.

Rather than give in to the anger, she turned instead to the only box left: Will's. She lifted the top gently and immediately all other thoughts vanished. The tears came. His stuffed dog, Dudley, was on top; he had kept that dog on his bed way past the age of stuffed toys. She had often heard him in his room next door to hers talking to it, long after he bragged that he needed to start shaving. There were sports trophies, his report cards, and his school photos. Lots of clippings of him from local papers, covering both his academic and sports accomplishments. The box was much fuller than hers.

There were quite a few photos of him alone or with their mom or dad, or both. Maggie realized she probably took most of these photos. There were baseball cards and a metal box of rocks, feathers, medallions, and other unknowable treasures. There were a few books she knew he loved, and his baby book. There were lots of letters from him from his time at summer camp; she found quite a few letters addressed to her. Her mother must have scooped them up, saved them, and put them here.

She went through everything in the box slowly, savoring them. It struck her how much more alive her parents looked in the photos when he was with them, excited and happy. It was not just because they were younger; they just looked as if they were so satisfied with their lives then, so full. His death had emptied a part of them that was never filled again.

She stopped to study his baby book. She was curious how he compared to her children. She looked for Ethan in him, but he was dark while Ethan was fair. As a baby Will resembled Izzy more than anyone. His development benchmarks were carefully recorded and exclaimed over. The presents and attendees for each birthday party until kindergarten were listed. Scraps of hair from his first haircut were taped in, as was the bracelet from the hospital, looking as tiny as they all did. Her mother's happy voice was everywhere in the margins, in perfect script with lots of exclamation points.

Their grandparents were also well represented in the box. Will, who shared his grandfather's name, had many photos with him. As the namesake, he was the clear favorite. She spent a good half hour with his baby book comparing it to hers. She considered how much more complete his book was. She would have thought that as the oldest, she would have more details, but her mother's entries in her book had waned, after Will's birth. Her mother seemed to have shifted her focus to him. Maggie could not imagine herself favoring one child over another as her mother seemed to.

Her birthday parties always had fewer attendees, all girls. The gifts were clothes or dolls. His parties were larger and always seemed to have extended family at them. Will's gifts were books, planes, building toys, and sports items. He even got money gifts and a piggy bank. She remembered buying one for herself, as no one else had thought she might need one.

The baby books supported her sense that her brother had been the focus of her parents' lives. It was also clear that boys mattered more. She was the afterthought. She realized now that instead of feeling bitter or jealous about this, she was glad. She, too, had doted on Will. If asked, she was sure he would have said his childhood was very happy. His was a short but happy life.

As she returned his baby book to the box, she found a manila envelope at the bottom. She looked inside, assuming it was his birth certificate. The birth certificate was there, followed by his death certificate, which triggered another wave of deep grief. Maggie could not remember ever feeling this devastated. She realized that lately all of her emotions seemed more intense.

Beneath the manila folder was yet another thick envelope. It contained a letter from her grandfather to Will on what appeared to be his sixteenth birthday. In addition to platitudes about his academic accomplishments, he wrote, "To follow in your father's footsteps, it is important to learn about business. I have signed you up for a subscription to the Wall Street Journal – read it daily and you will begin to get a feel for it. I have also attached ten shares of McDonald's, your favorite restaurant. I bought them for you shortly after you were born. Now that you are a young man, they are yours to manage. I will teach you about how to follow them when we visit next month." Will of course, had died shortly after this letter and the certificates had simply been stored away. Maggie now looked curiously at them.

They were red and white, with a beautiful detail of a man and woman standing in front of the familiar McDonald's shake, fries, and burger. It said something about being a "depository receipt" and a Bearer Certificate, mentioning that each certificate represented a Series E McDonald's share.

Maggie wondered if the shares were still viable. She could remember a dozen movies where share certificates made the hero a millionaire. Curious, she went to her computer and found a site called Yahoo Finance where she looked up the share price. A single share was now trading for more than $180. She was excited. It was clearly worth finding out if the certificates were still viable. She took a photo of one and then put them back in the box.

She moved the boxes back into her library, keeping out various photos she had found. She pulled down picture frames displayed about her room and out came some of the framed family photos with Neal. She replaced them with photos of her parents and Will. She even set a picture of Will, older and in a baseball uniform, next to her bed with other frames of her children. She realized it was nice to see his face again, to be reminded of him finally, even with the grief. She was glad she had opened the boxes.

Olivia had returned a day early from the UK at the end of the week, subdued by her brother's weakening condition. Maggie delayed her visit to her mother again when she saw how down Olivia was. Having her home again was welcome, it was wonderful to catch up with her. Maggie had really missed her company. Maggie insisted on making dinner that weekend for both Graham and Olivia, as a thank you for having had the house for Christmas.

To her embarrassment, Olivia had told Graham about Maggie's IRS dilemma.

Over dinner, he growled. "Damn IRS. I think they go harder after the innocent than the guilty. They know the innocent will break easier."

He offered his tax lawyer, or his accountant, to help. Maggie explained she could not afford them. She didn't want to admit to Graham that she was hopeful that the FBI would explain her husband was gone and that all her documents were missing. That should keep the IRS at bay. She had become resigned to her refund disappearing into the bureaucracy, at least this year.

"Well, you are clearly an *innocent* spouse, which is a good thing. That is the term they use. They could absolve you of all responsibility. But remember, since you filed jointly, they could, ultimately, come after you. They can reach into your paycheck for back taxes if they decide you knew what was going on. I know you probably signed your tax returns without even looking them over, but the IRS doesn't care. If they want to play hardball, they can." He took a deep breath and smiled at Olivia. "Olivia was the only one of my wives who ever paid attention to the tax forms."

"That's because I wanted to know how much you made. You never gave me a straight answer," Olivia explained. "At least I could find out on the tax returns.

Second page at the bottom of the 1040, easy. Besides, I had already learned the hard way never to sign a financial document unless you understood what it meant. Things can and do go wrong. Ugly bankruptcy with my first husband, the little shit. Took years for me to get back to even."

Maggie admitted she had been a wife who just always signed where Neal told her to. She never even took a minute to try to understand the taxes. A mistake, she told herself, she would never make again.

To change the subject, Maggie asked Graham what he knew about stock certificates. Olivia had previously told her that Graham's retirement activity was managing his investments, and that he enjoyed it.

"Stock certificates? Companies do not really do stock *certificates* anymore, Maggie. Gave them up in the eighties, I think. Shares are traded electronically now."

"Oh, well, I found what look like stock certificates in my parents' things this weekend. I'm not sure if they are real. I was thinking of checking with that Charles Schwab brokerage over in Brookline, but you might save me a trip."

Maggie scrolled through her phone until she found the photo and showed it to Graham. He squinted at it.

"McDonald's!" he said, surprised. "Looks interesting, but the print is too small."

Maggie said she would bring down the originals during dessert, and so while Graham and Olivia played footsies, idling over Maggie's cobbler, Maggie ran up to her room to pull out the share certificates. She came back and handed them over to Graham. He used the magnifying glass Olivia kept at her desk to pore over fine print. Finally, he sat back and pronounced they were likely to be real. Further, they seemed to be unsigned "Bearer" share certificates, so the shares would belong to the person who signed the back.

Maggie was excited. "Ten shares of McDonald's may be worth well over eighteen hundred dollars!" she explained. "It could replace the tax refund I was expecting."

Graham looked at her a little incredulously.

"I am not sure if you understand what this represents, Maggie. These are shares from *the seventies*. There have been multiple stock splits in McDonald's since then. I suspect these certificates represent a good many more shares than just ten."

"Stock splits?" Maggie asked.

"Companies used to like to keep their shares under one hundred dollars in price. It made people feel like they could buy a decent handful of shares. Now many company's shares are so expensive people feel like they can't buy them as individuals. For example, Amazon shares trade for thousands of dollars a share. Most people feel like they can't afford *one*, let alone ten shares. It shouldn't matter, but it does."

Maggie nodded, determined to listen closely.

"Anyways," Graham continued. "Companies back then used to regularly 'split' their stock when it got around one hundred dollars per share. To split it, the company simply divides its existing shares into multiple shares. Although, the number of shares outstanding increases, the total dollar value of the shares remains the same compared to pre-split amounts. While the split itself doesn't add any value, a stock usually goes up after a split This is because the stocks look more affordable after a split, so people feel they could afford to buy more. Demand for the stock increases, so the price goes up yet again."

"Wow. So how many splits do you think these have gone through?"

"Hard to say. Stock splits are rarer now for a number of reasons, but back then a company might have done it every few years or so. McDonald's was growing very fast back then, and its share price would have kept running up to the hundred-dollar mark. It probably split its shares every couple of years or so."

"Okay. So, if that's true," Maggie said slowly. "What does that mean for me?"

"Stock splits were usually two shares for one. That means that if you owned ten shares, after the split, you would now own twenty. You would have started with, say, one hundred dollars' worth of stock. Ten shares worth ten dollars each. After the split, you would have twenty shares worth five dollars each. If your shares here were split two for one, these certificates would represent twenty shares, not ten. If they split two for one again, your twenty shares would have become forty. Every time McDonald's did a split, you would have increased the number of shares you owned. I suspect these ten shares certificates could represent more than one hundred shares of McDonald's today. If they are real, they could be very valuable."

Maggie just stared at the certificates in amazement, doing the mental math in her head.

Graham continued, "But before you get your hopes up, I think you should head into Schwab—actually, call McDonald's first. They'll have a department called Investor Relations set up to help people who have shares in the company. There are a couple of identifying numbers on the back of the certificates" he flipped the certificate in his hand and pointed "these here, see? They are called CUSIP numbers, and they will use them to let you know if they are real. They will also tell you the best way to redeem them if you want to. If talk to them first, you can go into Schwab with a little more knowledge. The salesmen there are likely to suggest you open an account with them using these shares. You should know roughly how much they are worth."

Maggie nodded and made notes of his advice in her head, but she was still in shock. A *hundred* shares of McDonald's? It seemed unreal to her.

"My God!" Olivia exclaimed, clapping her hands. "It's like something out of a movie!"

Graham grinned. "Looks like we may be dealing with an heiress, my lovely. Does that mean we have seen the last of Maggie's cobbler? Might as well make the most of it," he said as he helped himself to another generous serving.

Maggie sent them along to the rest of their evening as she cleaned up the kitchen and headed back to her rooms. She was very excited and thought she might do a little research before bed, and see what she could figure out on her own.

She was up until well past two in the morning, giving herself a crash course on stocks and stock splits.

Maggie learned that shares, stocks and equities were all names for the same thing. A share represented a percentage of ownership in a company. It was a stake in the future profits of a company—assuming of course that it made profits. There was no guarantee a company would not lose money, or even fail completely, so there *was* risk involved in owning shares. Most small or new companies had shares that were held privately by owners or investors, but larger and older companies, like McDonald's, offered their shares to the general public. This meant anyone could buy their shares in public markets, which were called stock exchanges.

The two biggest stock exchanges were both located in New York City. The largest in the world was the New York Stock Exchange, the NYSE. The second largest was the National Association of Security Dealers Automated Quotations—a mouthful she would never need, or want, to remember. The acronym, NASDAQ, was far easier.

Maggie was a little confused by the Over-the-Counter or OTC stocks. These were not traded on exchanges, just traded between *broker-dealers*. These stocks often traded for pennies, so they looked a little sketchy to Maggie. She decided she would just avoid these stocks for the time being and ask Kate about them. She wanted to concentrate on the basics first.

Over six thousand companies, mostly US-based, traded on these two exchanges. Most countries had their own stock exchanges for their own domestic companies, although some of those companies also traded in the US under a slightly different "ticker."

A company's "ticker" was generally a letter abbreviation used for the company on the exchanges. It was short, to allow it to easily fit on the "ticker tape." This was a device that showed stock symbols and share values. The ticker tape was electronic now, but the name came from the ticking sound the original mechanical machine made as it spat out narrow strips of paper. Modern-day ticker tapes were the scrolls seen on the bottom of many business news channels.

Ticker symbols were usually the company's initials or, if they were taken already, some type of mnemonic. McDonald's ticker was "MCD."

The "Dow," or the Dow Jones Industrial average, was an expression Maggie had always heard on the radio. It was either up which was apparently good news, or down which wasn't. Really big drops made headlines. Now she understood that the "Dow" was simply an index of the sum of thirty large companies' share prices that traded on the NYSE.

The Dow's value was much greater than simply adding up the share prices of the thirty Dow companies on any given day. That was because the index was price weighted and adjusted for changes like stock splits, mergers, and other corporate actions over the years. Maggie realized she did not need to understand how to calculate the index; she just needed to watch the Dow to understand how the stock market was doing overall. Again, going up was good and going down was bad.

The companies Dow chooses to include in its index are among the largest and most established in the country. They come from a variety of different industries, because it is intended to represent the entire American economy. The thirty companies in the Dow have changed over time, but the index itself has been in use since 1896.

Maggie learned that today, most stock traders preferred to use the S&P 500 index as a better gauge of how the stock market is performing. This index was more complex, as it was made up of five hundred companies, big and small, rather than just thirty industry leaders. It uses a formula that weights the components based on size as well as share price.

There was also another index, the NASDAQ Composite Index, which was made up of stocks which traded on the NASDAQ. This index was considered a good indicator for how well *growth* stocks, like technology companies, were doing. Newer companies often chose to enter the market and list their company through the less expensive NASDAQ exchange rather than on the older more established NYSE.

Maggie now understood that the reasons for owning a stock were two-fold. First, there was the expectation that a stock's value would increase over time—and stocks generally did. Stocks had returned over ten percent a year, on average, over the past one hundred years. Recently, however, a ten percent return was getting harder to come by. Most articles she read said expecting six to eight percent return every year now was more realistic, perhaps even ambitious.

Either way, these returns generally assumed that someone would buy shares and then hold the stock for a long time, so returns could be averaged over good and bad years.

The second reason to own stocks was to collect dividend income, which was far more interesting to Maggie at this stage of her life. Dividends were payments made by the company to stock owners. The payment was generally a portion of the company's annual profits, but payments varied widely from company to company. Some paid the same amount every year, no matter what, even increasing the dividend over time. Other companies chose not to pay a dividend, particularly if they believed they could use their cash to grow their business. Dividends were not guaranteed. Companies could reduce or even suspend their dividend if they decided they needed their profits for other purposes, or if there were no profits to share in a particular year.

On average, dividends generally returned about two to three percent per year, although again there was a wide range. Some stocks, like utilities or telephone companies, paid a large, steady dividend of four percent or more. Others chose to pay little or nothing. What caught Maggie's interest was that a four percent dividend from a boring, solid company was well over twice as much as she was earning on her money in the bank.

Maggie now had a basic grasp of what stocks were. She turned her research to stock splits and McDonald's itself.

She soon found a table that showed all of McDonald's splits since 1971, and there had been many in its early years. After careful calculations and checking her numbers twice, it appeared that her ten shares of McDonald's had grown through ten different splits to 1,215 shares. By her reckoning this meant the shares, which had been trading at $180 when the exchange closed earlier that day, were worth about $218,700.

Maggie could not believe it.

She guessed that her grandfather had paid about four hundred dollars for the ten shares represented by the certificates. That was based on the stock price shortly after Will had been born, when McDonalds had been in its infancy. If this was correct, her grandfather's 1970's investment had grown to almost a quarter of a million dollars. She calculated that the shares had made about fourteen percent every year since her grandfather bought them. This did not include the dividends that McDonald's had paid.

It was a revelation. No wonder wealthy people invested in the stock market. Between dividends and stock appreciation, the stock market was a great way to make your money work for you. Maggie was hooked.

Maggie was so excited she could not sleep. She decided she was going to move at least some of her nest egg into stocks. If the McDonald's shares were really what they seemed to be, she was going to add them to her nest egg and build a "portfolio" of stocks. She would talk to Graham about it, maybe get some investment advice. She would try to focus on dividend-paying stocks, so her money was earning money.

She understood that stocks were a gamble—she got that. But investing seemed to be *educated* gambling. She could learn how to evaluate companies and then decide if they were worth investing in. Assuming no crazy events occurred, Maggie thought she could make a solid bet on a company she knew and believed in, like maybe Starbucks or Lululemon.

Stocks seemed like the only way her nest egg was going to get where she felt it needed to be. The bank interest she earned on her savings account just was not going to help her very much. Her salary alone was just letting her get by. She decided she was going to become an educated investor and build a portfolio of stocks. She may not be excited about coding medical records, but managing her own money? That could become the job that she loved.

CHAPTER 9:
COMPOUNDING IS A GIRL'S
BEST FRIEND

Maggie texted Tammy before she went to bed and asked for a personal day so she could try to get an answer on the McDonald's shares from the Charles Schwab office. She was too excited to wait. She also wanted to work out what was involved in buying stocks in the first place. Investing was a whole new world to her.

Since Maggie had come in one day on her week off to work a double shift, she was sure she could get the time off. By six a.m. the next morning, Tammy had texted her back: "Of course! We owe you. See you tomorrow."

Exactly at nine in the morning, she called the 800 number McDonald's listed in the Investors section of their website. She explained what she had found to a woman named Monica, who asked Maggie for the CUSIP numbers on the back of the certificates. She explained these numbers were used to identify stocks and other financial instruments. She also asked if the certificates were in Maggie's name. Maggie said they were unsigned "Bearer certificates." Clearly her grandparents had meant for Will to sign the shares, but he had never gotten to it.

After a while on hold, Monica returned to the phone and confirmed that the certificates' numbers were valid and did in fact represent more than ten shares. Maggie felt her heart racing. Monica could not say exactly how many shares until the actual certificates were transferred to the appropriate agencies. She recommended Maggie sign and notarize the certificates as soon as possible. Then Maggie should take them to a transfer agent. Maggie explained she had a Charles Schwab office close to her, and Monica said Schwab was a transfer agent who could take care of moving them into an account for her.

Maggie thanked her and sat in silence for a moment, trying to tamp down her excitement. It was not a sure thing. There could still be issues, like there had been with her IRS refund. She would wait until things were finalized but in the meantime she grabbed her keys and purse, and went humming happily down to the garage.

Maggie had found out her local bank had notary services. She arrived and learned that it was Doris, who happily notarized the certificates for Maggie. Doris then offered the bank's investor services department as a way to perhaps transfer the shares into an online account, but Maggie declined her offer. Maggie didn't say it, but she was worried what liabilities Neal's bank dealings might saddle her with if she banked here. To deflect any more offers of help, Maggie explained about her new job and her success at the tag sale. She apologized again for moving to an online bank. Doris dismissed her apology. She told her that while she had another bank, Maggie was a customer of theirs too . Maggie then excused herself and headed to Brookline to the Charles Schwab brokerage office.

Maggie arrived and explained her dilemma to the receptionist. Despite being a walk-in, she was shown to the desk of a young woman named Kate Freitas. Maggie showed Kate the certificates and explained that she wanted them transferred into an account that she could access online. Kate explained that she could certainly set up an account for Maggie, but she was not sure about the certificates.

After studying them for a few moments, Kate called over an older gentleman who sat at another desk in the open plan office. He smiled broadly when Kate handed them over to him.

"Goodness. Can't remember when I last saw actual share certificates. These would be collectables if they weren't worth so much. And McDonald's no less! Very nice. We will have to send them in to get them registered and then we can have a brokerage account set up for you," he said. "I may be able to get the actual certificates back after we get you set up, as a keepsake. Of course, they will have no value once the shares are transferred into an account."

He proceeded to pull up some screens and walk Kate through the steps she needed to get the shares into the system. Maggie then filled out the transfer forms with Kate. Together, they then set up an account for Maggie, and Kate showed her how to sign on. Maggie was determined to master online access to all her financial accounts.

Maggie explained to Kate she was completely new to investing and she was trying to learn. "Could you perhaps recommend a course I should take?"

"There are a lot of personal finance and investing courses, online and at community colleges in the area," Kate told her. "We also have a lot of information on our site. We offer loads of educational features. These days, all the bank and brokerage-house sites have them. Of course, you can always just call me. That's part of what I am here for."

Maggie said, "Well, if you don't mind then—it may be a dumb question, but what is the difference between a bank and a brokerage house?"

"A brokerage house is a middleman that facilitates you selling shares on the open market, on the stock exchanges. Brokerage firms generally make money via commissions they collect as financial instruments are bought and sold. Not all banks have brokerage services, but most of the big ones do. Stand-alone brokerage firms generally do not offer retail banking services, but the financial industry is changing pretty fast with all the new technology. Today there are brokerage firms that act a lot like banks, and vice versa."

"In the old days, brokerage houses had human advisors. A 'broker' directed investments and provided advice and support to his or her customer. Today, computers and the internet have changed everything. While there are still brokers and financial advisors, the types of information brokers and advisors used to have a monopoly on is now readily available to anyone with an internet connection."

"Charles Schwab is a *discount* broker. We let you do it yourself, or 'self-direct,' as we call it. Because you do not have a dedicated advisor, you pay lower commissions for each trade. There are also online brokerage companies who charge no fees to people. They are very popular, but people need to understand how they make their money. These companies' actual customers are third parties that make money off the flow of trades going through them, making just pennies or a percentage of pennies off huge block of shares. People trading on these platforms often complain about customer service and lack of transparency. We think beginners are better off with more established platforms with deeper financial resources and better educational resources."

Maggie smiled and said, "Yes, I have an online bank. I think that is as technologically forward as I am prepared to be at this point. I think I need to learn more before I am ready to do much trading on my own. I am going to be looking for a lot of advice."

"Be prepared, many human advisors will charge you. A lot of new investors rely on 'robo-advisers.' Basically, computers make all the decisions where to invest based on mathematical formulas called algorithms. There is almost no human intervention, except in the initial programming, and the fees are very low, or even zero. If you are looking for advice, you are better off learning on your own. At the end of the day, the best teacher is experience. Most people *learn by doing.*"

Maggie was alarmed, "Wait, computers making choices about what to buy or sell? What if something goes wrong?" Maggie asked. "Isn't there a lot of money at stake?"

"The exchanges and the Securities and Exchange Commission— the SEC— is monitoring machine trading. They are like the Wall Street cops," Kate said. "As to computers doing the trades, a lot of people worry about the market having too many machines making decisions. Basically, everyone is kind of waiting to see how it goes. Personally, it makes me a little uncomfortable too, but there have been a lot of benefits—like making the stock market more accessible to people. Currently, the benefits seem to outweigh the potential problems."

Maggie told Kate she wanted to stick with a self-directed approach to start with. She wanted to make her own decisions and she was not ready to turn her money over to a machine. She realized her father must have been one of the human advisors that used to control the market before computers. She wondered if he would have been out of a job in this new world.

Maggie thanked Kate for all the help. As she got up, she explained that she would go home and use the site to educate herself as best she could. She said she was going to focus on dividend paying stocks to start.

"Oh, dividends—that reminds me. Once we have the McDonald's shares in the account, do you want to enroll in their DRIP program? Or do you want the cash just put in your account?"

"What's a DRIP?" asked Maggie.

"A Dividend Reinvestment Plan. We can direct McDonald's to take your dividends and reinvest them in more McDonald's stock. That way you are always adding to your stock position. It is a smart way to go if you don't need the cash and believe the company will continue to grow. Also, since the dividends you get are based on the number of shares you own, if you use your dividends to buy more shares, you end up getting more dividends. It is compounding your returns—you know, adding returns to your existing pile to get even more returns in the future."

Maggie was suddenly curious. McDonald's did pay a good dividend, over $4.60 per share per year. It had been paying dividends on these stocks for years—where had that dividend money gone? Had it been reinvested? She wondered how to find out. She asked Kate who said it may have been re-invested and to check with McDonald's Investor Services. Maggie planned to call Monica when she got home.

For the time being, she told Kate that she would let her know about the DRIP program after the stock was showing in her account. Maggie knew she would be checking daily.

As she was heading out, Kate told Maggie that Schwab had a promotion going on currently for new accounts. They would be giving her five hundred free trades, good for two years. Maggie was thrilled. She doubted she would do more than even a hundred trades in the years to come. It looked like building her portfolio would be cost free.

Maggie had already decided she was going to be a "buy and hold" type of investor. She did not want to trade quickly in and out of stocks, chasing winners. She would put an emphasis on dividend-paying stocks so she could build steady income for herself. She did not need her shares to jump up suddenly in value; she just wanted slow and steady growth.

Maggie went home and spent the rest of the day watching educational videos on Schwab's website. They were helpful, but there were too many terms she didn't know and graphs she found confusing. She knew she needed to get familiar with the jargon before she could really make sense of the material. She found her online bank, Ally, also offered brokerage services and had educational materials as well, as did her original bank. There was a lot of information available; she just needed a better overview.

Most of the actual trading sites she visited seemed to make things even more complicated than the banks. Many were simply confusing, talking about Beta and Alpha and other terms she did not know. Many sites were very cluttered. There were even more graphs. Maggie felt overwhelmed.

Fortunately, Maggie found a site called Investopedia which described itself as the world's leading source of financial content on the web. Its definitions of financial terms were a relief to Maggie. Clear, easy to understand explanations for everything that confused her.

In the afternoon, she called McDonald's Investor Services again. They informed her they could not give her the information as to where the dividends were going until she was the shareholder of record. Maggie assumed this would take a while. They did assure her, however, that the dividends were being deposited in an account and had not been part of their DRIP plan. They also told her they had been paying dividends since 1976, although the annual payout per share back then was only about eighteen cents per share. Maggie knew that in those early years there had only been about thirty shares, so the annual dividends were not going to amount to much. More recently though, the dividends were larger and being paid on over a thousand shares. Those were dividends Maggie needed to track down.

The next day at work, Maggie avoided questions about what she did on her day off. Tammy teased her about being so tightlipped about it. Maggie felt awkward talking about the shares. She knew her co-workers would be thrilled for her but somehow it felt wrong to talk about her windfall when many of them struggled to support families.

To distract herself, Maggie got stuck into a knotty work problem she had been trying to understand since Christmas. One of the most frequent procedures that the hospital did had files that were very different, one much thicker than the other. Maggie had worked out that there were two different surgical approaches to this particular procedure. One involved a much longer stay in the hospital which should have a different code because a longer stay meant a higher cost. Maggie found the same code was used every time the procedure was done, even though the costs were clearly very different.

Maggie had pointed out the discrepancy to Tammy and she had asked Maggie to calculate how many files might be affected. It was turning out to be a big job. This puzzle, and her regular coding work, distracted her for the rest of the day.

As she drove home that afternoon she had a sudden inspiration. She called the director at her mother's nursing home and asked for the contact numbers for her father's attorney. When she called his firm, she was surprised to hear that her father's attorney, Mr. Randall, had retired over a year ago. The Gagnon Family Trust, which was her mother's trust, was now being administered by a new attorney. Maggie assumed that the news of Randall's retirement must have gone to Neal. Maggie was transferred to the new attorney.

"Hello, Dale Hanes here, Mrs. Mueller. Lovely to hear from you. Mr. Randall was very fond of your family; he spoke very highly of your father." Maggie thought he sounded young. She thanked him, explained about the certificates she had found and asked whether he had any knowledge about whether any dividends from the shares going into the GFT.

"I can't really say. There are too many income streams there to know them all. The GFT holds a great many shares you understand."

"Is there any way I can review the statements to allow me to work it out?" Maggie asked.

"I'd prefer to have a chance to meet with you in person," he replied. "Just to be sure you understand the documents. The GFT is not the largest trust we oversee, but its administration is complicated."

Maggie realized that this was actually a good suggestion. She had always left the issue of her mother's care to her father, and then Neal. Given Neal's disappearance it was time she stepped up. She had planned on visiting her mother this month, anyway. "Yes, that would be terrific, and in the meantime, could you see what you can find out about the dividends?" They then set a date for the following week.

Maggie arranged another day off work and headed down to Connecticut. First, she visited her mother, who was in bed asleep. She sat with her for an hour, holding her hand, and talking to her. She told her about the children and then about Neal, and finally all about her new life and friends. There was no response, not even a squeeze from her hand, but somehow Maggie felt better. Her mother's primary aide, a small Latina woman, saw Maggie with her mother and stepped in the room to give her an update.

She introduced herself only as Carmen. She knew families rarely bothered to remember more than her first name anyway and fewer still would ever use it. She explained to Maggie that her smother was now sleeping a great deal. They tried to get her out of bed at least once or twice a day using a lift. She was not able to walk on her own, but she was well otherwise, and her heart was strong. Carmen said she still did not speak beyond moaning when they transferred her. She did not seem to really see. She had cataract surgery three years ago, but there seemed to be little improvement in her eyesight. Carmen explained her milky eyes did not follow people moving about her room.

Carmen did not sugarcoat her mother's condition to Maggie. She did not suggest she was happy or even aware. She wanted Maggie to understand, though, that her mother was well taken care of and made as comfortable as possible. Carmen carried herself with an air of compassion and Maggie knew she was lucky her father had been able to pay for this level of care. She warmly thanked Carmen for all of her support. She realized she had been thoughtless, not acknowledging her mother's caregivers. She made a mental note to send the floor staff a belated Christmas gift.

Maggie left the room feeling resigned and very sad. The wing her mother was in was full of men and women in much the same condition. They were shadows of the people they had been, and Maggie hoped that they had families who were not as drained as she was when they came to visit. She doubted any of these people had ever anticipated that this would be the last chapter of their lives.

Maggie's grandmother had keeled over and died while picking strawberries in her beloved garden. Her mother had often commented how appropriate it was, she had been a keen gardener. She had always told Maggie she was not to let her father put her in a nursing home and yet here she was. Maggie was determined that her children should never let her get to this point. She'd rather they let her go before she ended up unrecognizable to them and to herself. She realized she should probably put this in writing for them. Maybe, she thought wryly, she could pre-pay a hitman to make sure it got done.

She continued with her morbid musings until she pulled into the parking lot of the law firm. It was an attractive brick building in downtown Greenwich. Inside, it had a large, comfortable reception and offices extending down two wings. She was shown to a warm, dark-paneled conference room. She was offered a coffee, and a rich latte arrived. She waited for Mr. Hanes.

When he arrived, Mr. Hanes looked older than Maggie had assumed, perhaps in his late thirties. He came into the room with a younger man who he introduced as his paralegal, Matt Daneau. Matt was struggling with a stack of documents and bound folders.

"Mrs. Mueller, a pleasure. So glad you found the time to come down and go over these documents with me. I know if I had simply sent them, they might have been confusing. It will be very helpful for both of us to go through them together."

As Maggie shook his hand, she said, "I have been looking forward to this as well, Mr. Hanes."

"Family trusts can be complicated."

"Yes, they can," Maggie dove right in. "I understand that my husband is the Trustee of the GFT, but I want to understand her financial situation better. My circumstances have changed recently, and I would prefer I take a more active role regarding my mother's care, rather than my husband."

Mr. Hanes paused, then cleared his throat. "Ah, well. Before we start, may I see some identification? Just a formality, you understand." Maggie showed him her license. "Wonderful. Well, that's the first thing, you see. Your husband has *not* been the Trustee on this account for some time. Your father changed it shortly before he died."

"What? Who is the Trustee then? Why was it changed?" she asked, alarmed.

"Well, you are, Mrs. Mueller. And your mother's executor as well. You should, of course, designate a successor if something happens to you. Mr. Randall still is. We can assign any attorney here, including myself, to take on that responsibility. With your approval and some minor documentation, of course. As to why it was changed, I'm not certain. I believe it was something to do with your father's concern over your husband's effort to have access to the funds. Your father wanted to make sure that your mother was taken care of, first and foremost. Anything that was left over was to go to you. He was not prepared for anyone to have access to it until after your mother passed. I'm surprised you weren't notified of this by Mr. Randall. There was a note in the file that said he had spoken with your husband, surely he told you?"

Maggie hid her shock that Neal may have tried to access her mother's money, even back when her father had been alive. He seemed to genuinely love Maggie's mother. He didn't remember his own mother, as she had died when he was very young. He had always treated Maggie's mother more gently than he had ever treated anyone else. She was sure this is why he always refused to see her in her current condition, he wanted to remember her as she was.

"My husband worked with Mr. Randall when my father died," Maggie explained. "I had very little contact with him, beyond a brief conversation to confirm a bank transfer of my father's estate. My husband is currently...on sabbatical. We have not been in touch. I have only recently come to understand that my contact details may have been difficult to find. I'm not very active online."

"I see. The Trust account had opted for electronic statements, so we assumed you were accessing them. If you have not, I imagine that you have not seen a statement recently." said Mr. Hanes. He then pushed over a twelve-page statement to her. The top page showed a healthy $1.9 million balance, which Maggie was delighted to see. Neal had given her the impression that the GFT was near insolvency. There was a box on the first page labeled "Estimated Annual Income" which suggested the account generated about $51,000 per year. This income would not be enough to cover all of her mother's annual care, but it helped.

The list of holdings in the trust was very long. It looked to include both stocks and bonds. There was something called "alternative investments" which Maggie did not understand. She looked the document over and decided she would research each and every one of the holdings to better understand what they were and what they earned her mother. She was pleased to find she understood the statement and most of its jargon, on a basic level, anyway. Her research efforts were paying off.

She spent a few more minutes studying the statement, then asked, "Given that the Trust's income is less than the cost of my mother's care, does the GFT have to use some of its principle every year to meet the shortfall?"

Mr. Hanes looked a little sheepish. "The GFT operates at a major deficit each year. The income does not even cover the costs of managing the trust, so the principle is always used to pay for your mother's care."

Maggie didn't understand and gave Mr. Hanes a puzzled look.

He explained, "Our management of the GFT is extensive. In addition to writing checks to the Residences, we pay for the preparation of the GFT's annual tax returns and your mother's tax return as the GFT's primary beneficiary. We distribute funds for your mother, pay her supplemental insurance, and review requests for particular items related to your mother's care and other duties. Any procedures or trips to the hospital require an ambulance and other additional costs. We review any extraordinary care before we write a check. I believe we authorized cataract surgery last year?" After an uncomfortably long pause, he added, "Of course, the investment firm charges management fees, as well."

Maggie was surprised the trust was losing money every year. She was also irritated at Mr. Hanes's lack of knowledge about the woman whose care he was supposed to be overseeing. "The cataract surgery was three years ago, Mr. Hanes. Can you please tell me, what exactly are your annual fees? How much of a deficit does the Trust run, on average?"

"Our fees run about one to two percent of the value of the GFT. As the value of the Trust has become smaller and your mother's needs have grown, that per centage has varied. The investment firm who actually manages the holdings within the Trust always makes sure there is adequate cash in the account for expenses so we can write the necessary checks, but their firm also charges its own fees. While the GFT generates income every year, once fees come out there is generally a shortfall. I am not sure exactly how much the Trust earns before fees, nor do I know how much the investment managers charge."

Maggie was surprised. As the administrator, she thought that Hanes should know what the investment managers charge. "Given the GFT's income is not covering its costs, how much has the Trust lost over the years?"

Hale sighed, rubbing the side of his face nervously. "Well, we would have to go through the records to determine the initial funding of the GFT to get that number. The financial markets have been relatively positive over the past few years, so I am sure it is well ahead in terms of value over its total lifetime. We only handle the expense details of the Trust when doing the taxes. The overall balance is not a direct concern for us."

At this, the paralegal, Matt, cleared his throat. "Uh, Mr. Hanes? May I?" Hanes nodded. Matt continued, "Based on my review, the GFT holdings have really struggled over the past decade. Interest rates have been almost zero for years, so the fixed income portion—that is, the money the Trust earns from bonds—has been very low. There have been both losses and a good deal of trading on the account, which means a lot of transaction fees. The principle is down from a starting point of over four million dollars in 2003."

Now Maggie was confused as well as surprised. If the GFT had over four million when it was started over fifteen years ago, it should have been earning a *lot* of money, despite the expenses. From what she understood so far about compounding, reinvesting the income the Trust earned should have meant the principle would have grown—unless, of course, there were significant losses.

In the early years, her mother's care had been far less costly. She had been able to feed and even bath herself, she had only had a part-time aide. Assuming even a conservative annual income of four percent on the four-million-dollar principle would have meant that the Trust used to earn over $160,000 per year, probably more. Even with taxes and fees, there should have been money accumulating in the account. On top of that, the stock market had been up pretty significantly the past few years—Maggie had learned that recently as well. Surely the stocks she was looking at in the statements had not gone down in value over that time. Where had the money gone?

Maggie turned her attention to Matt rather than Mr. Hanes. Matt seemed to have at least made an effort to get up to speed on the details. Maggie knew there was a lot of work ahead of her if she was going to get to the bottom of this.

She asked Matt for copies of all the statements dating back to the GFT's inception. She also asked for an accounting of all the expenses, both her mother's and those the law firm had billed to her. Maggie also wanted copies of all the tax forms they filed every year, for both the GFT and for her mother.

"And since I am the Executor, a copy of her will too, if you would."

Matt looked at Mr. Hanes for confirmation that he could execute her requests, and Mr. Hanes again nodded. As Matt prepared to leave, Maggie asked him whether he had found out anything about the McDonald's dividends, which had initially brought her here.

Matt grinned. "Yes. It took a bit of detective work. I stumbled on it by accident, really. It turns out that before the GFT, there was another trust set up for just you and your brother. This trust was dissolved, and the assets were consolidated into the GFT when it was set up. I noticed, however, that there was one asset left behind. It was a joint savings account in both you and your brother's names. As the law firm of record on the account, I was able to check the deposits into the account and they married up exactly to when McDonald's paid their quarterly dividend. The McDonald's dividends have been deposited into that account since the late seventies. The account is held by the bank your father worked at. There have been no fees charged all these years—an employee perk that has been carried over from that time. You are lucky that there have been regular deposits being made into the account. Forgotten accounts like these are often considered *abandoned* if there is no activity on them. The state of Connecticut could have claimed the balance." Matt softened a bit before he added, "I understand your brother is deceased, so the proceeds in the account are yours to do with as you wish."

Maggie was grateful for Matt's detective work. "I know there were only ten shares initially, and McDonald's did not pay much in dividends until recently. I can't imagine there is much money in the account."

"In the initial years, in the early seventies and eighties, the dividends were only about twenty dollars per year for the few shares you owned. By the nineties, though, after share splits, you were receiving closer to two hundred dollars a year. Of course, there is the magic of compounding interest. In the early eighties and nineties, interest rates on savings accounts averaged about seven percent per year or more. Those pennies grew."

"So?" Maggie asked. "How much is in the account now?"

"Well, in this decade, the account has really paid almost nothing in interest on the balance. As a result, the compounding impact has been pretty limited. The dividends, however, have increased over time. Between the early compounding and the increase in dividends, the balance comes to just under sixty thousand dollars."

The amount stunned Maggie. The early dividends had been literal pennies. McDonald's had only recently increased its dividend to its current level. How had she accumulated so much from what started out as pennies? She already knew the answer: *compounding*.

"Would you like the bank statements for the account? You have full access now that you are no longer a minor."

Yet another amazing windfall from Maggie's sentimental house cleaning. "Where did the statements come from?"

"The bank itself," Matt explained. "They were being sent to their trust department and filed there under your father's name. They had no contact information for you personally, but they had our firm's name, and Mr. Randall's contact details information as an original trustee. They were happy to work with us. They asked that you contact them as soon as possible so they can start forwarding you statements. You could also get online access."

Maggie genuinely thanked Matt. She waited while he left to copy documents for her. She chatted with Mr. Hanes, who was friendly. He asked, but Maggie declined to fill out the paperwork that would designate him the survivor Trustee in the event something happened to her. He was clearly disappointed. When Matt returned, he reminded her she might have some tax liability on her dividend income. *Great,* thought Maggie. *More taxes.* She thought now it might be time to get some professional tax help after all. Given her windfall, it looked like she could afford it.

As she gathered up the documents, she explained to both men that she wanted to spend some time familiarizing herself with the holdings in the Trust. She also wanted to understand all the expenses related to her mother's care. She needed to get a better idea of her mother's financial situation and how she was positioned going forward. She also asked for the Trust's checkbooks so she could write checks for her mother's care as needed. If Mr. Hanes was surprised by her initiative, he did not show it.

She thanked them both and headed out for the long drive home. As she started the car and pulled out, she calculated that if the law firm was charging 1-2% of the GFT balance in fees she was probably paying the law firm up to $40,000 a year in fees. Probably more. She guessed the investment advisor was also charging a lot. She was going to look to see if she could find a more cost-effective solution. Perhaps she could do some of it herself. It didn't seem right to pay someone to manage her mother's money and then have to hear about losses.

She turned onto Interstate 91 and put on the audio book which she had borrowed from the local library for the ride. She had started frequenting the library regularly again, given the cost of books. She had been pleased with all their audio offerings. She even had an app on her phone, called Libby, that let her download borrowed audiobooks while sitting in the library parking lot. She enjoyed listening to books more than music in the car.

The book today was called *Get Rich Carefully* by Jim Cramer. He was a well-known TV personality who worked on the CNBC business channel. His *Mad Money* TV show was one that she had started watching when she could, so she could get more familiar with the investment terms and companies. Cramer tried to make a dry subject like investing entertaining and clear. The librarian was a huge fan of his and had turned Maggie onto his many useful books.

Maggie had already finished her first investment read. It was short and easy: *The Little Book that Beats the Market* by Joel Greenblatt. She had built a pile of these "investment advice" books next to her bed. The basic books were great, but she was frequently overwhelmed by minutia and conflicting advice. She had decided to concentrate on basic concepts that they all agreed on rather than get tied up in all the details or specific strategies. She knew she would eventually learn by doing.

She arrived home just as the book was, ironically, touting the benefit of compounding. It was one key concept she needed to take to heart. Cramer had quoted Albert Einstein, who said that compounding interest is "the eighth wonder of the world" and "the most powerful force in the universe."

Maggie realized she had seen the proof of this due to her McDonald's dividends. Leaving pennies in the bank had truly paid off. Compounding worked. Maggie wished, however, that she could return to the era of high interest on savings accounts. She understood math well enough to see that the power of compounding was diluted in an era when you only earned 1 to 2% interest on your money in the bank.

As Maggie went upstairs, she thought about the second key takeaway she had learned from the McDonald's windfalls. Time was a very important consideration when it came to investing. The longer the period you had to invest, the better. The more compounding could do the work for you. Just as importantly, holding investments for a longer period meant you could average out the good and bad years. The value of the McDonald's shares and dividends had grown because they both had decades to do so.

Maggie bitterly regretted she had started saving so late in life. True, she might have twenty years to work, but maybe not. She might get Alzheimer's, or her health could simply decline. If she did, medical care could easily strip her savings, particularly if it went on for a decade or more like her mother had.

Maggie sat down at her desk and played around with a spreadsheet to work out where she might be financially in twenty years. She knew she wanted her nest egg to start working for her. Now she had some idea of how much she could contribute to it each year. Changing the values in the spreadsheet allowed her to understand compounding a little better.

Her ultimate target was to have two million dollars by the time she was seventy. It was a huge number. She had come up with it simply by assuming that if she retired at seventy, she should plan on having about twenty years left with at least one hundred thousand dollars per year to live on, before tax. She knew most years she would be able to live on less than half of that. The wild card was whether she would need hospitalization or nursing home care for some or most, of that period. Healthcare costs continued to skyrocket. If not for her experience with the cost of her mother's care, she would have been happy to target half that amount, or even less. Now she knew two million dollars was the only way to be sure her children would not struggle trying to arrange her long-term care.

Maggie saw on her spreadsheet that she could reach her two-million-dollar target *if* her nest egg earned four percent a year *and* if she was very aggressive in her savings, adding to it regularly. She would also need her salary to grow and have an emergency fund. Without a safety net to cover unexpected expenses she might have to raid her savings, which would make reaching her target even harder. She did not have time to make up any raids on her nest egg.

Once she had the spreadsheet set up, she tried a number of different scenarios. If she lost her job or could not save as much as she wanted, it was easy to see how she would miss out on her target. It was discouraging. Sadly, the best scenarios were ones where she had started decades earlier.

If she had been in her twenties or thirties, she only would have had to put aside five to ten thousand a year. If she had done that, she would have been free to do almost anything at sixty. She might even have had her father's "golden years" of travel and adventure. She would have had choices. Sitting back, she made a note to herself to talk with the children about their savings. She would encourage them to save as aggressively as humanly possible. Money saved in their twenties had at least forty years to grow.

Accepting the reality of the situation, Maggie reminded herself that twenty years was still a long time. Her household *liquidity event* and the gifts from Will gave her a huge jumpstart. She was way ahead of many of her peers, who were frequently faced with mortgage, medical or education debts. Many people, she now understood, could only live paycheck to paycheck. Most people probably avoided thinking about the future, expecting to deal with at some vague point. She wished she could somehow tell them that avoiding saving money now was only going to make it harder, later. She was grateful she even had the option of saving money.

She set a target of earning at least a four percent return on her nest egg. With the addition of the McDonald's stock and dividends, it was now worth more than five hundred thousand dollars. If it earned four percent a year, this five hundred thousand would earn twenty thousand dollars a year in extra income. Of course, she would pay some income tax on that.

If she reinvested what remained of this twenty thousand after tax every year and it *also* earned four percent from dividends and interest it would help her nest egg grow through compounding. If she also topped up the account every year with cash from her salary, she worked out that she just might meet her two-million-dollar goal in just about twenty years. It *was* possible. The investment advice books were right: compounding was going to be her new best friend.

CHAPTER 10:
FIXED INCOME AND THE PROBLEM WITH FEES

Maggie spent the next ten days researching and learning about every holding in her mother's Trust. She started with the stocks and was surprised that the GFT held hundreds, ranging from large well-known companies to small companies that barely traded at all. For some companies she held only one or two shares. The overall number of holdings was overwhelming.

She went back to the original portfolio documents, the first year of statements. She carefully studied the original holdings. These were stock and bonds her father had picked to generate the income her mother would need. He must have wanted a steady income stream with as little risk as possible to the initial investment, the principle. Given that her father was a banker with an insider's knowledge, his choices were likely to have been some of the best choices available at the time.

Maggie noticed that the heading on the original statements said, *Fixed Income*. She learned it was a financial term used for a portfolio of investments that focused on giving the holder a steady stream of income, not appreciation in the value of the stocks themselves.

Back then, the portfolio was valued at just over four million dollars, a fortune for that time. It had significantly fewer holdings than it currently held, only about thirty or so. While it had fewer holdings, the value of each holding—most of which were bonds—was much larger. Each was valued at least one hundred thousand dollars, with a few at twice that.

Maggie had heard about bonds but had never really understood what they were. She knew they were supposed to be less risky than stocks, but that was about the extent of her knowledge. She decided it was time to learn more.

Bonds, Maggie discovered, were a way government agencies or companies got money for large scale, expensive projects, like building a new school or factory.

They offered bonds to investors. The bond investor is lending the *issuer* part of the money required to fund the entire project. In exchange for the use of the money, the investor is paid a set interest rate for a specified time period. At the end of the time period, the full amount that the company or agency borrowed from the bond holder is paid back.

The total amount of the debt that a particular bond represented was called the *face value*. The interest payment was called the *coupon*, which was generally paid quarterly. Many of the coupons in the original portfolio paid eight percent per year. The date all the borrowed money was supposed to be paid back in full to the investor was called the *maturity date*. Many of the bonds listed in her father's original portfolio had clearly matured, as the date of their repayment seemed to have been ten to twenty years from when they had originally been issued.

Maggie saw, for example, that one bond in the original account had a face value of one hundred thousand dollars and had an eight percent coupon. This had paid her mother's Trust two thousand dollars per quarter, or eight thousand dollars per year. While not all original bonds in her portfolio paid eight percent, many were close.

The bonds her father had selected seemed to be long-term holdings. They generally matured well after whatever the bond had funded was up and running. They were ideal for a fixed income account, Maggie realized.

There were a lot of different types of bonds. Some chose not to pay a quarterly coupon and paid all the interest at maturity when they paid back the principle. Other bonds could be *called* by the issuer, being repaid before they matured so the issuer could take advantage of changes in interest rates. Maggie's father had seemed to concentrate on basic bonds without any unusual features. Maggie put aside trying to understand the various types of bonds at this point. She figured she could wait until she was looking at a specific bond that had these features to try to understand them.

Maggie also learned that there were agencies that rated bonds as to their risk profile. She did not understand how the ratings were determined but she knew she would concentrate on high quality bonds, ones rated as the least risky rather than *junk bonds*. Junk bonds offered higher rates of return, but apparently has more possibility of *defaulting*, that is not paying back her principle. Maggie had to be careful with the Trust holdings.

Maggie saw her father had chosen mostly government rather than corporate bonds. At first, she assumed this was because government agencies were less likely to disappear or go bankrupt. As she read on, she learned that the interest income from many government bonds came to the owner tax free. These were called municipal or *muni* bonds and were not taxed at the federal, state or local level as long as the owner lives in the same state or municipality that issued them. Most of the muni bonds that her father had bought were issued by Connecticut, so the income would have come tax free to her mother. Maggie's father clearly had disliked paying taxes as much as Maggie did.

Not only had her father's bond selections generated a lot of income over a long period, but they also limited the income tax the Trust had to pay. Her father's choices had been smart.

All of this explained to Maggie why bonds had been such a staple of her mother's *fixed income* portfolio. It was the type of portfolio that retirees could rely on to supplement their income. Maggie finally understood the term, "*Letting your money work for you.*"

Maggie initially assumed all bonds were held until maturity. Looking at the most current GFT statements, though, it appeared that bonds were also traded just like stocks. The prices they were traded for could be more or less than their face value. The price seemed to depend, in part, on how much their coupon paid and when they matured.

When her father's bonds had matured, the money that was paid back by the issuer appeared to have been reinvested in smaller bonds. These smaller bonds matured in fewer years and at a lower coupon, or interest, rate. As a result, the GFT's income had fallen over time.

In the past decade, the bonds that had matured were not reinvested in bonds at all. Over time, the portfolio had changed its mix, becoming increasingly geared toward stocks rather than bonds. She assumed this was probably due to changes in the stock market overall.

Maggie knew that interest rates had fallen a lot in the years since her dad had bought his bonds. Today, dividends on some stocks paid more than interest on most bonds. If the investor needed income these days, Maggie suspected he or she might be better off collecting the dividends paid by stocks rather than a two to three percent coupon on bonds. There was a trade-off, though. Stocks were riskier than bonds. And muni bonds produced tax free income.

Her father, who had selected the original holdings of the Trust, had clearly chosen holdings that he felt represented safe and reliable income for the Trust. When he set it up, bonds had made up over eighty percent of the Trust. The few stocks it held were well-known household names like AT&T and Duke Energy. These were names Maggie recognized.

She saw that her father had a preference for stocks that had a large *market value*. Market value, Maggie learned, was simply the number that resulted from multiplying the total number of shares the company had issued by the current price of the share. It could vary over time, even day to day, as the stock price varied. It was a common way to describe the size of a company. People talked about *large, mid, and small cap companies*—these terms just meant that companies were either large, mid-sized, or small companies when it came to their relative market value—or market *capitalization*.

She again assumed her father chose the larger, well-known companies because they were less likely to go out of business than smaller, less familiar ones. They were more reliable.

She wished she had taken an interest in her mother's investments while her father was still alive. She could have learned so much from him. The Trust had clearly been well managed under his watchful eye. She saw there was value in an experienced, attentive advisor, who had the best interest of his client in mind. He seemed to have maximized the Trust's returns.

Today, the Trust held only about ten percent of its value in bonds. The bonds it did have were small holdings of only ten thousand dollars each. While there were only a few bonds left in the account, there seemed to be a great deal of trading in and out of them. There did not seem to be any pattern in this trading, as far as she could tell.

Maggie also noticed the stocks were traded very frequently. She assumed, at first, that this would happen when there was a loss—a holding would be sold to buy a new, better one to replace it. However, that did not appear to be the case. Some stocks were sold at a very small profit, or even when it was about equal to what it was bought for.

Also missing from the current portfolio were the large stock holdings of well-known companies that her father had favored. These companies paid good dividends and the Trust had bought and held onto them for years. Her father had owned companies like AT&T, Wells Fargo, Chevron, and Duke Energy, among others. He had held over one hundred thousand dollars in each. After his death, these core holdings were sold. The Trust no longer held any of these familiar stocks. Apparently, no holding was safe after her father's death.

In the original portfolio, every single holding generated some type of income. The dividends and interest were usually paid quarterly. Maggie even noticed these income payments were staggered across months, so income was distributed evenly throughout the year.

Looking at the numbers, Maggie knew the interest and dividend income on the original portfolio would have easily paid for her mother's care, plus all the fees of both the attorneys and the bankers. There would still have been money leftover to be reinvested. When her father was alive, it was.

The portfolio had grown in its initial years. It had a value of over five million dollars at its peak, shortly before her father's death. He had clearly been a good shepherd of the money.

Almost immediately after his death, though, the statements had changed. The new format looked cleaner and crisper. It appeared to have more details. Oddly though, all the additional information only made the statement harder to read and more confusing.

After her father's death, most of the high-value, high-dividend bonds disappeared. What bonds remained were corporate bonds whose income would be taxed. Maggie did not see any income in the portfolio now that appeared to be tax-free.

There had also been a noticeable shift in shareholdings. Stocks in household names had shrunk, and the increase in the number of holdings made the statements longer and more complex. This trend had accelerated in the past five years; large dividend-paying stocks were sold to buy newer, smaller companies in a wider range of industries. Many did not even pay dividends. Bonds were replaced with smaller bonds, paying less. The portfolio had moved from a relatively simple set of holdings, primarily made up of bonds, to this new mash of equity positions.

Why? Maggie wondered.

The current holdings in the portfolio paid less than two percent in interest and dividends overall. This was a considerable drop in annual returns from the six to eight percent the Trust had enjoyed in its earlier years. The change in mix explained some of this drop, but Maggie also knew that market conditions had changed over the years.

To understand what had happened to the portfolio, Maggie focused specifically on the years since her father's death. She stepped back from the portfolio and looked at overall market returns. She was trying to understand if the problem was with the Trust's holdings or a broader problem with the market overall.

Maggie saw that from 2008 to 2010 there had been a major drop in the stock market. The stock market indexes told her this. In 2008 there had been a worldwide financial crisis, brought on by a major housing bubble in the US. This housing bubble had threatened the financial stability of the largest banks in America, who held many of these mortgages. Maggie remembered that the news then had been full of worries about a collapse of all the financial markets. It had threatened to bring about the end of the world.

At the time, she didn't really understand any of it or see any impact on her or her family. Maggie had been oblivious to the impact on her mother's Trust. Or, she thought suddenly, on her and Neal's personal investment holdings. *Or his company's holdings.* Wow, Maggie thought. She had never even asked Neal if it was affecting them, she just assumed Neal had it under control. It *must* have had some impact. She did not remember him ever saying anything.

Somehow, despite all the gloom, the world saved itself. She looked back and realized that she had only seen the financial crisis as a time when some people were losing jobs or, in dire situations, their homes. Everyone had seemed stressed about money. Neal and she, however, had never even discussed it. Was *that* why he had tried to access some of the funds in the GFT, she wondered?

She saw, looking at the charts, that the Dow and S&P 500 indexes slid over fifty percent from the high in October 2007 to the low of March 2009. Maggie now realized that anyone close to retirement around then, or relying on fixed income, was probably badly shaken by this drop in the value of their portfolios. It must have been heartbreaking to see half of the funds you have worked a lifetime to accumulate gone in a matter of weeks.

The crash also slowed worldwide economic growth. To try and reboot their economies, governments around the world lowered their interest rates to almost zero. The idea was that if companies could borrow money cheaply, they would use the money to grow their businesses. If they grew their businesses, they would hire more people, and that would get economies growing again.

But lowering interest rates also meant the people who needed to earn income off their savings—people like her mother—were going to be earning a lot less. Her mother's Trust account was originally earning six to eight percent but as the bonds matured and new bonds were bought, they paid less interest. Many companies also either shrunk or suspended the dividends they were paying during the crisis. For retirees, there was less money in their accounts and less income to be earned by that money. It was a double whammy for fixed income portfolios.

It was a difficult time for many older people. Those who had worked hard all their lives and saved responsibly for retirement found they had to continue or return to work. Not just were their retirement savings reduced because of the crash, but the money they had saved was barely earning anything to help supplement their Social Security checks. Pension funds began to have problems making their pension obligations. Anyone with money to spare was looking for ways to make money from their money, but there was simply no place to put it.

Looking at statements from that period, Maggie saw that the GFT *was* hurt by the financial crisis. The crash occurred just months before her father's death and it coincided with many of the bonds maturing. After the crash, it was extremely difficult to find new investments that paid as well as the old ones. Generally, the proceeds had been reinvested in stocks rather than bonds. Initially, though, Maggie saw this was a winning strategy. Stocks did rebound a bit initially.

As the financial crisis dragged along and her father passed, the new manager appeared to have panicked; many of the holdings were sold at losses as the crisis deepened. Maggie saw that there was a great deal of cash that sat in the account for years, earning almost no interest, perhaps waiting for an opportunity to reinvest. Unfortunately, by the time most of this money was put back to work, the initial market recovery was already very far advanced. Holding cash rather than stocks meant the Trust had missed a large portion of the rebound from the crash.

It was during this period that the shift from large, established companies to smaller, newer ones accelerated. Maggie suspected that the manager may have been trying to buy stocks that could appreciate quickly to make up for the losses. It did not appear he or she made good choices.

There were relatively few bonds bought, and these bonds were smaller. Many paid less than three percent. In what she assumed was a bid to make more money, someone had purchased over a half million dollars of Puerto Rican bonds, which were paying a very high dividend at the time, but these bonds were sold at a substantial loss in 2014. She vaguely remembered something about Puerto Rico having to undergo something like bankruptcy. So not all government bonds were safe.

The most confusing of the current holdings was something called "Alternative Investments." It was a heading that materialized a couple years after her father's death. It grew to over one million dollars over a period of five years. She could not see any returns. There were only two companies listed here and she could not find any public information on them. She was not sure what she was looking at.

Two weeks later, Maggie felt she had a good enough handle on the GFT. She called the investment firm who managed it. She was shuffled around for a while until she finally got a hold of a man who said he was familiar with the Trust and its holdings.

"Hello, Jesse Brennan, here. So sorry it took a while to get ahold of me. I've only recently been assigned to the portfolio. The old manager has recently left the firm. Let me see," Maggie heard paper rustling, "My paperwork here identifies you as the Trustee on this account. Can I have the account number and your Social to confirm who I am talking to?" Maggie gave him the information he needed. Jesse then went on to give her his background and, in passing, mentioned he had once worked for her father's old bank.

Maggie was confused. "But aren't you still part of Dad's bank? This account was originally held by them; I have the statements."

"No," Jesse said. "Our investment company is independent. We are a stand-alone advisory firm. We recently merged with another independent practice from another bank."

Jesse then explained to Maggie that the financial crisis had spawned a number of these independent advisory firms as struggling banks had to shed staff.

Unemployed advisors set up their own shops, often taking their old clients with them. Her father's name meant nothing to Jesse.

"But your company name and logo are both so similar to his bank! It is very confusing." Maggie said impatiently. Now she understood why the statement had changed format. Looking closely, she saw that while the colors and logo on the statements looked similar, there was a different name in the small print at the bottom of the page.

She asked Jesse how the Trust had been able to move from her father's bank to a stand-alone firm without her consent. Jesse told her that as he understood it, her husband, as the former Trustee, had authorized it shortly after her father's death. He suggested that it probably happened before the paperwork replacing him with Maggie had come through. Maggie pointed out that ignorance did not seem like an adequate excuse, but Jesse simply said he would have to defer to his legal department on the issue. Everyone on his end, he assured her, had acted in good faith.

Maggie was frustrated. It was not a good beginning. She then asked Jesse what he thought about the portfolio's performance.

He did not miss a beat. He smoothly observed that the Trust had experienced some "performance issues." He then made a point of emphasizing that these problems arose before his time. He felt that the current holdings were performing adequately. Jesse suggested it might be a good time for them to get together to review the objectives of the Trust.

Maggie had not expected Jesse to admit that his company had mismanaged her Trust. She asked him incredulously, "*Review objectives?* The only objective the Trust is to provide income for my mother's care. Nothing has changed. Look, let's not waste time. I want to understand why there are so many holdings and the rationale behind the frequent trading."

He began a long spiel about the need to "diversify" and how small and middle-sized firms had more growth potential than larger ones. He mentioned his focus was on stock appreciation. He told her that the reduction in the proportion of bonds in the portfolio was because there was so little "yield" in bonds currently. He told her that by the firm's performance benchmarks, the fund had done well.

When she pushed him, she discovered the benchmarks he was using to measure his firm's performance were simply random ones selected from time periods that showed large losses, making the Trust portfolio's losses look good by comparison.

Jesse defensively assured her that everyone in fixed income was having a difficult time finding ways to generate income on holdings. Interest rates were simply too low.

Maggie asked him to explain the "alternative" investments. She was furious to find out the funds had been directed to an in-house investment group. The returns had been negative for the past four years, and yet the Trust managers chose to *top up*, meaning to put even more money into these firms. Jesse said they were expecting a liquidity event soon but could give her no specifics. It was like throwing good money after bad, as far as Maggie could see.

Maggie was at a slow boil. These people were supposed to be professional financial advisors, yet she felt she had more innate money sense than Jesse. How, she berated herself, could she have let this go on for so long? She had assumed the firm was being responsible, that it had her mother's best interest at heart. She never realized that firms would treat other people's money so carelessly.

It was the answer to her last question, though, that made everything click, "What are your fees for managing this portfolio?"

Maggie heard the intake of breath over the phone and then the pause. Finally, Jesse said, "Well, in this type of portfolio, this size, we take one percent of the value of the portfolio annually. Of course, we also have minor fees when we execute trades, part of our *expense ratio*."

"Expense ratio? You mean there are fees in addition to your one percent management fee?"

"Well, yes. There are costs associated with the trading itself; we have to pay the exchanges to execute our trades, recordkeeping expenses, custodial services to hold fund assets, legal expenses, accounting, and audit costs. That type of thing. Mutual funds and exchange traded funds all have them. They generally run from one to three percent, depending on the type of fund and the managers."

Maggie was confused. "I thought the *expense ratios* for stock funds had to do with payments to their managers, the ones who decide what to buy and sell in the fund's portfolio. Why do you have a one percent management fee *and* also separate fees for executing the trades?"

"Well, our management fee is modest relative to most firms. The additional fees are to handle costs specific to the trades themselves. Think of them as execution fees. Of course, if you had advised us to limit trades on the account, we would have. That would have reduced fees. We *actively managed* the Trust to try and improve its performance."

"Can you tell me exactly how much we paid last year in these *execution* fees? I mean, on top of the management fees?"

"Well, we do not track that number as such."

"Estimate it for me then." Maggie said sarcastically. "How much does the Trust pay per trade?"

"On equity trades we charge five cents per share. On bonds, fifty basis points, depending on the size of the purchase."

"From looking at the most recent statements, it looks like you do a lot of trades, particularly in smaller companies where the shares cost less than ten dollars. At five cents a share, the cost would add up quickly." Jesse didn't reply. Maggie sighed. "What are *basis points*?"

"A basis point is 1/100 of a percentage point."

"Then, why don't you just say that you are charging half of one percent of the value of the bond to trade it, rather than using jargon like fifty *basis* points?"

"The term is just an industry standard, I think," he said. His voice sounded more relaxed moving to generic topics rather than answering questions about the Trust.

"So, from looking at the monthly statements for the last couple years, I see that there has been a tremendous amount of churn in all segments of the portfolio. The smaller companies in the portfolio have less expensive shares, so a charge of a nickel per share means the cost to trade those smaller companies is costing the Trust substantially more than trading in shares of larger companies with more expensive shares. I really haven't studied it, but it appears there are thousands of shares traded each month in this account, mostly trades in smaller-value stocks."

Maggie pulled out the latest statement and continued. "In last month's statement, for example, I see you traded in and out of a company whose shares are five dollars each. On four different dates, you traded ten thousand shares—fifty thousand worth of stock. Each of these transactions would have generated five hundred dollars in fees for you—that's two thousand for the month on trading shares in just this one company. Not one of these trades booked a profit of more than twenty dollars for the Trust. On two of the trades, you actually *lost* money and repurchased the same shares at a higher price! Just looking at this statement, I estimate there would have been over five thousand dollars in execution fees this month alone."

There was silence on the other end of the phone. It only made Maggie angrier. "I can't say for sure," Maggie said. "But it also looks like you are also trading bonds *every* month too, averaging fifty thousand dollars' worth of trades. At one half of one percent, that would be $2,500 in fees every month just on bond trading. Did you really need to trade bonds that frequently? Whatever happened to buy and *hold*. All up, I estimate you are earning at least $7,500 per month in trading fees on this account, on top of the management fees you charge. It looks like your firm earns almost one hundred thousand dollars per year on just *trading* fees in this account—and there is a management fee of one percent as well? That is at least another $18,000! All this on an account that has consistently lost money. The Trust pays you more to manage the money than it actually pays for my mother's care! As the Trustee, I am not happy."

"I understand your concern," Jesse answered smoothly. He seemed to have been expecting this challenge all along. "The manager who handled this Trust was recently let go. In large part, it was because he was a risk taker and was clearly far too active on the account. He had a broker friend who managed small and midcap shares for the Trust. That broker was also let go for poor performance."

"And the Puerto Rican bonds? The Alternative Investments?" Maggie snapped. "How did those decisions get made? Just one single manager has the ability to put that much money at risk? Where are the controls? Why did no one there make any effort to contact me about the annual performance? Oh, all that was before your time too, I imagine." Maggie said angrily.

Again, Jesse was calm. "Well, we understand your frustration. The only contact we have had is with the law firm. They were our designated point of contact. You were not listed on the account as Trustee, I am not sure why. Dale Hanes called to alert me to your role only this past week and he sent over the paperwork. Our firm has taken all care, but we are not responsible for losses. You understand that all investing involves risk and there is no guarantee regarding returns. We know that the portfolio requires rebalancing and we are prepared to undertake this at our cost. There will be no transaction or management fees. We want this cleaned up and better managed, going forward. We are even willing to renegotiate fees."

Maggie wanted to throw the phone. She had not expected this open admission of mismanagement. She had hoped for a rational explanation for the poor performance.

She knew she was done with this particular investment advisory firm. Her father had been a wise and disciplined advisor; Jesse's firm had clearly been the opposite. Tense with the futility of dealing with Jesse, Maggie spit out, "Yes. Jesse. *Clearly* it needs to be streamlined and rebalanced. It should focus only on generating income as was set up to do. Before we do that, I want a full accounting of the fees paid by the Trust over the past five years, in detail, by the end of the week. Going forward, send everything to me. Absolutely *no more trades* on the account without my specific approval. Also, I want to know the liquidation process for the alternative investments. I want the money as cash."

Jesse readily agreed to everything and was clearly relieved to have finished the call. Maggie hung up still shaking with anger. Was it fair to call them thieves? She wondered if there was legal recourse for this type of thing, maybe malpractice? But she knew from her reading that most advisors worked under the umbrella of "all care but no responsibility." In the end, she returned to blaming herself. Yet again, she had just assumed Neal had everything under control.

Until today, Maggie had had respect for people who handled other people's money. Her father had been scrupulously honest, even returning pennies to a store if they gave him the wrong change. He had always said his integrity and reputation was worth a great deal more than mere money.

But Maggie realized the issue of fees was larger than just unscrupulous advisors taking advantage of naive investors. Money management fees were always going to take a bite out of investments returns. Fees were frequently small and hidden, people often paid them without even realizing it. They were rarely spelled out in clear, unambiguous terms. No invoices sent out. It was lucky if fees were even itemized on a statement.

In the past, when market returns averaged six to eight percent, management and advisory fees, even commissions on trades, still left a solid return for investors. Now that market returns were averaging closer to three or four percent, particularly on fixed income accounts, fees of one to two percent could halve the returns of a portfolio. This would greatly reduce the benefits of compounding.

The Trust account had shrunk in the past decade because of market conditions and a change in the mix of the holdings. It had also suffered more because the fees had outstripped the returns and eaten into principle. Eating into principle had, in turn, reduced the Trust's ability to generate income and reduced the principle even more. In some respects, Neal's departure was lucky. It had forced her to catch the problem before her mother's money was completely siphoned away.

In Maggie's study she had learned that in her father's era, well before the internet, investing had required manual research and experience. Banks like her father's and trading firms employed armies of analysts. Trading was done on trading floors by humans with decades of experience and who managed incomprehensible amounts of paper. Investing was work, involving research by thousands of professionals. There were many, like her father, who were honest and skilled at their work. And there were others, like Jesse, who seemed almost unconcerned about their clients' needs. These unscrupulous advisors needlessly *churned* accounts to generate extra fees. Many clients would not know which type of advisor they had until it was too late.

Today, automation was the rule and fewer people were involved. Information was readily available on the internet, so research costs fell. Maggie learned that fifty to sixty percent of daily trading is estimated to be done by machines, and as a result the cost of trading had come down substantially. Excellent research on companies was available to everyone with access to a computer, at the click of a keyboard.

As a result of all this new technology, Maggie knew fees in the industry were coming down fast. It was a serious point of competition between banks and brokerage firms. Yet, it appeared that the GFT had been paying more in management fees over these past few years than ever before.

Maggie had never expected the Trust to have had so much money. She had always assumed there would be little left after her mother's death. Neal had always complained that the Trust was not going to last.

Now she knew the Trust could probably carry her mother for whatever time she had left. This belief assumed that the principle would not be stripped away by an unscrupulous manager or a major market downturn. Before Neal left, she believed that if the Trust ran dry, she and Neal would meet any financial shortfall. She knew in her current situation, alone, she could not afford to be that unlikely cushion. She had to protect the GFT at all costs.

Her taking control would make a difference. It would at least stop the bleeding. She knew she had her mother's best interests at heart. She would develop a plan. She would find someone better to manage the Trust. She would find the right firm, and then decide if they were worth their fees. It would take time, but she knew where to start. Getting rid of Jesse was the first step.

She wanted the GFT money moved as soon as possible. Jesse's firm had done enough damage. Thinking about her options, Maggie remembered Kate, the young broker at Charles Schwab. Kate, she assumed, could help Maggie get the account transferred to Charles Schwab for the time being. She would put the money into large, dividend-paying stocks, then try and manage it herself until she found a proper advisor.

When she hired someone this time, though, she would make sure she understood the fees involved up front. Transaction fees, expense ratio fees, advisor fees—whatever people were calling them, she would ask about them all and make sure she understood them and the impact they might have on returns. She was not going to let the Trust income get eaten up by fees if she could avoid them. She was happy to pay advisors, but only if they could prove their worth.

Maggie was uncomfortable at the thought of managing the Trust, even in the short term. Realistically though, she believed she could not do worse than Jesse's firm had done. With a little luck, and a cooperating market, she might even do better.

The law firm would also have to go. She could write checks and find an accountant to do the taxes. If she managed it, she would be sure that the person writing the checks had her mother's best interest at heart. It was well past the time for her to step up.

As nervous as she was about all the changes she was making, Maggie knew one thing at the very least. Going forward the Trust would be practically free of fees. She now realized that this alone would improve its returns dramatically.

CHAPTER 11:
UNDERSTANDING LIMITS

After work the next day, Maggie went directly to Charles Schwab and explained her dilemma to Kate, who was delighted to help. The Trust account could easily be moved, Kate assured her, especially since Maggie was the sole Trustee and had the full authority to change managers. As the value of the account was over one million dollars, Maggie would get the current promotion Schwab had for large new accounts: unlimited free trades for two years, as long as she stayed with them for more than a year.

"No fees at all?" Maggie was thrilled at the prospect.

"Not from us," Kate assured her.

Maggie asked Kate whether she should have Jesse's firm liquidate the holdings in the Trust or if she should have Schwab do it. Kate said she could take care of it. Maggie gave her a copy of the most recent statement. As Kate flipped through the list of holdings, she just shook her head. When Maggie described the churn and the fees, Kate was matter of fact about it.

"Many of these smaller advisory firms are dying, and they know it," Kate said. "Unscrupulous companies will churn to generate fees. They can't compete with online services like us. It is general knowledge now that simple, low-fee index funds generally have higher returns than a basket of stocks selected by an advisor. Even robo-advisors, that is companies that have computers picking stocks, generally do a better job. Only really wealthy people have advisors these days."

Maggie was unsure that all human advisors were bad; her father had seemed to select good stocks. But she understood Kate's absolute confidence in technology. It was a twenty-something belief, Maggie thought. She always wondered how younger people would cope if the power were ever to go out indefinitely.

Maggie asked Kate to look at the alternative investments in the GFT account, which she said looked odd. Kate shrugged. "Looks odd to me too." she agreed. She asked to keep a copy of the statement and said, "Leave everything to me, Maggie. I will do a bit of sniffing around. It's my job to help people move accounts to the firm. I'm good at it!"

As they went through the necessary paperwork for the move, Maggie asked Kate if the two years of free trading on the Trust account could extend to her personal trading account as well. Kate got up and checked with her supervisor, the gentleman who had admired Maggie's certificates. Maggie could see from Kate's desk that he was nodding his head in agreement.

Kate returned to her desk and said, "It was good that you thought to ask. I wouldn't have known that was possible."

Maggie wanted to take advantage of the free trade offer. She knew that many of the online firms were charging close to five dollars per trade, as did both her old and new banks. Maggie explained to Kate that she had money from two other accounts she wanted to add to her new trading account.

First, she showed Kate the statement from the dividend account in her father's old bank in New York. Kate produced new paperwork to also transfer this money into Maggie's brokerage account. She said she would arrange to have the McDonald's dividends posted to the account from now on.

Then Maggie said she would also like to transfer $250,000 from her Ally account to the Schwab account. Kate looked at Maggie with wide eyes.

"Any more cash rabbits coming out of your hats?"

Maggie laughed and said no, that was pretty much all of it. Maggie mentioned that she had considered using Ally for her trading site, as the commissions were as low as Schwab's, but the free trade offer had made the decision for her. Ally's trading commissions would have eaten into any profits she made.

Maggie had decided she would still use Ally as her day-to-day bank. She already had her paychecks automatically deposited there and had recently opened a separate emergency fund account there.

After they had finished the paperwork, Kate asked if Maggie knew what her first trade would be.

Maggie was prepared. "I think AT&T. Phones are not going anywhere, and it pays a dividend of over six percent. I am trying to earn as much income as possible in this account."

Kate looked at her screen and said AT&T was trading between $30.50 and $30.56 per share today. "What price do you want to pay?" she asked.

Maggie did not understand the question. She could choose the price she paid? Kate pulled up Maggie's account on the Schwab site and swung the computer screen around so they could both see what she was doing. Kate was going to explain by showing her how to enter an order to buy a stock in her account.

"You will begin by going to the *Trade* tab, and then select *Stocks*. When the page came up, Kate showed Maggie how to fill the boxes.

First you put in the ticker symbol for the company. For AT&T, the ticker is just 'T.' If you don't know the ticker, just type the name of the company and the computer will generally give you the ticker. Tickers are like a short nickname that makes entering trades easier. After a while, you get pretty familiar with the tickers of the common companies."

"Second, you select what you want to do, the Action. Most of us just use the Buy or Sell option. Ignore the other terms like *sell short*. These are terms related to trading options. Most people will never need to get that sophisticated in their trading. Options require a bit of experience with the market. Finally, you put in a quantity. That is the number of shares you want to buy. Alternatively, you can put in a dollar value of how much you want to spend, and the computer will calculate how many shares to buy for you."

Maggie was nodding as Kate went through the screen with her. It was all pretty straightforward so far.

Kate continued, "This next box is very, very important. It is the *order type*. A lot of people just pick *Market* here as it is the first choice. This means that the price you pay is whatever the market is trading the stock for at the moment your order arrives. However, stock prices range a lot on any given day, or any given moment. There is always a *bid* and an *ask* price. The bid price is what people are willing to pay for the stock, and the ask price is what people want to sell it for. The bid/ask range can be a couple pennies or a couple dollars for the bigger stocks. Market orders frequently are supposed to give you the best price at the time you place the order, but given the range, it may not be. If you put in *market price*, you may find yourself wondering if you got the best price possible. Some firms send their orders to third parties to execute trades and these firms can make money by just delaying a couple seconds or shaving the price a fraction of a penny on either side."

"Then, what *should* I pick?"

"I always tell people to pick the *Limit* option. When you do, the machine then asks you what price you *want* to pay for the shares, what is your *bid*. I tell people to have an idea before they buy a share as to what they want to pay. Pick the low end of the bid/ask range, or even go below it. The price you want to pay often comes to you over the course of a day. If the price does not go that low, you will not get the share order filled on that day. If you really want to buy the stock that specific day, you can always choose to change the price. The trick is to be patient when you can. Watch the range the stock trades in over a couple of days or week. I tell my clients it is better to wait a couple of days for the price to come to you, rather than feel regrets when seeing an immediate loss. Whenever possible, buy a stock on a day it is trading down. That way you can feel pretty smart when the price returns to the price it was trading at before and you see a profit. A lot of stocks trade in a noticeable range."

Maggie thought the limit order tip was very useful. She and Kate finalized her order to buy AT&T. Maggie entered an order to buy a hundred shares for a limit price of $30.40, below the current bid price.

"Timing or duration is this final box here, and that asks how long you want your order to last. Generally, I tell people to do it for just the day. Alternatively, you can choose GTC, or 'Good until Cancelled' and the order will stay in the system for up to thirty days waiting for the stock to get to the price you are willing to pay. It is cancelled if it does not fill. This can be dangerous, though, as stock prices can be very volatile. I generally tell people to select *same day*, and re-enter it the next day if you don't get filled. You can get caught out with GTC orders if the market has a sudden drop, or the particular stock you want has unexpected bad news." Kate saw Maggie looking at curiously at the other timing terms, "Forget the other timing options for now, Maggie. When you are learning, stick to the basics. Use a *limit* order. Buy or sell the *same day*."

Maggie noticed a box on the screen which would let her reinvest dividends, a DRIP option, but she told Kate she wanted the cash in her account for the time being. They left that box empty.

At the bottom of the screen was a button marked "Review." Kate told her that was a critical step.

Maggie clicked on it and a preview of her entire order appeared. It gave her one last chance to look over what she had entered to make sure there were no errors. Kate told Maggie that she should always review this carefully. The computer would give her a warning for an obvious mistake, like a bid that was well over the asking price, but it was easy to mistakenly add an extra digit somewhere and get burned. Like buying one hundred shares when she wanted ten. She should always check.

Finally, at the end of the review page was a *place order* or submit button. Maggie clicked on it and the order was done. Maggie had entered a price below where the stock was currently trading, so her order status was *open*. Kate then set up electronic notifications on Maggie's account. It would send a text to her when her order filled. Maggie could not wait to get home and work out what other shares to buy.

As Maggie was leaving Kate asked, "Do you want me to set up a *sweep* for the cash in the account? We have a money market fund that is currently paying just about two percent in interest." When Maggie looked confused, Kate explained, "A money market is a fund that invests in high-quality short-term debt and cash equivalents. It is as close to risk-free as you can get. A sweep means that we put your cash into the money market until you are ready to invest it. That way, it will earn interest for you in the meantime. Just call me when you need cash and I put in an order to liquidate it."

Earning almost two percent in an investment that was close to risk-free sounded like a good idea. Maggie said yes to the money market sweep. She thanked Kate for all the help. She hoped to learn how to sweep for herself.

As she drove, Maggie thought about simply leaving the cash from liquidating her mother's Trust in the money market fund Kate had talked about. There would be no loss of principle and she could still earn about two percent a year in income. Maybe more, if interest rates rose. It wasn't much, but the money would be safe and there would be no management fees. It might be the way to go.

She would have to eat into principle a little each year to care for her mother, but that might be fine. It would last for at least ten to fifteen years. It might be the better, safer, choice than reinvesting the principle in stocks. She thought she might run the idea by Graham and see what he thought.

Arriving home, Maggie saw there was a Jeep in the driveway. It was an unusual car for Olivia's typical visitors. She drove around back to park in the second garage and used her internal stairs so as not to interrupt Olivia and her guest.

Maggie had just changed into jeans and a sweater when there was a knock on her door.

Olivia was normally in the habit of throwing open the door to announce herself. This knock was soft, as if she did not want anyone but Maggie to hear. Maggie answered it with a question mark on her face.

"You have a dilemma downstairs," Olivia said with a sly look. Maggie looked at her blankly. Olivia continued, "A 'gentleman caller,' as we used to refer to them. I thought for a minute that it was that missing husband of yours, but he gave another name. I was still suspicious, but he was polite and nervous rather than guilty looking. He almost left a couple times, but it turns out he is fond of both dogs and Johnny Walker, so we're almost family now."

"Does this polite and nervous man have a name?" Maggie asked with a smile.

"Yes, yes, he does. But he said to let you know that your *aviator* was here. Sounded like a very sexy nickname to me. He tells me he hasn't seen you since you ran off and married someone else. So, I guess that's one reason he's nervous."

Maggie couldn't sort out the wave of emotions that hit her—there was panic, pleasure, confusion, excitement, regret, and shame. The last two lingered. Olivia watched as the emotions washed over Maggie, reddening her face.

"So...not expecting him?" she asked. It was more statement than question. Olivia was clearly very curious.

"No. Not really. Not ever, actually," she said. Her mind was elsewhere, replaying a night from over twenty-five years ago.

Olivia stopped Maggie's daydreaming. "I don't think he's leaving until he sees you. You might want a minute to freshen up."

Maggie could not come up with any excuse not to see him. She knew Olivia was right; there was no avoiding him.

Olivia went back downstairs. Maggie took her time getting ready, nervously changing three, then four times. She added make-up, fixed her hair. There was no getting over it—she was old and fat. She ended up back in jeans and a cashmere sweater set. At the last minute, she changed from slippers and put on pumps with kitten heels. He was probably still tall.

His back was to her when she stepped into Olivia's living room. The crown of his hair had thinned, and somehow it made him dear to her. As he stood and turned to greet her, she realized why Olivia had thought it was her husband. The hair was a soft, wavy blond, the face weathered and tan, but still terribly handsome. There was no room for doubt—it was an older, taller Ethan standing before her.

Shit, she thought.

Olivia only stayed a minute more. She scooped up the spaniels and announced she was taking them for a walk. Maggie and her guest just awkwardly stared at one another. After Olivia left, Maggie broke away, said nothing, and walked to Olivia's bar area. Turning her back to him she poured herself a drink with an unsteady hand. He said nothing either, which was pretty typical, she thought wryly. She looked down at her drink and realized she didn't even know if she liked Johnny Walker, but she didn't care—she needed to do something with her hands. This was going to be painful.

His name was Brody Cavanaugh, after his grandfather, a pilot who had gone down in WWII. He and his father had been obsessed with flying. Brody had started lessons at fourteen and went on to study aeronautical engineering at the Massachusetts Institute of Technology. He had been an officer in the Air Force when he was there; the government had paid for his school.

She met him in the fall of his senior year. They had been put in the same sailboat on the Charles River by friends trying to matchmake. Each had assumed the other one knew what they were doing, but neither had been in a sailboat except as a passenger. She had deferred to him, but finally took over with an exasperated sigh when the boat failed to even come close to home. It took her two tacks to get back to base, and he deftly caught the dock before she crashed into it.

They both got out of the boat agreeing they would never be sailors.

Despite the earlier tension, now that they were safely on shore, he surprised Maggie by asking her to dinner. He was quiet, even shy, she guessed. His friend knew enough about Maggie to know she could be genuinely interested in any-thing. She would pull him out of his shell. Dinner that night went much better than the sailing. It was all about flying and the Air Force. Maggie admitted she would like to learn to fly; it seemed so adventurous. She asked about the types of planes he liked and what he wanted to do in life. He had plans, he said. He was going to start a specialty airline after he got out of the Air Force in four years. He wanted to do tours of the National Parks, give people a chance to see them all, to have a book where kids could collect stamps of their visits.

"So many of the parks are hard to get to," he said excitedly, "I built my flying hours visiting them. They are all so different, but each spectacular."

Maggie thought it all sounded very romantic. They stayed late at the restaurant. He kissed her chastely on her cheek at her front door after he walked her home. They agreed they wanted to see more of each other. It quickly became an intense relationship.

He took her to airports and showed her the various types of planes he flew. He explained how they worked and how far you could go with each different type. The first time she flew with him, he let her take control of the plane. She thought she was probably in love—though it wasn't clear whether she was in love with him or with the flying.

That same night, they had not been able to get through dinner. They couldn't stop touching each other. Maggie leaned in and slowly stroked his leg under the table, moving up his thigh until he had to pull her hand back onto the tabletop. Her suggestive looks and teasing comments had Brody calling for the check while their plates were still half full. She did not object. He took her home, where they made love for the first time. She never told him that she was a virgin. It was absolutely perfect. The foreplay, the pace, the teasing and the climax. It could not have been better. He told her he was not an experienced lover, but everything about the sex had been exactly right for her. She simply didn't believe him. In a heady rush, she thought this was surely the only man for her. She felt more alive than she had any time since her brother had died. Suddenly life seemed full of possibilities.

Over the next months, they spent as much time together as they could. They walked the Esplanade, went to movies, and hiked the suburbs. They developed pet names for each other—he was her *aviator* and she became *Trix*, short for aviatrix. They flew when they could, and she planned to learn to fly too.

His upcoming graduation presented a problem, though. He had orders to return to Colorado immediately afterward, and he would be there for at least three more years. They both knew that neither was ready for marriage. Maggie wanted a career, but Brody did not know what she would find to do in Colorado. There was not a lot happening around his base. As the date of his departure approached, they became prickly with one another. Neither was willing to admit how much a separation was going to hurt.

Maggie's parents came to Boston for a visit just before he graduated. She had been excited for them to meet him. She had kept the duration and intensity of their relationship to herself, simply describing Brody as a friend. It might have been an error not to let her parents know how much she cared for Brody.

Her father selected the most expensive restaurant in town, and they all went out to dinner. From the beginning, her father seemed less than impressed with Brody. Maggie knew her father did not think highly of the military. Early on during the meal, her father made a poor joke that suggested pilots were little more than highly educated bus drivers. Brody's MIT degree did not help either. Her father was a Harvard man.

Brody took her father's ribbing well, but Maggie could see he chafed. At one point, he started to explain his dream to start an airline. Her father brutally picked it apart, starting with the issue of how difficult it would be to finance. Brody got defensive and they finished the dinner on a tense note. As they were leaving, Maggie pulled Brody aside to try and smooth things over, but Brody just shrugged her off, thanked her parents, and headed home alone.

From this point on, they began to fight more openly. Minor things set them both off. Despite Brody's quickly approaching departure, they did not see each other very much. Brody had finals and he was swamped, so they only met for quick coffees or short meals. He did not come by her place and stay over like he used to. Maggie found she often preferred to be alone rather than sparring with him in person. She was angry and frustrated, but also ached to see him. They simply failed to connect like they had so effortlessly before.

During Brody's finals' week, Maggie's father called and asked her to please escort a young man from his bank around Boston. He was going to be there for a few days to recruit from Harvard for the firm. Maggie agreed.

Neal Mueller was considered a catch, or at least Maggie's father thought so. After meeting Brody, her father had decided a timely intervention in her social calendar was in order. Maggie might have presented Brody as a friend but Maggie's father had seen more in their interaction that just a friendship.

Maggie found she liked Neal - he was darkly handsome, incredibly charming and *very* interested in her. He had met her mother at multiple firm functions and told Maggie how lucky she was to have a mother so beautiful and clever. He explained to Maggie that he had been raised by his dad after his mother had died.

He had then added that his dad had succumbed to cancer while Neal was in college. He said he looked up to Maggie's dad as a father figure.

As their first dinner progressed, she contrasted Brody and Neal. Brody had always been all about *his* plans and *his* interests. They could spend all day at some airport without Brody asking a single question about her or her life. Neal's interest, however, was in Maggie. It was a welcome change. Neal also made her laugh, which Brody certainly hadn't been doing, lately.

The next night, Neal called again. Maggie had not spoken to Brody in over three days and was frustrated. She knew he had finished an exam that day and she had had a really lousy day. She wanted to share it with him. Despite complaining she was tired, Neal finally cajoled her into meeting him at her neighborhood restaurant for a quick dinner. Halfway through, Neal put down his fork and reached out for her hand.

He then startled Maggie by saying, "I know this is sudden, but I just want you to know, Maggie, I am not dating anyone. Your dad tells me you aren't either. Last night was really special for me. I mean, I really like you, *a lot*, and I would like to date you. But I want to make it clear, I am looking for a wife. Not just a girlfriend."

As chance happens, this was the same day Maggie had been sidelined at her workplace because a male consultant had taken credit for her work. She was feeling demoralized and directionless; she felt like her career was going nowhere. Neal's timing could not have been better. She suddenly saw herself as a wife and even a mother. This idea did not feel as dull as it usually did. Her plans for a career seemed to be washing out. The work setback had planted a seed of doubt about her abilities, much like Mr. Harris had done in middle school all those years ago. Marriage was suddenly a possible—and attractive—alternative.

Maggie took a minute and slowly said, "Thank you, Neal. I am really flattered. I like you too. My dad is wrong though, Neal. I am seeing someone. But he is about to move to Colorado, so I don't know where it's going."

Neal smiled. "No problem. Let's just see how things work out then." He smiled at her mischievously. "But you should know that I don't give up easily, Ms. Gagnon. Consider yourself warned."

They finished their meal and he assertively kissed on her cheek when he said good night.

Brody finished his exams and packed for Colorado. Their last night together was awful. They tried to be civil to each other, but they fought. They argued about everything, both unwilling to admit their true feelings. Their pride got in the way. Finally, in frustration and not ever understanding why, she bitterly told him about Neal.

Brody went crazy, calling her unfaithful and a tease. She stormed out of his place and was not sure whether she would ever see him again. She was devastated and heartbroken. She hoped he would call, and then told herself she would hang up if he did. She was sorry she had mentioned Neal and wondered why she had. When the phone did not ring, she did not even consider calling him herself. She felt like she did not deserve him.

After weeks of silence from Brody, she let a relationship with Neal begin to develop. He called from Connecticut daily and even drove two hours each way to take her out to dinner or for weekend dates. As summer passed into fall, Maggie and Neal finally slept together. After Neal left, Maggie cried. Neal was an experienced, adventurous, and even a playful lover. He introduced Maggie to things she had not imagined, but there was something missing. Sex with Neal was not going to be anything like sex with Brody. She couldn't explain it even to herself.

As time went on, it did not change. There was no spark like there had been with Brody, and during sex she was rarely gratified. She never told Neal this, because he never bothered to ask. Maggie play-acted her satisfaction with him, finally understanding the term *faking it*. Neal was happy, so that was that. After just three months together, he casually asked her to marry him, testing the waters. She ignored him. He asked regularly thereafter. She always smiled and said maybe. Drove him crazy.

One day in early winter, Brody showed up at her work unexpectedly. He had a bouquet of wildflowers. Maggie only hesitated a moment; her heart was racing. She made excuses to her new boss and left early. They were politely cautious with one another. He took her to their favorite bar. One drink led to three, and then dinner and wine. They finally went back to her apartment to talk. There, they both apologized for how they had left the relationship. Brody blamed himself, said he was too immature and self-centered. She put her bad behavior down to anger, stubbornness, and fear. As they talked, it was clear that they had both matured a little, though neither realized it.

Finally, Maggie admitted she was seeing Neal. She tried to make it sound casual, but the tone of the evening shifted. Anxious to get the closeness back, Maggie leaned in to kiss Brody and ended up in his lap. They eventually moved to the bedroom, and the lovemaking was like old times. No need for Maggie to pretend. The gratification was real and deep. She was sure that they could put things back together again. She knew then she loved Brody, not Neal.

In the morning, Brody simply got up, dressed and woke her to kiss her goodbye. He said he had an early morning flight to catch. While his words were brusque, he tenderly brushed through her hair with a practiced hand. He looked tired and devastated. He said nothing specific about seeing her again. It was on the tip of her tongue to ask, to tell him she loved him, but she could not bring herself to say it. Looking back, Maggie realized she had been too afraid. Since her brother's death, and her parents' stepping back from her life, Maggie had built strong walls around herself.

This second goodbye, so short and tender, somehow felt more final than the dramatic first one. Maggie convinced herself Brody was saying it forever. After he left, Maggie could not get out of bed for the rest of the day. She called in sick to work. She was sure Brody had left her for good.

Neal showed up that evening with long-stemmed red roses. She had told him a thousand times before that she did not like roses, but she kept quiet this time. He carelessly shoved them in with the ones from Brody. He said he had called her at work, found out she was home sick, and had come to take care of her. Instead, they had sex. Neal always expected it of her when he made the two-hour trip. Later, when he awoke hungry and playful, she got out of bed to make him something to eat. She had not really expected him to even know how to take care of her.

Later than night, back in bed, he asked her yet again if she would marry him. This time, she just tiredly said yes. She knew at least her parents would be thrilled.

Any second thoughts about the engagement disappeared when she found out she was pregnant. Neal was excited. He wanted lots of children. The wedding was accelerated. Ethan was born dark-haired and with Maggie's eyes. He looked enough like Neal that she never even considered any other possibility. When Brody finally called almost a year later, she coldly told him she was now a wife and mother. He curtly wished her a happy life and hung up. Her first and only great love was now one more thing she would simply box away in her memory.

As the years passed, Ethan's hair lightened. Perhaps he looked less like Neal, but no one really noticed. Only when Ethan began to obsess about planes did a small doubt surface for Maggie. She tried to redirect his passion as it niggled at her, but her parents spoiled him and planes popped up everywhere in her world. When the girls came along, the three children shared enough traits in common that Maggie put the plane obsession down to boys being boys.

By then, Neal had started his own firm with some friends. His work was all consuming. Neal's travel ramped up and soon he was only home on weekends, leaving early most Sunday afternoons for another week on the road. The children were left to Maggie and she let the whisper of a doubt fade. Life just moved along.

But today, looking at the man himself, she was reminded of that old doubt. In fact, Maggie was sure anyone could see the resemblance, and that Olivia in fact had. For her, it was clear that this was Ethan's biological father. She did not know where to begin. Reluctantly, she turned from the bar to face him.

Brody gave her a deep, sad look. Finally, he looked down at his drink and then back at her. "Well, Maggie. You have something to tell me?"

Maggie's heart sank.

CHAPTER 12:
UNEXPECTED BENEFITS

Brody waited, and Maggie looked down, unable to meet his sad eyes. Finally, she just quietly asked how he had found her. He shifted, clearly relieved to answer such a straightforward question, "It wasn't easy." He went on to explain how, over the years, he had looked periodically for her on the internet. He said he was curious as to how she was getting along. He had been surprised that he had neither found her nor her parents on Facebook or any other social network. He had never known Neal's last name.

This year, though, when he Googled her maiden name, he found the YouTube video Charlie had made. It had been dedicated to Maggie's parents, and the last name was unique enough. He had watched Charlie perform with her students and she reminded him enough of Maggie that he followed her to her Facebook page. It had not been updated lately, but there had been family photos.

"I recognized you in the photos immediately. Then," Brody paused and looked meaningfully at Maggie, "I saw Ethan." The disappointment in his voice gutted Maggie. He cleared his throat and went on, "The next step was easy. I found your old address contacted new owners and they gave me a forwarding address, which led me here."

Maggie sipped her drink and sighed, then gestured Brody back to the sofa and sat down opposite him. She wanted to take his hand but instead gripped her glass with both of hers. She leaned forward and the words tumbled out.

"Look, Brody, I am truly sorry. I can't even begin to imagine how you feel." Maggie paused, sipped her drink, and then began again, "I just didn't think it was possible. Even now, I am not one hundred percent sure. But looking at you, well, anyone who knows Ethan would have to see the resemblance."

"I know it sounds unbelievable that I wouldn't know. But it was immediately after that last night we had, that I got engaged. On the rebound, I guess. Neal and I had to accelerate our wedding when I found out I was pregnant. Ethan didn't look like you when he was born; we all thought he resembled Neal. My parents said he was the spitting image of my brother. The girls came so quickly after Ethan was born, and I was just so busy with babies, it didn't even think about it. The only thing that made me pause was when his plane obsession surfaced as a toddler. But I told myself all boys do the 'cars, planes and trains' thing. I didn't think that a plane fetish could be genetic. As he grew up, the resemblance may have evolved, but my memories of you had faded. Maybe I just didn't want to see it." She sipped her drink again, unable to meet his eye. "Honestly, I would have tried to contact you if I had known. Honestly? If you weren't here in front of me now, I don't think the question would have ever come up for me again."

Now Brody looked at his glass. "Funny way to start a catch-up conversation." Maggie heard the sadness in his voice. He added softly, "I would have liked to have known, Maggie. I have two wonderful girls, but a boy would have been something special for me. You may remember, I'm very close to my dad. The father/son thing has always meant a lot to me."

"So, you have children? Got married?" Maggie was desperate to change the topic of the conversation. She needed something to ratchet down the tenseness she was feeling. To give herself a chance to process the reality of Brody being here, in front of her. To try and work out what his showing up would mean to her family. To Ethan.

"I was late getting married; my girls are still in high school. They live with their mother. I think I might have a pilot," he said proudly. "I was away a lot when they were growing up so we aren't as close as I would have liked. I was flying for a couple different airlines. My wife wouldn't move away from her hometown. She wanted to be close to her family, especially when the girls were small because I wasn't there to help much. I understood but being away from them was grueling. It always felt as if I was getting ready to leave right after I got home. And there was nothing else for me to do, in that town. It was a farming community for the most part. I looked for other jobs, but there was never going to be anything else. My life has always been about flying – it's who I am and what I love. Of course, the money was good which meant I could give the girls everything they needed and then some. At first, my wife and I fought about the constant separations. I was furious she wouldn't move. I think after a while she just gave up on us as a couple. She ended up with her hometown sweetheart. He has been great to the girls. I'm lucky in that respect, I guess."

It sounded a little lonely to Maggie. "Where do you call home now?"

"Well, I move around a fair bit. I ended up leaving the airlines and cashed out the investment properties I had accumulated over the years. Then I bought an FBO, then another, and finally a private air charter company. Eventually, I found some additional investors and we bought more planes. I ended up owning an airline, of sorts, after all. I'll admit, your dad was right all those years ago. Access to money is the critical success factor in my business. That, and not getting too caught up with the latest toys. Now I have a place in New York and a couple of apartments near our other FBOs. I can't really say I am based anywhere, unless you ask the tax office. They will tell you I'm from Miami."

"FBO?"

"Fixed Base Operator. It's the building that private planes use when they land at an airport. We make money on aviation fuel, for the most part. We charter a full range of private planes and manage a number more for private groups and companies."

"Do you still fly?"

He finally smiled. "Whenever I can, Trix." The nickname slipped out effortlessly, and he looked up at her like he wanted to take it back. He relaxed when he saw that it made her smile.

He asked about Neal and she talked about the life she had just left, raising the kids, the house and Neal. She talked a lot about the children, Ethan especially, and her parents. Somehow, after a slow beginning, the story accelerated. She did not feel the years of separation or the awkwardness of the Ethan situation. They caught up as if it had been a year since they had seen each other, not a lifetime.

To her surprise, even her life this past year tumbled out. She skipped over the FBI, but then later backtracked and even told him about that. She just bulldozed ahead, relieved to get the whole story out. She finished with telling him about her cash flow problems and how she came to be living here with Olivia.

Brody listened and asked a few questions. His disapproval of Neal was clear. He was sad to hear about her mother's situation and her father's death. After a comfortable silence, he returned to the issue that had brought him here.

"Did you ever think about reaching out to me, when you had those doubts about Ethan? I was easy enough to find. My name and the word *pilot* works in Google every time."

Maggie gave her best answer, the same one she told herself whenever she toyed with the idea of checking to see what he was up to over the years. "We left things so badly. You didn't say anything about wanting to see me again. Then you didn't call for a year. I thought the message was pretty clear. I can tell you now that I was devastated."

Brody looked at her in disbelief. "I thought *you* were the one who didn't want to see *me*. You were the career girl, having fun with the guys. I was just an enlisted pilot with big plans and no money to back them up. And stuck in Colorado for three years. After you told me about Neal, I was furious. I had thought we had something pretty special, indestructible. Suddenly I realized you had never *said* you felt the same way. You used to send out a lot of mixed signals, Maggie. Independent one minute, waiting for me to hold a door the next. I was pretty shy and naive back then. It took a lot for me just to pick up a phone and call a girl. You were beautiful, intelligent, and just so perfect. Once I knew Neal was in the mix, I just lost my confidence. I just did not see how I would ever be able to compete with someone your father had blessed, it just killed me."

Maggie looked down at her drink again, ashamed she had hurt Brody so deeply. She had only dated Neal as a favor to her father. Telling Brody about him had only been to try and goad Brody into declaring himself before he left for Colorado. She had not really considered how he must have felt. *Selfish, foolish and so young*, she thought to herself

Brody continued. "All that time we dated, you never said anything specific about how you felt about me, or us. You rarely called me. It felt like I was always the one chasing, Maggie. When I told you, I had to go to Colorado, you barely said a word. And then your parents disliked me so much after that silly dinner. Rich girl, poor boy. I thought you gave up on me. When you told me that you were dating Neal that night I left for Colorado, I figured it was over." Brody continued, now looking at Maggie. "You know, I had to work up the courage just to bring you those flowers that day. I flew into Boston just to see you. I had tried to get over you, but I just couldn't stop thinking about us. When I found out Neal was still in the picture, I knew. You never said anything that night about breaking up with him, or how you felt about me. That last night just felt like a goodbye."

Memories of that night flooded back to Maggie. They hurt even more, with Brody here before her. *How had she let that opportunity slip away?*

Brody continued, "I tried to call you about six months later, hoping that you had moved on, but your number was disconnected. I tried your consulting firm and they said you weren't there anymore. A couple of months later, the guy who introduced us admitted he had been to your wedding. He knew I was crazy about you, so he hadn't wanted to tell me. I didn't believe him. I looked up your parents' number and called your mother, telling her I was a friend from college. She gave me your number. It was another couple of weeks until I had the courage to call you. When you told me you had a baby, I knew it was done. I figured I hadn't really known you at all. You were not the independent career woman after all."

Maggie was shocked. His view of their relationship was the complete opposite of how she had thought he felt.

"It shook me, Maggie, to hear you were married with a baby. I had thought I had all the time in the world to get you back, that you would be there when my service was up. I thought you would be busy with your career and just needed some time to live a little before eventually settling down. We were both so young. I just wanted to make something of myself first. Prove to your parents I was good husband material. I didn't date again for years after that call. My wife had to ask me out."

Brody looked world weary. Maggie was ashamed to realize that their relationship ending was as much her fault, maybe even more, than his. She had always blamed him. It had never occurred to her to reach out to him, let him know how she felt.

She touched his hand and said, "I am so sorry, I know it sounds pathetic now. Back then, taking the lead in a relationship just wasn't something I felt I was supposed to do. I was waiting for you to say something or do something." She smiled sadly. "So much for women's liberation."

Brody just reached over and grasped her hand, holding it for a moment. He seemed about to say something but then softly dropped her hand, gathered himself and changed the subject. He asked if she had some recent photos of Ethan. She showed him the ones she had taken of Izzy and Ethan at Christmas. They talked about how well the kids got along. She told him about how thoughtful their gifts had been.

"You know, I would like to meet him," Brody said.

Maggie hesitated, then said honestly, "I can't stop you, Brody. You obviously have a right to meet him. Even have a relationship with him if that is what you two decide you want." She continued, "I am worried, though. The kids are dealing with a lot just now. I think we both need some time to work out how you will fit into the picture. I just would hate for you or even me to lose Ethan over this. He is so angry with Neal right now. Could we give it some time?"

Brody was disappointed but he understood. Surprisingly, he shifted the conversation again. "Would it help if you and I spent some time together? I would like to really get to know the mother of my son. If Ethan knew we're friends, it might be a starting point in my relationship with him. If things go well, we could explain everything to him. I would like him to know that I would have been part of his life, if I could have been."

Maggie was torn. She realized she *would* like to get to know Brody again, both as Ethan's dad and as a person. To understand the man that the boy she knew had grown into. But was this the best way to introduce him to Ethan, as her *friend*? She didn't know. It might work.

Maggie was surprised that she felt as comfortable with Brody now as she had during that first dinner, despite the revelation about Ethan. Time had not changed that. She did not have any male friends. She realized she missed just having a man around. But if Brody entered her life, Ethan would probably meet him sooner or later, and their resemblance was so uncanny he might make the connection all on his own. She knew Ethan would probably take it badly, maybe even condemn her. He might find it hard to believe that she didn't know. There was no good or easy way to break this type of news.

She was also worried she might mistake or misinterpret Brody's interest and somehow sour their relationship. She realized, with a start, that she still found him very attractive and there were unfamiliar feelings resting just below the surface. She did not know how to respond to any of this.

Olivia's timing was perfect. It was as if, Maggie cynically observed, she had been watching at a window. Maggie and Brody had reached an impasse and were both staring at their drinks. Olivia bustled in with the dogs and announced dinner for all of them was on the way, courtesy of Graham. She would not take no for an answer and sent them both into the kitchen to set the table while she changed. As Brody set the plates that Maggie handed him onto the table, he asked, "Are you ok with me staying for dinner?" Maggie nodded, grateful that he had asked. They were both feeling the situation out.

Dinner was surprisingly fun. The conversation flowed and there was a great deal of laughter over life stories. Brody cornered the market on tales, a true raconteur. His life was full of dramatic twists and turns, revolving around his life as a pilot in the company of very wealthy people. He had a number of clients who were wonderfully eccentric or famous, and he now counted many among his friends.

Brody had been to the Oscars, as well as quite a few legendary Hollywood parties. He was circumspect with client names. Olivia tried but could not even pry initials out of him.

The only people he seemed to harbor contempt for were political clients— of both parties. He flew a number of them during campaign season, and they had a sense of entitlement that never ceased to amaze him. Politicians were the ones most likely to insist they should fly through hurricanes. They just weren't geared to reality.

Brody had been almost everywhere in the world. He and Graham compared stories about places and people. They were like old friends before the night was out.

They all cleaned up together, delaying the evening's end. Brody collected everyone's numbers before he left that night. He pecked Olivia on the cheek when he left, then turned to Maggie to do the same, though a little more awkwardly. Olivia closed the door behind him.

She turned to Maggie with a wide grin and simply said, "Well!" Olivia winked at Maggie but left it at that. She and Graham turned in for the night.

When Maggie got back to her room, she found the drinking she had done was taking its toll. She treated herself to a hot bath then headed straight to bed. When her phone dinged shortly after ten p.m., she was surprised. It was a text from Brody thanking her for the wonderful evening and saying how much he enjoyed meeting Olivia and Graham. He was going to be in Boston again on Saturday. Could they perhaps walk the dogs together?

She smiled. This was a different Brody. In the past she would not have expected to hear from him for days. She smiled when she texted back that yes, she would love to. She also told him she had had a good time, too. No more missed communication between them, she decided. She suggested he come by sometime in the early afternoon. She went to sleep already looking forward to it.

Maggie had woken up in the morning with a heavy head, and a shift in her thinking. She realized that her concern about a relationship with Brody was a distant second to the numbing prospect of talking with Ethan about this additional father. He was already so angry at Neal—what would it mean for Maggie's relationship with her son when she told him? Would he resent her when she did?

Maggie realized that since she had moved, she was talking with her children more, sharing more of her life with them. Ethan, in particular, had not just helped with the move but had gotten to know Olivia and the dogs. He had been so kind to her recently; he called her a couple of times a week and texted regularly. He had even asked her to join him and Hannah for dinners. That was unheard of a year ago. She did not want to lose this new, closer Ethan. She hoped that an inspiration would strike about how to tell him. She was afraid of what might happen if it didn't.

She left for work early to avoid Olivia's probing. Shortly after arriving at work, she noticed that she had missed a text telling her the *buy* order for one hundred shares of 'T' had been filled yesterday. It had gone to the *Unknown Senders* file. She moved the number into her Contacts so she would get all future notifications and sat back, thrilled. She owned stock. Stock that she had bought for herself.

She used her work computer at lunch to check her Schwab account. The money from both Ally and her father's bank seemed to have posted as well. Under the *positions* tab her AT&T stocks appeared, up a couple pennies from what she had paid for them. A profit!

All the transfers, together with the McDonald's stock that had also posted, meant the account had over $500,000 in it. It changed everything for her, seeing the total there. This was what she now thought of as her net worth, give or take the value of her emergency fund and car. She believed, barring another huge downturn in the stock market, her target of two million dollars in twenty years was very achievable. The relief she felt made her giddy. Who said money could not buy happiness?

She used her lunch hour to call the law firm handling her mother's Trust, then Jesse at the investment advisory firm. She let them both know that she would be terminating their services. She used the excuse that she wanted advisors closer to her home. The law firm said they would send a final bill. Jesse tried to talk her out of leaving, but in the end said he would coordinate with Kate on moving the Trust to Schwab.

She and Brody had already exchanged a couple of short texts. She was grateful that he did not use the childish emojis the kids relied on, his words were enough to keep her smiling.

When Tammy returned from her lunch, she asked what Maggie was so happy about. Maggie had not realized she was grinning. She skipped telling her about her date with Brody—too much teasing potential there—and explained instead that she had just bought her first stock. Tammy congratulated her and told Maggie the only stock she owned was probably in her 403(b).

"403(b)? Is that like a 401(k)?"

"A 403(b) is like a 401(k), but for non-profits like this hospital. 401(k)s are for private employers who pay tax. I had a 401(k) that I was able to roll into my 403(b) when I started here. They are basically the same thing."

Here at last, Maggie thought, was someone who could explain a 401(k) to her. "What exactly is a 401(k) or 403(b)?"

Tammy said, "They are employee sponsored retirement savings plans. A lot of employers offer them. It takes a fixed amount out of every paycheck, before tax. In our 403(b) plan the hospital matches 50 percent of what I put in, up to 6% of my salary. Their match is free money from them to me. I don't pay taxes on the income the account earns until I take it out when I retire. It compounds, because the income is just re-invested. They give you a choice of a bunch of different investments to choose from, about ten different kinds, I think. I don't really understand the choices, so I just followed the hospital's suggestions and selected a fund that is intended to switch into more conservative things as I get older. A target date fund, I think that's what it's called."

"How much can a person put in these plans?"

"I think the limit is now about nineteen thousand per year, but I can't free up that much cash. I would like to put in fifteen percent of my salary—that's what payroll told me I should be doing—but who has that much free cash with two kids? It's great though, because what I do save comes out of my paycheck before tax, and so it reduces my tax bill. And because it comes out every paycheck, I really don't miss it."

"Suppose someone has a lot of money but has never had a 401k or 403(b). Can you make up for lost time and put a lot of money in?"

"Beyond my pay grade. I am not thinking much about retirement these days. I have to get the boys through college first. I may have to take some money out of my retirement plan or maybe borrow against it. I want to avoid withdrawals, because you pay a penalty, ten percent, I think if you take it out before retirement. I will get my money six months after I turn fifty-nine, but that is too late to help with college. Haven't you signed up for it yet?"

Maggie knew she was not part of any employee retirement plan. She decided to check with the payroll office. She had been meaning to go up and see if her doctor was covered under her new health insurance, anyway. The retirement plan question made it important to get up there today.

After work she went up to the payroll office to talk to their benefit specialist, Carla Ponte. Maggie found out that she would become eligible for the 403(b) at her six-month work anniversary, which was quickly coming up.

Carla told her, "The maximum you can contribute annually is currently $19,000, although that changes occasionally. The hospital will match your contributions 50 percent, up to 6% of your salary. It is one of the most generous benefits we offer. Since you are over fifty, you could contribute up to $7,000 more each year as a *catch-up*, for a total of $26,000, all in pre-tax dollars."

Maggie was amazed. "The hospital will really *match* how much I put in?"

"Well, yes, fifty percent. Not to exceed 6% of your annual salary. That would mean about $3000 dollars a year for you. Some employers do not match at all, but the hospital is very generous. The amount you can contribute changes periodically as the government changes the rules. Of course, most people can only afford to put in about five to ten percent of their salaries, but we recommended to try for fifteen percent. You'd be surprised—despite what a great deal it is, many people choose to not participate in the program *at all*."

Maggie knew she was not going to be one of those people. She would immediately put in at least fifteen percent of her current salary into the 403(b). The hospital match alone would be about $3,000 of free money. It would mean she could easily make her retirement savings target, which she had aggressively set at $10,000 a year. Taking advantage of the hospital's match to her 403(b) would be like getting a 6% raise.

She asked, "Can I use my own money to contribute to this plan? Money beyond my paycheck?"

"No, a 403(b) is an employer payroll-based plan. It only comes through your paycheck. You can't just add more to it on your own. You can designate a higher-than-normal percentage of your salary to go into the it at different time of the year, though. There is no limit on how high that percentage is. If you have a month when money is not tight, you can up the percentage. Or cut back the percentage if you need more cash in a particular month. You just can't go beyond a total annual contribution limit of $26,000."

"And what is an IRA? Is that another type of 403(b)? I hear about that one too."

"An IRA is an Individual Retirement Account. That is totally separate from the employer-based plan. You just do that on your own, with a bank or broker. You can put in up to seven thousand per year, since you are over fifty. Only six thousand for the younger folks. Most IRA contributions are tax deductible, and the interest or dividends that the IRA earns also accumulates tax-free. Of course, like our retirement plan, there is a penalty if you access it before retirement."

Carla continued, "There are different types of IRAs, before-tax and after-tax ones. Most bankers or brokers can advise you and help you set them up. IRAs are not something we get involved with."

Maggie nodded and make a mental note to talk to Kate about setting up an IRA. She would move some of her nest egg into one so she could defer paying taxes on any income it generated.

She didn't need to use the income her savings generated just yet. She certainly did not want to pay taxes on any investment income she earned, if possible. She felt like the government was already getting its fair share of her paycheck.

She also wondered if she could push most of her salary into her 403(b). She wanted to maximize the hospital's match. Maybe she could use her investment income to live off of instead of her salary. She didn't want to miss out on the free $3,000.

Maggie was excited. She had no idea that something with such a confusing name could help her save as much as it would. Carla gave her the 403(b)-enrollment form to fill out. Maggie designated fifteen percent of her salary to go into it as soon as she was eligible. "There goes most of my recent raise," Maggie quipped to Carla.

Carla smiled, "I know if feels like a lot, but remember, you will be putting money every other week into the stock market on a defined contribution plan. This means you are putting money into the market on a regular fixed schedule, regardless of what the market is doing. This is called *dollar-cost averaging* and it can be a very powerful way to invest. You may buy some stocks when the market is high, but will also buy low, so you will get the average price of shares over time. Also, you can change the contribution percentage online any time you want. Some people start with a lower percentage and then increase it if money is not too tight or if the stock market falls, to try and invest more when stocks are on sale. While you are limited in the total amount of your contribution, but you can decide the timing of it over the course of a year."

Carla then gave Maggie a list of funds she could choose from. This confused Maggie. "Why can't I just pick what investments I want? I was planning on buying shares of specific companies."

Carla explained that the hospital's retirement plan was managed by another firm. The hospital did not have the expertise to do it. This company, an investment firm, selected which stock funds to offer in the retirement plan. It was a short list. Maggie would have to choose from their menu of thirty fund offerings. She could not buy individual stocks or choose options outside the menu. Carla had the name of an advisor that Maggie could contact to help her decide which funds to pick. Maggie, remembering Jesse, declined the offer and instead asked Carla about the stock funds on offer.

Carla told Maggie that stock funds were a basket of stocks that met criteria set up by the people who managed them. Some funds focused on growth stocks, others on international shares. Many just replicated a stock index. The most popular ones in retirement accounts were those set up to change stock holdings based on the age of the owner. They moved holdings into more conservative investments as the person got closer to retirement age. They were called *Target Date*, *Age Specific* or *Age Appropriate* funds.

Maggie thought it was a bit odd that many of the funds offered by the plan shared a name with the company who administered the fund. The management company was basically recommending many of their own products. "Isn't that a conflict of interest?" Maggie asked.

Carla just shrugged and said, "Just the way they do it. The idea behind the 403(b) or 401(k)s is that it is basically a *set and forget* investment. Because it comes out of your paycheck every week, people generally don't even pay attention to their retirement accounts. Most people don't even bother to look regularly until it starts getting close to retirement. They just assume Social Security will make up most of what they need."

The mention of Social Security caught Maggie's attention. She had not factored in any payments from them into her retirement thinking "How do I know how much in Social Security I will get?"

Carla smiled, "You should be getting an annual letter from the Social Security Administration that tells you. Or you can call or go online and check with them."

Maggie made a mental note to check this as soon as possible. Now that she was working, she wondered how much her retirement payment might be. She had another thought as she looked at the list of funds. "How much do I pay in fees for this firm to manage the account?"

"Depends. All the funds themselves have an expense ratio, a percentage that tells you how much you have to pay in fees. For example, if you bought one thousand dollars' worth of a fund and the expense ratio was one percent, the fees would be ten dollars per year. Ideally, a low-cost passive fund, one which simply mimics an index can have fees as low as 0.1%. Mind you, I have seen active funds that are managed by well-regarded professionals who charge as high as three percent."

"But what do I pay the company that manages the retirement fund for the hospital. The company that holds these funds for me?"

"It's funny, I was trying to work that out on my own account just the other day—and I couldn't. The information is not readily available. I know there are fees in addition to the expense ratio on individual funds. I think there is another fee on top of those, but it is not clear. I personally try to pick funds with the lowest expense ratios, but I am not sure of the additional fees. Can I get back to you on that?"

Maggie was surprised that even Carla was unclear on fees. Maggie told her she wanted to do a bit of research on each of the 403(b) fund options herself so she would know which funds to pick. Carla told Maggie she could take her time and promised she would have the answer on fees for her next time they spoke. Carla explained that once Maggie was enrolled, she could also change her fund selections online—for a small fee, of course.

The final thing they covered was whether Maggie's doctor was part of their healthcare network. Maggie was relieved to find she was, so there was no change necessary. She discovered that she did not have the proper insurance identification card, nor her insurance number. The benefits manager had her sign yet more paperwork and told her to watch the mail. She should have her new card shortly. She also told Maggie that the high deductible on the hospital plan would make her eligible to set up a tax deferred Health Savings Account, or HSA. Maggie had already researched what a HSA offered, another way to save taxes, and she had added it to her list of things to talk to Kate about setting up.

As Maggie headed to her car. As she walked out, she found herself humming happily. She stopped when she realized she was doing it. She *was* happy. It might have been the successful completion of her first stock trade. It could have been finding out about retirement plans and the *free money*. It might even be the simple fact that she could keep her doctor. But as she reached her car, Maggie laughed at herself. Being honest, it was not any of today's unexpected benefits that had lifted her mood. It was Brody, and the simple fact that she was looking forward to the Saturday dog walk.

The weekend seemed to take forever coming. Their walk, however, was not the pretty hike Maggie and Brody had envisioned. Brody had done some research and found a trail around one of the many large New England ponds that dotted the area. The website assured him it was passable in the snow because it was well travelled and packed down.

He had not, however, known that Bunny used a stroller that lacked snow tires. Or that Buster would be unwilling to walk once snow froze to the hair on his small paws. Maggie struggled as she pushed Bunny, who refused to share her ride. Brody carried a shivering Buster in his arms. They got quite a few bemused and pitying looks from other dog owners after they turned around a mere half mile in and trundled back to the parking lot.

The dogs settled gratefully into the back seat of the Corolla. Maggie and Brody looked at one another and tried to work out an alternative plan. "I feel pretty silly," Maggie sighed. "I should have known the dogs were not up to full scale hike."

"Don't worry, I have always thought of myself as a dog person, and I knew they were older. I should have asked about whether they had limitations." Brody said. "Can't we just leave them in the car?" The dogs were already well on their way to a long afternoon nap.

"Bunny will need her meds in a couple of hours, and I don't know if a cold car is OK for her. I think we are out of options; they need to go back home." Maggie knew the house was empty, as Olivia was back in England with her brother. She realized that being alone indoors with Brody made her uncomfortable. Why did she feel so awkward? She had told herself all week that this was not a date, just a dog walk with a friend. Now, with the aborted walk behind her she found herself thinking about the sailing disaster they had when they first met. This walk seemed like a replay of that first date. Was this some kind of sign?

When they arrived home, both dogs headed straight to the kitchen for water and a nap on one of their many beds—this one adjacent to a heating vent. Brody brought his hiking knapsack in from the car and Maggie was charmed by the surprise lunch he had packed for their hike. Pickled vegetables, cheeses, French bread, and Italian dry-cured hams. There was even a thermos of tea and tiny, carrot cake whoopie pies for dessert. She tried to remember—had she ever told him carrot cake was her favorite?

She added a salad that she had in the fridge and thought about wine. She decided against it, nervous about the message it might send. This time with Brody was about friendship, she reminded herself, not anything else. It was going to be a minefield with Ethan as things stood. She did not want to complicate things even more.

Over lunch, they talked more about their lives and the trials of being parents. They agreed they had been lucky—no health dramas, good students, no drugs or discipline issues. Maggie talked about the stress that Ethan's learning disabilities had caused him. Brody told her that he, too, had trouble with reading. He said he was lucky because he had always wanted to be a pilot. Short of certification tests, he said there was very little reading and writing involved with his job. Now, as the boss, someone else handled most of the paperwork.

Maggie realized that while she could discuss the kids at length, she could not actually remember much about *her* life, specifically. She could not decide if the lack of strong memories was a reflection on the life she had led or just her feelings about it. The years she had spent raising the kids were almost a blank for her, she had simply lived in the background of their and Neal's lives. The subject of Neal and where their relationship now stood was carefully avoided by both of them.

Brody's part of the conversation was surprisingly personal, reflective, and insightful. He talked about the mistakes he had made in his relationships and what he had learned from them.

Brody was close to his parents, who were both in their nineties. They were still living in the house in upstate New York that Brody had grown up in. His father was forgetful and grumbled about doctors, but still flew with Brody whenever the opportunity came up. Brody explained to Maggie that his Dad woke every morning and did a round of army calisthenics that Brody doubted even he could do.

His mother had more trouble getting around but was still very sharp. She was frail and only really left the house for medical appointments or to visit friends in the local nursing home. She didn't drive but his father still did, slowly and carefully. Never on highways, anymore. They were close to Albany, so good medical care was available when they needed it. Brody felt that when they passed, he was sure that they would be one of those couples that went within hours of each other. He sounded almost wistful about the prospect.

Maggie, in turn, explained in more detail about her father's death and her mother's Alzheimer's. Brody was surprised he had not seen her father's obituary online. Maggie realized she had not notified the papers or even prepared one. She had just assumed the lawyer, who had handled everything else, would have done it. Now she regretted that she had let his passing slip by with so little acknowledgement. She had always felt like her parents had distanced themselves from her, now she saw she had been complicit in the distancing.

She told Brody that she envied his parents, their health and longevity. She was particularly happy that they were able to stay in their own home, together, so late in life. She wondered how many people got that chance.

Brody stayed quiet for a bit, then asked, "Do you think if we stayed together, we might have been one of those couples?"

Maggie thought about this. It was a very leading question. She looked at Brody and answered, "Too hard to say. There was a moment when we might have gone in another direction. But we both pulled back from that. Neither of us was willing to cross the line into the next phase. Things may have been different if I hadn't found out I was pregnant, and then married Neal so soon after. It's funny. Some moments come along that unexpectedly offer a big choice. To make the choice seems so overwhelming that you do nothing, and then the decision is made by default. You don't even realize the implication until much later. Then, you are so busy just getting on with your life, the fact you even had a choice fades from your memory."

Maggie sat back in her chair, letting the past, and her regrets, wash over her.

She continued, "I understand now why all those philosophy courses talk about living an *examined life*. I think if you just stop once in a while and give yourself time to look at the big picture, you might realize the implications of those types of choices. I think I might have made better decisions for myself in the long term, rather than just letting my life rush by, if I had stopped to think about my life's direction once in a while. Had made a choice to do things for myself, rather than for others all the time."

Brody looked at her, surprised at how philosophical she was getting. He had always admired her willingness to engage on a topic. He smiled a little and said , "Yes, I am finding that is one of the advantages of getting older. Reflection and then, sometimes," he paused and looked at her meaningfully, "…regret."

Maggie nodded ignoring the opening he had given her. "I think that is the oddest thing about where I am in life right now. The benefit of Neal disappearing is that I had to stop the drift my life was in. Now I have time to ask the big questions, like, 'how do I want to live the rest of my life?' Or even the basics, like '*am I happy*?' I just hadn't ever stopped to ask myself any of these before. I never really realized that I could set the agenda, rather than simply react to whatever came along."

Maggie stopped then, shaking her head and feeling a little silly for getting so philosophical. She decided to redirect the conversation. "Do you mind if I ask you a really, really, personal question?"

Brody grinned, "Ask away."

"Have you done any financial planning for your retirement?"

Brody's blank expression clearly showed this was not the direction he was hoping the conversation was taking. "Financial planning for retirement?" he asked, a bit incredulously.

"Yes, you know. 401(k)s, IRAs. Investments overall. I know it *is* pretty personal, but Neal left me in a bit of a mess. I have just become eligible for a 403(b) at work and I'm also now responsible for the Trust that pays for my mother's care. I'm going to be making some big financial decisions over the next few weeks. I'm trying to learn as much as I can, as fast as I can, but it's pretty daunting."

Maggie then explained to Brody about her taking over the Trust from the investment firm. She proudly told him she had bought her first stock for her own account just this past week. She was going to spend tomorrow doing more research. If she could find the right stocks, she was going to wade in deeper on Monday when the stock market opened again. She was nervous. She was new to personal finance.

Brody was clearly disappointed with the shift away from the conversation they had been having. He was a little surprised that she had opened up to him about her finances. Talking about money *was* pretty personal, he suddenly realized.

He switched gears and began slowly, "Well. I am not really thinking about retirement at this point, but I do have a plan of sorts. I had a 401(k) that I built up over the years at the airlines I worked for. Every time I changed jobs, I took it with me and consolidated it, or rolled it into my new employers' 401(k)s. I always maxed the contributions out to put away as much money as I could. Every airline had slightly different plans - but I always made sure that I maxed out on what they matched."

Maggie asked. "What about the type of investments in your 401(k)? How did you select which ones to pick?"

"Whenever the 401(k) administrator asked which funds I wanted, I just selected a fund that matched my age profile. I assumed they moved you into less risky things as you get older. I only realized a lot later that I might have been better off if I had done a little research and selected funds from their menu with better performance records. Honestly, I did not really pay any attention to my 401(k) until I quit work to buy my first FBO. After I left my last employer, I moved the money to a broker to manage. He converted it to an IRA since I was self-employed.

He selects the funds I am in now, mostly index funds. My accountant advised me to add the maximum tax-deductible amount to it each year.

Brody stood up and began clearing their lunch dishes. "I did give some serious thought to raiding my IRA those first few years when I started up the company, when I was always short of cash. But I didn't touch it, because of the penalties. I did end up borrowing against it once, using it as collateral for the loan, but I paid the loan back as soon as I could. My advisor said you should only raid an IRA if you are facing foreclosure or bankruptcy."

Maggie rose to help him clear. She pulled down two coffee cups and gestured to them, Brody nodded his head and said, "Black, please."

Brody continued, "These past few years, we have done so well that our company now offers all our eligible employees a retirement plan. I have even moved my own IRA into that. I add a lot more to mine now than I could before. I am in something called a SEP, and there are some restrictions because I am an owner, but to be honest, that's all I know. My accountant takes care of it all. I will say, whenever I check it, I am always pleasantly surprised by how much money it has in it."

Maggie asked, "So, if you don't know too much about it, you probably don't have any recommendations for specific funds or good investments?"

"Sorry, not at all. I don't follow the stock market, never have. When I was younger, other pilots would tell me about absolutely 'sure things' they had heard about from some insider. I would put money in, and always got burned. I learned the hard way that there are no *get rich quick* options. Like they say, if it sounds too good to be true, it probably is. I also learned to never, ever, trust a 'rumor' about a company being bought or some new drug that would cure cancer. It is a sure way to throw money down the drain."

Maggie was a little surprised Brody knew so little about his retirement investments. As a businessperson and a man, she assumed he would be well versed in the stock market. She was learning that men were generally no better informed than women about their finances. Men also seemed less likely to do the research Maggie did. She now realized that Graham's interest in investing was not the norm. She guessed that, despite what she had always assumed, many people with strong business backgrounds didn't follow the stock market at all. They simply didn't have the time or the interest, and just relied on their brokers or financial advisors, hoping that these third parties would do their jobs effectively. Like their dentist or doctor. Maggie now knew, though, that if the advisor was like Jesse, they might be disappointed, *or worse.*

They took their coffees into the living room. With the dogs settled down for the afternoon, Maggie showed Brody, Olivia's vast collection of DVDs, explaining how Olivia refused to *steal movies*—which is what she thought streaming services did. She would not listen to Maggie's defense of Amazon or Netflix, further explaining that her loyalty to paying for an actual DVD was because she had had a stint as an actress. Olivia thought every creator or performer should get his or her due. She hinted that her screen debut was in her collection somewhere, but never would tell Maggie which DVD.

They selected a classic black and white film neither could remember seeing, *The Big Sleep.* They both loved Bogart and Bacall, movie stars their parents had introduced them to. Maggie sprawled on the sofa and Brody chose an overstuffed armchair. After it was over, they guiltily chose another, and by the time the second movie finished, they had almost moved into dinnertime. They briefly walked the dogs around the estate and then decided to head into town to get something light to eat.

They were laughing as they walked up to the front door after dinner. Maggie reached for her house keys and put them into the lock. She then turned to face Brody. It was a cold, clear night and both of them stood stiffly facing each other, hesitating and then shuffling their feet to stay warm. Neither said anything. They both felt the expectation hanging in the air but were equally shy about how to end the evening. Finally, Brody thanked her for the day and moved in to hug her in a quick, simple embrace. When he pulled back, she instinctively reached for his arm. He did not hesitate. He stepped forward, this time to kiss her quickly on her lips. Maggie was not sure how to react, but Brody did not give her time to say anything. He just grinned happily, said "Good night, Trix." He then turned and almost ran down the walk to his car. Maggie turned the lock and then pushed herself inside a little breathless. She did not look back.

Maggie went up to her room, questioning herself as to what was going on between them. It was clear that Brody was angling for something more than just friendship. She did not know how she felt about that. She was still married, at least in name. Being honest, she knew it was gratifying to be pursued, no question about that. She felt more attractive since Brody had come into her life. She had even decided that her weight really wasn't that bad after all.

She stopped the thought as it was forming and chided herself out loud. *"Really, Maggie, is that all it takes? Your reflection in a man's eyes? Shame on you"* She wanted to be better than that. It was frustrating that she was beginning to feel so independent and strong, and yet she still craved the acknowledgement from a man that she was attractive. Was that her conditioning, or just human nature? Too deep a question, she thought. Sighing, she undressed, grabbed a book, and headed into her bathroom to treat herself to a long soak before bed. She was going to think about that kiss, though.

CHAPTER 13:
MAKING CHOICES

The next morning, Maggie let herself sleep in and then got to her computer just before noon. She knew her research was going to probably take the better part of the day, but she was ready. She knew it was time to put all the things she had learned to good use.

Maggie's immediate focus was on her mother's Trust. She was going to try to understand if she could replicate what her father had originally done. She wanted to set the Trust up as a *fixed income* account, the objective was to generate a steady income with as little risk as possible. The holdings in it did not need to grow, just stay steady and generate income for the next ten years. She also wanted the portfolio to be pared down, so the statement was back to a few pages if possible. She agreed with what she had read, that she should know what she owned. She doubted that would be feasible if she had more than fifty holdings. She was going to try and limit herself to about thirty different stock and bonds. That would mean investing in big chunks of about fifty thousand dollars each. It was a lot of money, and she was nervous about making these types of decisions. She told herself that if Kate and Graham thought her choices were weak, she would just leave the entire Trust in a simple money market fund.

Maggie reviewed her mother's expenses. The cost of her room, board, administrative expenses, and aides exceeded the annual income the Trust generated. Maggie estimated she could get her mother's essential expenses down to about eighty thousand per year, maybe less. The cost was still staggeringly high to her. Far more than she earned at the hospital.

Her mother had not worked outside the home. As her father's widow though, she got his full Social Security check every month and Medicare. Both of these payments were made directly to the nursing home - they barely paid one quarter of what her care cost. But they helped reduce what the Trust needed to pay.

The facility where her mother lived was the best in Connecticut. Maggie was sure that if her mother had been without financial means, she would have died many years ago in a publicly-run nursing home. They did not have the resources to provide around the clock care for all their residents, let alone the daily doctor visits Maggie's mother had. Maggie imagined how hard it was for families who did not have the means to afford anything else. She had learned that almost half of all people end up in nursing homes at the end of their lives, although few plan they will.

Maggie toyed briefly with the idea of moving her mother closer to her, perhaps finding a less expensive alternative. It had taken only a few calls to learn her mother's type of care would be even more costly in the Boston area. It also seemed unfair to dislodge her mother from her "home" of more than twenty years, where she was clearly very well cared for.

Looking at the expenses, Maggie still worried the Trust might run out of money. In part, this was because the care at the Residences was so good. Many of the patients in her mother's ward were well into their nineties. Despite being bedridden, Maggie's mother could easily live another ten years or longer. On top of the day-to-day care, any medical emergency involving an extended stay in a hospital ICU could cost tens of thousands of dollars. Maggie could also see that many of her mother's incidental expenses were not covered by either Medicare or her private insurance.

Maggie decided to put a quarter of a million dollars of the Trust's funds into a money market fund like the one Kate had recommended. Since the money market fund at Schwab invested in short-term debt securities like US Treasury bills, Maggie knew it was a pretty safe investment. Money could be moved in or out of the fund simply by making a phone call to Kate. It was almost as liquid as cash, but it still earned almost two percent per year. If she put about three years of expenses into a money market, the Trust would have the cash to carry her mother through if the market crashed. Three years should be enough time for the market to recover.

Maggie knew if she put the entire Trust in a money market, it would not earn enough to cover the cost of her mother's care. She would have to eat into the principle every year. Maggie's plan was to increase the Trust's income by buying bonds and stocks of solid, well-established companies that paid a strong dividend.

Her last invoice from the law firm, for her half hour meeting with Dale and Matt, had been over one thousand dollars. She was indignant, but she paid it. She was done with them. The investment firm had been harder to extricate the Trust from, but Kate had proved herself very capable in that regard. Whatever she had said to Jesse's firm had hastened the liquidity event of the "alternative investments." Everything had been liquidated, and Kate had pulled the Trust's cash over to a Schwab account. Jesse and his firm were also out of Maggie's life. The lack of fees from both these firms would save the Trust over a hundred thousand dollars a year.

Maggie started by focusing on bonds for the portfolio. She knew the basics from her initial review of the Trust after she had gotten back from meeting with the lawyers. Her father had relied on these to form the backbone of the Trust. If she could buy government bonds paying eight percent like her father had, she would just scoop up however many she could with $1.5 million in the Trust and call it a day.

She looked at a couple online sites that sold bonds. She thought she might find a couple to ask Kate about. Unfortunately, most government bonds were paying much less than five percent. In fact, even bonds issued by corporations paid less than five percent. After an hour of searching, she finally gave up. She needed to see if Kate could help her find bonds tomorrow, since she just couldn't seem to find any online. She decided to pivot to stocks. There was plenty of online information there.

Maggie had learned that the *riskier* a stock, the greater its potential return. This account, while it needed income, had to be minimal risk. She needed to find conservative investments with a good income stream. Stocks like new internet companies or biotechs searching for a cancer cure were too risky for the Trust. The crazy 'meme' stocks that filled the financial news were way too speculative for Maggie to even think about. Their stock prices were divorced from the reality of their value.

Maggie was going to *invest* not *trade*. Investors generally bought stocks expecting to hold them for a year or longer. Traders moved in and out of stocks quickly, even daily, for short term profit.

Maggie had spent a lot of time reviewing various stock sites before settling on Yahoo Finance and Morningstar. These seemed the most straightforward sites to her. Both gave access to the basic information she needed—the stock price, its trading history, key financial ratios, and analyst reports and recommendations.

Her reading had taught her that there were two basic approaches to evaluating stocks: fundamental versus technical analysis. Fundamental analysis focused on the company itself. It involved reviewing financial statements and company-specific information. Technical analysis assumed the stock price already reflected this information. Stock *technicians* were more concerned with statistical analysis of a stock's price movement. As a beginner, Maggie decided to concentrate on fundamental analysis for the time being. She assumed technical analysis required more math than she currently had at her command.

Stock sites had an overwhelming amount of information on them. As Maggie became more familiar with them, she found herself focusing on just a few key indicators that her investment books and Graham had recommended.

As it turned out, Graham was turning out to be a big asset to Maggie's stock market journey. After her phone call with Jesse, she had vented her fury at his firm over dinner with Olivia. She told Olivia she had decided to take over the management of her mother's Trust. Olivia had eyed her warily.

"Big job," she said simply, "Graham would be a good person to talk to about it." She explained he now spent a good portion of the day trading stocks, happier than he had ever been before. "It's a profitable hobby, for him," Olivia grinned.

At Olivia's request, Graham came by the next night and gave Maggie a crash course on stock selection, delighted to sit down with her to talk about investing. He taught her that she shouldn't look for a good stock but should rather look for a *good company*. After she decided on the company she wanted to invest in, she should then decide whether that company's stock was at the right price to buy.

He was impressed with the work she had already done. He complimented her on the books she had read. He suggested she consider getting the Wall Street Journal to follow daily business news, just like Maggie's grandfather had suggest to Will in his birthday letter. Graham insisted that investing well was not hard, it just took some effort to learn terms and pay attention to the world. "And a little basic math, of course. I learned as I went. Now, I probably do better than most of the financial advisors I used to use. It's not hard, Maggie—professionals just try to make it look that way," Graham said firmly.

He encouraged Maggie to begin her study of a specific company by first reading an analyst report or two on it. They were written to help investors understand and choose stocks. They would help her understand the industry the company was in, their market and products, and their competitors. He told her she could get analyst reports from her broker or through the website she traded on. These reports were usually free.

He explained that analysts who wrote the reports worked for a variety of financial firms. Banks and brokerage firms used the information internally to help their managers and clients invest. Graham warned Maggie that analysts varied in their knowledge, skill, and independence so it was usually helpful to look at least two or more reports.

"How long are these reports?" Maggie asked. She inwardly groaned as she envisioned days more of research. Graham smiled and pulled up his trading account and clicked on the research tab. He then asked Maggie to sit next to him so they could look at a real example. Maggie suggested AT&T. When Graham downloaded the Morningstar analyst's report, Maggie was relieved to see it was only sixteen pages, the initial eight of which gave her a great understanding of the company.

She asked why Graham he chose the Morningstar report. She had seen that his brokerage firm offered two other company's reports as well. Graham replied, "Morningstar is my favorite source. They only do independent research. Some analysts work for firms whose clients can be the very companies they are writing about," he said. Other companies that wrote analyst reports Graham liked included Standard and Poor's Capital IQ, Argus and Reuters. All the major banks and brokerage firms also had in-house analysts. Graham warned against Maggie relying too much on stock sites like Motley Fool or Seeking Alpha at this stage. Many of the authors on these sites already owned the stocks they recommended, so they might be a bit biased, trying to get others to buy the stock and send the price higher.

Together they skimmed through the Morningstar report and Maggie found it very useful. The analyst presented the pros and cons of the stock, the major issues management faced, what regulatory concerns there were and even a little history. The end of the report was a set of financial tables related to the company. They looked daunting to Maggie

"After you read a report or two, you will begin to get a feel of companies and industries," he said. "I know the quantitative tables at the end look dense, but you don't really need to study them in any great detail. The math you need for basic analysis is nothing more complicated than what you did in fifth grade. It simply involves averages, ratios and simple addition and subtraction," he promised.

To begin with, he said, there were four statistics she should always have on her radar when looking at a company she was going to rely on to pay dividends.

"No one statistic tells the whole story," Graham opined. "But for basic analysis, particularly for dividend-paying companies, I think you should look at four key things."

"First, remember that at the end of the day, companies are in business to make money. They need to pay its employees, suppliers, etc. Money left over generally goes to building the business or paying dividends to shareholders. So, I always begin by looking at a company's *cash flow*. Cash flow is the actual cash a company generates. It is a separate line item on a company's income statement. It is different than a company's earnings."

"Earnings," Graham explained, "can be manipulated somewhat by the company's accountants. But cash is cash."

"How can earnings be manipulated?" Maggie asked with alarm. She was worried that she might miss something.

Graham started to explain, "A company can have *negative* earnings but still have a positive cashflow, for example—" When he saw Maggie's confusion he stopped and smiled sheepishly. He said, "Okay, let the accounting issues go for now. I guess I can be guilty of making it too complicated too. Just remember for now that *cash flow* is key. You should stick to companies that have shown they have an ability to consistently generate cash. Since you are looking for companies that pay good, consistent dividends, you want to see that a company generates a positive, consistent cash flow so the company can cover the cost of paying the dividend."

He and Maggie looked over the financial tables on the AT&T Morningstar report. The page showed a consistently positive cash flow for the past five years, over thirty-nine *billion* dollars just in the latest year. AT&T definitely met Graham's first criteria. He told Maggie that she could also find out the cash clow by looking at the financial tab of the stock on Yahoo Finance. Financial statistics like cash flow could be found on a variety of financial sites.

The next Graham told Maggie to look at the *payout ratio*.

Graham explained that the payout ratio measured the proportion of a company's after-tax earnings it paid out in dividends. It was generally reported as a percent. If it was 75%, that meant that 75% of the after-tax earnings was used to pay dividends. While there was no "right" number, if the payout was greater than one hundred percent, it meant a company was paying out more in dividends than it actually earned. Some companies occasionally borrowed money to pay their dividend. Maggie agreed with Graham that that did not sound like a sustainable strategy.

Maggie looked on the Morningstar report and saw that the payout ratio for AT&T had ranged over the years. It was currently about seventy percent. That sounded high to Maggie, but it was actually lower than it had been in previous years. It meant that the cash AT&T earned was sufficient to pay its dividend, even at the currently high level. In fact, AT&T had consistently raised its dividend for the past twenty-five years, making it what Graham called a *Dividend Aristocrat*. Based on this, the dividend seemed safe. This was a second positive check for AT&T.

The third thing Graham told her to look at was the debt a company carried. He said, "Like people, having a lot of debt can be a problem for a company. Of course, the amount of debt a company has depends a lot on its particular circumstances – debt loads vary by industry and whether a company needs to borrow for a particular situation like building a new plant or acquiring another company."

"I use a statistic called the debt (D) to equity (E) ratio, or the D/E ratio. It is calculated for you by most of the financial sites. In general, 0.4 or lower is considered a normal dept/equity ratio. That means that for every $40 dollars a company has borrowed, it has $100 dollars in stockholder equity. Higher ratios, 0.6 or higher, means company is considered a higher risk."

Maggie had not thought about companies having debts. She realized she would never have even thought to check. "How will I know if the debt a company has is too much?" she asked.

"Over time, you begin to get a feel for the statistical differences between industries. It's not critical to know them right away. You will get familiar with them over the years. All things being equal, though, if you are looking at two competitors in the same industry, the one with the lower debt ratio is probably healthier, financially speaking."

Maggie knew she was not interested in companies with a lot of debt, particularly for her mother's Trust. She was relying on them to pay a steady dividend.

She worried that if a company was paying back high amounts of debt, particularly if interest rates rose or the company had a bad year, it might make it harder for it to pay its current dividend.

She checked AT&T's statistics. The company had debt ratio of over 0.7. Her first reaction was panic. "Graham, I bought AT&T and it has massive amounts of debt! I should have done this basic research before buying the stock. I'd done a cursory review and got excited by its dividend. Yahoo said that a lot of analyst recommended it. I simply relied on what I knew about the company and those recommendations. Did I make a mistake buying it?" she asked.

"Maggie, don't worry," Graham reassured her. "From what I can tell, you have done more research than most people. It's a common mistake for new investors to simply buy stock in whichever companies they hear good things about. Or one that a friend or someone on the internet recommends. Frequently, this does not end well. Doing a bit of research and a little math is simply too much work for many people. For those types of investors, I recommended passive index funds with the lowest possible expense ratio. Working off recommendations alone, you will get burned. You, however, are willing to put the work in, so let's look a little deeper at the AT&T debt."

Graham then asked Maggie to look at Verizon's D/E. It was even higher than AT&T's. Relative to this peer, AT&T looked healthier financially. Taking Graham's advice, she checked the telecom industry overall and she found that telecoms and utilities had some of the highest debt ratios in the stock market. This was due, in part, because it was very expensive to build out and maintain their large communication networks. However, given that phone companies and utilities had regular steady cash flows, having relatively more debt was not as concerning as it might be for other companies. Phone companies appeared to have enough cash flow to easily pay back their debt. This made her more comfortable about AT&T's debt level. She added another, albeit smaller, check to her list.

The final ratio Graham said to pay attention to was "P/E," or the Price to Earnings ratio. This ratio could tell Maggie how relatively expensive the stock was, especially as it related to its competitors. The ratio was calculated by dividing the current stock price (P) by the earnings per share (E). It was a common ratio that all the financial pages included in their summary.

"The current stock price, the P, can be found by just looking up the price of the stock on any financial website. The earnings per share was slightly more nebulous," Graham explained. There were various company earnings that could be used. Most P/Es used the company's actual earnings from the past year (earnings from the *trailing twelve months* or the TTM earnings). This was called a *trailing P/E*. On most financial websites, the P/E shown was the trailing P/E.

Some analysts, however, preferred to use the company's estimates of what it will earn in the upcoming twelve months. This was called the *forward P/E*.

Graham told her he looked at both trailing and forward P/Es. One spoke about past performance, while the other was a best estimate of the future.

Maggie decided she would focus on the trailing P/E for the time being, because it was based on known facts. She didn't know if she could trust a company's management when they estimated their earnings in the upcoming year. She imagined that with experience, she would become more confident with forward P/Es.

Graham agreed that as Maggie was just a beginner, the trailing P/E would work for her.

When they had finished looking at AT&T, Maggie told Graham it had been her first stock purchase. She said she wished she had looked at it closer, done her homework.

Graham said, "You probably can't go wrong with AT&T. It won't appreciate much in value but if you are investing for dividends, it is a solid start. Just repeat the process we just went through for the other stocks you are considering. When you do the work," he said, "you will be more confident about your choices. Just remember though, circumstances can change, so be prepared to re-evaluate a stock if the company does something that changes its earning potential."

He closed up his computer and said, "Enough for your first night. When you have settled on other possible selections for the Trust, I would be happy to review them with you. You're a good student, Maggie. Remember it takes time to get up to speed on this, you have plenty of time to become familiar with all these terms and companies. Rome was not built in a day."

Maggie thanked him for the time. She was grateful that he never even hinted that managing the Trust was beyond Maggie's abilities. Instead, he said, "Remember, Maggie, no one is going to take as much care of you or your mother's money as you will yourself. Yes, it requires some work, but not as much as people think. Being in control of your own finances is the ultimate stress reliever."

Maggie left Graham that night with a definite confidence boost.

Today, she was putting all his coaching to the test. She did not expect to become an expert on every stock, but she did want to understand what she planned to own.

She pulled out a pad and wrote <u>Shopping List for Trust Holdings</u> and then wrote AT&T and then added $30 in parenthesis next to it – that was the price she would like to pay for it. The page looked very empty after that first entry.

Maggie knew the Trust's portfolio should be diversified, meaning that stocks she bought should be spread across a range of industries. Diversification was encouraged in all her investment books. It made sense. If any one industry had problems, like when oil prices sank and the energy industry suffered; others might benefit, like transportation companies who would get cheap gas. Diversification could soften the blow from any one industry or segment getting hit by a sudden shock.

The business community divided stocks into eleven sectors. Each sector was then divided again into multiple *industry groups*. She decided she would try and find a stock or two in each sector. She believed this should diversify her holdings sufficiently. Key for her was finding one that paid a good dividend and was relatively low risk.

Maggie looked for *best in breed* in the industries she was reviewing. This was the company that was considered an effective leader in a particular industry when compared to its competitors. Unfortunately, how the best in breed was determined varied somewhat by analyst. Generally, however, Maggie found there was a usually a consensus among analysts regarding which companies in a particular industry were the strongest. This was based on things like their earnings, financial health, and management teams. For the time being, she would rely on these analysts' opinions. She knew it would be a while, if ever, until she could say which company was best in breed based on her own opinion.

Maggie's target companies would be: 1) well established, 2) make good money, and 3) have little debt. She also wanted her companies to sell products or services that she understood and that were in steady or growing demand. She was prepared to accept a lower dividend if it meant a company was solid and she understood what they did.

Her investment books seemed to agree with Graham's recommendations on which ratios were important.

To find stocks with high dividends, Maggie used an online *stock screener*. Many sites used complicated criteria she didn't understand. Finally, she settled on using the Yahoo Finance screener that let her pick her screening criteria: size of a company, it's industry, P/E, dividend yield, and D/E. She would look up the payout ratio after she had selected a specific company. She also added the stocks her father had selected when he had first started the Trust, since all of them still operated today.

Ideally, Maggie wanted her stocks to pay a dividend that would give her a five percent annual yield. This meant if she invested ten thousand dollars in that stock, it would earn her five hundred dollars a year. She soon found that some industries had high yields, like telecoms, but others had little or no yields, like many major internet companies. She soon realized she was going to need to make compromises. A five percent yield for the entire portfolio was ambitious. If AT&T paid a 7% dividend, some other company could pay 3% and the portfolio might average out to 5%.

Kate had shown Maggie how to access Morningstar analyst reports through their platform. Kate had agreed with Graham, Morningstar was a great resource because of its independence. Using the Charles Schwab site, Maggie could now get Morningstar and other detailed analyst reports for specific companies.

She began with the *communications* sector, since she had already done some of the basic analysis with Graham. The screener gave her the names of a number of other telephone companies she wanted to look at as well.

Maggie looked at the P/E ratio on the other telecoms. She understood how to calculate it but was unsure what it was really telling her. She saw that AT&T had a current P/E of 10, Verizon a P/E of 14, and T-Mobile and Sprint had P/Es of 20 and 80, respectively. If P/E was a measure of relative value, AT&T appeared to be the least expensive of the four telecoms.

Maggie checked and saw that AT&T's stock price had ranged over the past year from a low of about twenty-eight dollars to a high of nearly forty. As it was currently trading at about thirty dollars a share, it was relatively cheaper than usual. *Is it cheap for a reason, Maggie wondered?*

She looked at Yahoo Finance and saw around thirty analysts who *covered* the company, that is they studied and wrote reports about it. Most of the analysts were recommending to *hold* not *buy* AT&T. This meant the analyst community was basically neutral on the company. There was nothing in the analyst's views to suggest the company was in trouble.

The average price target, where analysts thought it would get to within the year, was thirty-five dollars a share. This was well above where it was trading now. This suggested that there might be potential for the stock to increase in value. She did see someone recommending a price target as low as twenty-five and another a high target of forty-three. She concluded there would probably be some price variability over the time she owned it, but again, she really did not care if the price varied day to day or year to year. She just wanted stable dividend income. She wanted to know that the dividend was safe, and the ratios Graham had taught her helped her understand that it probably was.

Maggie read the Morningstar report on both Verizon and AT&T. The analysts liked both companies. They considered Verizon's network the best, but said AT&T represented a better value at its current price. So, it *was* the price that mattered. The lower P/E reflected that the stock was relatively less expensive. This was the final check for Maggie.

Overall, her work had shown her that AT&T had the highest current dividend of the group. Its cash flow was terrific and its dividend, despite the relatively high payout ratio, was considered safe. Its D/E was reasonable for the industry. Overall, AT&T seemed like the best choice for the Trust's needs.

She sat back and realized that she was prepared, assuming Kate and Graham agreed, to put $100,000 of her mother's trust in AT&T shares. She knew she had her father's approval too, since AT&T had been one of his initial purchases for the Trust.

Maggie's final thoughts were about the price she was willing to pay for AT&T shares. Kate had told her to set limits. She had decided on $30.00 per share, below what she had just paid for her shares. The price had dipped since she had bought it.

She had already bought one hundred shares for her own account at $30.50 per share. She knew she would get two dollars a year in dividends, or fifty cents every three months for each share she owned. This was roughly a 6.5% yield. Since she had bought her shares, the price had fluctuated above and below what she paid. She was happy with the price she had paid but thought she could do better for the Trust. She was also aware, though, that the price one paid for a stock mattered, particularly as it relates to dividends. The cheaper you were able to buy a stock, the higher the percentage dividend yield on her investment. She played with AT&T's price to make sure she understood this.

If AT&T stock price rose to thirty-five dollars per share and she bought it at that price, she would still get two dollars in dividends per share. That would mean each share now *yielded* only 5.7%. A good yield, but not 6.5%. The lesson was, the higher price paid for a stock, the lower the percentage yield. This was because while the stock cost more, the dividend stayed the same—two dollars per year. The dividend amount was fixed, the percentage yield varied.

Conversely, if the stock price dropped, the dividend *yield* got larger. If she got a chance to buy AT&T for twenty-five dollars and it then paid her two dollars per year in dividends, it would mean each share *yielded* a whopping 8%. It would be great to get a stock like AT&T at this price, she thought. Buying a stock when it was down, or *on-sale* as Maggie thought about it, would give her a better yield on her money.

Maggie knew the market had been down lately. It could go down more. Maggie thought she might not buy all the stock for the Trust at once. To build a $100,000 position in AT&T, she would need to buy about three thousand shares. It might be better to buy one thousand shares now, then wait and see what happened in the market. If AT&T went down, she could buy more, and her investment would have a better yield. If it went up, she could wait and see if it came back down. *Stepping* into the market in thirds was a conservative approach that many of her investment books recommended. It made more sense than buying all her shares at once.

Maggie decided she was not prepared to pay more than $30 per share for AT&T, based on what she had learned. Buying it for less than $30 a share would be an opportunity, in Maggie's mind—unless, of course, something happened to the company or if the stock market suddenly dropped. When conditions changed, she would need to adapt. She did not need to follow the market or a particular stock minutely, but she needed to keep track of daily shifts or big news that would directly affect her stocks.

She spent the rest of the afternoon sorting through other industry segments, repeating the kind of analysis she had done in the communication sector. By the time she finished, she had decided on two to three possibilities from each industrial sector. All of her choices were large companies, *brand name* stocks. Many were companies that had been in business so long, her father had also chosen them.

These companies generally paid good, steady dividends. She had a telecom, three energy companies, two utilities, a financial stock, four different consumer goods companies, two healthcare stocks, one raw material manufacturer, two tech companies, and a real estate option. Every sector was represented.

She planned to work through these stock ideas with Kate tomorrow and see what she thought of her selections. She would also check with Graham. Her plan was to put about one million dollars in these stocks little by little over the next few months, and then see if she could get bonds for the rest. She was staggered when she thought about the amount of money she controlled. She vividly remembered scrounging around for spare change when she had found her coin collection. She had come a long way very quickly.

She felt good about the work she had put in today. If she could get these stocks at the prices she wanted to pay, she might reach her target *rate of return*, her five percent per year. She was realistic, though, and reminded herself of what she had read in all the broker's disclaimers—that the past is no guarantee of future performance. The best choices in the world could still hit air pockets. She was not naive enough to think that a single day of research was enough to make her an expert at picking stocks, but thanks to Graham she no longer felt one needed to be an expert - she just needed to do the homework.

The last thing Maggie did was email Kate. She asked her to move all the cash currently in the Trust into the money market account she had mentioned. It would pay just over two percent until they agree what to buy. She also sent Kate the shopping list of stocks she had selected, and finally she asked her to help her find some bonds to round out the Trust's portfolio.

As she got up from the computer, she checked her phone. Brody had texted her a couple of times throughout the day to ask how she was going. In her last text she had sent him, she was grumbling about all the choices she had to sort through. His response to this text had been flirtatious but direct: "Perhaps, for a change of pace, choose 'us'? My research suggests our dating could yield excellent dividends."

She didn't know how to answer him. Most days she found herself stumbling over reminders that Neal was still missing—someone mentioning a husband's promotion or a news story about some financial misdeeds. She worried about him then, but she still harbored enough resentment to keep any deep concern about Neal at bay.

The children still started almost every conversation with her asking for any news. Her answer was always the same: that the FBI had told her they were still looking for him. Judge Munoz told her there was news of sightings on occasion, but he was unwilling to give any specifics.

Maggie had conveniently walled off her developing feelings for Brody, but now he was specifically requesting that they breach that wall. She had left his request unanswered for most of the evening, not sure what to say. She knew she owed him a reply. As she got ready for bed, she simply texted, "Need to sleep on it." He replied with an emoji, a thumbs up. She finally understood why people used them—they were satisfyingly vague.

She wondered about her children. If she said yes to Brody, should she then tell the kids? If she simply let Brody into her life and they found out after the fact, she knew the children would be hurt. They would assume she was letting Neal go, perhaps even think of her as unfaithful. They deserved her honesty.

Maggie had been reaching out to all the kids more frequently than she had in the past. Her structured Sunday calls had become more informal. There were frequent midweek catchups. Now that she had a job, was learning about investing and had Olivia and the dogs to update the kids on, she had a lot to talk about. In response, she also found them sharing more. First it had just been Ethan who called to check in on her, but then the girls started to call more frequently. After the dinner with Ethan and Hannah, Izzy had made a point of asking her to come into the city for meals. They had been getting together every two weeks for dinner. She was finally developing the relationship she had always wanted with her kids.

She decided it was probably time to at least discuss the possibility of a man in her life with them. She texted all three children, apologizing for not making her usual Sunday calls. She used the abbreviation, NDU which they had developed. It meant *No Dad Update*. She then asked Izzy and Ethan to dinner one night during the week, their pick. She also made a date for a video call with Charlie. Before she said yes to Brody, she needed to begin to discuss letting go of Neal with each of them. If she got cold feet, she would just tell Brody to wait.

As she fell off to sleep, she tossed and turned so much she almost reached for one of her few remaining sleeping pills. The potential conversations with the kids about her broken marriage worried her. Then there was the constant tension over the eventual Ethan conversation. And, of course, all the worry about managing the money her mother relied on. But when she finally fitfully drifted off, she slid into sleep realizing that what was bothering her the most was the problem of how to answer Brody's question.

CHAPTER 14:
STOCK AND BOND BASKETS

Shortly after Maggie arrived at work the next day, Kate emailed back. In response to Maggie's request, she offered a 4 p.m. meeting which Maggie agreed to. She also told her she would need a call from Maggie to verbally confirm moving money into the money market. E-mails, or any electronic communication, was not accepted when it came to transferring large sums of money. As Maggie settled down to her files, Emma Biers, another coder, approached her. Emma was one of the department's youngest staff members.

Emma was a college graduate, unlike most of the coders. She acted superior with them despite her being the youngest coder in the office. Tammy had told Maggie that Emma had somehow expected Tammy's recent promotion, despite Tammy's seniority and superior skills. Tammy's frustration with Emma's attitude was clear. She had explained to Maggie that Emma had only taken the coding job after an unsuccessful job hunt post completing college. Tammy understood Emma felt the job was beneath her but could not understand why she just couldn't get over it. "It's like the girl never faced a setback before," Tammy said as she shook her head. "I always tell my boys *life is rarely fair*. You have to accept the defeats and move on. Once you get your foot in the door anyplace, make your own luck. Emma just takes her disappointment out on us."

Emma also had a bad habit of taking personal calls during work. All the other coders had taken to wearing headphones when she was in the office, as she rarely followed Tammy's instructions to limit her calls. Everyone rolled their eyes whenever she picked up her phone, which was far too frequently. If she had not been a quick and efficient coder, Tammy would have let her go.

This morning, Emma was clearly angry. She growled at Maggie, "My friend in the finance department told me that you wrote a memo about a coding error which might be shortchanging the hospital on reimbursements. I coded some of those! They are going to think I'm an idiot. What gave you the right?"

Maggie grimaced; Emma was clearly out of line. She fought her irritation and smiled, "I think there's a misunderstanding. The memo was based on work I did over the holiday break, when you were off. I never mentioned which coders were involved. It was Tammy who instructed me to outline the two different interpretations and then to send the report along to Finance. They're going to discuss it with the insurance companies. No blame, just a query as to how to handle things going forward. The hospital may be undercharging for the procedure. Since we don't have access to either the costs or the charges for procedures, it's up to Finance to tell us which codes to assign."

Emma raised her voice and said, "It *is* a question of right or wrong. My coding is right. I applied for a position in Finance, and this makes me look bad!" By now, everyone in the office was listening. Realizing this, Emma reddened in embarrassment and stormed off. Tammy and Maggie just exchanged smiles, shrugged, and went back to work.

Later in the day, Emma stopped Maggie in the break area and quietly apologized. She said with a catch in her voice, "I'm sorry, Maggie. I'm having a terrible day and took it out on you. My friend in Finance told me this morning that they hired someone else for the position there. I'd been counting on it." She breathed deeply and said in frustration, "I am working in a job that doesn't even require a college degree, yet my college loans are killing me. I know I'm well paid for what I do, but not enough to get me out of the financial hole I'm in. I live with too many other people because it's all I can afford; I can't seem to save any money. And coding just doesn't offer much of a career path. I have been here almost two years and I'm going nowhere."

Maggie was sympathetic. She knew her children were lucky to have parents who had paid in full for college. Less than a third of parents could afford to, that is if they could afford college at all. Maggie doubted whether her children had ever even thought about how much college cost. Izzy was the only one among her roommates who was looking at purchasing real estate—it was just a dream for her friends. Ethan was able to contribute to a 401k at work, taking the maximum match because he had no college loans. Most of their more ambitious peers worked two jobs just to try and pay off student loans, to get out from under the debt. Others worked to try and help their parents with the debt they had taken on to put their children through college.

Maggie said, "I understand, Emma. It sounds tough. Have you been looking for other jobs where your college degree would help?"

"Everywhere. I keep sending out resumes. I'm worried that the lack of forward momentum in this job looks bad. There is no promotion available for me here. I don't have any family contacts; I am on my own. I feel like I just can't get started. I wish I had thought more about the impact of college debt. Or that I worked before or during school, so I had more contacts and experience. I am not sure going to college even made sense for me. I just went because my parents wanted me to, and all my friends were going. So many jobs here in the hospital just require technical degrees rather than college. They pay good money and offer career paths. I could be debt free if I had gone another route." Emma sounded bitter when she said, "A college degree does not guarantee anything anymore."

Maggie gave her an understanding smile. "My kids are just starting out too. It's hard. Tell you what, how about if I ask them for any contacts they might have? Maybe they know of a job at their firms. Your degree is in finance, right?" Emma looked surprised and smiled warmly. She thanked Maggie for being so understanding. She said she would send Maggie her resume, that she could forward it to anyone. She was happy to have a chance to expand her network. Maggie was glad she had given Emma a chance.

Just after 4 p.m., Maggie arrived at Kate's office bringing them both afternoon treats of tea and scones from the hospital bakery – surprisingly good scones for institutional food. The stock market had closed at four, but that didn't worry her. Maggie wanted to put her money to work as soon as possible, but she was not just going to rush in.

Kate had looked at the list Maggie had sent. She said, "Wow, Maggie, you really took the time and did the homework! My new clients, especially the men, usually come in with *hot tips* or an *inside scoop on a sure thing*. They say women are more emotional. In my experience, when it comes to money, women tend to be more rational. You certainly prove the point. Not that I am sexist in any way," Kate grinned.

Over tea, Kate told Maggie that she thought her stock picks were sound ones for a fixed income portfolio. They were solid companies that were not going away anytime soon. She agreed their dividends were relatively safe compared to other, higher yielding options. She was happy Maggie hadn't *reached for yield* and put riskier stocks on the list. She cautioned Maggie that her very conservative stocks were unlikely to appreciate a great deal, but that they were also less likely to slide as much when the market experienced its periodic downturns.

They discussed the criteria Maggie had used: P/Es, the cashflow, company debt, and the payout ratios. Kate said Maggie's screening criteria were good ones, particularly for fixed income. She also suggested Maggie also pay attention to management of the companies.

"Management? How do I find out about that?"

Maggie realized that statistics regarding the strength of management was not usually found on any of the sites she had looked at. The books she read always talked about good management but seemed to rely on how *well known* the CEO was rather than using quality measures of any kind. It seemed to Maggie that a "good" CEO was simply the one that hired the best public relations firm.

"Well," Kate admitted, "learning about a company's management is harder and more subjective. There is usually some mention of it in analyst reports. Really though, it is something you get a feel for over time by reading things like the Wall Street Journal and watching the business news channels. You can also watch senior management being interviewed by Googling videos of them. They are frequently on the news when they report earnings, or their company is in the news. They usually talk about their company's performance or prospects.

There are also sites that will tell you when senior management is buying or selling company stock. Companies are required by law to report that. All of these sources can help you get a feel for what management thinks of the company going forward. For example, if management is buying stock, that probably means they feel that the company's future prospects are good. A lot of selling can tell you there is a problem. And, just for fun, look for women in senior management. There are studies that show female CEOs have, on average, outperformed their male peers. This is probably because they have to be so much better than men to even get to the top. It is a minor thing, but I always check it."

"That's interesting." Maggie remembered she had picked General Motors, who had a female CEO, over Ford on her list. "I'll look at that going forward. And check for YouTube videos. I like to see how people handle questions. Changing subjects though, any luck on finding me some bonds to buy?"

"Bonds are different from stocks," Kate explained. "I know you understand that, but they are different enough that there are dealers who specifically focus on bonds and bonds alone. They don't do stocks. Remember, stocks give holders a cut of a company's profits, so values can change based on a company's performance. Bonds are contracts that will give you a fixed income over a certain period with a set repayment schedule. Bond dealers don't really spend a lot of time analyzing the government agencies or companies who are issuing bonds, they rely on bond ratings. Bond traders tend to look at the big trends in world markets and focus on interest rates. Their universe includes trades in treasuries, government and corporate bonds."

"Treasuries?" asked Maggie

"Those are the bonds issued by the US government, our Treasury. They pretty much set the bar for interest rates in the country and are considered the lowest risk of all bonds, because they are backed by the Federal Government. Currently, Treasury yields are too low to interest you as part of your portfolio. You are indirectly invested in them, though, through the money market fund you are in. Government bonds are different than Treasuries. They can be issued by any government agency, like a township, city, or state, to raise money for infrastructure projects. The big advantage of government bonds is that you do not usually pay any tax on the interest they pay you. Corporate bonds are slightly different. They trade like stocks but are not necessarily offered on stock exchanges. Corporations can issue bonds to lot of different ways to different people, so you generally need a specialized broker. And you have to pay income tax on the interest a corporate bond pays you."

"So, do I have to call a bond trader to find bonds to buy?"

"Well, you could. We have people here that specialize in them. The bond market has changed a lot since the financial crisis in 2008. Since interest rates are so low now and bonds now yield so little, they are a lot less popular. There are fewer bond salespeople because there is less money to be made."

Maggie said, "Yes, I keep reading about the financial crisis in 2008 and how it changed things in the financial markets. I hate to admit it, but the news then just went right over my head then and now it feels like ancient history. I feel a little silly asking, but what exactly was the financial crisis of 2008 all about?"

Kate laughed, "Oh, Maggie. It is too complicated for me to explain it all to you today! You know, you should watch the movie <u>The Big Short</u>. It gives a great explanation of what happened, plus it is terrifically fun to watch. It makes things pretty simple and it is great cautionary tale. A lot of everyday people got caught up in the crisis back then, they really did not understand what they were doing. Everyone was talking about how to get rich quick, until it all came crashing down. It will help you understand what we call *market bubbles* and perhaps learn how to avoid them. All the silly *meme* stocks remind me of that time. Watch the movie, I'm sure you'll enjoy it."

Maggie made a note of the film title and they talked about movies for a bit. Maggie then asked, "So, given how low the rates are and how I have to use a special bond broker, should I just give up on bonds and just do all stock?"

"Well, *all* stocks is a way to go, but there are other options. And diversification is important. You could do corporate bonds, since there are more of them around and some trade on the exchanges. They are higher risk than government bonds, but they do perform relatively well. There are also *preferred* stocks you could consider. Preferred stocks are almost like bonds, but you get a dividend rather than interest. If a company goes bankrupt, the preferred stockholders get their capital back right after bond holders are paid. Common stockholders get whatever is left."

Maggie took a minute to absorb this. She had not realized that some owners did better than others if a company failed. It seemed that ordinary people like her who owned common stock were last in line when something went wrong when investing. This was part of the reason she wanted to focus on large, established companies that were unlikely to fail.

Kate continued, "I think, for now, you should consider a bond mutual fund or bond ETF, instead of individual bonds. It is a basket of bonds, like a mutual fund for stocks. The yields are a little lower because you have to pay a management fee to the fund, what is called the *expense ratio*. But a bond fund is a great way to diversify your risk. By buying bond funds a small investor can buy a well-mixed group of bonds. There are even bond funds that offer only municipal bonds so the interest they pay is tax free."

Maggie had run across the term *mutual fund* when talking to the 401k advisor at work. She knew that ETFs, the abbreviation for exchange traded funds, were like mutual funds. She was not sure, however, what the difference was between them. And now Kate was talking about bond funds. She was getting confused. She said, "I know I should probably know this by now, but what is the difference between mutual funds and ETFs?"

Kate smiled, and said "I'm not surprised you are a little confused. You are learning a lot of new terms, Maggie. Mutual funds and ETFs are simply baskets of stocks. They are meant to limit the risk that comes from owning just one or two stocks. Remember, beginner investors generally do not have a lot of money to buy a variety of stocks and bonds, like you are doing. However, diversification is important. The best way someone with limited cash, say below ten thousand dollars, can diversify is to buy a basket of investments. These baskets can include stocks, bonds, derivatives of each, or even other assets like real estate. There really is no limit. Managers generally select what goes in the basket. Baskets that mimic established market indexes, are frequently just "managed" by computers with minimal human intervention."

Maggie nodded. This was what she had thought mutual funds were. "But when my father selected holdings for the Trust, he didn't choose any mutual funds or ETFs. Are they a new thing?"

"Maggie, your mother's Trust had enough money to buy stocks outright, so your father created his own basket of stocks, his *portfolio*. By buying stocks outright, he did not have to pay any fees to outside managers. He also received all the dividends the companies paid. If he had wanted to include a mutual funds, he could have picked one; they did have them back then. I'm told mutual funds took off in the 1970s, when mutual *index* funds came into being. These mutual funds mimicked stock indexes like the S&P 500 or the Nasdaq. At the time, were revolutionary; they were very inexpensive to manage as they did not require stock picking. Managers just invested in the stocks that made up the index. These index funds were the first *no-load*, low expense ratio funds. They drove down mutual fund fees dramatically, which boosted returns to investors. Vanguard Group pioneered these index funds. They became a real powerhouse in low-cost index funds. That is why Vanguard is still involved in or manages so many retirement plans and pensions today. They might even be the company who manages your 401k."

Maggie said, "I was going to ask about fees for these funds. What does *no-load* mean?"

"Gee, Maggie. You really focus on fees." Kate continued, "The fees for mutual funds are complicated. First, there is the *expense ratio*. That is the ongoing fee that you pay every year to the fund managers. It gets deducted from your total return. If you have one thousand dollars invested and the expense ratio is one percent, then you pay ten dollars a year for the managers to manage the fund. Remember, some types of mutual funds have legitimately higher expense ratios. For example, mutual funds that invest in international stocks have higher fees simply because trading international stocks costs more."

"Well, that makes sense," Maggie agreed.

"What people don't realize is that there are frequently even more fees for mutual funds, many of which are hidden. There are four key areas to ask about. First, there can be an upfront commission when you first buy a mutual fund. A *no-load* fund does not charge this upfront commission. Second, sometimes you will also be charged a *redemption* fee when you sell your mutual fund shares, particularly if you do this within five years after you buy it. Third, there are *short-term trading* fees. Since mutual fund investments are intended to be held for the long term, you can also be charged a *short-term* trading fee if you buy or sell shares within a thirty to ninety-day window, even if the fund is in your 401k. Finally, there can also be a service fee for marketing costs related to the fund. This marketing fee can be in addition to the expense ratio."

Maggie shook her head in bewilderment. "There are so many sneaky ways for people to charge fees!" she complained.

"All up, it is almost impossible to work out the fees for some funds, as they are simply deducted from your returns at the end of the day. People need, though, to try and understand these fees before they commit to a particular fund. Almost identical funds can have significantly different fees. Mutual funds currently dominate in 401ks and other retirement plans and their fees do vary, sometimes a lot. ETFs are catching up though in terms of market share. They now make up about 20% of funds being offered. ETFs don't have the extra fees mutual funds often have, like upfront commissions or redemption fees. They are going to continue to grow in popularity. I hope to see more in employer sponsored retirement plans in the future."

Maggie was grateful that Kate was willing to spend the time explaining this. While she was willing to read to teach herself, listening to someone explain things made it clearer.

"Again, if they are both baskets of stocks how exactly how are ETFs different from mutual funds? Besides having lower fees," Maggie asked.

Kate started again, "ETFs, or Exchange Traded Funds, are very similar to mutual funds. The major difference is that shares in an ETF trade exactly like common stock on an exchange. Their price fluctuates throughout the day and you can buy or sell shares whenever you want. Mutual funds only trade once daily, after the market closes. At the end of the day, the value of its holdings can be calculated to set the mutual fund's share price. Mutual funds are less liquid than ETFs, and the volumes traded each day are lower. They are meant to be held, not traded. ETFs tend to have lower fees and they trade more frequently. They are easier for the average investor to access, and they have become an attractive alternative to mutual funds."

"If you can trade them like stocks, they do seem easier," Maggie agreed.

"Yes. While ETFs are rarely offered in 401k plans, in part due to regulations. I think this will change as the whole fund industry is being forced to lower fees. Technology has changed the entire cost structure of the industry. There is now a race to offer the lowest cost fund possible. ETFs generally win in that regard. The other advantage is that ETFs invest in a wider range of assets. There are commodity, currency, and bonds ETFs. Some target specific countries or industries, and others only invest in *socially responsible* corporations. There are some that let investors bet on market direction to help hedge against market downturns and lots of other speculative arenas. Some get very technical and be highly leveraged. Even I don't understand exactly what some ETFs do, and I work in the industry! To be honest, I can't see you in these speculative types of ETFs. They can be dangerous."

Maggie agreed. "No, I don't see myself interested in the more speculative ones either, but I do hear about them. It is helpful to know what they are. I think if I did invest in an ETF, I would choose a low-cost or zero-fee ETF index fund, based on the S&P 500. That sounds about my speed for now."

"I would go that route, too," Kate said. "For clients who come in to open an IRA or simply have less than ten thousand dollars to invest, I always try to steer them to an S&P 500 stock index fund to start. As they get older and have saved more money to invest, I recommend a mix of funds, some growth and some fixed income. Every year, I tell them to reassess. Change the mix. This is what *target date funds* do, they change the mix of holdings from mostly growth to more fixed income as you get older and head into retirement, but they do it less frequently. You can do it yourself though, Maggie, rather than paying fees to managers to do it for you."

Maggie considered this. "But what if you are my age with limited savings?"

Kate said, "Look, everyone's financial situation is unique. Most people have not saved enough for retirement, so *target date* funds can be a problem. You'll need more growth in your portfolio if you have not saved enough. That is why it is so important to start young. That way you do not have to take as much risk when you are older trying to play catch-up. You need to think about your *risk-profile*, Maggie. How much risk you are willing to take in exchange for growth."

"Are index funds risky? You are making it sound as if that is the route I should go," Maggie was not sure if Kate was trying to advise her invest in these funds or not.

"I am not advising you either way, Maggie. Funds can be an important part of any portfolio, especially if you want to invest in a particular niche you are not familiar with, say European companies, small cap companies or even biotechnology companies. There are specialty funds dedicated to specific areas that are managed by people who know these niches very well. You have a fair amount to invest for your mother's Trust. You may want to invest in stocks directly rather than pay a management fee to an index fund, no matter how little they charge. If you own the stocks outright, you also get all of the dividend income. You could then use ETFs to fill in areas where you have gaps, like bonds. There is a mutual bond fund from iShares, MUB is the ticker I think, that pays over 2%, tax free. That might be a way to add bonds to your portfolio without having to buy a bond outright."

Maggie was warming to the idea of some low-cost funds in her mother's Trust and perhaps even in her personal accounts; they made a lot of sense. She asked, "How do funds do over the longer term?"

Kate answered with a grin. "Well, that varies. You need to understand that there are two different types of funds: *active* and *passive*. Active means that human managers have to pick the right stocks and do it at the right time. They buy and sell stocks more frequently and do a lot of research, much like what you are trying to do. As a result of all this work, their fees tend to be higher. These are managers who are trying to beat the market. If you choose well, or just get lucky, you can find a fund manager who regularly outperforms the market. But, like they say, *past performance is no guarantee of future performance*. It is hard to find a manager who consistently outperforms. Over the past few years, in general, active managers have actually underperformed average market returns."

Maggie grimaced. After Jesse and all his failures and hidden fees, she was wary about money managers. She was not surprised that active managers often failed to outperform basic index funds.

"Passive funds, on the other hand only try to match the performance of the market," Kate continued. "It's more of a *buy and hold* approach. As I said, increasingly, these types of funds are managed by computers, not people. Many people worry that computers performing trades is problematic. In fact, some of the more recent, really rapid drops in the stock market have been blamed on the computers working off algorithms."

"I have to admit, I am a little leery about computers, too," Maggie said.

"It's understandable," Kate said with a nod. "There is a reason, though, that passive funds have grown so much. There is a famous book, called *A Random Walk Down Wall Street*, which says it is pretty clear that passive outperforms active—not because passive index funds do so much better, but because active managers do so much worse. There is a statistic that says the S&P index outperforms eighty percent of the mutual funds out there. Furthermore, since the expense ratios for passive funds are generally lower than active funds, the investor ends up with more cash in her pocket investing in passive funds. Remember, paying someone 1-2% to manage a fund, when the return is only 2-4%, effectively halves your return. This is even more damaging over time as you lose the ability for those lost returns to compound."

Maggie got it. "So, if you are just trying to simply match the market, not beat it, a passive index fund would be the way to go. Are the bond funds like that, too?"

"Yep. Also, actively and passively managed. But be careful though—some of these bond funds, especially those with higher yields, have *junk* bonds in them. Junk bonds are bonds rated BB or less. These bonds are usually not considered what they call *investment grade* bonds, so they have a higher chance of default. Because they are higher risk, they have a higher yield. Be careful with junk bond funds."

Maggie knew all about bad bonds. She explained to Kate about the Trust's Puerto Rican bonds and the money the Trust had lost. Maggie said, "I understand what you mean about not buying *junk bonds*, but who decides what is and isn't *investment grade* in bonds?"

Kate explained, "Bonds are rated by companies called credit rating agencies. Their job is to assign a rating for *credit worthiness* of debt. They give ratings similar to your credit score, but instead the rating is applied to the specific debt of the company, government, or other issuing agency. While people get numeric credit scores, bonds get letters. A bond will be rated AAA, AA, A, down to Cs, Ds or even Fs. Just like school."

"Each of the three major agencies vary in the letters they use; there is not a standard system. They sometimes add pluses or minuses, a capital A or a lowercase 'a.' Regardless, junk debt is generally BB or below. Surprisingly, even BBs rarely default—only about 1.5% of all the BB bonds go bad. Bonds with ratings of BB and higher are called investment grade, and very rarely default.

"I was looking at bond funds for a client recently. One called 'Vanguard Corporate Long-Term Bond Fund' caught my eye. It is made up of investment grade bonds and yields over 4.4%, has a great performance record and very good reputation. There are a couple others I can go through with you, too, but a fund might be a better way to go in terms of bonds, rather than buying a single bond that pays very little in terms of interest. Remember though, interest rates are supposed to be going up, so attractive bonds may start coming up in a year or two. You might want to swing out of your bond fund then and go into individual bonds."

"There are also ETFs designed for a fixed income account that pay a relatively high dividend. They hold stocks or bonds with high payouts; sometimes they hold both. We can look at some of those as well, if you like."

Maggie liked the idea of a *fixed income* ETFs, so she and Kate spent a half hour working through options.

To research ETF and mutual funds, the process was almost identical to stocks. They entered a ticker into the financial website and up came the fund's trading history and basic information. As Kate had promised, there was usually a list of the top ten holdings in the fund, so Maggie could easily see what the managers were choosing for their portfolios.

Kate and Maggie agreed on three bond funds, all of which paid more than Maggie's target of four percent. The plan was to start trying to buy both the stocks and the bond funds Maggie was looking for the next day. They would try to fill out the Trust over the next three months

Maggie knew the stock market had been struggling lately, down from its highs of earlier in the year, so some of her selections were already *on sale*. She worried the market might go down even more, so she wondered if it was the right time to buy. She was going to get Graham's advice as well, when it came to the timing.

For the time being, both women agreed on a price Maggie was willing to pay for each of the stocks and the bond ETFs. At Kate's suggestion, Maggie put orders in for one third of the total number of shares she was eventually trying to buy, at prices well below where they were currently trading.

Kate called this fractional way of buying *legging in*. It was the same as the *stepping in* Maggie's books recommended. By buying her positions a third at a time, Maggie would not be as disappointed if the stock market dropped, and she lost money. She could look on that drop as an opportunity to get another third at a lower price and reduce her average cost. Ideally, she would buy her final third for even less, so she would have dropped her average price per share even lower.

They agreed it might take a while to get all the orders completely filled and the portfolio completed. It required being patient, but it was the more logical way to build a portfolio. Maggie understood this. Kate echoed what her books said, "You can never time the market. You are better being patient and letting the price come to you rather than jumping all in." Her mother's money was earning almost 2% in the money market fund in the meantime, so Maggie felt she could afford to wait.

It was well after five when Maggie got up to leave. She realized everyone else in the office had gone, and she apologized for keeping Kate so late. Kate smiled back and said it was a pleasure.

As she was leaving, Maggie called out, "And Kate, I want to talk to you about setting up an IRA and a Health Savings Account. Let me know what I need to do."

Kate laughed, "Of course you do. I'll get the paperwork ready." As Maggie left, Kate locked up behind her and Kate chuckled to herself. *Maggie hasn't missed a beat learning about the smartest ways to manage her money.* She wants an IRA and an HSA in addition to her two stock portfolios, not many people went much beyond an employer supported retirement plan, she was taking advantage of all the tax deferred savings she could. As Kate returned to her desk and packed up to leave, she said aloud to the empty office, "At the rate she's going, I'll be taking that woman's financial advice in a year's time."

Maggie drove home feeling better about investing overall. Kate's reassurance had finally allowed her to feel comfortable about stocks and how to evaluate them. She would open her IRA and HSA next time she saw Kate, so she could fund both accounts and get the money in them invested as well. While she was not ready to offer anyone else stock advice, she was confident she could make solid choices for herself.

She now felt she knew enough to look more closely at her 401k options. She would select from its menu of funds options a fund that had low fees and mimicked the S&P 500 index. She understood it was critical to check a fund's fees, its holdings, and its performance over time, just like she would with a stock. She would not blindly take the advice of a human resources administrator who may not be any more educated than she was. She would not simply rely on the *target date* option.

It was a wonderful feeling to understand her overall financial picture. To be able to take control. She had a salary, a budget, emergency savings, retirement accounts, and even *investments*. She felt like a fully functioning adult for the first time in her life. She was even feeling good about her mother's Trust, knowing she could actually manage it after all. It was all coming together. She felt more confident and in control of her life than she had ever imagined being. Neal's departure had truly rebooted her life. She was surprisingly grateful.

Of course, she wanted to know that Neal was okay. The kids needed to know where he was too. Until he resurfaced and their relationship was resolved, she could not truly enjoy her newfound freedom. She knew she was moving toward leaving her marriage with every day that passed, but she didn't want to hurt Neal. She knew her eagerness to leave her old life behind would make her seem ungrateful to him. He would be hurt.

As her mind turned to Neal, naturally last night's anxiety over Brody's potential role in her future also resurfaced. She admitted to herself that her feelings for him were getting stronger. The children's possible reactions to Brody made her uneasy, particularly Ethan's. His relationship with his father had always been strained, but she did not fool herself into thinking Brody could simply slide in and neatly replace Neal. And even if some type of understanding could be reached between Ethan, Neal and Brody, she knew the girls would rise to defend their father. They would not be happy to find a new man in their mother's life. There was simply *no way* that introducing Brody into her family was going to go smoothly.

As she continued home, her earlier satisfaction with herself faded, replaced by frustration and uncertainty. *Two steps forward, three steps back,* she thought to herself grimly. Neal was the crux. One way or another, she had to have him back. Maggie felt tension rising, and she gripped the steering wheel more firmly. As she aggressively passed a delivery van, she thought to herself, *managing money is a hell of a lot easier than managing relationships. And,* she added to herself, *a lot more gratifying.*

CHAPTER 15:
GROWTH AND RISK

As if he had heard her thoughts, Judge Munoz was waiting for her in the driveway in his black Expedition. He had been waiting for a while, in the cold, and was grateful to be invited in for a coffee. Maggie avoided asking about Neal immediately, concerned that this personal visit was the way the FBI broke difficult news.

Olivia was away again in the UK, with plans to treat herself to an open-ended holiday in Portugal afterward. Maggie had heard her discussing places to stay with Graham, so she assumed he was joining her. Their lives were on another level from most people in retirement, Maggie thought. *Go for it, Olivia,* she had cheered in her mind.

Munoz followed Maggie into the kitchen. She watched him looking around Olivia's house, trying to make some determinations about Maggie's living situation. Maggie simply explained she was taking care of the owner's dogs and left it at that. He did not ask her any more questions about her household arrangements.

He settled into a bar stool at the counter. "No word from Neal? I have to ask," he said, offhandedly.

Maggie breathed deeply; she was surprised she had been holding her breath. So, this was not going to be one of those dramatic *bad new*s visits. "No, I haven't." She continued, "Before you ask, the children haven't heard from him, either."

"Not even Charlotte?"

Maggie was startled. Charlie? Did the FBI think Neal was in Guatemala? She had not reached Charlie last Sunday on the weekly check-in. She was so busy with her stock research she hadn't given it a thought. Only Ethan and Izzy had responded to last night's text. She searched her mind and realized it had been well over a week since she had last heard from Charlie.

As Maggie served Judge his coffee she honestly said, "I haven't heard from my daughter in over a week. Should I let her know to keep an eye out for her dad?"

"Couldn't say. I was just checking in with you." Munoz sipped the coffee with a casual indifference that maddened Maggie. He then continued, "But on another note, I was contacted by an IRS agent regarding your personal tax situation. I told him that we had our own people liaising with his superiors regarding the joint returns filed in prior years. He agreed to leave the issue in our hands for the time being."

"Thank you." The tax situation sounded ominous to Maggie, but she could also play at nonchalance. "Any chance you could get my tax refund cleared?" she jokingly asked. "I sure could use the money."

"I am afraid that is not my department, Mrs. Mueller."

They sat in silence for a moment until he cleared his throat and said, "Do you mind if I ask you a personal question?"

Maggie tensed. Was this "personal" personal? Or was it FBI, "I-want-information-for- my-investigation" personal? She liked Judge Munoz. After weeks of check-ins, she even trusted him a bit—but she was still wary.

Judge continued, "We have family situations like yours quite often. Husbands gone missing, or simply arrested. Your reaction to everything has been a little, shall we say, unique? Most wives are either furious with their husbands and threaten some physical damage or we get tears. A few, usually wives of really bad guys, get their lawyers out so fast we barely see them again. You have been both accessible and forthcoming with us. As a matter of fact, on the day we arrived at your home, you were pretty calm and composed. It seemed like you were either expecting us or were simply unconcerned. Which was it?"

Maggie saw no reason not to be perfectly honest. "I think you misread the situation. It was shock you were seeing. I had only learned the day before that our accounts and credit cards were frozen, or whatever it's called. The money issue was more of a crisis for me than Neal disappearing. He has travelled so much in our marriage, his absence just felt like an extended trip. No access to money, however, felt like a catastrophe to me. Since then, I have had to deal with house foreclosures, raising cash, finding a place to live, and then a new job. Neal's disappearance has simply been on a back burner." Maggie sipped her coffee, then continued, "You have to understand, I had never given a thought as to how my life was funded. From the time I was young until the day before you arrived at the house, money was simply there. Now I think about it all the time."

"So, do you think your husband will try and contact you? Are you two close?"

Maggie thought about the question, "Honestly, I think Neal *would* have tried to contact me by now—if it were important to him. I have left forwarding addresses and phone numbers; the kids have my information. I expect the girls will hear from him before I do. He and my son are not close."

"Mrs. Mueller, if you really are as indifferent to your husband as you seem to be, why are you still married?"

Maggie answered as best and honestly as she could. "In retrospect, inertia, I think. Of course, now I don't know where to serve him papers. I can't divorce him even if I wanted to."

The agent smiled. "Nonsense. That is a made-for-TV myth. People divorce missing spouses all the time. Not that I would want to be accused of recommending something like that. It is just that you should be aware that it is easier for government agencies, all types of government agencies, to believe someone is an *innocent spouse* if the parties are divorced."

Maggie was surprised to hear you could divorce a missing spouse. When she asked him about the process, Munoz did not have any specific details. He recommended going to see a lawyer or going into the local courthouse to speak to a clerk in family court. "Generally, though," he explained, "it's pretty simple. A person usually just publishes a notice in the paper with the intent to divorce. After a set period of time, if the missing spouse is not heard from, a judge rules that the parties are divorced. There are rules specific to each state though," he cautioned. "You would need to check about Massachusetts."

Maggie was immediately suspicious that his recommendation might have something to do with trying to flush Neal out. Thinking it over, though, she realized the option of divorce was now on the table for her. They both talked a little more about Maggie's new life and then he thanked her for the coffee. As he rose to leave, he said he would let her know about any new developments. He then patted the dogs and left.

After a small dinner, Maggie tried to call Charlie, but no luck. Maggie wondered if Charlie had heard from Neal and was avoiding Maggie because of it? She texted her a message asking her to call back as soon as she had a chance. Maggie mentally added Charlie to her anxiety list.

Maggie's original plan for the evening had been to figure out what to do with her nest egg. Worrying over Charlie and thinking over Munoz's divorce discussion intruded on her plans. She checked her phone every few minutes as she cleared away her dinner and went upstairs to change into pajamas. She sat down at her computer and tried to concentrate.

Unlike her mother's Trust fund, her personal needs were not simply about income and preservation of principle. She needed growth so her nest egg would appreciate and perhaps earn a higher rate of return, which meant taking on more risk.

Maggie had given a lot of thought to her investment *risk profile*. That's what Kate had called it. She had spent a lot of time over dinner trying to understand just how comfortable she was with risk, and she really struggled.

She knew that from an investment perspective, people who were *risk-averse* did not like losing principle and were supposed to be willing to accept lower returns because of it. *Risk-seekers* were people who wanted appreciation in their portfolios. They were willing to accept big swings in the value of that portfolio with the expectation that, in the end, they would have a greater return than risk-averse investors.

Conventional wisdom said that as you got older, you became more risk averse. This was because you had fewer years left to earn replacement money in the event that the market swooned. Older people were supposed to weigh their portfolios more towards bonds, which would tend to hold their value in market swings. Plus, bonds offered a steady income. She understood the theory, but it did not fit her reality.

She read that a simple rule of thumb was that the percentage of bonds you should have in your portfolio was simply your age. For a thirty-year-old that meant thirty percent bonds, and for an eighty-year-old it meant eighty percent. That formula seemed too simplistic to Maggie. In fact, she found most age-related recommendations too simplistic.

There was nothing "standard" about being fifty years old and in your first job in over twenty-five years. Maggie thought about her nest egg in terms of her *growth profile* rather than *risk profile*. How much did she need her money to grow? How was she going to get where she wanted to be, financially, in twenty years? What did that mean for managing her money now? How aggressive would she have to be with her investments?

As Kate had implied, her situation was not unique. Between mortgages, paying for college or even caring for elderly parents, many people her age lacked substantial retirement savings. People who lived paycheck to paycheck, like many of the coders she worked with, didn't even have the option of taking advantage of the hospital's 401k offer. They planned to start putting money aside at some unknown future date. Or work forever. Maggie knew that a lot of people saving for retirement needed to make up for lost time, like she was doing. If someone needed to play catch-up, that person was going to need investments that grew in value, rather than simply generate income. It meant taking on more risk than older people probably wanted to during the second half of their lives.

Maggie learned that an all-stock growth portfolio was supposed to yield an average of about nine percent per year. On the more conservative end of the spectrum, keeping her money in a money market fund would yield just about two percent. Her Excel spreadsheet told her she needed an average of about a six percent return every year to reach her goal, assuming she would also be able to add ten thousand dollars to her nest egg every year.

It was an ambitious goal, but she knew she was well ahead of many of her peers. She was starting off with a solid nest egg, free accommodation for the time being, and a good salary that included healthcare coverage. She was lucky that her mother was taken care of and that she did not have anyone else who depended on her financially.

She expected that she would only have her savings to rely on in retirement. She had called the Social Security Administration and found out she was not currently eligible for Social Security. She had not worked long enough to earn the forty credits she needed to qualify for it. It would be years of working before she did. She *was* eligible for some of Neal's Social Security, even if she divorced him, as they had been married for over ten years. But it would only be a very small amount. And she would not be eligible until she was well into her sixties.

The woman she had spoken to at the SSA had also explained that Social Security was not intended to be enough to live on in retirement anyways. It was only intended to make up about 40% of a retiree's income. The rest of it was supposed to come from employee sponsored savings plans like 401ks and personal savings. She had also told Maggie that, unfortunately, almost a third of retirees rely on Social Security for 90% of their income. That meant they, mostly women, were living in poverty. For another sixty percent of people, it made up half of their retirement income and they struggled. Maggie had decided she would not plan on Social Security at all – she was determined to use her savings to fund her retirement. Getting any Social Security at all would be a bonus for her.

Maggie sighed as she returned to her portfolio. She was worried about creating a retirement portfolio that was all stocks, but bonds just would not give her the returns she needed. She decided she would put thirty percent of her holdings into conservative, fixed-income stocks, and seventy percent would be in stocks or EFTs that paid some dividends but also had some growth potential. Unlike her mother's Trust, she would have to take more risks. That mix of stocks and bonds should give her a return of about six percent per year, if she was smart about her choices.

She would keep her portfolio simple. She had about $500,000 in total. She would find ten to twenty stocks or EFTs and make them core holdings, adding to them over time. Each position would have a value of twenty to twenty-five thousand dollars. She knew she was going to have to sell some of her McDonald's shares to diversify her holdings, but she thought she would wait to sell until after the quarterly dividend was paid next month.

If any single stock position grew to be more than fifty thousand dollars in value, she would reevaluate it. She would then *trim* the holding, selling part of the position, or maybe even sell all of it. She wanted to keep her portfolio balanced, not let any one sector or stock get too big or too small, in order to stay diversified. She would also not get greedy. She told herself that if a share gained more than 20% within a year after tax, she would consider selling it.

Any dividends her stocks earned would be deposited back in her investment account as cash. She liked the idea of a dividend reinvestment program, a DRIP, but she knew she would be actively watching her account. She felt she would be better able to deploy her cash because she was watching the market closely enough to be nimble, to buy when the market pulled back.

Maggie understood that stocks occasionally went on sale when the market dropped. A sale could occur any time, and last for hours, days or even weeks. A drop of greater than ten percent was called a market *correction*. There might also be an unexpected drop in a specific stock she liked because of some short-term issue, like bad publicity or when they missed earnings due to an unusual event. She had prepared a list of stocks she wanted to buy so she would be ready when the stock went on sale. She would keep her eyes open and had set text alerts to tell her when one of her stock selections suddenly dropped in price by more than five percent. She knew market corrections could occur any time. Maggie just hoped she would not panic during a market drop and be afraid to buy.

If, by the end of year, she found she was not making good choices with her dividend income, she could always go back and select the DRIP option for the shares that offered them.

Maggie had also decided she would max out the annual payment to her 401k. If needed, she would use the dividend income coming in from her nest egg account to supplement her living expenses. She would also start an IRA and put money into an HSA, both contributions would give her a tax deduction and the money would grow tax free until she needed it.

Maggie knew that her investing time frame was about twenty years, if she was lucky. After that, she would be like her mother, looking for income and a pres-ervation of principle.

She wished, yet again, that she was still in her twenties. Adults in their twen-ties had about forty investing years ahead of them. They could afford to be in the riskier growth stocks. Their returns would probably average about eight to ten percent, or even better over that time. If they just saved as little as five to ten thousand dollars a year, and it compounded, they could enter their middle age confident that they would have very few money concerns later on in life. What a difference it would be for them relative to their parents, who were probably feeling very insecure about their retirement.

Maggie realized that was what she missed most about her life with Neal; the fact she had never worried about her financial future. It had been a false sense of security, but it was a sense of security, nonetheless. Now, she did not see a time ahead when she would not have to scrimp and save, to question the necessity of every purchase. Worse, now she had the added anxiety of what might happen if there were a major stock market decline, or if she couldn't work for some health reason. What a difference saving early in life would have made.

Because of all she had learned, Maggie had begun talking to her children about the power of investing when they were young. She had been surprised at how interested they had been—but then again, younger generations were uniquely aware of financial issues. Many had felt the impact of the financial crisis. Some had parents who had lost jobs, or even had homes foreclosed. Many of them were currently *in* a financial crisis, living at home, delaying starting their lives because they were buried in debt or unable to afford a home of their own.

Maggie thought about Emma, unable to get out from under her college debt. She imagined she was one of those people who was not contributing to her 401k at work. Emma was probably focused on simply paying down her college loans. Maggie knew this was a mistake. Emma should be taking advantage of the 401k despite her debt. Maggie wondered if she should perhaps share her new insights with her. *It would have to be part of a casual conversation*, she thought. Maggie suspected that a lecture about money coming from her would not be welcome.

Fortunately, none of her children seemed particularly surprised by Maggie's growing passion for personal finance and the investment world. They did not know the extent of her financial struggles, but they seemed to understand her moving out of the family home was not a simple downsizing. They respected her for finding a job and "helping out" Olivia. They were impressed with her self-education. And they were happy to listen to her suggestions on how to save money and what to potentially invest in. Maggie was touched that they listened to her.

Izzy even sat down with her one Sunday afternoon and worked out a budget with Maggie. They both came to realize how much Izzy was wasting on food services and simply eating out, especially her daily coffee addiction. It added up. Izzy was inspired to clamp down more on her spending when Maggie admitted to her all the things she was now doing without so that she could increase her savings.

Maggie had been shocked to find that Izzy had saved a good amount towards a down payment on a property, but that it was just in a savings account. On Maggie's advice, Izzy had moved it into a money market fund and also moved her banking to a less expensive, online bank. Now Izzy had even started sending her links to websites of property she was looking at, asking Maggie's opinion.

Maggie was gratified that her financial advice was helping her children. What surprised her was that talking about finances with them was actually helping them all connect more. Maggie realized that talking openly about her finances was helping teach her children critical life skills. She no longer saw herself as an ATM for her children. Talking with them about their respective finances created a welcome intimacy between them.

Maggie returned to her portfolio. Using the Yahoo stock screener, she looked for stocks.

She researched stocks and funds that met her search criteria. Because she also wanted *growth* with her portfolio, she had added a new ratio to her stock evaluation process, the PEG ratio.

The PEG ratio, or Price/Earnings to Growth, is calculated by taking the company's P/E and dividing it by the growth rate of its earnings for a specified period. Maggie learned that, *any value below one was considered desirable*, but like all the ratios, it varied by industry. Similar to P/E, a PEG ratio could be trailing or forward. A trailing PEG used the historical growth rate of the company. A forward PEG used the estimated earnings growth rate, usually provided by management. Maggie found it was useful to look back at earlier periods to see if management met its prior growth projections. It gave her a way to assess how realistic their current projections on growth were.

Maggie had already started to develop a list for her personal portfolio. The easiest thing was to piggyback off the stocks she had already selected for her mother's portfolio. Most of them would work for her as well. She now checked the PEG ratios on them and found only a few had values below one. She had selected them based on value alone, but now the PEG ratio added another useful dimension.

Given these PEG ratios, she realized that the future price appreciation of some stocks may not be as great as she hoped it would be. She re-ranked her list, putting companies with a lower (which meant better) PEG ratios ahead of other choices. Her investment portfolio would be similar to her mother's, but more geared toward growth. If she gave priority to stocks with lower PEGs, assuming all other things being equal, they might afford her better price appreciation, or growth, over time.

She knew if she purchased her selections at the price she had targeted, she would get the stock at a good price. She believed that in addition to getting dividends, her selections would gradually appreciate in value over time. She generally set her price target by looking at the yearly range of the stock and then picking a value somewhere in the middle, assuming at some point the stock would return to that value. It was a *reversion to the mean* assumption that she had read about in her books. Of course, the stock also had to fit her other criteria; a low P/E, limited debt and strong cash flow.

Investing with growth in mind complicated her choices. She understood she would probably pay more for the stocks of companies that were growing rapidly, like technology stocks or social media companies. She also knew smaller companies would probably grow faster than larger companies. It was easier to double your revenue if you were a small company rather than, say, Amazon. Then there was also the question of companies in other countries. Many countries, like China and India, had national growth rates that were greater than the US, so their major companies might grow faster. There were just too many factors that influenced potential growth stocks – Maggie felt overwhelmed.

Adding growth as a criterion for choosing a stock also made it harder to evaluate the stock. Estimating future growth relied primarily on management or analysts' estimates about the company's earnings potential. She knew it would be a while until she would be able to work out who regularly overestimated or underestimated their growth, if she ever could. She wanted growth, but growth at a reasonable price. How could she to determine a good price to pay for a stock that was growing rapidly?

And then there was the problem that growth stocks rarely paid dividends. They generally used their cash to re-invest in themselves and grow. Maggie liked dividends, trading them for potential future stock price appreciation was a trade-off that made Maggie uneasy.

She thought back to the funds Kate had talked about. Maybe the better way to capture growth was to select stock funds focused on growth. Was there a fund focused on growth that also paid some type of dividend? That would be ideal.

A quick Google search gave her the answer, there *were* growth funds that paid modest dividends.

Something clicked for Maggie and she reached for the list of funds offered in her 401k. There were *growth* funds listed there. When she had signed up, the administrator simply directed her to age-specific funds. After her talk with Kate, she had checked and found that the target date funds on offer in her 401k were actively managed, so she knew her returns would be reduced by fees.

She looked up the tickers for each of the growth funds offered in her 401k. She then looked up each one on Yahoo Finance, checking its performance, its expense ratio, its rating, and what their major holdings were. She ended up selecting an *aggressive growth* fund with a low expense ratio. It had four out of five stars on the Morningstar rating system. It also had a solid performance record over the past three to five years. When she checked this fund's performance against its competitors, she found there were almost identical funds from other companies that had lower expense ratios and even better performance. Unfortunately, these competitors were not on offer on her 401k menu, so she marked them instead as possible additions to her personal portfolio.

Selecting the aggressive growth fund in her hospital 401k was riskier than opting for a target date fund. Its annual returns varied dramatically, but on average it had earned over ten percent a year. She thought she would balance it out with less aggressive growth funds that paid dividends in her nest egg account. This mix of an aggressive growth in her 401k, and some additional growth funds in her in her personal trading account made sense for her particular situation.

She wondered how many people simply ticked the age-specific fund in the 401k without understanding whether or not that was the right choice for their personal situation. She remembered Brody saying he had done exactly that. Maggie thought it had probably worked for him because he had done it over a lifetime of earnings. She did not have that luxury.

People who had not been able or willing to put money aside in their twenties or thirties needed more aggressive growth to catch up. If they had raided their 401k to help kids with college, like Tammy worried she might have to do, or for some family emergency, that too would require *catch-up* investing. She realized that a 401k allocation was not something anyone should simply set and forget, regardless of what people say. It deserved time and attention. Maggie resolved to learn how to access her 401k online and check in on it at least quarterly.

While she worked, she found the divorce discussion she had had with Judge Munoz kept slipping back into her mind. Finally, she gave in to the niggling and stopped her stock search. She turned instead to researching divorce in Massachusetts. She found out that what he said appeared true. She could divorce Neal without him being physically present, no need for the dramatic *serving* of *divorce papers* that television shows played up.

She sat back. She wondered if she had latched onto the divorce idea because of Brody. She knew the fact that she was married made it easy to explain why she was holding him at a distance. Then again, if she stayed married and let Brody into her life, started sleeping with him for example, would it make her something less in the eyes of her children? Would she *feel* like something less?

And just like that, her thinking coalesced. She *did* want a divorce, and she wanted it before Brody became part of the equation. Agent Munoz was right; she was basically indifferent to Neal and his situation. There was no anger or frustration with him, just disappointment that the kids were getting short changed and resentment that she had been left high and dry. She, of course, loved him as the father of her children. Unfortunately, though, their relationship had died without either of them ever admitting it.

She knew that Neal's disappearance had turned out to be a positive change for her. Even with all the money issues. She felt more connected to people, she had a purpose, and she had new friends. She would probably never own a new Hermes bag again, but that seemed like a ridiculous goal now. If there were going to be major legal issues brewing with Neal, it would be better to be clear of them, at least legally. She could not afford to have her newly found financial security shattered by Neal for a second time.

She called Izzy and Ethan and invited them for Sunday dinner. She told them she had something important to discuss with them, so no backing out. She had not heard back from Charlie yet, but she texted her to let her know she would have to be available for FaceTime then too. That it was important, a family meeting. She would tell them all together.

She turned back to her portfolio to stop her from envisioning the children's reaction. It took a while to chase out the visions of their tears and anger. She settled herself in and tried to concentrate again.

She turned back to her list of funds. She had decided to take a look at what stocks the growth funds were actually holding. She could do that on the Morningstar site, her favorite site for basic stock data. She figured if a particular stock was a major holding in most of the growth funds, perhaps it might be a good option to add to her portfolio as well. As she started moving through screens, the numbers began to swim before her. She realized she was crying. Enough of the numbers for tonight.

As she got up to get ready for her bath, she realized she felt like talking to Brody. She was not ready to tell him about her divorce decision. The children deserved to hear it first, anyway. It surprised her that she just wanted to hear his voice, see how his week was going. For the first time, she called him just to say hello. When she told him there was no reason for her call, she could hear the surprised grin in his voice. They talked about nothing for an hour or so. Gratefully, he did not bring up the dating question. After her bath, she fell asleep instantly, exhausted from the night before.

Next morning at work, Maggie's phone buzzed repeatedly between 9:30 and 10:00 a.m. She saw that the market had fallen over two percent at opening and some of her limit orders for her mother's Trust were filled. The Trust now owned stocks again. She spent most of the day worried the stock market would fall farther, but instead it reversed and began a steady climb up. She was thrilled when it closed at 4 o'clock, to find she had modest profits on all of her newly purchased shares. The profits would probably not last, but at least it made her first purchases for her mother's Trust seem like a success.

Just as Maggie was preparing to leave for the day, Tammy came over and told her they were wanted in Finance. It was about her coding memo. Tammy walked up with Maggie and introduced her to Edward Grimes, who reported directly to the hospital's Chief Financial Officer, the CFO. Ed was heavyset and balding, but probably younger than Maggie. He said he was delighted to meet her, lingering with his handshake, his palm sweaty. He ushered them into his office, guiding Maggie with his hand nestled on her lower back. Maggie stiffened, given his uncomfortable touch, and she took an instant dislike to him.

He motioned to chairs in front of his desk, while he went around and sat heavily in his oversized leather one. He smiled and said, "Quite the coup for you little ladies. We got your memo, and there was a bit of confusion about it for a while. I got my best analyst on it, though. He talked to the insurance companies, and you were quite right. The procedure was being coded incorrectly, the reimbursements well below what we think it costs." He continued gleefully, "We managed to renegotiate the reimbursement rate and have worked out the correct coding from now on. The real news is that we got three years of retroactive reimbursements, so a real windfall for the hospital. More than three million dollars. We'll also be making a profit rather than losing money on the procedure going forward. Wanted to thank you both in person."

Tammy and Maggie beamed at each other. It was wonderful to be acknowledged, and the impact was a lot more than either of them had imagined. Maggie was moderately disappointed that there was no discussion of any type of bonus for her initiative or effort.

Grimes continued, "So, we were wondering. Should we be looking at the coding across all our most common procedures to see if there are similar issues? We thought someone from coding could work with a costing analyst here in our office to make sure there is a better match between reimbursement from the insurance companies, the actual costs of the procedure, and the coding."

Tammy hesitated, then said, "We are short on coders as it is, Mr. Grimes. We might have trouble staffing it."

Maggie then spoke up, looking meaningfully at Tammy, "We do have a young coder, Emma Biers, who could maybe work with you. If Ms. Withers thought she could spare her, of course. She is very good at coding, a college graduate with a degree in finance."

"Hmm, a *young* lady, you say? Well, she would have to work up here in our office, with the analyst. We would find a desk for her. She would come back down to you when the project is done. Say, in six months or so?"

Tammy said she would take a look at it and get back to him. As they left Grime's office, Tammy looked at Maggie with a funny expression on her face and said, "That project was yours for the taking. I was hedging just because I didn't want to lose you. The Finance Department would be moving up in the world. The office has windows, nice coffee, and a nine to five schedule. Why put Emma up for something as plum as this opportunity?"

Maggie looked at Tammy and said seriously, "Because, Tammy, she needs the chance more than I do. It would be a great opportunity for her." Tammy looked a bit incredulous. Smiling, Maggie then added, "Besides, I like the flexibility of my schedule and, face it, we all hate wearing headphones."

CHAPTER 16:
OPTIONS ARE NOT STOCKS

Maggie returned to Kate later in the week to talk about her portfolio. She was still conflicted. She wanted appreciation in addition to dividends, but most of the growth stocks she had looked at—like Facebook, Apple, Netflix or Google—did not pay any. These FANG stocks also traded with P/Es well in excess of twenty, and their PEG ratios were unfavorable. From her current way of looking at things, these growth stocks were too expensive for her to own on their own.

Maggie had looked at these popular growth stock's trading history over the past five years. When they did drop, they often dropped a *lot*. For the most part, their stock price eventually recovered and moved even higher. But that frequently took some time. She worried about buying a growth stock which dropped after she bought it but then it did *not* recover. It happened. Or if they dropped when she was close to retirement and there was not enough time for them to come back. She understood now why people who selected growth stocks had to be willing to stomach major variations in a stock's price. Growth stocks clearly worked better for people who had longer investment time frames.

To work her way around the risk of owning the large well-known growth stocks, Maggie had focused instead on stocks in the same sector with lower P/Es and better PEGs. She also screened to find those with dividends. She found that there were companies like Cisco or Seagate, who were considered growth stocks but they had better PEG ratios and also paid dividends. These were the types of choices she wanted Kate's opinions on.

Kate was again impressed to see the choices Maggie was considering. Kate said that every single one was a stock that she would be happy to have in her own portfolio. "What are the criteria you are using when you chose stocks?" she curiously asked.

Maggie's explained that her stock picking criteria remained relatively simple. She liked companies with good cash flow, that appeared financially healthy, and had strong management. They also had to be trading at reasonable P/Es and PEGs.

"I always try to pick the company that looks like the best among its competitors," Maggie said. "Then, on your advice, I add a tick when the company has a female CEO. I need growth companies, but I have to buy them at a reasonable price."

"And how do you decide what is reasonable?" Kate wondered.

"If the stock meets my other criteria, I set the price I'm willing to pay by looking at the annual trading range for stock. Then I target a price at the low end of the range, usually at a level at least five percent below where it is currently trading. I also check the price targets set by analysts, to make sure I'm paying well below the target. I want there to be some room for the stock to run up. I'm willing to be patient, to let the price come down to point I feel comfortable buying it. I like buying when things are discounted a bit."

They moved on and talked about the stock funds Maggie had selected. Both were ETFs she had found when doing her internet research. One focused on growth companies. It held all of the popular FANG stocks and a number of other growth stocks as well. While Maggie was worried about the risk, she had decided that a fund that pooled the risk across a range of companies might not be as volatile. Plus the ETF she selected had a very low expense ratio and seemed like the safer way to go.

The second ETF Maggie had selected focused on stocks from small and midsized companies. Maggie's stock selections generally involved large well-known companies. She had decided to use an ETF to diversify into some smaller companies. Again, Maggie just didn't know enough about the specifics of these smaller companies, but her research showed her that smaller companies generally had more opportunity to grow over time.

These two funds would form the main *growth* part of her nest egg portfolio. She was going to devote about 20% to these two funds, or about fifty thousand dollars to each. Both ETFs had very low expense ratios and, as a bonus, paid a small dividend. Maggie was hoping for appreciation on these funds in addition to relying on the dividends. They both had a solid history of good performance over the years, and both had grown at a rate greater than seven percent per year. She told Kate she also planned on adding an aggressive growth fund in her 401k.

"The rest of my portfolio is just going to be made up of large *blue chip* companies across a range of industries." Maggie explained to Kate, "Do you know why they are called *blue chips*?" Kate shook her head, "It's because in poker the blue chips hold the highest value."

Kate laughed. "How appropriate that it would be a gambling term!"

Maggie feigned mock indignation, "*I'm* not gambling, Kate. Well, maybe I am a little, but it's *educated* gambling. I do the homework. And I am starting out small, only buying a third of what I eventually want to hold."

Kate said, "You could also consider another purchasing method. It is called, *dollar cost averaging*. You may have heard of it, it involves buying stocks at regular set intervals—for example, every month or two. The normal month-to-month variation in the market should have you buying stocks at both high and low points. This generally gives you a better average price for your holdings. Easier to have a set investment schedule rather than trying to catch the best price."

Maggie said, "Yes, I know about dollar cost averaging, it's how my 401k works. But I think I want to put the orders in myself, try and catch stocks on sale. I'm happy to watch the market initially, it should help me get a feel for it."

Kate hesitated for a moment and then said, "A third way you might want to buy stocks is using options, particularly if you want to get in at a bargain price. The problem is that you may not be *'put'* immediately, so you may have to wait to get the stock into your portfolio. But you would get to keep the premium in the meantime."

"*Options? Puts?*" Maggie said uncertainly, "I've heard the terms, but I don't know what they mean. They sound pretty sophisticated for a beginner like me."

"Well, option trading is not something we necessarily encourage people to do, especially someone who is just starting out. Option contracts are riskier than stocks. You need to educate yourself about them, make sure that you clearly understand the potential downsides. Most people get in trouble by trading options on the margin—that is, using borrowed money to trade with. But you're pretty conservative. I can't imagine you'd be comfortable working with borrowed money, so I think options could work for you."

Maggie was confused. "I would never borrow money to buy stocks! But *margin* is not the issue, I just don't know what *options* are."

"OK. I am going to explain it as best I can. But Maggie, promise me you will not try to look this up on the computer tonight. It will overwhelm you. You really don't want to get caught up in all the *bull calls* or *butterfly spreads*, or any other fancy option strategies. What I am talking about is plain, vanilla, all-American, cash-covered *put* options."

"I promise I won't look anything up tonight," Maggie said with a wry smile.

Satisfied, Kate continued. "An option is simply a contract. It is a written agreement to buy or sell a stock at a certain price on a certain day. Most option contracts expire on the third Friday of every month. I am not sure why that is the expiration date, but it is. You can buy or sell these contracts at any time on the US markets. The best way to learn about options is to actually trade them. You get in a rhythm and become familiar with the nomenclature."

"Why would I use them to purchase stocks? Could you give me an example?" Maggie asked.

"Well, let's see. Your list says you would like to buy AbbVie, the healthcare company. I see here that you would like to buy it for eighty dollars, but it is currently trading at about $95.50 per share. It looks like you think the P/E is too high. Right now, the stock seems too expensive to you."

"If you could buy it for eighty, it would be more than ten percent below where the stock is currently trading. Right now, the simplest way for you to buy the stock is to put in a limit order for eighty dollars and wait and see if you get it for that price. It may be a while before it gets there, or it might not reach it at all. While you wait, your money just sits in your account, not working."

"Alternatively, you could use options and put your cash to work. You create or *write*, a *cash-covered put option*. Let me break down what the term means. *Cash-covered* simply means that you have the actual cash in your account in case you are *put*, that is if you forced to buy the shares. You will not have to borrow money. The term *put* means that you are writing a contract that lets someone *put*, or sell, their shares to you at the contractually agreed price."

"For example, when you write an option contract says you are willing to pay eighty dollars per share for AbbVie on or before the third Friday of the current month. If the share price drops to or falls below that price, you are contractually obligated to buy the shares for eighty dollars. If it drops lower than eighty, you are *still* going to have to pay eighty for that share. That's the catch."

"But why would I do that? And how is it different from a limit order?" Maggie was still confused.

Kate smiled, "You do it because when you *write* or create that contract, you can sell it. There are tens of thousands of these option contracts trading every day. The person who buys that option contract will pay you a *premium.* The premium varies from pennies to dollars per share, but it can add up. Think of it like an extra dividend."

"Why would someone pay me for creating a contract like that?"

"The person buying the contract from you wants insurance in case the stock falls in value. If the stock price goes below the price set in the contract, what is called the *strike* price, they can still sell it to you at the price you agreed to in the contract. In this case, eighty dollars. It could be that they bought the stock for less than eighty, and they want to lock in a profit if it falls suddenly. Or they may be buying the stock now and want to limit the amount they can lose if it goes down after they bought it. Very often, the people buying options contracts are investment managers in large funds trying to *hedge* against potential losses if the market suddenly drops. They just pass the cost of buying this "insurance" onto the holders of the funds. It can be part of the expense ratio."

Maggie pursed her lips, "I'm still not sure why *I'd* want to do this versus just using a limit order."

"It is confusing. The best way to learn about options, is to actually trade them. Let's use the AbbVie example." Kate turned her computer towards Maggie so she could see what she was doing. "First let me tell you that each option *contract* represents one hundred shares. Ten contracts would represent one thousand shares. Since you are looking to buy a lot of shares in the next couple of months, I thought you might find options useful."

"Say you want to buy five hundred shares of AbbVie at eighty dollars per share. That means you need to *write* five option contracts. These contracts usually expire on the third Friday of a month. This month, the third Friday will fall on March 19th."

Kate clicked on a tab marked *option,* and then another marked *chain.* Then she selected *all strike prices.* A table of numbers appeared with a highlighted center row labeled *Strike.*

"This is the AbbVie *option chain.* On the right side are the put premiums for each strike price on the March 19th date. See here," Kate pointed to the highlighted strike price of $80 and moved her finger to the right. "The *premium* you would get for writing a contract at an $80 dollar strike ranges from $0.75 to $.85 cents per share. If you were to write a put option to buy 500 at $80 on the 19th, and you sold it for say, $0.80, you will get four hundred dollars put in your account the same day. You know, 500 time 80 cents. If, by the 19th of March, the share price has not fallen down to eighty dollars, you will not be *put* the shares. That is, you will not have to buy them. We say the option has *expired* and you simply keep the premium. The four hundred that was deposited to your account when you sold the contract."

Maggie was beginning to understand. Kate continued, "If you had simply put in a limit order to buy the shares for eighty dollars, you would not have gotten the shares either. By using options, at least you make four hundred dollars. When you use options, you get paid while you wait for the shares to reach the price you want to pay."

"The risk is, if the share price falls below eighty dollars. You will get *put* the shares, meaning you *have to buy them* for eighty dollars per share, as per your option contract. Given, however, you were already paid $0.80 for the contact, the *actual* price you pay for the share is eighty dollars minus the $0.80. This means that the price you actually pay for the shares is $79.20, which is less than if you simply had a limit order in for eighty dollars."

"Now, Maggie, be aware. The risk is that if the price for an AbbVie share falls below $79.20, you will lose money. But if you were planning to buy the shares anyway at eighty dollars, you can consider yourself lucky that you got in for $79.20, less that you would have paid with the eighty-dollar limit order."

Maggie understood the math. The option contract did not sound overly complicated, perhaps it was worth a try. Kate saw Maggie shaking her head, warming to the idea of options.

"Remember though, Maggie, AbbVie stock can fall dramatically. It could be a poor earnings report or a bad drug trial. Alternatively, the whole market could drop and take down both good and bad stocks equally. It happens. If AbbVie fell to sixty dollars a share, you will lose money having to buy it at eighty. In general, though, using cash covered *puts* to populate a portfolio is another way to wait to get the price you want. You may even get in for a better price than you wanted. Trading in options can work well if you write option contracts for stable stocks that you are willing to own at the right price."

"Why do I get to keep the four hundred dollars if I'm not put?" Maggie believed she understood why but wanted to make sure.

"Because it was the price someone paid you for taking the risk to *write* the contract. It is the price someone was willing to pay you for creating their insurance. The great thing is that you can do it again for the next month, and the month after that, if you want. It can be like an extra dividend. And if you leave your cash in a money market fund while you are waiting to be put, you can also earn interest on the money while it is waiting to go to work."

Maggie was thinking hard. She understood the risk, but if she was going to buy the stock anyway, then why not? "And I have to have cash in my account to write a *cash-covered* put option?"

"*Yes,* either actual cash or you have stocks that can be converted to cash, to pay for the stock if you get put. A lot of people who write put contracts use borrowed money, or margin, to do it. It can get ugly for people very fast if the market or the stock falls suddenly."

Maggie nodded. She definitely didn't plan on taking that kind of risk. "No margin trading for me," she said.

Kate continued, "While we are talking about them, the other type of option contract I think you should consider is what is called a *covered call*. See here on the option chain? While the right side of strike price has put premiums, on the left side are call premiums. Selling put contracts involve you having to buy stock, selling *covered call contracts* mean you are agreeing to sell shares you already own to someone. You said you were planning on selling some of your McDonald's stock to diversify your portfolio, weren't you?"

"Yes," said Maggie slowly. She was still struggling with the *put* option concept and was not sure she wanted to complicate it more.

"Well, suppose you wanted to sell half your position. Five hundred shares," Kate said. "You could write an option *call* contract. This time, you agree to sell—rather than buy—five hundred shares at a set price at a set time. MCD is trading at $200 today, so let's assume you want to sell them for $210 each. You could write five call option contracts, representing five hundred shares at a strike of $210 for the third Friday of the month."

"And that what would I be paid to write this contract?"

She turned back to her computer. She changed the ticker and brought up a new option chain for McDonalds. "Let me see. Today, at the close, a call option contract for McDonald's shares at a $210 strike price was trading with a premium of around $1.50 for each share in that contract. If you had sold five contracts today, $750 would have gone into your account. If the stock goes above $210 by the third Friday, you will be *called* and you *have to sell* the five hundred shares for $210. Remember though, since you already collected the premium of $1.50 per share, you will *get out* of McDonald's for $210 plus the $1.50 or for $211.50 per share. If it does not get to $210, you again get to keep both the stock and the premium."

Maggie was not sure about options but with a little more convincing, she and Kate agreed to give it a try. To practice, they entered an AbbVie *put* contract. Kate showed her that she would select *sell to open* for a put at a *strike* of eighty dollars for March 19th for a premium price of $0.80. Then she did another *sell to open* for a call for her McDonald's shares at a strike price of $210 for March 19th at a premium of $1.50.

Maggie could not, however, actually enter an option trade. Kate explained that option trading, of any kind, required some additional paperwork. Option trading was riskier than stocks, and an additional form needed to be registered. This form was intended to ensure she understood the risks involved in options. Kate printed out the option trading form that Maggie needed to fill out and sign. They went through it together.

The form began by asking Maggie about her income objectives, which was easy: income and capital preservation. Then it asked about her trading experience, and she put "less than one year."

It then asked for her liquid net worth, her annual income, her total net worth, and her employment information. She marveled at the fact she understood all these questions and the terms, which she would not have, even six months ago. She quickly answered them all.

Then it asked what types of options she would like to trade. On Kate's advice, she selected *cash covered puts* and *covered calls*. She made it clear to Kate that she did not want to trade on the margin, ever.

Kate said she would submit Maggie's paperwork and guessed she would probably be approved for *level one*. Most bank and brokerage firms had four or five levels.

"You could have filled this authorization form out online," Kate told Maggie. "But I think it is better when you clearly understand what the form is asking for, and most people don't. I have had people with almost no stock trading experience, fudge their answers and end up asking for the option trading levels that let them write calls without actually owning the stock. They can lose a lot of money if the stock shoots up unexpectedly and they have to buy stock at the higher price so they have it when the contract expires. *Naked calls*, that's the term for these types of option contracts. Really can get ugly."

Kate said that once Maggie's approval came through, she would help her place her first option trades. She encouraged Maggie to watch the premium prices on the McDonald's and AbbVie options chains over the next few days. They fluctuated a great deal every day, much more than the underlying stock prices, and it would help her get a feel for the ranges for those particular contracts. Kate emphasized that using options was generally considered trading, not investing, so watching the market and trading in *real time* mattered.

Maggie left Kate's office feeling pretty intimidated. Up until now, the stocks and bonds were relatively clear to her. She was becoming familiar with terms, various companies, and investing principles. She realized she still needed to learn a lot about investing, but she saw how she could get there. This option stuff seemed way out there. And it was trading, not investing. That meant paying attention to the market when it was open, didn't it? It sounded a little like day trading, which she knew required paying a lot more attention than she had time for.

When Maggie got home that night, Olivia was back. She had cut short her vacation to go back to her brother after he had had a fall, only to find her brother feisty and unappreciative. She had given up after two days with him and decided to come home. She was already complaining she should have stayed in Portugal, where it was warm and sunny.

Regardless, she was glad to see Maggie and excited to hear about the results of her coding detective work, her catchups with Brody, and her trading. Maggie had made soup on Sunday, so she served herself and Olivia. Over dinner she asked Olivia about divorce lawyers. Olivia laughed and said she kept hers on speed dial.

She looked at Maggie seriously then, and asked, "Are you sure? Your first one is always the hardest. And you have children. It will be tough on them."

Maggie explained that Agent Munoz's visit had sparked the issue. He alluded to the fact that if Neal was in trouble with the government, a divorce might help keep her out of it. She also said she was not sure what she felt about Brody or even where it was going, but it felt wrong seeing him if she stayed married. At the very least, it was not fair to Neal.

Finally, Maggie admitted that she wasn't angry at Neal about all of this. Actually, she was indifferent. That was what settled it for her. Didn't they say indifference was the opposite of love?

Olivia agreed that marriage without love was pretty pointless—unless, she grinned, there were financial considerations. But given that Maggie seemed to be flourishing in the financial arena, Olivia said it was unlikely she would need a man in that regard.

"Other areas, maybe," she mused, then winked at Maggie.

Olivia already knew that divorcing a missing spouse was straightforward. Her first one had skipped out on her, she explained. All she ever saw of him after he left was his debts. She agreed to give Maggie her lawyer's name once she had a chance to give her a heads up.

As they ate, Olivia launched into a lurid tale about how, after her first marriage had ended, she was not just broke but had to declare bankruptcy. She had not known that cosigning on credit cards and mortgages would mean she was fully responsible for the debts when he skipped town. She had not known that he had maxed out so many cards. The credit card companies had not been sympathetic to her situation. The debts he had racked up had been in the tens of thousands.

The marriage had ruined her credit for ten years and left her broke. Olivia said she didn't have an education or a career to fall back on, so she had to rely on a different set of assets, she cupped her chest to illustrate. Maggie suddenly realized that Olivia's breasts were unnaturally large for a woman of Olivia's small stature.

"Fortunately," Olivia went on. "Certain men—the dense, insecure type—are pretty conditioned to the idea of having to pay for the privilege of having an attractive woman on their arm. All you have to do is find a way to put yourself in their path, and you are set. It doesn't take that much more to get a rock and wedding out of them. The only problem is actually having to live with them afterwards."

Olivia said she never felt a twinge of guilt about taking advantage of her second husband, a real estate developer. It was a purely transactional relationship, not built on love, and they both knew it going in. They had a lot of fun prior to the marriage. He always tried to get to the "right" parties and made a point of being seen in all the "right" places. Olivia had even hoped she would grow to love him. Unfortunately, she had to insist on her own bedroom three months after her wedding. "He waited until after marriage to let me know about some pretty perverted sexual interests which I was not prepared to indulge him in."

"He kept other women on the side for the raw stuff," Olivia continued. "Overtime, I realized he was not simply an overweight frat boy. I saw him stiff business partners and even valets. He was petty and narcissistic. His businesses were all a house-of-cards, but he had borrowed so much the banks were nervous that it would blow up on them if they pushed him to pay it back. Mind you, I still got a nice settlement during the divorce five years later – money he had borrowed from some sucker I imagine. The settlement was only paid after I signed a non-disclosure. I knew he was a crook. If people saw him for what he really is, his whole empire would fall apart."

Olivia rose and began rinsing off dishes. "In the end, though, I don't think I got enough. I should have gotten hazard pay. I almost suffocated under him on more than one occasion. Thank goodness he thought a 'long' love-making session was anything more than five minutes," Olivia said with a laugh.

"Mind you, I always drew the line at having children with him. I'm not one of those women who rush to have a kid, just to guarantee a lifetime of financial support. I didn't want to subject the world, or the poor child, to such weak genes. Big men with small dicks, it's just the worst combination. The insecurity of the man was frightening."

Maggie colored a little, as Olivia was getting increasingly graphic. She quickly changed the subject and asked Olivia about Graham instead. Olivia who had been angrily drying dishes, stopped, and smiled dreamily. "Graham? Well, in comparison he was just perfect," she said. "Just a little too gullible and trusting. He swept me off my feet after I had sworn, *sworn*, I would never marry again."

Olivia went on to say that their marriage had been wonderful from the beginning. "We tried for children, but I must have passed some invisible line because it never happened. It didn't matter, really," Olivia said, looking down at her feet. The way Olivia said it, had Maggie suspecting that it probably did matter.

Olivia shook herself a little and then, clearly searching for a word, said, "Maggie, I have to tell you, it was *exquisite* to be so perfectly matched with someone both physically and intellectually. We shared political views and books, liked the same music and movies. Where our tastes differed, we complemented each other. He loved to dress me, and I him. We even joked about having the same thoughts at the same time. We always marveled that growing up in different circumstances, in different parts of the world, could result in two people being so well matched."

"It does sound quite wonderful," Maggie said.

Olivia sighed. "My only regret in life was that I was not able to forgive him for the secretary. So cliché. He said it only happened once and I think that's true because the morning after, he seemed broken somehow. He put it down to a night of heavy drinking, but I knew something had happened. I couldn't pry it out of him." Olivia paused while she put away another dish.

"She called me later in the day, just to tell me, of course. I threw him out of his own house that night. Both of my first two husbands had been unfaithful, but I didn't love them enough to care. Graham's infidelity was different. It was shattering. I'm not the type of person who blames the other woman—it was all on him. She didn't hold a gun to his head. I sometimes wish, though, that I hadn't been so damn decisive." Olivia paused here, before continuing, "But then before we could really talk about it, there was a baby in the equation."

She went on to explain that the secretary, Marilyn, had pleaded a pregnancy just weeks after Olivia kicked Graham out. In her fury and hurt, Olivia hastily filed for divorce and told Graham to get out of her life. Graham protested but Olivia refused to even speak to him. He had dutifully married the secretary, but the pregnancy, if there had even been one, never developed. Graham was back on Olivia's doorstep within the year. It took time, and Graham was persistent, but Olivia had gradually let him back into her life.

Now, Graham and Marilyn lived apart, but she refused to divorce him. He wanted to marry Olivia again, but she resisted, so he just stayed married and ignored his wife.

When Maggie asked, Olivia said, "I don't know why I won't marry him again. Maybe it is the excitement of something illicit about the relationship, the freshness of not living together. The romance of it all." Olivia sighed, "Or maybe it's just that you can't go back, but you can move forward."

Olivia went on to tell Maggie that her attraction to Graham was based on his underlying confidence in himself and in her. He told Olivia that he loved the way she challenged him, both intellectually and emotionally. It was very sexy. He liked her strength, her independence, and her curiosity. He encouraged Olivia in everything.

Maggie realized that she sensed Graham's type of confidence in Brody too.

Olivia glanced over at Maggie who was wiping down the counters. She saw the faraway look in Maggie's eyes. Misreading it, she asked "What attracted you to your husband?"

Maggie sighed. She let go of her musings about Brody and said, "Neal and I were compatible. And my parents were very encouraging - they loved him. I was also pregnant. I married him because it was what everyone expected me to do."

Maggie realized that while she was talking about Neal, she was remembering the Brody of that era. He had been too self-centered and shy, simply not ready to marry. He seemed different now. Maggie went on to say, "I doubt I will ever have what you and Graham seem to have. You two are like a matched set." *And you both revel in it*, Maggie thought. To change the subject, she said to Olivia, "I pity Graham's wife for accepting her life of rejection. She must be a sad, silly woman."

"*Stupid* woman is more like it." Olivia snorted. "She should have more respect for herself. Graham would set her up financially, if she agreed to a divorce. Then she would be free to redirect her life. She just likes to tell people she is a 'Mrs.' Somehow, that makes her more important than if she were single."

When Olivia spoke again, it was as if she had read Maggie's earlier thoughts.

 "You know. Don't discount the potential of your relationship with this Brody character just yet. Relationships ebb and flow. It is not constant, and sometimes it takes a while for sparks to catch fire. There is something between you two, Graham and I both think so. You both have to be less cautious, less careful. Life is short."

They finished up in the kitchen, and Maggie hugged Olivia goodnight, saying how glad she was that she was home. Maggie meant it. Coming home to Olivia was a huge improvement in her life.

As she went up to her rooms, though, she became pensive. Why had she allowed herself to live so long in a relationship which had diminished her so much? Why does any woman? Was she like Graham's wife, staying in a marriage just because it made her more legitimate, somehow? Worthier?

No, she told herself. It really had just been inertia, like she had told Judge Munoz. More passivity about her life. What a waste. She wondered if Neal had been feeling the same way. He had never said anything, but then again, she had never asked. It was as if they both had been too polite to point out the shortcomings of their relationship.

She realized she was also frustrated with herself. She was being tentative with Brody. It was especially odd given how she had charged ahead in so many other things. She knew it was more than just being married. What made her so cautious with her feelings? Olivia's *carpe diem* attitude was so inspiring.

As she bundled herself into bed, she told herself that she was going to have to take Olivia's advice and take some risks if she wanted a richer life. It was like stocks: more risks, more reward. She just had to accept that there might be some bigger emotional swings than she had had in the past.

A few days later, Kate called Maggie to tell her that her option trading approval had come through. She said she would call Maggie the next morning, shortly after the open, and would walk her through how to enter the options and what premium prices to set for both. They also agreed to put some limit orders in for some other stocks Maggie wanted, again at prices well below what they were currently trading, to see how they would go.

The next morning, Maggie spoke to Tammy and arranged a break from 9:30 to 10:00 a.m. to work with Kate. Maggie was yet again grateful that coding let her set her own schedule to some degree.

She had brought her own laptop from home, and at 9:25 she headed to a quiet corner in the hospital cafeteria. She got on the phone and took instructions from Kate. She wrote a put contract for AbbVie and a call contract for McDonald's.

She was surprised that the contract's possible premiums were presented in a range, just like stocks. There was a *bid* price and an *ask* price. The bid was the price people were willing to buy at, and the ask was what people were willing to sell at. The option market was like the stock market.

This morning, the premium for the AbbVie put contract was in a range, from $.64 to $.71. She decided she would ask $.70 and see what happened. The McDonald's call was ranging from $1.80 to $2.00, so she decided to sell her call for $1.90. If she was put, she would be buying five hundred shares of AbbVie. If she was called, she would be selling five hundred shares of McDonalds. Unlike stocks, options really felt more like gambling. She felt guilty admitting to herself, but that made it a little bit fun.

She put in some additional *day only* limit orders on stocks she wanted, all at prices well below where the stocks were trading. They would expire at the end of the day, but she would be watching her option contracts closely every day, so she could renew them each day if they were not filled.

Then she checked on the Trust account. She had decided to add another bond ETF that she had found. Once all the orders for the stocks and bonds were filled, she will have finished putting the remainder of her mother's money to work.

By the time she had finished her other entries, her phone was dinging. She had been filled on both her option contracts. Stocks, bonds, and now options. It was a brave new world. She *was* starting to embrace a little more risk. *Carpe diem* after all.

CHAPTER 17:
ENHANCING RETURNS

Sunday night, Maggie made a roast dinner for Ethan, Izzy, and Olivia. Both children had met Olivia and now treated her like a trendy grandmother. Ethan teased her about her technology illliteracy and Izzy admired her style and directness. Olivia, in turn, genuinely seemed to enjoy them both. Maggie was a little torn seeing Olivia fill a role her children barely remembered her own mother playing, but then again, her mother never could have competed with the novelty of having been an exotic dancer.

After dinner, the children came up to Maggie's study and they got Charlie on Maggie's laptop. "Hey, you're alive!" Ethan chided. "I've been trying to catch you for weeks. Beginning to think you had gotten lost in the jungle somewhere."

Charlie apologized, "We had a bad storm, knocked a local tower over. No internet. We have real third world problems here, guys. You live the high life there in your first world bubble."

After the usual ribbing between the siblings concluded, Maggie began, "All kidding aside, you three. I have something to tell you all and wanted to do it when we were all together." Maggie looked nervously down at her lap and Izzy and Ethan exchanged worried looks. "As you guys know, there has been a tremendous amount of change in my life recently. I know this is going to be hard, but as part of that change I am planning to get a divorce. Your Dad and I have been moving in this direction for some years, but his disappearance has really decided it for me." There was silence for a few minutes.

Initially, their response seemed muted. Ethan's eyes seemed to water, but his expression made her think they were angry tears. Maggie couldn't tell who the tears were directed at.

Charlie looked sad, her hands playing with something offscreen, but she was silent.

It was Izzy who became their spokesperson. "*What?* Look, you need to wait," she said definitively, "You need to talk with Dad about this, at least wait until he's back. It has only been six months. You're just frustrated, and you are letting your emotions carry you away. You're moving too fast."

Then Izzy suddenly shifted and was angry. "I mean *why* are you moving so quickly? I mean was this all planned? Is Dad even aware of what is going on? I mean the sudden sale of the houses, getting rid of all our stuff. Does Dad even know? Or is he in on it somehow?"

In the silence, Ethan asked her dryly, "So, is there someone else? Has Dad buggered off with someone, somewhere?"

Maggie fought to stay calm and tamp down her own tears. "No, Ethan. There are no other people in the mix. Dad and I have been drifting apart for years. His disappearance left me in the lurch financially, but I have resolved all that. On my own. Now that I have settled in here with Olivia, it is time to take this step." She did not mention the issue of being the *innocent* spouse in a legal action. It was all already overwhelming for the children as it was, that detail could wait.

Maggie explained the process, "First, I will advertise to give Dad a chance to contest it. If he resurfaces and does, of course we'll talk. But, let me make this clear, I doubt your father will be able to change my mind. In fact, I don't think he'll even object." She then went on to remind them that Neal had given her no advance warning of his departure and had made no effort to contact her. Of course, his disappearance worried her, but the divorce was not intended to punish him in any way. It was just part of effort to get on with her life. "With the house sold, I am sure you kids understand, there is no going back to the way things were," she finished.

All three kids then hashed out the pros and cons with her for a while, clearly angry and upset, but eventually they lost their energy.

Charlie, who had been the quietest of the three, excused herself from the call, telling her mother she would accept any decision. As she signed off, she said, "But if it was me, Mumma, I would wait a bit longer before moving anything forward."

Maggie was surprised that Charlie seemed to give up. She had always been the peacemaker in the family, championing them as a family unit. After Charlie hung up, the other two excused themselves immediately. Ethan said he had already called an Uber back to the city and would drop Izzy off.

When their car came, he kissed Maggie on the cheek, not meeting her eyes. Izzy said goodbye, crossing her arms when Maggie tried to hug her. They were not happy, and it hurt Maggie to see it. *Adult children*. What a perfect phrase, she thought.

Within the hour, Charlie called her back. She didn't say much, just talked about when she might be coming home. As she spoke, she held up a piece of paper to the camera while she talked over it. Maggie was shocked to see it was a short note in Neal's handwriting. A thousand questions raced into Maggie's mind. The note said:

Love you all, baby, but I'm in a bit of a mess. Sorry for the cone of silence. Need to stay out of the US while I work it through. Will be in touch when I can. All is good, I'm safe. Tell your mom not to hate me too much. Love and hugs, Dad.

Once she had shown the note to Maggie, she pulled it down and while still talking about a potential trip home, held up a second note in her own handwriting: "Is someone listening?"

Maggie marveled at her foresight and simply shrugged. If they were listening, Maggie worried they might be able to see the screen too. Well, she would probably hear from Munoz if that was the case.

Charlie's next note said, "How bad is it? Shake your head *yes* if you think I need to come home." Maggie shook her head with an emphatic no.

Next note said, "Are you okay?"

Maggie smiled and gave a thumbs up.

The final note, clearly written on the fly, simply said, "Hold back on divorce – Dad needs you."

Maggie groaned inwardly and wondered if it could be true. They then talked a few more minutes about the weather, Olivia, and the dogs. Charlie finally said she would call Maggie again next Sunday as usual. She held up one last note: "Call me if anything happens."

Maggie regretfully let her go, planning her own set of placard questions for her next call.

Maggie was surprised that she was so profoundly relieved about Neal's note. He certainly was alive. He also seemed to know what was going on and he was on the run, but safe. It was all very dramatic. She was curious how Charlie had come by the note, but decided she was glad she didn't know. She could quite honestly say to Judge Munoz that she had not "heard" from Neal if he asked.

Charlie was smart. Maggie had not considered that the FBI, or anyone else for that matter, might be listening. She supposed it was possible. Had she done anything that could be viewed as suspicious? Was the new money in her brokerage accounts under review? A lot of the money that she raised had been in cash. Did that look suspicious? She thought it might.

She knew she would have to be careful going forward. If she was under FBI surveillance, it would show that she had not been in contact with Neal. But her phone and computers might be bugged. If Neal was in a lot of trouble, the FBI might have gotten permission to listen. She needed to make sure Kate was clear on where her money had come from, in case anyone ever asked. She assumed her money trail was pretty clean if anyone was looking.

She knew she should tell Izzy and Ethan about the note as soon as she could, but it had to be in person. She decided to go into the city early tomorrow to see them.

Did Neal's resurfacing change how she felt about the divorce? Not even a little bit. She would call Olivia's lawyer and put things in motion, no matter the cost. She would also be more guarded about what she said on the phone going forward.

The following day, both Ethan and Izzy were visibly relieved when Maggie told them about Charlie's note. She had gone into the city at dawn and managed to catch them both in the morning before each left for work. She mentioned that they were going to have to be careful when talking or texting about Neal, and that they should not let anyone else know about Charlie's note.

"I am not sure what is going on with your father, but I don't want to have any of you kids pulled into it. I am not asking you to lie, of course, just to be circumspect." They agreed to wait until Maggie found out more. Izzy asked, "Does this mean the divorce is on hold?" Maggie shook her head, and they both let it go. Perhaps, Maggie thought, they had come to understand her position a little better in the past twenty-four hours. Maybe her children were adults after all, she realized.

*   *   *

Maggie's life moved along. Brody became a regular feature, flying into Boston from wherever he was working once a week. He put together some pretty creative dates, which delighted her. There were picnics, a museum opening, and even a drag show.

He did not push about Ethan. She did not tell him about her conversation with the kids or her decision about the divorce. She would let him know when she felt it was time.

They laughed a lot and enjoyed one another's company. The ritual at the front door at the end of the evening had moved from a polite peck into something longer and more intense. She felt like she was sixteen again, waiting for her father to pull open the door and glare. It was kind of fun.

She contacted Olivia's divorce lawyer, a woman named Alex West. Maggie had been persuaded to have a private detective do a cursory check for Neal's whereabouts. This was to prove to the judge that *every effort* had been undertaken to locate him. Since there were no custody issues and Maggie had said she did not want, or expect, a settlement or alimony from Neal, Alex assured Maggie the divorce should be straightforward. She said she would give the detective two weeks, then file the petition and advertise. She told Maggie she might be a free woman within three months.

The fee Alex quoted seemed suspiciously low to Maggie. She confronted Olivia on the issue, but Olivia just waved it off. Olivia reminded Maggie that she herself was tight about money. It was only logical that her divorce attorney would be a good value. Maggie was not convinced but let it go.

Since Maggie had taken a more active role in her mother's care, she had begun to receive and pay her mother's bills. She even caught a mistake in one: an ambulance charge for a doctor's visit that should have gone to the insurer, not to her. She contacted the doctor and arranged for him to make house calls going forward, so her mother would not need the ambulance. She wondered how many unnecessary charges like this had slipped through when the law firm had handled the bills.

She also went back to H&R Block to have her mother's and the Trust's tax returns prepared. She asked for Robbie, who remembered her. She proudly told him that she was doing her own taxes based on his advice. She explained, however, she needed a professional to do her mother's and the Trust's taxes.

She explained to Robbie that she had spent hours going over the Trust's statements, expenses, and the prior tax returns. She did not understand much of it. She gave her best at summarizing the investment-related expenses, but the investment firm's paperwork had been difficult to understand and collate. The lawyers' fees were even harder to understand. She just wanted one, simple annual invoice. She gave Robbie everything that she had pulled together and wished him luck sorting it out.

When she came back a week later, Robbie explained neither the Trust nor her mother owed any taxes. All the income of the Trust flowed through to care for her mother. Since her mother's medical expenses exceeded her income, she would owe no tax. Regardless though, both her mother and the Trust *did* need to file a return, even if there was no income.

He shook his head when he handed her back the thick returns from prior years. "Remember what I told you, about how the thicker the returns, the more questionable things are?" he said. "These guys fit the bill. I am sorry to say this, but they look like crooks that have been bleeding your mother's Trust dry."

Maggie felt satisfied having her suspicions confirmed, even though she knew she would never be able to fund any kind of legal battle to get any money back.

She showed Robbie the new, slimmed down statements she was getting from Schwab, and he smiled. "Well, next year we will be able to get your tax filings for the Trust and your mother down to a couple pages, by the look of things. You seem to like things clean and tidy. We tax preparers like that."

Maggie thanked him for the help. As she gathered up her papers, he added, "Hey. You know you can pay yourself a salary from the Trust. It is a perfectly legal thing to do. Of course, you would have to report it on your tax returns as income."

Maggie told Robbie that taking a salary at this point was not an option. For now, she was working for her mom, not herself. She had just slimmed down the expenses and didn't want to add more. As she left his office, she had a fleeting thought that if she did take some sort of salary from the Trust, it might help offset the loss of her hospital salary that had resulted from increasing her 401k contribution. She would have to see how well the Trust performed, and maybe revisit the idea sometime next year.

With her mother's and the Trust's taxes now filed, Maggie checked it off her to-do list. The Trust was now earning money and its expenses were under control. It was a huge weight off her shoulders.

Managing the Trust was actually only a minor time commitment. She felt closer to her mom and more like a good daughter, being directly involved in her care. She felt better now that she had pulled the Trust from its former managers. There was still a risk of a market downturn or a health crisis with her mom, but she felt confident now she could manage any challenge.

At work, she asked Payroll to have twenty-five percent taken from her salary to fund her 401k. Carla Ponte was impressed. Maggie selected the *aggressive growth* fund she researched rather than the target date option. The holdings in her personal portfolio would balance this choice. She designated her children as beneficiaries of the 401k, otherwise she learned it would just default to Neal as her husband.

Her first paycheck, minus her 401k contribution, was sobering. She had been accumulating cash in her bank account for her emergency fund, but now there was not going to be anything left over. She thanked fate that Olivia had come into her life. Given that she had no rent costs, health insurance expenses, or utility costs, she only had to cover her day-to-day living expenses. She could get by with the high 401k savings commitment. Putting aside so much for retirement was a luxury she knew many working families did not have.

Maggie had come to terms with the fact that most of the luxuries from her old life were now gone. She was not truly living paycheck to paycheck. Her cash-flow issues were self-imposed, and she had money to fall back on. She did occasionally miss the pampering and shopping without a thought as to the cost of things. She was often frustrated that she needed slimmer lunches and dinners the day or so before her paycheck got deposited. The end of the month was lean financially. She watched every cent she spent.

Maggie now regularly asked for overtime and Tammy was happy to give it to her to help cover Emma's absence. The extra income helped a lot, and Maggie was disciplined enough to put it all into her emergency fund, now earning two percent at her online bank.

As it turned out, Emma loved her new job in Finance. Tammy had made sure she understood that Maggie was the reason for her getting the job. Maggie periodically sent up suggestions to her regarding other reimbursements to review. As a result, Emma was doing really well upstairs, and considered Maggie her mentor. Maggie had even successfully coaxed Emma into starting to contribute to her own 401k. It was a good feeling, being able to provide practical advice. She often smiled thinking that Emma might have an easier retirement someday as a result of her coaching. As an added benefit, the medical records office was now a lot quieter as a result of Emma's relocation. It was a win-win for everyone.

Maggie was still nervous about the options contracts she had written. There was no reason to be, she told herself, as she had made relatively safe bets. But options were more complicated than simply buying stock for long-term investing. It was *trading* not *investing* which she had never envisioned herself doing. She checked the market when she could but felt guilty taking time from work.

Finally, Maggie asked Tammy about taking an hour from 9:30 to 10:30 a.m. to monitor the stock market as it opened. She explained she would take the time in lieu of lunch and that she would use her own laptop. Tammy looked at her over her glasses and asked, "Taking up day trading?"

Maggie looked embarrassed and assured Tammy it was more of a learning exercise. "I am trying to get a feel for the stock market to help me understand my mother's Trust holdings." Maggie had told Tammy about firing the people managing her mother's money. She had said she was going to try and manage it herself. "Now that I'm her trustee, I'd like to better understand the stocks she holds. It is not going to be forever," she assured Tammy. Maggie realized that she was uncomfortable admitting that she actually had her own account to monitor.

Tammy hesitated only for a moment, "The stock market? Isn't that like gambling?"

"No," Maggie assured her. " Generally, gambling relies a lot on luck. The stock market is about using information to take calculated risks."

"Well, still sounds like gambling to me. Let me know how you go, though. Wouldn't mind taking *calculated* risks. Do let me know if you figure out how to get rich quick," Tammy laughed. "You're welcome to spend your lunch hour watching stocks if you want to. It's all about output here and you code almost as fast as me, and I'm the best here. Please though, keep what you're doing private. I don't want anyone watching over your shoulder and getting any ideas."

Tammy allowed Maggie to create a workspace for herself in a small file room down the hall from the main office. Maggie found she could code while she watched her computer screen. Most of the time she spent checking the value of her put and call contracts, which usually mirrored the moves of the underlying stock. She also tuned into CNBC on her phone and listened to it while she worked.

Maggie noticed that the premiums on options moved more dramatically than the underlying stock prices. If a stock moved one percent, the option premium could move ten percent in value. Most of that was due to the simple fact that the options premiums were just smaller numbers—dollars and cents rather than share prices which were generally in the tens or hundreds of dollars per share. The other factor was that the option market was simply more volatile. Options were like opinions on stocks, and they could change radically over the course of the day. Stocks prices also shifted throughout the day, just not as much as the option premiums.

As the days went by Maggie also noticed that the premiums on her option contracts were also influenced by market or stock volatility. If the market was swinging wildly, or the stock itself was, option premiums seemed to increase in value. If options contracts were like insurance, then increased volatility was like weathermen predicting a bad hurricane season, prices when up.

Maggie began to find the first half hour after the market opened exciting. She would check the CNBC business news channel site for the *pre-market* report every morning when she got up. In addition to news about what may impact the market or specific stocks that day, there was always an indication of how the market would *open* relative to the close the day before. Events, both geopolitical and economic, could positively or negatively impact the open. The *up or down* projections were generally right initially, but frequently the trend did not hold. By 10 a.m., the market could be headed in a totally different direction.

The stock market was heavily influenced by news and rumors, political or economic. More than anything, it disliked uncertainty. Announcements about a poor economic indicator, like a slowdown in economic growth or a rise in unemployment, could send the market tumbling. She noticed many announcements, both national and company-specific, were timed so they came before the market opened or after the market closed at 4 p.m. Clearly, this was to give the traders time to digest the news. But tweets, rumors, and news still happened during the day. These, particularly ones about takeovers, tariffs, or accounting irregularities, could make a stock soar or plummet.

In that first half hour of the market, a lot tended to happen within Maggie's accounts. Her limit orders were frequently filled. By 10:30 a.m., the market seemed to settle on a rhythm for the day. Often, there was a slow up or down trend with gradual changes in direction throughout the day. Unless, of course, there was big news story or a tweet or an unexpected policy decision. Then there could be a huge, sudden swing in one direction or another. There was no set pattern; anything could happen. Maggie marveled at how quickly things could change, only to revert back the next day or week.

Maggie now tried to get home in time to actually watch CNBC during the last half hour before the market closed at 4 p.m. It seemed that the last half hour was when the greatest volume of shares seemed to trade. She learned that much of this volume was often simply machines closing out of positions for the day. CNBC's program, The Closing Bell, usually summarized the trading for the day. She picked up a great deal just by listening to all the market traders and analysts CNBC interviewed. She found that for every opinion about the market, there was usually someone with an opposite view.

Maggie learned that shares were also traded by professionals in the hours outside of market open. Graham had warned her about trading either after- or before-hours. He said the after-hours market had less liquidity, wilder stock price swings and more competition from institutional investors who were usually less price sensitive. Maggie saw an *after-hours* trading tab on her brokerage account, but she taught herself to ignore it. After-hours activity often seemed exaggerated, and the share prices could ricochet. Too risky for Maggie.

She began to watch the volume of stocks trading in addition to the direction of the market. There were red and green bars at the bottom of her Yahoo Finance market index chart, which indicated total share volumes. It gave her an indication of how active the market was. More activity usually meant there were more traders with greater conviction about the direction of the market, one way or another. Lower volume seemed to mean more uncertainty. Fewer people were willing to buy or sell, instead choosing to *sit out the market*.

Maggie got used to the daily shifting stock prices. There was a column on her account holdings page marked *Unrealized Loss/Gain*. It told her whether she had a gain or loss on her holdings on any given day, at any given time. This gain was *unrealized* because she still owned the shares. To *realize* a gain or loss on a stock, she would have to actually sell the shares.

Unrealized gains or losses were also called *paper* gains or losses. In this modern age, unrealized gains showed on her computer screen, not on a paper statement, but the term remained. Maggie learned to not get to attached to paper gains, they could be gone as quickly as they appeared.

The day her option contracts had sold, Maggie had been confused about how they appeared in her account. As Kate promised, the cash from each contract she had sold had shown up in her account as cash. Three hundred and fifty dollars for the AbbVie put contracts, and nine hundred and fifty for her McDonald's calls. The contracts were listed as a *holding*, just like her stocks, but her account showed the options' *cost basis* as a *negative* number.

Maggie understood the term *cost basis* when it came to stocks. It was what she had paid for the stock. When shares were sold, the cost basis was subtracted from money she received, the result being her realized profit. When the option expired, what was her profit if her *cost basis* was negative? She was confused.

She puzzled over this for days, working it through in her mind. Finally, she realized that the potential *profit* from an option contract had already been deposited in her account: it was the cash she had received when she sold the option contracts. The option's cost basis was negative because while the cash was in her account, it was not *really* a profit yet. It was only a potential profit, because she still had an open option contract, which was a liability. Since it was a liability and not yet an asset, she understood why an option contract showed up as a negative. As long as the contract existed, she might not get her profit. It would only be a *realized* profit when the option contract expired or was closed.

The unrealized gains or loss on her options contracts also fluctuated. This was because options contracts were constantly changing hands and premiums changes constantly. The value of her option contract was the option premium multiplied by the total number of shares represented by the contract. Her contracts sometimes showed a positive value, or profit, and sometimes a negative value, or loss. Just like stocks.

Maggie was surprised that the value of her option contracts changed so much daily. Sometimes her unrealized gain on a contract was very negative, other days positive. It could move between negative and positive in a single day, sometimes sharply. The option's premium value generally seemed to mirror the stock movement, albeit amplified.

Maggie noted that if AbbVie's stock price was down for the day, her put option became more negative and often showed a loss. Maggie assumed this was because as the stock price went down, it came closer to the put's strike price. As a result, the premium people were willing to pay for their "insurance" went up because it was more likely that the person selling the contract would get put. Conversely, the put became less negative—or even positive—when the stock price went up, because the likelihood she would get *put* went down and people would pay less of a premium for their "insurance."

The McDonald's calls had a similar relationship. When the stock moved up, and it was more likely to be called, the value of the option contract became more negative. She might then show an unrealized loss. When the stock fell, and the call option was less likely to be *exercised*, the option's unrealized gain became less negative or even went positive.

One key difference between stocks and options contracts was that options were also affected by time. This was because, as the option came closer to its expiration date, the likelihood of it reaching a particular price became clearer. With certainty, there was less price fluctuation. Since the strike prices Maggie had set were still far from the price where the underlying stocks were trading, the premium prices for her contracts got smaller as they both seemed increasingly unlikely to happen.

As it got closer to the third Friday of March, the values of both options contracts started swinging a bit more dramatically, in addition to the overall value for the premium dropping. Both contracts began to show an unrealized gain more frequently as they moved closer to the 19th of March. It was as if time was working on her side.

Maggie also used the hour she took every morning to learn about her trading screens. She would take a break from coding to click on tabs to see where it took her. There was a lot of information on the brokerage site's screen, and a lot of Greek letters. Gradually, she learned to tune out most of it. The screens made trading look more complicated than it needed to be, she thought. She assumed most of the additional information was something the more sophisticated day traders used. She put herself firmly in the KISS school of thinking—Keep It Simple, Stupid.

Maggie concentrated on the market's general movement, watching whether the line graphs that showed the major indexes—the DOW, the S&P 500, and the Nasdaq—were going up or down. She wanted to understand if there was any rhythm or pattern. She learned to create a split screen on her computer that allowed her to watch her unrealized gains column in her account while she also watched the indexes. She did not neglect her coding. She only glanced up every few minutes to watch what was happening.

Occasionally there was a sudden spike in the graphs or in a particular stock. She stopped coding then and tried to work out what had caused the sudden change. She found a site called Seeking Alpha that usually explained specific stock spikes. The CNBC site was also helpful, as it usually had a headline that explained a sudden market shift.

She was tempted on a couple occasions to sell her AT&T shares. They were now showing a nice little unrealized gain since she had purchased them, and she worried she would lose it. But then she thought she would have to wait until it went back down to buy it again, and she might lose the dividend. She realized that up until now she had only focused on what price to buy a stock at. She had assumed she would simply hold all of her selections forever. But watching the markets and listening to CNBC, she realized that there were situations when she might need to sell. Companies had failed strategies, stocks spike on merger news. Things that she liked about a stock, could change. She made a mental note to research when it was best to sell.

As time went on, she found herself checking the prices of her holdings on her phone throughout the day. She felt she was getting a little addicted to it. She liked to guess the direction and follow swings closely to try to understand what drove them. It was exciting for her, a lot more exciting than coding—but coding paid the bills.

On the morning of March 19th, neither AbbVie nor McDonald's was close to the strike price on their respective contracts. By the end of the day, both contracts were trading in the pennies, basically at zero. After the market closed, she was not sure what to expect. She felt deflated. She called Kate.

"What do I do now?" Maggie asked.

Kate laughed. "Enjoy how clever you are! You just made $1,250 in less than three weeks. Of course, you will have to pay Uncle Sam his cut. Today, the contracts you wrote expired. They ceased to exist. You are free and clear—and get to keep the premiums you were paid for creating the contracts in the first place. They're realized profits. And of course, the best part is that you are free to write them all over again for next month's expiration date!"

Maggie was stunned. She was still having trouble understanding how she had just earned well over a week's salary by simply trading a *promise* to do something. It was kind of thrilling. Like conjuring money out of thin air. It felt almost immoral.

It dawned on Maggie that she now had three ways that stocks could make her money: appreciation, dividends and trading options.

"I'm a little shocked," she said to Kate. She fell silent for a moment. In just a few months she had gone from knowing almost nothing about the stock market to this: her money working for her in ways she had never even knew existed. It had not been *that* hard. Doing some research, watching the business news, reading. Maggie breathed in deeply, appreciating what she had accomplished.

She then said to Kate, "I really stunned that it's so easy. I'm already thinking about next month's..." Then she remembered what Kate had said, "Wait, you guys don't take the taxes out of my trading profits?"

"No, you're going to have to have put aside cash to pay taxes on your profits at year end. Trading profits are generally treated like regular income, unless you have held the stock or the option contract for over a year. Then it is a long-term gain and has a different tax treatment."

Maggie said, "So, does your firm tell me how much I owe in tax?"

"No, everyone has a unique tax situation, so we really couldn't do it accurately. You'll get a statement from us at year's end called a 1099. It is like the W-2 you get at work. 1099s cover investment and interest income. It will tell the government how much you have earned in all your accounts with us for the year—the interest, the dividends you collected, and any trading gains or losses."

Maggie almost swore. *Taxes.* Yet again, she had not considered taxes. She thanked Kate for helping with her first option trades and said she would call her on Monday to do it again. Maggie decided she would send Kate some flowers to thank her for all the help especially as it related to options. She wanted to share her good fortune.

Maggie realized she was hooked on option trading. She decided to see if there were any other stocks she might write contracts on. She also decided to put the cash aside for any taxes in her emergency fund. She would set up a separate tax account if she found she was making more than a couple thousand dollars a year trading. It was unlikely, but she did not want to be caught out when she filed her taxes.

Her taxes had been simple last year. She had used the 1040EZ that Robbie recommended, but vaguely remembered that she could not use it if she had dividend income. She also realized that she had not reported the five thousand dollars in McDonald's dividends paid into her brother's and her bank account last year, or in the prior years. She may not have known about the income, but she knew she would have to make-up for not reporting it.

Furthermore, if she sold the McDonald's shares she might owe tax on the profits from that sale too. It could be a huge number, which would then put a major dent in her principle. Should she just leave the McDonald's shares alone?

Despite the victory on her options, all these tax questions now running around in her head left her feeling deflated. She had been so confident that she was on the other side of the learning curve when it came to investing. She had simply not considered the tax issues.

She suspected she had moved away from the simple one-page return to a more complicated tax return in just a year. She had visions of pages and pages of tax returns. Plus, she knew the IRS was looking at her taxes from earlier years. She was going to need professional tax advice.

Fortunately, Maggie had asked Olivia and Graham to have dinner with her that night. She had wanted to share her option outcome with someone, for better or worse, and she knew Graham would be interested. He would probably know someone who could do her taxes.

Dinner was Thai take-out, Olivia's favorite, which Maggie was proud to pay for. Olivia insisted on opening champagne when she heard about the success of Maggie's option trades. Graham, too, was very impressed. When they asked, Maggie managed to explain the basic principles of *cash-covered puts* and *covered calls* to them.

Graham, of course, knew about trading options, but usually avoided them. They were too complicated to really interest him, he explained. He did like day trading, but it tended to be on stocks where he anticipated a big move. He was very fond of the *mega* cap stocks like Amazon and Apple, which he bought and sold regularly. Maggie knew Graham was probably working with a great deal of money to be playing with Amazon and Apple, as these shares cost hundreds—if not, thousands—of dollars each.

Maggie asked Graham whether he thought her success was just beginner's luck. She stressed that she was only going to do puts on stocks she wanted to own and covered calls on the stocks she already owned. These were the simplest of option types, from what she understood. She wasn't seeing that much risk in these types of trades, and she wasn't going to put on a lot of positions. Was she missing something?

Graham began, "Maggie, I am sure you understand that there is a difference between investing and trading. Investing is what you do with a 401k, where you add money on a regular basis but rarely change its holdings. Income from an investment account is generally reinvested until there is a need for that money sometime in the future. Usually later in life when you are not working and need it to supplement Social Security payments.

"*Trading*," Graham continued, "is more of like a job. And it sounds like you will be *trading* options. I trade, and I am in front of the screen for the better part of most days. You have to keep up on the market, economics, and politics. And then there is the company-specific information for the companies you invest in. You move in and out of holdings frequently, even daily. You also have to make provisions for taxes. Most importantly, you have to be able to withstand market swings. It's risky and exciting, it feels like you are at the race track all day. For me, personally, I love it. I don't know if you're there yet."

Graham paused for a moment when he saw Maggie's disappointed look. He patted her hand and smiled. "In terms of the options you are doing though, Maggie, you should be fine. It sounds like you are using option contracts just to fill out what you want to buy and to add to the dividend returns you are looking for. I don't see that much risk if you keep your positions small and set strike prices ten-to-twenty percent beyond where stocks are trading. Especially if you are enjoying it."

Graham then went on to talk a little about his trading. He told Maggie he did trade most days, but he also had weeks he did not look at it. He traded more for fun than profit, although he did well enough to keep at it. He particularly loved *earnings season*, when companies reported their quarterly earnings and gave guidance on how much they expected to earn going forward.

"That's the time to play, Maggie," Graham said with a chortle. "Big changes when companies report earnings. Sometimes stocks can rise or fall by twenty percent or more! If you like to trade, you'll learn to love earnings season."

Maggie smiled and decided to talk to Kate about *earnings season* the next time they chatted.

Olivia interrupted Graham and deftly moved them both off the investing discussion. She found it all a bit dull. She gave them both an update on her brother. Olivia proudly said he was simply too stubborn to die. They also discussed some issues they were having with Bunny, who was increasingly unwilling to move around and was disinterested in her regular meals. Olivia was hand feeding her for the most part.

"Oh, Maggie, I forgot to tell you!" Olivia suddenly exclaimed. "Graham's half-sister, Libby, is moving back to Boston. She married an Australian and moved to Sydney over three decades ago. Unfortunately, her husband Dane, died last year so she is relocating back here. Grace, her only daughter, has married an American who works for a company downtown. Libby decided she wanted to be close to her daughter given that she's pregnant with Libby's first grandchild."

Olivia went on to tell Maggie that she was excited for her to meet Graham's sister, who was almost twenty years Graham's junior. She explained that she and Graham had spent long happy vacations with Libby and her husband in Australia. Olivia was of the strong opinion that Australia's laid-back approach to life rubbed off on people in a very good way.

Not wanting to get back onto financial topics and bore Olivia, Maggie waited until after dinner to ask Graham about her tax dilemmas. When Olivia went into the living room to select a movie, Maggie quickly explained her concerns about taxes on her option trades and the tax impact of selling the McDonald's shares.

She explained to Graham that she had done her taxes herself last year. This year, she knew she was going to need help—and she was worried that Robbie, her young accountant at H&R Block, might not be up to the job.

Graham smiled. "Goodness, Maggie. You are trading options, and you are worried about the complexity of taxes? The only reason anyone worries about taxes is because he or she is making enough money to have to pay them. They can be complicated, and mine certainly are. But yours? I *have* to assume they aren't that bad, at least, not yet. I understand your concerns though. How about this?

My company accountant is not busy now that I have scaled down my activities so much. I still pay him a full salary. George is one of my oldest friends. He has been with me for over fifty years. I am always looking for things to keep him working, so he doesn't feel like I am giving him a hand-out. Why don't you give him a call and go through your situation with him? He'll give you an opinion on how to handle all this. I'll give him a call tonight and let him know you will be in touch."

"Gosh, Graham, that would be fabulous, thank you!"

"George should be able to estimate a figure for you to put aside for your taxes at year end. He may also have some suggestions on easy ways to reduce your tax bill going forward. I have to say, I always rely on tax professionals when it comes to tax issues. I don't like to get on the wrong side with the IRS; that can be a long and complicated process that just wears you down. You should be fine, though. And by the way, if you go in to see him, take some of that honey of yours. George has one hell of a sweet tooth."

Olivia came back complaining she just wasn't in the mood for anything in her collection. She suggested perhaps a game or going out for a movie.

Maggie remembered the movie *The Big Short,* that Kate had recommended. She had really wanted to see it and asked if Graham and Olivia were interested. Graham was willing, he had also heard of it. Maggie assured Olivia that despite the subject matter being the financial crisis of 2008, it was supposed to be funny.

Maggie went up to her rooms and brought down her computer to show them a preview. They both thought it looked great. "Do we all watch it on your computer?" Olivia asked suspiciously.

Maggie went into the living room and turned on the TV. Olivia was shocked to find she had a *smart* TV that had Amazon preloaded. All Maggie had to do was sign in into her Prime account, which she had splurged on, and they were good to go. Graham laughed at Olivia's grudging acceptance of streaming. "Need to take her kicking and shouting into the future," Graham observed.

They poured themselves nightcaps and Olivia snuggled against Graham. Maggie found herself a soft blanket. They all watched the film and marveled at how much fun it was. It actually made clear how the entire financial world had been on the edge of catastrophe. It was sobering.

After it ended, Maggie said good night and made her way upstairs, still thinking about the movie. As she drifted off to sleep, she realized that the stock market meltdown that the film depicted had actually happened; it was not a dramatic device. As a result, her dreams were filled with plunging graphs, market chaos, and empty bank accounts. Investing did involve risks, her dreams whispered to her. She did not sleep well.

CHAPTER 18:
DEATH AND TAXES

"Short-term gains?"

Another new term for Maggie. She was meeting with Graham's accountant, George Cohen, in his home office not far from Olivia's. They had been talking about her investments and her option trading income.

"Yes, there are different tax rates for short-term versus long-term gains. Short-term gains, gains on something you have held for less than a year, are taxed at a person's personal tax rate. Profits from option trading—or any kind of trading—are usually short-term. Long-term gains, or *capital gains*, are gains from things you have held for over a year. That will be your McDonald's stock, if you sell it. Those types of gains are taxed at one of three different rates."

Maggie nodded, keeping up so far.

"If you are single and make less than $39,000 total—salary and everything—in a year, you do not pay tax on *any* capital gains. If you make between $39,000 and $426,000, you pay a fifteen percent tax on capital gains. If you make more than that, you pay twenty percent. Generally, the tax authorities make wealthier people pay more. Given what you have told me, you will probably have to pay fifteen percent. When you add all your overtime and your dividend income to your salary, you'll be well over the $39,000 threshold."

Maggie shuddered at the fifteen percent figure. It made her wonder if she should just leave the McDonald's shares alone and just collect the approximately 2.6% dividend. It was less than she wanted to make on her portfolio but if she sold some shares to diversify, as she had planned, she would have to immediately give up fifteen percent of any profit she made to pay the tax owed to the government.

George continued, "People generally pay more tax on short-term activity because it is taxed like income, and their personal tax rate is usually higher than fifteen percent. As a result, you need to be mindful of when you buy and sell stock. If you hang onto a position for more than a year, you only pay the long-term capital gains tax, fifteen percent."

Maggie frowned. "So, fifteen percent is actually lower?"

"Usually," George said. "Capital gains tax is why buy and hold is popular. People do not want to get hit with taxes, trading in and out of stocks all the time. If they hold a stock over a year they get taxed at the lower, long-term capital gains rate. Trading, rather than investing, can create a pretty big tax bill at the end of the year. You have to document everything. It really complicates a tax return."

In Maggie's imagination, her simple tax form multiplied and multiplied.

"Also, you generally pay lower taxes on dividends, again only fifteen percent for your tax bracket," George said. "Taxes are why getting money into a tax-deferred IRA or a 401k is all the more important—it is all tax free until you withdraw it. You need to look at your investment returns *after* tax to really understand how well you are doing."

Maggie found George very easy to talk to. He was avuncular, slow and deliberate in his speech. His office was cluttered and dusty. The coffee he had made her was instant with powdered cream. It was all very old school.

He wasn't what she had expected of an employee of Graham's, who always looked like he had stepped out of an ad for Breitling watches. Graham always wore expensive Italian shoes and beautiful, crisp white shirts. But maybe that was Olivia's doing, Maggie mused.

Maggie admitted to George that she did not know what her actual tax rate was. She and her husband had filed jointly in prior years, but she was divorcing him and would be filing as a single in the years ahead. She proudly told him that she had done her first tax return just last year but hadn't thought to calculate her effective tax rate.

George took her copy of her 1040EZ and her latest pay stub. "Is this what you expect to make again this year?"

Maggie shook her head, "I only worked a few months last year, and I have had a raise. My salary, with regular overtime, should be well over fifty thousand dollars this year. I also have a nest egg worth about five hundred thousand dollars, about half of which is in that McDonald's stock Graham told you about. My dividend income, once I complete my portfolio, should be about another seven thousand a year. I have started to trade options too and may make three or four thousand more. And I will get interest on the cash in my money market as well—that might be another thousand or so. All up, I think my investment income should be between twelve and fifteen thousand dollars. That would bring my total income to about seventy-five thousand dollars a year." Maggie said proudly. She had been very pleased with herself when she first estimated this figure. It was almost double what her starting salary had been.

Based on this estimate, George told Maggie her effective tax rate would probably be twenty-two to twenty-four percent. He told her she should put aside about a quarter of the profit she made trading option contracts, or any other trades she did, for paying federal taxes at year end. He said he would work out the Massachusetts state tax holdback as well and get back to her with a figure.

She told George that she liked the fact the hospital paid her taxes for her every two weeks. It made everything easier. While she had been frustrated seeing how much tax came out when she got her first W-2, at least she knew her taxes were paid. It was daunting to her that she was going to have to put money aside for a year-end tax bill.

George then said, "If you are going to be trading things like options contracts, you must discipline yourself to put aside tax money every time you have a successful trade. You don't want to be caught out at the end of the year, not having enough for your tax bill. If you wait, you might have to sell stock at a loss to raise cash to pay a tax bill. I have seen it happen. Mind you, if you end up with losses at the end of the year instead of gains, you can *refund* yourself the money you have put aside."

He laughed when she asked if she needed to pay FICA on her profits. "No, just tax. But it's still hefty, considering you have already paid tax on the money you are using for investment in the first place. Now you are paying tax on it again, as that post-tax money earns money. People call it *double taxation*."

Maggie said, "I was planning to sell some of the McDonald's stock to diversify my portfolio. I am nervous having half of it in a single stock. If I sell some, though, I assume I'll have to pay a lot of capital gains tax and it will reduce my principle. If it takes money to make money, then I assume having less money means *making* less money. Should I sell it? What would I owe in taxes on it?"

"The tax bill on that particular sale may be tricky," George replied. "While Graham told me about your windfall, he did not tell me where that came from exactly."

Maggie went into detail about finding the stocks certificates in her brother's things, and then getting them signed over to her and deposited.

"So, you and your brother were both minors when he died? I assume he had no will. Legally, the shares would have passed to your parents when he died, not to you," he said. Maggie had not thought about this. "Are they living?" he asked.

Maggie explained her father had passed away years ago, but her mother was still alive. Unfortunately, she explained, her mother is both mentally and physically incapacitated. Maggie explained, "I'm the trustee on my mother's Trust and her Executor. If that makes any difference."

"Hmm. Well, for the time being, do not sell the shares and don't write options on them. I need to do a little digging on that one." George looked thoughtful. "Have you read your mother's will?"

"Yes, it's very short. Everything she has will come to me when she passes. She is healthy, though, and I'm told she has a strong heart. Sometimes I worry a little that her Trust fund could run out if she has any major medical events. It was being depleted at an alarming rate these past few years, though I think I've stemmed the bleeding. The income her Trust generates does not cover all her expenses, so I have to dig into principle every year to pay her bills. She has Medicare and supplemental health insurance, but there are still bills that are not completely covered."

"What is the current value of her trust?"

"About $1.9 million. I know that sounds like a lot, but her care costs well over one hundred thousand per year. It is staggering how much it costs. She is in her mid-eighties but there are a lot of residents on her floor who are well into their nineties. My grandfather lived to ninety-seven George looked at her sympathetically. "Yes, the expense is staggering. Sounds like she is at a facility that does a wonderful job caring for her. Other options can be a little, well, *grim*."

Maggie could tell by his expression that he had firsthand experience.

They talked a little more. At her request, he walked her through the additional form she would have to file with her taxes next year regarding her investment income. He also highlighted how the tax form, the 1040, differed from the 1040EZ. It was a pretty minor difference.

She thought she could still handle filing her taxes at year's end, doing it on her own. She kept great records as part of her budgeting. She had created a row of jars on her desk for all her receipts, one marked health, another food, etc. She was doing it to get a better understanding on where her cash was going, but she realized it would help with her taxes as well. Once they had gone through the form, Maggie realized her taxes appeared manageable and she felt a lot less stressed.

As they were wrapping things up, Maggie finally admitted that she was having an "issue" with the IRS. This raised George's eyebrows. There was no way to half-tell it so the story poured out: Neal being gone, the FBI, the Trust's mismanagement, her not reporting the unknown dividends, and her refund being held up. Maggie bit her lip and said quietly, "Honestly? My biggest concern is that I might be liable for something enormous, since I co-signed on our old taxes. I just never asked about anything."

"Do you have copies of your past returns?"

"No, nothing. Neal appears to have taken all our paperwork." Maggie explained she had planned to pick copies up from the IRS, but the FBI agent had told the situation had been bumped up to a higher level. He said the IRS agent she had talked to was not involved any more.

"Well," George said, "this is getting interesting. You have a right to those returns, and you should have a look at them and see what kind of trouble your husband may have gotten you into. If you would like, I have a power of attorney here. It gives me the right to act on your behalf as your representative with the IRS. Would you like me to take a look?"

Maggie was torn. More than anything, she would like to understand what was going on with the taxes—some insight, perhaps, into what Neal had done. She worried, though, that she might trigger something that could rebound on her. The IRS scared her, she admitted to George. For no other reason than rumors. She had no real experience with them.

George understood her concerns, but said, "Better out than in, as they say. You need to have some idea what you are up against, and information is power. The more they keep you in the dark, the more you are beholden to them. I imagine they like you a bit uncomfortable. Without information, they can frighten you into doing something you may not want or need to do. They are *your* returns; you are entitled to them. I would get them if I were you."

Maggie realized George was right and told him so. He then rummaged through his files and produced a power of attorney form for her. They filled it out and then she signed it. As she was leaving, she pulled out a jar of her honey from her only remaining designer bag, prettily wrapped, and handed it to him as a thank you for his time.

She asked him if he would please keep track of the hours he spent on her case. She needed to speak to Graham about it. George guessed where she was going with the request and said, "If you are worried about payment, I'd just ask that you keep me in this honey. Love the natural stuff, had it as a child because my dad kept bees. Store-bought just doesn't compare. I haven't found any regular source for it. It's like gold to me. I use it every day at breakfast."

Maggie thanked him again. He told her he would be in touch once he got copies of her returns and had a chance to go through them.

By the time Maggie got home, the sun was going down. The house was darker than normal, no lights on in the kitchen. At first, she thought Olivia must not be home. It was Friday night. Maybe she had gone out.

She let herself in and heard muffled sobbing. She found Olivia in the living room with Buster in her lap and a drink and a bottle at her side. She was, Maggie guessed, more than a little "sloppy." Olivia's face was wet, her perfect make-up running. Maggie sat down next to her, concerned.

It took Olivia a moment to get it out. Bunny was gone, she sobbed. She had been put down at the vet that afternoon with Olivia by her side. It was not just age that had been slowing her down, but probably cancer as well, the vet suspected. And she said that Bunny was in pain. Olivia made the decision that it was time. Bunny was almost eighteen, after all. She had lived a long and wonderful life.

Olivia said she had been fine initially, staying strong at the vet. She had broken down when she got home and saw Bunny's things. She told Maggie she was surprised it was affecting her this way. She knew Bunny had lived longer than anyone expected. She was only a dog. Olivia never thought of herself as someone who mistook her pets for people.

Maggie listened as Olivia went on. "I suppose it is partly what she represented to me. Graham bought her for me when we finally accepted there were not going to be any children, even with all the miracles of science. I was a little blue back then. I was indifferent to her at first, but she was *so* persistent. You never knew her when she was young. Smartest little thing you ever saw, and so much energy. Twice the work the two of them are now. She swam, you know? Loved to swim. Had to pull her out of the water all the time, worried that she would swim herself to death. I've ruined some great boots wading into the water after her."

Maggie said she would have liked to have known Bunny back then. They talked about the type of puppy she had been, and how the little dog had taken over Olivia and Graham's lives in some ways.

Olivia explained, "We got Buster to distract Bunny from aging; she had started to slow. She was over ten then but she really rallied and mothered him. I'm sure getting Buster added years to Bunny's life."

Then they talked about Buster and how he'd cope without her, both of them laughing about dog antidepressants. They then talked about dogs in general, and what they could mean in people's lives.

Finally, as Olivia got control of herself, they agreed to order take-out from the steak house so Buster could also help celebrate Bunny's life. Both women were sad, but Buster looked even more so. The little dog seemed to know that there had been a major shift in his life. Both women ended the night sadly acknowledging that time moves on, drinking toasts to Bunny until they were both flushed, befuddled, and ready to sleep.

Graham had been in New York when Bunny died. Olivia had called him from the vet, and he appeared at the house the next morning to spend the weekend there. He looked as devastated as Olivia had been, perhaps more so. Very pale and sober. He picked up and cuddled Buster rather than his usual reaction, which was to tease and bait him.

Olivia smiled when she saw the way Graham babied Buster. She had told Maggie he had always doted on the dogs, although he rarely admitted it. She believed if she had given him custody of them, it is unlikely they would be together today. He might not have pushed for those initial visits with her.

Brody arrived at the house a little later that same morning. He and Maggie had a hike in the Blue Hills planned. When he heard the news, he hugged Olivia and told her how sad he was for her. Olivia spontaneously invited him to stay the weekend. He readily agreed.

Maggie quickly pulled Olivia aside and told her she had to offer Brody a guest bedroom. Olivia's eyes widened mischievously. "Not there yet? Time's a wastin', you know." Maggie blushed.

They decided to cook a feast for dinner, a wake of sorts for Bunny, with apple pie for dessert. The hike was postponed as Maggie was feeling a little less than energetic after her prior evening with Olivia. The men were excited all out of proportion at the dessert proposal.

"What is it about men and apple pie?" Olivia asked Maggie.

Maggie and Brody shopped for groceries, and he picked up what he needed for an impromptu overnight. They cooked together, but Olivia took over the apple pie making. After dinner they played card games from their respective childhoods, then took a second dessert course and finished the pie and most of the ice cream. Both Olivia and Graham bemoaned the lack of proper custard in America.

Olivia and Graham went up to bed, leaving Maggie and Brody alone. They started slow dancing to silent music in the kitchen, and as Brody's kisses became more urgent, Maggie pulled away.

"Hey," she said softly. "I need to say something here. I would *really* like to take this where it is heading, more than I think you know. But I have a problem, and his name is Neal. I know it is old fashioned of me, even silly in this day and age, but I am still married."

Brody looked hesitant. "Which means what?"

"Well, I haven't said anything to you yet, but I have a lawyer and I am moving to divorce Neal. I had hoped to be further along by now. I am waiting to hear from her. She was supposed to call me and hasn't."

"Oh, wow, that *is* a step forward," Brody said watching Maggie closely to try and read her reaction.

"I've told the children. They are upset, but they know my plans. I don't know exactly what you and I are doing, but it feels like it is something very real. I'd like to be able to introduce you to the kids, but at the right time and with a clear conscience. I think, too, we need to do that to be fair to Ethan. If you two are going to have a relationship, it should be built on solid ground."

Brody looked down, his frustration clearly written on his face. "Yeah, I get that. I understand and it sounds like the right thing to do. I can wait, hard as it is. But please, Maggie, for the love of God, call your lawyer first thing Monday morning and put a stick of dynamite under her. I want you to be free. I want to meet Ethan, and your girls and," he barreled on without taking a breath, "you need to be free because it seems like I to want to marry you."

It took a moment for both of them to realize what Brody had just said. They both knew it was partly the alcohol, but now that it was out there, he hesitated before plowing on.

Brody stepped back and looked Maggie in the eye. "Look, Maggie, this thing between us has never felt to me like a casual *getting to know you* flirtation. These past few weeks have been nothing like my other relationships. I didn't even feel like this when I was dating my wife. It's a deeper involvement for me, more permanent, more like a partnership. And I am desperate to move back to a physical relationship again, as you can no doubt tell. I want us to be together."

Maggie was speechless. She knew he had feelings for her, but she had no idea they ran this deep.

He went on, "I have not felt this way about anyone since the last time I was with you. Looking back, I am frustrated that I held back then out of fear of looking like an over eager fool. I just figured I was in the midst of a run-of-the-mill, twenty-something passion. If I had known then how rare it was to find the type of chemistry we have, this connection, things would have turned out differently."

Maggie looked at Brody and said softly, " It doesn't feel casual to me, either."

In her mind, Maggie had rationally put her feelings down to being older and not wanting to waste time. She finally admitted to herself that her feelings were very intense when it came to Brody, particularly her physical desires. Up until now, she had chosen not to look at them too closely.

He looked at her questioningly now. "You know, all of that just came out. I thought I'd raise the marriage issue at the right time, do it the right way. I just wanted you to know where I see this heading. A benefit of being older, I guess. You have learned what you want, not to waste time." His eyebrows knit together. "But was I wrong to say it? Have I overstepped? Is it too soon? Never?"

Maggie embraced him again and cuddled into his chest. She began talking into his sweater. "Not totally unexpected but startling still the same. I can't give you an answer if this is a proposal. Yes, it's probably too soon, given I *am* still married. But not *never*. I'm more than a little nervous about how we tell Ethan. More importantly, I have just started getting my life going again and finding my feet. Thinking about starting another marriage now seems like I would be stepping out of the life I am just starting, a little like going backward, maybe."

He pulled her away and looked at her face. "Backward? You think I want you barefoot and pregnant, taking care of my every whim? Have you seen my lifestyle? I need *independence* in a wife, not someone waiting for my footstep at the door every night."

Maggie sighed, "Well, you know what you want in a wife, but I don't know yet what I want in a husband. Or if I even want a husband at all. I haven't given it a thought beyond knowing what I don't want. I need to work out what my *baseline life* is like, and then figure out what I want to add back in."

Maggie's position was not something Brody readily understood. Maggie said she was having trouble understanding it herself, or even articulating it clearly. They moved into the living room and talked for another hour or so, Brody mapping out all the different scenarios of what their life together could be. Life in Boston, or one of the other places he had a place to stay. Getting a house, or not. Travel, working together, or her keeping her job at the hospital. He was open to anything.

Maggie listened. It was wonderful, being wanted and having someone trying to build a life with you. Brody's plans excited her, but nothing was egging her on to say, "Yes." She was not even close to being ready to commit to anything or anyone. She knew she needed more time for herself before she was ready. Finally, she said, "Nothing has to be resolved tonight, Brody. I'm just so overwhelmed by all this. Thrilled too, I think. But definitely overwhelmed. Let's call it a night." Brody sighed heavily. "I get it, too much too soon. Damn Graham and his excellent taste in wine." They chastely hugged each other goodnight and went up to their separate rooms.

Maggie was the first downstairs in the morning and made herself coffee, humming happily. She had gotten raspberries and sour cream when shopping with Brody, and with them she made muffins and then, inspired, a quiche. Brody was the next one down about an hour later, complaining he had not been able to sleep until he had had, not one, but *two* cold showers.

When he saw the quiche and muffins, he joked they were going to have to accelerate a wedding if she cooked like this every day. They flirted with each other and were both giddy. If he was disappointed by her reaction last night, he did not show it. Brody asked if he could tell Graham and Olivia about the marriage idea and enlist their help in winning Maggie over. She pleaded with him to hold off. Maggie knew that Olivia would not let it rest.

"That's the point." Brody grinned.

It was just after ten when Olivia finally came down to the kitchen with Buster in her arms. She was pale, without any make-up. For the first time since Maggie had known her, she looked her age. Her hair was combed neatly, and she was dressed but it was just a bare minimum. She cuddled and kissed Buster, keeping him in her arms, but did not say anything.

"Olivia?" Maggie knew then. She didn't know how she knew, but she did. She felt the sorrow reach deep into her bones. Her eyes welled up. Olivia finally spoke, almost in a whisper.

"Graham died in the morning sometime. I tried to wake him. He was still warm, but he wouldn't wake up. He's cooler now. I think we need to call someone. His wife should be told."

Brody was up and over to Olivia in a moment, enveloping her in a hug. Maggie followed, tears rolling down her face. Buster did not complain, despite being squashed. They stood for only a brief moment until Brody pulled away. He took charge and had Maggie get Olivia a coffee, which she spiked with a bit of whiskey from the bar in the living room, while he went upstairs. When he came down, he shook his head at Maggie.

"I've called the police and explained the situation." Brody said. "They are on their way over. We will get things sorted for you, Olivia. There is nothing to worry about. We will take good care of him."

The police arrived shortly after. Brody showed them to the bedroom. Graham was in pajamas, tucked neatly in bed. He looked older, his face gray and slack. His clothes were neatly put away and his reading glasses were folded on the bedside table. The police were surprised to hear that this was not his home. Graham had a closet filled with his clothes and the bathroom showed two sets of toiletries. They were even more surprised when they heard Olivia was the ex-wife, not the current one.

Eventually, the police went downstairs and gently spoke to Olivia. They all moved into the living room so that Olivia would be more comfortable. She spoke in a monotone. She explained the evening, the dinner, and the cards. She said they had gone to bed and had sex like they always did. Then they talked a bit, and both fell asleep. Nothing unusual, no angry words or wild sex, just another night together, like so many others. Olivia explained they had both been a little flat, as one of their dogs had died that afternoon. Neither of them had been feeling particularly frisky.

In the morning, Olivia explained, she awoke at sunrise and went to the bathroom. Coming back to bed, she noticed how still he was. She called him and tried to shake him awake. She could not feel him breathing, and she said she knew then. She lay down and talked with him until he began to get cold. She knew then that she should get up and tell someone. That it was done.

She told the officers, Graham's current wife should be contacted. She explained that they lived apart, that Graham had his own place in Boston. She asked Maggie to get her address book for her and then gave the policemen both Graham and his wife's information. While the officers exchanged looks, they did not ask questions.

They did ask Olivia about Graham's health. She explained he had had some minor strokes over the years and was on blood-thinning medication. He had not had any pills last night, of course, because he had not expected to be here. He came because of the dog's death. She did not have any of his pill bottles here, so she couldn't say exactly what else he was taking. She gave them a key to his apartment so they could check there.

The medical examiner and the paramedics arrived while the police were talking with Olivia. They went up and examined Graham, then gave the room a once over. Brody repeated what he had heard Olivia say about the strokes. The examiner checked the bathroom for pill bottles and the bedside table. He took photos. He wrote things up on his clipboard and checked off answers. After ten minutes or so, he told the paramedics they could move Graham's body. Everyone was respectful and subdued; there was a practiced ritual to the process.

Olivia started when the stretcher came down the stairs. She started to rise and then sat back down, trembling. Graham left the house. Maggie's silent tears started again. Olivia did not get up, nor did she shed a tear. Her replies to the questions were dry and matter of fact. To know Olivia was to know how out of character her every word sounded; there was no life in them at all.

Maggie sat with Olivia the whole time. Eventually she was asked to step into the kitchen and also questioned about the evening before—same questions, similar answers. The police asked about Maggie's relationship to Graham and then about Olivia and Graham's. Maggie explained, tears coming again to her eyes, that theirs was a loving relationship and that she had never heard them say a single cross word to one another. When asked about Graham's wife, Maggie simply shook her head and said she had never met her. The police were straightforward and professional. After they finished with Maggie, Brody was called into the kitchen. Afterwards the medical examiner and the policemen huddled for a few moments. The medical examiner came over to express his condolences to everyone before he departed, the police followed shortly after.

In two hours, it was all done. Everyone had left. The three of them faced each other in the living room, Maggie and Brody both looking at Olivia. No one knew what they were supposed to do.

CHAPTER 19:
ESTATE PLANNING

Olivia was a mess, literally and figuratively. Brody went back Sunday night. He had a meeting he needed to attend. When he hesitated about going, Maggie insisted he leave. He asked Maggie to keep him posted about the funeral.

Maggie emailed Tammy on Sunday night and asked for the week off to stay at home to take care of Olivia and Buster. If anyone doubted a dog could be depressed, they would only have to look at Buster to know it was possible. Olivia, meanwhile, just looked blank.

Olivia stayed dry-eyed. She wore the same clothes she had worn the day Graham died—Maggie suspected she was sleeping in them. She put meals in front of Olivia that she only picked at, and Buster followed suit. Olivia excused herself and kept to her room, most often sleeping when Maggie quietly checked in on her.

Tuesday morning, more to have something to do than because she wanted to, Maggie called the divorce lawyer. The conversation was not what Maggie expected. The lawyer, Alex West, began a little haltingly.

"I didn't call you because my private detective, Rick, is being circumspect, which is quite unusual for him. Umm, were you aware the FBI was involved in your husband's disappearance?"

Maggie said she was. "I'm sorry, is that a problem? It's some trouble with his firm, I think."

Alex said grumpily, "Well, it becomes a problem when FBI agents show up at Rick's door and ask him to *cease and desist* contacting people associated with your husband. They do not look fondly on investigators who insert themselves into one of their investigations."

"Who would your investigator be contacting?" Maggie was suddenly worried that the children might be pulled into this.

"Former business associates, his roommate, his acquaintances. I don't think Rick had gotten very far. It was only a few hours after he spoke to your husband's roommate that the FBI arrived on his doorstep discouraging any additional inquiries."

"Roommate?" Maggie was confused. She didn't think Neal had kept up with any college friends.

"The woman who shares his work apartment in the city. It looks like he was operating his business offices from there, the apartment I mean. Since your husband travels a great deal, they had an arrangement where she lived there rent-free in exchange for basic secretarial services."

At this point, her voice softened a bit. "Rick was a little suspicious of the relationship, I'm sorry to tell you. She was a pretty tight-lipped young lady. He had intended to follow up and confirm his suspicions but hasn't been able to make contact with her again. He seems to think she is being watched."

The news of an apartment in the city was a surprise to Maggie. The woman was an even bigger one. Oddly, she found she really didn't care if there had been anything going on between them. She just wondered how she had missed the signs. And Neal was operating *his office* out of the apartment? What had happened to his firm? She exhaled heavily. Clearly there was something major going on. She was frustrated at herself for being so blind. "Look. I really don't care about this woman or what her relationship is to my husband. Can I just get the divorce going? I don't need cause or anything."

If Alex was surprised at Maggie's lack of interest in Neal's female roommate, she didn't show it. "If there's not an issue on your end with the FBI, I'm happy to do that. The paperwork is ready. I can start the process today."

"I've no issue with the FBI as far as I know. I've spoken to them on multiple occasions. They have never suggested I was being looked into. In fact, it was the lead FBI investigator who told me it was possible to divorce a missing spouse. So yes, please file and start advertising and keep me posted on progress, I'd very much like to get this divorce behind me."

After she got off the phone, Maggie found she was actually shaking a little. Neal had another life she had known nothing about. The distance between them, that she had assumed was just a product of familiarity, was more than that. Neal had been actively keeping things from her for some time. No wonder her FBI contact was so vague with her, he must have assumed she knew more than she did.

It made her angry, but also more than a little sad. What a waste of a life for both of them.

She needed company so she went to find Olivia but again found her asleep in her room. Maggie closed her door and then brought her laptop down to the kitchen, in case Olivia woke up and wanted something to eat. To distract herself, she pulled up her investment account page. The market was down so she wrote a put contract for AbbVie and then two others, all expiring on April 21. Since McDonald's was down as well, she was not even tempted to write a call. She would wait until the stock was having an up day, it would mean a bigger potential option premium.

She then phoned Brody to let him know she had followed up with the divorce lawyer and things were in motion. She didn't say anything about Neal and the other woman, she was not sure why. He asked after Olivia and she said it was more of the same. People called Olivia, but she always kept the calls short. She was tired and listless. She was sleeping a lot. Maggie said she was just giving Olivia time.

Brodie asked about the funeral arrangements and Maggie realized she had no way to know when the funeral would be. She Googled Graham's name while on the phone and found a glowing obituary. She learned a lot about Graham's life that she would have liked to talk with him about. It sounded like he had lived large—had Olivia been part of all that? There was no mention of a service. No mention of Olivia in the obituary at all, it just noted that he was survived by his current wife.

On Thursday morning, the bell rang. Maggie opened the door to find herself staring at a solid, striking, and well-tanned blonde about her age with a suitcase in tow. She introduced herself as Libby Owens and asked after Olivia. Maggie took her coat and showed her into the living room. She said she'd see if Olivia was awake.

As she headed upstairs, she saw the woman get up and circle the room, touching photos and other items. Maggie hurried to Olivia's room and knocked softly. Letting herself in, she found Olivia curled up on her bed with Buster. She was about to let herself back out when Olivia opened her eyes and said she wasn't hungry. Maggie said gently that it wasn't lunch she was there about; it was a guest for Olivia. A woman named Libby Owens.

Olivia roused herself. She gathered up Buster and went to the bathroom to brush her teeth and wash her face. Maggie was surprised to see that she added lipstick as well. Olivia told Maggie to join them; she was in for a treat. This was Graham's little sister.

Olivia and Libby fell into deep embrace with one another, both becoming teary eyed. Libby was quick to tell Olivia that she had only learned of Graham's death two days ago. Even then, it had only been by chance, as one of her son-in-law's acquaintances had forwarded the obituary to him.

As she pulled away from her and prepared to sit down, she snapped, "That bloody bitch didn't even call me."

For the first time in days, Olivia smiled a weak smile. "I think she might be a bit cross about where he died. She knows you and I are close."

Libby explained she had come directly here from the airport. She had not bothered to contact Graham's wife yet. Olivia insisted she stay with them at the house. Maggie went into the kitchen to prepare coffee for them and overheard Olivia tell Libby about Graham's last day. It was poignant in the retelling. Olivia had paid attention to details that Maggie hadn't noticed that night, like how Graham had snuck an extra sliver of pie or that he had allowed Brody to win at a card game he was just learning for the first time.

Olivia assured Libby that Graham's death had been painless and quick. She told her how much Graham had been looking forward to her relocating to the area. She apologized for not calling directly, but she assumed that the wife was supposed to handle notifications. She smiled wryly and said, "I thought I had stepped on her toes enough."

When Maggie returned with a tray of coffee and muffins, Olivia officially introduced her as a close friend, rather than a tenant. This pleased Maggie more than she could have imagined. Libby mentioned to Maggie that this was the house she grew up in. She had known the woman who had lived in Maggie's wing. She then winked at Olivia, as she explained, "I was very close to her."

Olivia smiled at Libby, and then turned to explain to Maggie that after Graham's mother's death—and the housekeeper's divorce from the landscaper—close quarters had done its magic. Libby was the result. Graham's dad and "Mrs. Potts," as Graham had always called Libby's mom, had married. Libby was a late-in-life child for both of them. Graham adored his unexpected little sister.

Maggie had not picked up on that before, that the house had actually belonged to Graham's family. This led to Libby telling her about Graham's mother, who she had referred to as "Saint Anne." Libby, of course, had not known her, but Graham's memories enshrined her. His mother had been English and had died of an untreated infection. Graham was only a teenager at the time. After his father, then stepmother died, the house came to him. Libby was already living in Australia. The house had always been kept as an homage of all things English. Libby laughed and said that Graham always considered Olivia his *crowning English acquisition.*

Libby was full of happy Graham stories and Olivia's color returned as Libby pulled remembrances and family legends out for both of them to hear. Maggie realized the stories were more for Olivia than her, who perked up listening to them, adding details and expanding on the stories. Maggie saw that some of her color was coming back. After an hour or so, Olivia asked Libby if she would call Marilyn, Graham's wife, and see about the service time. She said she would be there no matter what.

Libby excused herself to make the call. It wasn't long before Maggie heard Libby's raised voice. Libby barked "No right" and "disrespectful" until she angrily stalked back into the room, clearly well beyond livid. "She had him cremated! Against his specific wishes. She does not want him buried. She is keeping the ashes," Libby sputtered. "*And get this*, she had a memorial service! Yesterday! Did not even try to call me, had it at her apartment in the city."

Olivia stirred to life, feeding on Libby's fury.

"Graham had all his wishes for a service laid out," Libby raged. "He spent years refining it! I even have a copy. There's a family plot. Who disregards all that?"

Olivia's eyes flared to life. "Someone who knows the cemetery plot next to him is the one he bought for me." Suddenly, she began to look like the Olivia that Maggie had always known.

From that moment forward, Libby and Olivia became united on a warpath. They made plans to meet with Graham's lawyers and find a venue for the service Graham had specified in his will. They wanted Graham's ashes and they wanted to give him the service he had so carefully laid out. These had been his last wishes, and they were going to be granted.

As the tension grew over the next week, Olivia admitted she had been foolish not to remarry Graham when he had asked. She had never envisioned that his wishes would not be followed, or that a wife of three years could trump one of over twenty. Her lawyers pointed out that even children could not override the current spouse's position, unless specifically contravened by a legal document. Olivia smiled when she learned that Graham had created just such a document. Graham had had so much foresight—he made sure his wishes would be adhered to, by law, if necessary. Anyone who knew him well, would not have been surprised.

Olivia also took comfort in the fact that most of his old friends had been bewildered when they had gone to the service at the apartment. As the week wore on, she spoke to most of them. They all gossiped about how odd the wife's service had been. It had been all *her*. There was no discussion of Graham's life or death, beyond her alluding to his unexpected death as having been the result of *a stroke while on a business trip.*

Libby made sure word got out about the real circumstances of his death and the impending "War of the Ashes," as she called it. Graham's true friends, and there were many, all rallied around Olivia.

Friday morning, Olivia and Libby manned the phones, coordinating lawyers and the potential service. Maggie stayed up in her room, watching the market and her account. Since the market was down again, she wrote three more put option contracts for stocks she wanted to buy, now extending up to her *cash* limit for her cash covered puts. She could not write any more put contracts to sell unless she added cash to her account. She had been happy to find out that the McDonald's stock counted as collateral in terms of the cash covered puts. However, because it was stock and not actual cash, the value of the collateral was discounted by a percentage set by the brokerage firm – after all the McDonald shares could fall in value unlike actual cash.

She knew it was a little risky, effectively using these shares as collateral. If the put contracts were actually exercised, she would have to sell the McDonald's shares to raise the necessary money to buy the shares she was put. She set the strike price for the put options twenty percent below where the stock was currently trading. She felt it was unlikely she would be put. While George had told her not to sell call options on McDonald's, she figured she was safe using them as collateral for her put contracts.

When she finally went downstairs for a late breakfast, she found the kitchen table covered in papers. As part of his estate plan, it turned out Graham had a lengthy outline for his *End of Life Celebration*. It was very detailed and well over ten pages long.

Olivia showed it to Maggie. It was quite specific as to the service, the burial, and the reception. It listed the music, the order of service, and even the drinks to be served at the reception—Pimm's Cups, whatever they were. There was a playlist of English bands he had danced to in his youth and some poetry he wanted to be read.

Every guest was to be given the school scarf from the English university he attended for his graduate degree in economics—he had two boxes of them stored in Olivia's basement. He wrote he liked the idea that people would remember him when they used them. Like Graham himself, the scarves were warm, snug and very British.

In addition to the witnessed will, Graham's lawyers had also given Olivia copies of Graham's power of attorney, living will, and trust documents. His power of attorney would have granted her broad power over his financial and property holdings not to mention authority to make healthcare decisions for him. He had even added a healthcare proxy to absolutely ensure Olivia had complete control over his medical care. His living will set out what he wanted in terms of care in the event he was unable to make his own health care decisions. Then there were trust documents that neatly packaged up his assets so that the courts would have limited need to be involved. It was all very clear.

Olivia was also the co-executor on his estate, along with his long-standing attorney. There was even, what looked like to Maggie, personal, handwritten letters addressed to both Olivia and Libby. Both opened envelopes were on the table as well. He had carefully planned his estate so Olivia and Libby would know exactly what he wanted and have the least stress possible.

Olivia wouldn't need many of the documents now, but she was still grateful for them. "Look, Maggie," she said as she held up the power of attorney, "Graham gave me full say when it came to his health and finances. Can you imagine the cat fight that might have happened at the hospital when Marilyn found out? I would have had complete control over how his medical treatment should go. Can you imagine if he hadn't granted me this? If Graham had been in a coma after the stroke? Marilyn could have left him on life support forever. She wouldn't have wanted to trigger the will. He might have wasted away as a living husk."

She looked out, staring into space, and went on softly, "Of course, we had talked about how we wanted the end of our lives to go. We planned on going together, of course. Preferably during a dramatic romantic moment. Like that old couple in Titanic. But I guess given Graham's living will, he was a little more practical than he let on. Maybe it was the strokes that made him cautious," Olivia paused here, thinking about this.

She continued as Maggie helped herself to coffee. "He had told me multiple times, in passing, that he did not want to have machines breathing for him or any extraordinary efforts to extend his life. He did not want his last days spent in pain or hooked up to machines in a hospital bed. Clearly, he wanted to make sure I listened. He actually wrote this it all out, in this living will. I think he knew it would help me be strong if it ever came down to it. That everything was in writing I mean. A legal document."

Maggie had not heard about living wills. She guessed this was one of the reasons Graham had been so keen to divorce Marilyn and remarry Olivia. Obviously, new wives could trump other family members, even adult children, when it came to end of life medical care. It was good to know there were legal ways to designate who you wanted to be making those decisions.

Libby then said to Olivia, "Marilyn would also have been furious about that power of attorney too, since it covers finances. No raiding the piggy bank for her if Graham became incapacitated. A power of attorney would have given you full control over Graham's accounts and financial affairs. From what I can see here, it is clear that Marilyn is not listed as a co-owner on any of his bank or investment accounts. She just has a small joint account that he pays a monthly stipend into. If he had been incapacitated in anyway, you would have had full control of the money. It's pretty clear which of you he trusted."

Maggie was startled to hear Marilyn also had only access to a small joint bank account. She suddenly wondered if Neal's excluding her from their accounts had been a lack of trust, rather than a simple oversight. Graham had clearly made a deliberate choice.

Olivia sighed. Maggie moved behind her and embraced her in a hug, almost spilling her coffee on Olivia in the process. Olivia patted her hand and continued,

"I am just glad that his will designates me as his executor. Now that we have his death certificates, I'm able to get the lawyers going to fight Marilyn."

The will itself was a long document, very well-thought out and detailed. Olivia explained to Maggie that Graham's wife had been left the spacious, multi-million-dollar apartment she was living in and all the goods inside. There was also a three-million-dollar trust that would provide her an income until she was six-ty-five, at which point she could have access to the principle. It was clear Graham did not trust her with money.

Most of his estate was left to Olivia and his sister. There were, of course, behests to his favorite charities. He had sat on the Board of many of these. Not surprisingly, these behests were also specific. Money was directed for this partic-ular project or that building. He had clearly kept the charity behests updated with *codicils*; he was not one to let his money be frittered away.

Graham also made provisions for his company to be wound down and the proceeds to be put in another trust which George Cohen would run. Remaining employees would be paid their full salaries until their respective retirement ages and health insurance paid in perpetuity. He had always fully matched their 401k's. The five or so employees who were left, including George Cohen, found them-selves generously provided for.

Olivia had already been deeded the house in the divorce. While her gener-ous alimony would now end, another trust had been set up for her which provided her with a very good income. The lawyers had cautioned Olivia and Libby that there would be taxes owing as Graham's full estate far exceeded the Federal and State estate tax exemption limits, but again Graham had created a special account he directed be liquidated which would cover most of these. Olivia said, "Even after funding the other trusts, and making his behests, there's plenty left over. He made sure I will never have to worry about money again."

When Marilyn's lawyers heard about the will, they of course challenged it. They insisted Marilyn was entitled to half the estate. Furthermore, they requested a multimillion-dollar payment from Olivia *for pain and suffering* in exchange for the ashes. It was extortion, plain and simple. Olivia wanted to just pay it, to finally be free of Marilyn. Libby however, in true Graham-like manner, said she would not be bullied and insisted on putting the entire matter before a judge. They were waiting for a court date.

The following Monday, Maggie went back to work. Charlie had not heard from Neal again, and Izzy and Ethan were too concerned about Olivia to talk about much else on her Sunday evening check in with them. That morning, at the open, there was a huge spike in value in one particular stock. The company had reported excellent earnings that morning, beating expectations, and had said the upcoming quarter would be better still. The shares had soared. She called Kate, who advised Maggie to buy the contract back right now.

Maggie said, "I can do that? Buy the contract back before it actually expires?"

"Sure," Kate had said, "That is why the daily prices fluctuate so much; people buy and sell option contacts all day. You don't have to wait until expiration."

With Kate on the phone, Maggie put a price in the middle of the bid/ask range. The order was executed immediately. "So, what does it mean?" Maggie asked confusedly.

"Well, you no longer have that contract. You bought it back, and it is gone. You take what you sold the contract for, and then subtract what you just paid to buy it back. That is the profit you just made on the trade."

"That would mean I just made six hundred dollars on a contract I wrote just last week."

"Correct," Kate agreed. "If you watch, a lot of these earnings-related jumps drop back later in the day. That is why I suggested you close it right away. You may be able to reopen the contract later in the day, if you want. In fact, you may be able to sell it for at least what you sold it for originally. I may not have talked about it with you yet, but it is corporate *earnings season*. It lasts three to four weeks every quarter, starting about two weeks after the quarter ends. Public companies, those that trade on the exchanges, are required to report how they performed in the latest quarter, and most provide guidance on upcoming earnings. It can be a very volatile time in terms of stock prices of specific companies. Traders can make or lose a lot of money in these three weeks."

Sure enough, when Maggie checked after she got home, the stock price had dropped back again. On the conference call that came after the earnings headlines, analysts had asked questions of senior management. During the call, the CFO had suggested some of the projected gains in the next quarter were due to an accounting change, rather than an actual growth in revenues.

The stock had then slipped back below the price it was the day before. It was as if the spike never happened. It was just before 4 p.m., so Maggie quickly re-wrote the contact, selling it for more than she had originally been paid for when she opened the option contract for the first time a week ago. She had made six hundred dollars just by buying it back in the morning. Instant money. Now she was going to try to do it again.

When she had first seen the jump in the shares that morning, she had immediately regretted that she had not bought the stock itself, rather than the option. When it fell back later in the day, she felt better; she had not missed an opportunity. She would have liked to have had enough money to get in and out of the stock itself, rather than just the option, but that required more capital than she had at her disposal.

She suddenly heard Graham's voice in her head talking about earnings season, "That's the time to play, Maggie. Big changes—sometimes stocks can rise or fall by twenty percent or more. If you like to trade, you will love earnings season."

She felt as if he had sent her the price jump on her option contract as a sign. She smiled.

There was a minor celebration in the house the following week when the lawyers got their hearing before a judge and he ruled the ashes were to be returned to Libby immediately. Graham's estate plan, he commented, was extensive and well prepared. It was likely to withstand *any challenge*. It seemed like he was warning Marilyn's lawyers. Marilyn pulled her objections to the will, unwilling to deplete her trust by paying the lawyers any longer. Olivia and Libby booked the venue they had selected and set a date. Graham would have his service and his party.

George Cohen had called Maggie earlier in the day. She returned his call after dinner. She began by offering condolences regarding Graham, "You two must have been close. You knew each other for *such* a long time." George hesitated on the phone and she could almost feel him fighting back tears. Finally, he gruffly said, "Yes. Graham was probably my closest friend. Knew each other forever. You have no idea what an extraordinary person he was. Saw me through some very tough times. I know Olivia and I are going to miss him terribly." He paused here, gathering himself. "Let's get down to business, shall we?"

"I got copies of your joint returns from the past few years and have gone through them. It was not as bad as I feared. Your husband's company had been failing, then took a real turn for the worse about three years ago. He had losses but they look legitimate. I think the reason for the FBI's interest are a couple of shady looking *capital raises* he did. Foreign companies. I'm not a forensic accountant, but if I have to guess, it looks like he took money from problematic sources." Maggie waited for an explanation.

"Not sure, of course, Maggie. But I think the FBI might be looking at your husband for money laundering, rather than fraud."

Maggie hesitated. She knew money laundering was bad, very bad, but she had no connection with his company and certainly knew nothing about how he funded his business. She was devastated at the severity of the crime. Neal had obviously been in serious trouble for longer than she had known and had probably been under tremendous stress. He hadn't shared any of that with her, nor had she bothered to notice. How unhappy he must have been. How oblivious she had been.

"Wow, George. That is a shock. It's really bad, isn't it?"

"I think it depends on a lot Maggie. Don't jump to any conclusions, it will be lawyers who sort things out. Based, though, on what I see, I am going to request your refund, see what happens. If there is more going on, or they are looking at you specifically, it might flush things out."

Maggie sighed, which George heard.

George thoughtfully changed the subject. "I also spoke to a lawyer about the McDonald's shares. Legally, they belong to your mother. Your parents would have inherited them when your brother passed. I suggest that the shares be left alone until your mother passes, do not sell them. The shares would become yours as her heir, and the cost basis—for purposes of calculating capital gains—would be the price of the shares when your mother dies, not your brother's death. A higher cost basis means a smaller capital gain. Less tax to pay."

George continued, "The dividends, however, are clearly yours as per your parents' wishes. Going forward, you'll have to make some minor tax payments, 15% on dividend income, but that's all. I will look into re-stating earlier years returns to reflect the dividend income you had over the years, but it is a relatively small amount so don't worry too much. We have to wait until your husband's things settle anyways before we can do anything."

Maggie was disappointed about the McDonald's shares being off limits, but she understood why. There had been no clear will. With a start, she realized that without a power of attorney in effect for her mother, it was only because she was Trustee on the Trust account that she could make financial decisions for her mother. She contrasted her mother's lack of preparedness about her end of life, to how Graham had thought out every eventuality.

Maggie realized she lacked even a basic healthcare proxy for her mother. There was certainly no living will with her mother's wishes concerning her own care. Maggie had never discussed it with her nor had her wishes had never been spelled out in any document. The Residences would continue to make medical decisions based on simply keeping her alive, not on the quality of her life. She doubted her mother would have wanted a respirator or a feeding tube.

Maggie honestly didn't know whether the Residences were willing or legally able to follow any of Maggie's directives. It was in their financial interest to keep her mother alive as long as they could, by any means possible. She wished her parents had been more prepared. Or that she had thought to ask them about what they wanted while they were healthy and able.

Graham had prepared a will, an outline for the funeral he wanted, a living will, set up trusts and even executed a power of attorney. He made sure Olivia would have full control over health and financial matters if he had faded into dementia. It made things so much easier for everyone. It took away so much stress at a difficult time. She realized that Graham had made Olivia's life much easier by facing the reality of his own death.

She realized with a start that she, too, had none of these documents. Like everything else in her life, she had left it all to Neal. Had she ever discussed any of this with him? With the kids? When the divorce became final, she was going to have to make some decisions and make them soon. Her children deserved the gift of clarity. There would be a will, a power of attorney, and a living will. She would meet with them all together and work out how to divide responsibilities. Being prepared for the end of her own life was one final thing that Graham had taught her.

Graham's service the following week was part High Mass, part Irish wake. His ashes rested at the front of the ballroom at his favorite hotel. A slide show played on a screen behind it, the story of his life. Everyone had also been asked to bring any photos they had of him with the explanation on the back of where it had been taken and why. Libby and Olivia were going to sort them into the slide show so they could get a photo book published.

The "service" turned out to be a bit of a roast. Graham had selected the speakers in advance and may have cribbed them in what to say. The stories revolved around the theme of "Graham the Delinquent." There were musical interludes and fabulous food. Guests were asked to rotate tables periodically, like an elaborate game of musical chairs. Women moved to the tables to the left, men were to move to the right. People were confused and laughing. Olivia smiled and tsk'd, "*Mayhem by Graham*, should have made him a cologne by that name. He likes a party that goes a little off the rails."

Maggie found George Cohen's speech, the final one of the evening, the most touching. It was a tribute to all things Olivia. He made clear that was Graham's view as well. He told the story about them meeting, and even made reference to Graham's "unfortunate wife" who could never, *ever* measure up to the love of Graham's life. He had the audience raise a toast to Olivia. Maggie was glad Marilyn had opted not to attend, although she was not even sure she had been invited.

All of the speeches were to end in champagne toasts, Graham's orders. It was a bit like an English wedding. By the time the service ended, most of the audience were either pretty happy or a little maudlin. Or both.

Brody of course came to the service. As did Ethan, his girlfriend Hannah, and Izzy. The children were among the only dozen or so guests under thirty, most of the rest of whom were children or grandchildren of family friends. Maggie made sure Brody was Olivia's escort for the night, not hers. She introduced him to Ethan and Izzy as an old friend from college days. Izzy hesitated on meeting him, watching her mother for any clues. Maggie kept her cool and sat next to George Cohen for the night. Brody kept his attention on Olivia. If either of the children saw the resemblance of Ethan to Brody, they certainly didn't acknowledge it.

Brody was grateful to finally meet Ethan, albeit briefly. He explained to Izzy that he had known her mother when she was working in Boston, which surprised Izzy because she had never known Maggie had even held a job before. He kept his conversations with both of them very brief, then moved onto other guests. He told Maggie later that he was afraid he would reveal too much. She could see that meeting Ethan had been a very emotional moment for him.

Before the night was done, Izzy was wrapped up in two young men who did not leave her side. They were grandsons of close family friends and were clearly grateful for her being there, the only female close to their age. Ethan, Hannah, Izzy, and the boys left together shortly after the speeches, so Brody and Maggie could finally relax. The big introduction they had agonized over, had gone smoothly and unnoticed by everyone else involved.

Maggie then moved tables, finally going to sit next to Brody and Olivia. Libby and her daughter, quite pregnant, joined them. It had been, they all agreed, a lovely party. A perfect send off for Graham, just as he had planned it would be.

CHAPTER 20:
BULL AND BEAR MARKETS

Spring rushed into summer, Maggie went into the gardens more and more often. She enjoyed coming home from work and getting dirty, but only after the stock market closed of course. She had found homes for her transplants and they were all doing nicely. Buster fussed around her while she worked, occasionally walking off with tools just to get Maggie's attention.

Olivia was delighted with the garden's transformation. Maggie was a miracle-worker, she told anyone who asked. Flowers bloomed everywhere, shrubs were suddenly shapely and full of buds. Maggie promised Olivia that there would be golden raspberries and tomatoes before long.

It turned out that Olivia loved the hives and wanted to try her hand at beekeeping. She bought her own beekeeper jacket and, as Maggie had expected, was fearless with them. She demonstrated harvesting honey for anyone who visited. Maggie had to remove a few full frames and keep them in their laundry area, so Olivia did not disturb the bees every time she wanted to show off her harvesting skills to friends.

Olivia kept Graham's ashes in her bedroom but didn't talk about him very much. Any mention of him tended to silence her. Libby understood that Olivia wanted to be buried at the same time he was, so she never said a word to Olivia about her waiting to inter the ashes. Sometimes Maggie would overhear Olivia talking to Graham in her bedroom.

Olivia and Libby became close all over again. One night, when Maggie came home and found them cooking together in the kitchen, her heart tugged. It was almost like having Graham there again.

As time when on, Maggie had completed the purchases of all the stocks in her mother's Trust. They were performing nicely. It looked like its annual income would exceed her five percent target by a comfortable margin. She was pleasantly surprised there had been some capital appreciation there, as well. The stock market had continued to rise after she had bought her stocks. It was expected to continue to rise - a classic *bull* stock market. Its gradual rise had been going on for years now, many young traders had never known anything except higher, and then higher, returns. Kate told her it was a continuation of the longest-running bull market on record. Maggie's worry about a market crash, which had dogged her in the weeks after watching The Big Short, faded.

Maggie had been closing puts almost daily, taking profits of as little as fifty dollars when she could. She was averaging over five hundred dollars per week on her option trading, and it was really adding up. She just regretted that she did not have more capital to work with. If she had more cash, she could write more cash-covered puts. She refused to use the margin money that Schwab made available to her. It was too risky to gamble using other people's money, even if it looked like a relatively safe bet. Overall, she had become very comfortable selling option contracts.

She had already filled most of the stock positions she had wanted for her own account, a few by being *put* shares at great prices when option contracts expired below her strike price. Almost all of the stocks she had bought, even those she had been *put*, were now showing modest profits. Her holdings were up more than she could have hoped for, over six percent already, and the year was just half over. Even her 401k had over five thousand dollars in it. Maggie was feeling very confident about her investing skills.

Now that Maggie had so little cash in her account, Kate repeatedly warned Maggie to limit her option trading. Her shares were treated as a cash-equivalent when writing cash covered puts but were not valued 1:1, like the actual cash she had when she opened the account. Kate explained that the formula that Schwab used to calculate the cash equivalent value of the stocks she held could change depending on market conditions and the specific stocks that were held. She assured Maggie that Schwab would notify her if she needed to liquidate shares to cover an option trade. She told Maggie that her account had a *margin* facility. That meant that Schwab would loan her cash to cover a transaction if Maggie was short cash, charging her interest of course.

"I know you don't want to trade on the margin, Maggie," Kate explained, "but it can be useful to use margin if you have a sudden need for cash. It is like a low-cost *line of credit*. Our interest rates are very low. Mind you, there is a limit to how much you can borrow on margin, depends on the value of the stocks and cash you have in your account. The limit is very generous though. Gets some people into hot water."

Maggie was grateful the margin safety net was there in case she needed cash, but she had no plans to ever use it to fund her trading activity. Kate had warned Maggie that Schwab had the right to liquidate her shares if Maggie was short cash to meet an option contract or exceeded her margin limit. Kate was very clear on this point.

"But we will warn you if you are short cash in your account, and usually give you a couple days to raise the money yourself," Kate explained. "Just be aware, if the market crashes, option contracts can become problematic quickly. In extreme situations, Schwab may have to ask you to raise cash immediately because of its regulatory requirements."

Maggie had taken the warning to heart and pared down her option contract trading once her portfolio began to fill up. It was frustrating to limit her trading activity but using margin was not even slightly tempting. Maggie was too risk adverse to even consider it.

The divorce lawyer had advertised the divorce, but of course there had been no reply. Maggie told her that it was possible that Neal was out of the country. The lawyer had simply shrugged, "No problem, I'll request a court date. Once we have a judge's ruling, your divorce is final. Let me see, I think I can get you something next week."

When Brody heard the news he insisted they take a vacation together the day after the divorce was final. He would arrange everything. Maggie thought it would be a little odd, celebrating. As a result, she avoided committing to anything. She told Brody she was simply nervous and did not want to jinx anything.

It was a Thursday morning of that same week. Maggie had just made coffee and gone into her little trading annex in the file room. Tammy had let her continue to have her daily hour at the stock market open as it had not interfered with her work. Maggie looked forward to the open every day.

When Maggie checked the pre-markets that morning, she saw it was going to be up slightly. She was a little late getting settled that morning. When she finally opened the screen, she immediately panicked. The Dow was down over *one thousand points*, twice as much as she had ever seen it drop. She immediately checked the news feed.

There was a US military plane down in the disputed South China Sea. The Chinese were denying any involvement, but the President was ordering the entire US Seventh Fleet into the waters to search for debris. It was a massive military force and an extraordinarily aggressive response before anything was known. The market appeared to be in a tailspin.

She returned to the Medical Records office where everyone was talking about the downed plane. They too watched a computer screen with a live CNN feed. As the US fleet moved closer, the market kept dropping. Maggie watched the news with everyone else, keeping an eye on the market on her phone.

Some of the stocks her option contracts were written on had moved well below her put option strike prices. She knew she would have to come up with the cash to buy these stocks when expiration came, if not earlier. The contract holders could choose to *put* the stock to her at any time. With this decline it might be sooner rather than later, if they wanted their money. Maggie understood now why there were so many buyers for the contracts she wrote. Having stock "insurance" was probably a great relief when the market was dropping like this. She realized that she didn't have any.

The market continued to drop, heading into *correction* territory, a ten or more percent drop in the indexes. It easily reached this level before the day was through. Maggie was shocked at the speed and extent of the market drop. Kate had once told her the market was an escalator going up, but an elevator going down. Now she understood. On her way home from work, Maggie tried to call Kate to see if there was anything she should be doing. She found that the lines were busy. She sent Kate an e-mail and got back a brief note, which looked like a standard reply. Summarized it said: don't panic, hold tight, this too shall pass. Maggie did not find this message reassuring.

All night, Olivia and Maggie watched the news. China had allowed some US naval ships in to search a very limited area. The rest of the fleet was literally lined up along the Chinese coast in an extremely aggressive posture. The Chinese government was incensed. It, too, had begun to move its fleet in position. It felt as if the US and China were on the brink of war.

The next morning, Maggie exhaustedly checked the pre-market right after she checked the headlines. Another thousand-point Dow drop showed in the pre-market. They were beyond a simple correction now. The question was whether or not they were heading into a bear market—that would be twenty percent down from the market's year-to-date high which was just two weeks ago.

Maggie knew that a bear market, unlike corrections, usually took at least a year to recover rather than the days, weeks or months a ten percent correction might take. She felt like she was doomed; all her plans, all her savings would go up in smoke. Sadly, it could get even worse if someone on either the Chinese or US side did something stupid—and the news suggested that could happen. She was close to panic.

When the market opened at 9:30, she was in her little cubby, ready. She almost didn't look, knowing it was going to be very painful. She finally told herself she was being silly. Part of owning stocks was accepting the bad with the good. She steeled herself and looked first to her mother's Trust account.

She was shocked to see the Trust's holdings were down less than four percent that morning, after having dropped almost ten percent the day before. The bond funds were not just flat—they were up. She still had the cash she had pulled out and put in the money market fund. It had obviously not moved at all. Her mother would be fine if this bear market took a few years to recover, even if some of her dividend payments stopped. Maggie was grateful that she had kept some of the Trust in cash, in the money market fund. Overall, her mother's portfolio, while wounded, was doing relatively well when compared to the market meltdown.

When she turned to her own portfolio, however, it was a wreck. The option premiums on the put contracts she held had gone through the roof. In contrast, her call options were almost all very positive. The premiums for the calls had fallen as people now seemed to think the stocks were unlikely to reach her strike price. She closed her calls and made over seven thousand dollars. Normally, she would have been thrilled with that outcome, but it barely dented her losses.

The put contracts made her actual stock losses look even bigger. Looking at her account balance, she had lost almost one hundred thousand dollars in just two days. It was like losing more than two full years of salary. She was angry at herself for not keeping more money in cash, for being so vulnerable. She berated herself for thinking that investing was so easy.

When she looked at individual option contracts though, it was not as bad as it looked at first glance. Since she had set the put strike prices at least ten percent below where they had been trading, and had gotten good premiums, she saw she may not lose as much money as she thought. The *unrealized* loss that was showing was actually significantly larger than the actual loss she would have if she was put at the price the stock was currently trading at. This was because while the call option premiums dropped as the market fell, the put premiums had skyrocketed. People were willing to pay a lot more to insure their holdings in a falling market. Fear drove the put premiums up. Maggie realized that if the market did not fall a lot more, she was going to be put at prices a percentage or two below where the stocks were trading today. If things stabilized, she realized, she might just be okay.

This observation was a relief, but it was short lived. She realized that if she put all the shares she had contracted to buy, she would have to sell some, if not all, of her other shares to raise cash to pay for the stocks. Unfortunately, some shares were now down almost *twenty* percent. She told herself the good news was that she would have to pay less tax as her capital gains would be much smaller. But almost as quickly she realized she would need to have cash to pay the tax, which would further reduce her capital. She realized that she may *have* to use her margin facility after all.

More concerning for Maggie was that all of her cash-covered puts used the value of her shares from two days ago as collateral. Now many of these shares were trading for almost twenty percent less, would Schwab want more collateral? Would they insist she sell her shares, at a loss, to cover her *puts* or would she be *forced* to borrow on the margin? She really had to wait to see what happened. She felt very vulnerable, she was in over her head. She felt as powerless as the day she learned her credit cards were not working.

She began to think about getting out of the market altogether. It took a lot of self-control for her not to simply panic and just start selling. She turned the screens off and just breathed. Finally, she decided her best course of action was to just ignore it for the time being and wait until there was a clearer view as to the extent of the crisis. She would figure out what to do when, and if, the put contracts were exercised. She wished she could talk to Graham.

When she got home that evening, she had a black hole in the pit of her stomach. She had listened to the news all the way home, and everything still sounded grim.

As she pulled into the driveway, she again saw the familiar black Expedition in the driveway. She tried to figure out how Judge Munoz, the Chinese standoff, and the market sell-off fit together. She went inside and Olivia met her at the door, saying a gentleman had just arrived to see her. Olivia looked concerned but left as soon as Maggie stepped into the living room. Agent Munoz must have said something, she thought. Olivia would have stayed otherwise.

"Mrs. Mueller." Maggie knew immediately by his tone that the news was bad. It was in the way he said her name, the way he held himself. "I have some difficult news for you. Perhaps you'd like to sit down?"

Maggie walked slowly over to the couch. She was trying to compose herself but not really succeeding. *Neal was dead,* she told herself. How had she not known this was all going to end badly? "It's Neal. Tell me," she said, bracing herself.

"No, it's not about Neal. I'm here to tell you that your daughter, Charlotte, has gone missing in Guatemala. We're doing everything we can, working with local authorities. We have a team on the ground there and are following up on very good leads. We're optimistic," he finished gently.

The news was like a body blow to Maggie. Charlie? *This was about Charlie?* How could she be missing, and why was the FBI involved? Maggie felt a deep keening inside herself. She needed to go to Guatemala, to find her. Was this somehow Neal's fault? Did he know where Charlie was, who had taken her?

Agent Munoz continued as if he could read her thoughts, "We have your husband there as well, ma'am. He's working with us. We're confident we will be able to have a positive outcome. He is providing us with a great deal of information. We're honestly doing everything we can."

"I need to be there," Maggie said instantly. "Tonight. Charlie will need me. I want to speak with him too, to see Neal. Please, can you arrange this? Where should I fly to?"

Munoz only hesitated a minute, then gave her both the city and the name of which hotel to book. She wrote them down. He said he couldn't give her any more information at this time, but that when she arrived there, she was to ask for him. He would be there and would update her as soon as she arrived.

Maggie started to ask questions, but he held up his hand. He said he was sorry to bring her such difficult news, but he needed to catch a plane. He had wanted to deliver the news personally, but now he had to excuse himself. He was already late. He nodded to her curtly and let himself out.

Maggie sat in a fog for a moment after he left, but quickly roused herself. She called Brody and explained briefly. She said she needed to be in Guatemala City as soon as possible—did he know the best way? He asked her to hold on, then came back on the phone.

"I'll be there in forty-five minutes; can you get to Hanscom Airport? At the FBO there. Wait for me. I can't get clearance to get into Guatemala on such short notice, but I can get you to Miami. There is an American flight that leaves there tomorrow at around 4 a.m., which will get you to Guatemala City by 6 a.m. Remember your passport."

Maggie called out to Olivia, who followed Maggie as she ran upstairs to pack. Olivia could see the fear on Maggie's face as she explained what the FBI agent had told her. She packed a week's worth of clothes, her computer, and her passport which, she thankfully realized, she always left in her travel bag, not in the file drawers that had been cleared at the old house.

She kissed Olivia goodbye and said she would call as soon as she knew anything. She started to order an Uber but Olivia would have none of it. She grabbed Buster, who was anxiously following them around, sensing the fear and reacting to the commotion, and went to change shoes and get her keys.

At Hanscom, a small airport in Bedford, they rode around to the FBO located on the far side of the airport. Olivia, of course, had flown out of there many times, but it was a first for Maggie. The luxurious waiting room had thick carpeting and granite counters. There was a coffee bar and, opposite it, a setup for drinks. The waiting area was empty except for an attractive young woman behind the desk who greeted them and told them their flight was *eight minutes out*.

In less than ten minutes, Brody strode into the lobby and pulled Maggie into a deep hug. "It'll be fine, Trix. She'll be fine." He gave Olivia a peck on the cheek and a concerned look but then took Maggie's bag from her hand and made a motion towards the door, "All good to go?"

Olivia gave Maggie a hug as well and asked her to call or text as soon as she got to Guatemala. She looked small and newly vulnerable as Maggie looked back at her and waved. Maggie and Brody stepped onto the tarmac and then went up the stairs onto one of smaller private jets in his company's charter fleet.

They took off as soon as their belts were fastened. She had expected Brody to be flying himself, and to be perched in the seat beside him like they had done when they were young. This was new, flying private. She and the children had always flown commercial. Maggie noticed that there had been no security to clear them; they had simply walked on. They were the only two people on the plane except for the pilots.

Brody made her a stiff drink from the plane's bar, then made one for himself. He asked her to tell him everything she knew and this time she did, including what George had learned when he saw the returns—suspected money laundering. She let herself breathe and then cried a little. She then apologized, wiping her tears away, saying she never cried. Actually, she then corrected herself, she had been crying a lot lately. First it had been Bunny, then Graham, and now the Chinese and the stock market crashing. "I just don't want to cry over Charlie," she explained to Brody. "Charlie shouldn't see her mother crying."

A moment later, Maggie's mind switched gears and she began to rail against Neal. She told Brody she knew this had to be his fault. Clearly this had something to do with him and his disappearance. She blamed herself for being so oblivious the last few years they had been together. Had she told Brody that Neal might have a mistress? That he had a secret apartment in the city? Brody didn't look particularly shocked at this news, just grim.

They were both quiet for a few moments. Finally, in a soft voice, Maggie admitted that she was actually terrified. Everyone knew there were gangs in Central America, violent drug gangs. Charlie was young, she was beautiful. She could be in very serious danger.

Maggie switched gears again and said, "What do you think it means that Judge Munoz, the FBI agent, agreed, no *encouraged*, me to come to Guatemala? He never even hesitated. Did he think I can help with something? Was Neal holding back?" Maggie then fired off possible scenarios to Brody as her mind ricocheted from one possible outcome to another, each progressively grimmer. Finally, Brody unbuckled his seat belt. He came and sat on the arm of Maggie's chair to pull her to him. She turned and cried softly into his chest until the tears were gone.

When she finally sat back, he rose and made her another drink. He apologetically offered her a trail mix bar, explaining that he hadn't had time to arrange any catered food for them. She took the bar gratefully, then asked for another, admitting she had not eaten much. She smiled at him and asked about the plane. She knew he could not resist. It gave them something else to talk about.

Brody explained it was a Cessna Citation Excel—not the biggest plane he chartered, but one of the most useful. He gave her a little tour of the tiny eight-seat cabin and introduced her to the pilots. He showed her the small televisions which tracked their progress and showed her that they would get to Miami in about two hours.

To fill the time, they talked about the Chinese threat and checked the internet, using the plane's Wi-Fi, for any updates on the standoff. She booked the hotel Munoz had told her to. She checked the market averages, but not her accounts. The Dow had slid another 1500 points, but now Maggie just added this news to the overwhelming sense of dread she felt. She really couldn't care less about the market in the grand scheme of things. She asked Brody if he thought she should call Ethan and Izzy, but he said to wait until tomorrow. That way, she could have the most up-to-date information to share with them. She didn't know if she agreed with him or simply took his advice because she didn't want them to share her anguish.

Brody told her he had arranged her ticket to Guatemala, as he had connections. He brushed away talk of payment. He explained that being in the industry, tickets were inexpensive for him. He asked for her passport and checked her in online. He looked at her for a moment, then admitted that he had booked a ticket for himself as well.

He said he would come along for moral support, or *muscle* if needed, playfully crooking his arm Popeye style. She smiled at the thought of Brody up against Judge Munoz; she had a picture in her mind of a hawk hitting a brick wall. She said no thanks but asked if she could keep the option open. He didn't argue.

Brody consciously moved off the topic of Charlie's disappearance and instead talked about Olivia's slow recovery. They talked a bit about Graham and how much they missed him. They discussed the help Libby had been in terms of getting Olivia out and about, and how she too had now become a close friend of Maggie's as well. Maggie told Brody that Libby was pushing for a new puppy in the house, but Olivia was making excuses.

They talked blandly about Maggie's work and Tammy's oldest going to Wharton for business on a full scholarship, marveling that he had started his own little high-tech recycling company in high school. Brody talked about employees and his girls. Eventually they ran out of things to talk about, and just held each other's hands.

The flight seemed to take forever. When they landed, Brody went to the FBO desk and picked up an envelope.

"Here is a copy of your itinerary and boarding pass. Let's grab some dinner at the hotel; you should sleep. You have to get up early, and it's probably going to be a long day."

"What about this plane?"

"The guys will grab some dinner. They go when I go. That's the beauty of flying private." He smiled and headed out to a car parked out front. The driver took them to the MIA Hotel, which was actually in the International concourse, which meant only a short distance for Maggie in the morning. She wouldn't have to worry about getting to her gate.

They had dinner in the hotel restaurant, Vienna, on the seventh floor. The restaurant was modern but bland, with equally generic food. Neither of them cared or even noticed. They went up to Maggie's room and Brody paused on the threshold.

Maggie knew it would be easy to invite him in, but this was not the time to cross that bridge. They kissed and he held her for a while, reassured her again that things would work out. He let her know he could get to Guatemala quicker than she imagined, if it became necessary. She only had to ask.

Maggie was sad to see Brody head back down the hall to the elevator. With a last look, she went into the room and changed into her pajamas. She knew she should sleep, but her mind was racing. She wanted to take one of her old anxiety pills she had saved for emergencies, but she was afraid to take a pill in case she missed her flight. She slept badly and was already awake when both her phone alarm buzzed and then the wakeup call came a few minutes later. She was one of the first passengers waiting at the gate.

The flight got in on time and outside the airport she found an English-speaking taxi driver to take her to the hotel. The man behind the reception desk was sleepy and told her the check-in time was not until the early afternoon. She asked if there was a room available now and just paid for it, using the credit card she had paid off almost a year ago and had kept for emergencies. She had hoped to never have to use it again.

She was tired and knew that she should sleep. She wrote a message for Judge Munoz saying she was here and in Room 326. She gave it to the clerk. He said he did not recognize the name, that there was no Mr. Munoz registered as a guest, but he took the envelope anyway.

Maggie was awakened by a knock on the door at 10:30 a.m. Judge Munoz was there, dressed casually for once and looking tan. She did not remember him being tanned yesterday in her living room. Without asking, he swept past her into the room and looked around. He seemed satisfied that she was alone. He did not sit.

"I was not expecting you quite so soon," he said. "I thought you would have missed the commercial connecting flights."

"Friends in the industry," she replied. "Any news?"

"I just arrived here myself. Our people say things are moving, but nothing to report yet. Would you like to see your husband?"

"Of course, but I would much rather see Charlie."

"Get dressed and come with me."

Maggie dressed quickly while Munoz waited in the hall. She stepped with him into the elevator and was surprised when he pushed the button for the top floor rather than the lobby. They arrived and went directly into a large suite with four or five similarly dressed men and women scattered about looking at computer screens, sorting through stacks of papers and on phones. Maps were scattered everywhere. Everyone only glanced up at Maggie and Judge for a moment, a few acknowledging them with a nod. They then turned back to their work, all business. Two men had guns in holsters over their touristy shirts. It jarred Maggie.

Maggie noticed that there were bottled tans for everyone here. *Tourist casual* must be the dress code for FBI agents in Central America, she thought.

Munoz walked over to a double door at the end of the suite and knocked. He opened it without waiting for an answer.

Inside, Neal sat watching CNN.

It was unreal to Maggie. All that had happened since he had walked out of her life almost a year ago...and here he was, just catching up on the news.

"Neal, your wife is here," the agent announced. He then excused himself and closed the door behind him.

Neal looked aghast when he turned and saw her. Clearly, he had not been told she was coming. Tears started in his eyes. He rose to embrace her, but she crossed her arms and shook her head. He stopped and sat back down. "Mags, I am so, so sorry about all this," he began. "*It's all my fault.* Things just got out of hand. It was never supposed to get this bad."

He paused as if he expected her to say something. Maggie just stared him down, so he hung his head and waited. Maggie continued to glare. Neal had the only legitimate tan she had seen so far. He was flabby, not his usually lean, athletic build. He had shaved his hair very short and it was difficult to tell its exact color, but it was either lighter or there was a lot of gray. He was dressed in clothes she recognized, but they were tight, faded and ill-fitting. Despite the tan and the weight gain, Neal somehow looked wasted and shaky.

"Who has taken her, and why?" Maggie seethed. Until she had seen Neal, she could not have imagined ever being this angry.

Neal stuttered. "Look, I'm really not sure who exactly, but they are probably working with my Russian partners. I'm pretty sure of that. I'd been moving some money through my company for them. I knew it was wrong, but it was only going to be the one time. Like I said, things just got out of hand."

"Out of hand?" Maggie repeated incredulously. Her breathing was ragged.

"I kept trying to back out, Mags! Then a lot of money went missing. The Russians got angry and I couldn't work out what to do. They threatened me, and you guys too. I knew they went after family members to pressure people. I figured the only way to keep everyone safe was to disappear until I could work things out and figure out how to get the money. I honestly thought it was only going to be for a few weeks at most. I went silent so they wouldn't think I cared."

Maggie looked skeptical. "So, a few weeks became almost a year?"

Neal looked down and shuddered, "They found me when I was in Texas, Maggie." He then looked up at her and said emphatically, "They left *a fucking dead dog* on the kitchen table. It had been cut wide open! Christ, it was right out of a movie. A dead, bloody dog. Their note said it could just as easily be one of our kids. I just freaked and left the country. First, I went to Mexico, then by road through Central America to here. I just bought a cheap van, which I slept in. Used cash everywhere. Came close to not making it, a couple of times. I had to pay a lot of bribes to get across borders. It took months just to get here. You know how bad my Spanish is. I have been lying low forever. I came because of Charlie. Given time, I thought I could contact her and let you all know what was happening."

Maggie felt a small pang of sympathy when he described his flight, but it was quickly drowned out by the rolling waves of fury she felt. "You involved Charlie in this?" she seethed.

"Look, Maggie. I waited a long, long time to contact her," Neal said. "I just wanted to make sure I hadn't been followed and she would be safe. A month ago I gave a note to one of her students. Then, finally last week, we met for the first time. She looked so great and was so happy to see me. I got all the news about you and Ethan and Izzy. I am so sorry about the houses, Mags, it's all my fault. It was how I ended up finally giving in into the Russians. I just ran out of ways to raise any money. Without it, there was no chance I was ever going to get us out of the hole we were in. Taking their money was a Hail Mary."

Maggie closed her eyes. "So, it really *was* you that caused all of this. How could you have let it get so bad? The day the credit cards stopped working, I thought it was just a mistake. Then came the FBI and the foreclosures. I still thought it was probably just a misunderstanding or maybe a tax problem. At worse, a securities fraud issue or some larceny at your firm. I worried about how I would manage, about *my* potential liability. I never, ever, in a million years thought there was the slightest chance one of the kids will be targeted. Of you being involved in anything truly criminal."

"But that's the way they get to you, Mags! Family. Like I said, it's why I left, to protect you and the kids. They think I have the money, and I don't. They left a note where I was staying right after they took her. It said if I told them where to find the missing money, she would be let go. No harm to her. I don't have the money, though. That's when I went to the US Consulate, for help. Then these guys all showed up out of the woodwork." He gestured to the team outside. "I hadn't even considered that the FBI would be looking for me. I thought it was all about the Boris-es."

"Boris-es?" Maggie asked.

Neal sighed. "Yeah, Boris and Natasha? Bullwinkle? I have a friend, Natasha, who had introduced me to her cousin, whose name I couldn't pronounce. I had run out of money and Natasha said it would be risky, but she could make sure it worked out. We began to refer to her cousin, and then his partners, as the Boris-es. It was a joke."

"Is Natasha the woman in your city apartment?" Neal's eyes narrowed and he looked a bit like the old Neal. He bluffed his way through, "Yes, Natasha, she's my secretary. After the cash problems started, I had to downsize and move to a smaller space. The apartment was cheaper than office space and Natasha was willing to work as my secretary in exchange for living space. It was a good arrangement."

"*Secretary*? I've heard otherwise, but I don't care what your relationship is with her at this point. Our marriage was being held together by threads anyway, before all this. During Charlie's family update, did she mention that I'm divorcing you? Next week, I believe."

"Yes, yes, she did." Neal said slowly. "She was trying to get me to fly home and stop you. I think she saw my heart wasn't in it. I knew you were done years ago. I am just surprised you waited this long. I told her you'd be better off without me." He paused a moment and looked at her as if seeing her for the first time, "It looks like you are. Thinner. Beautiful, actually."

When he said this, they both paused and looked at each other for a moment, lost in time. But then the moment passed.

"So, what do you know about Charlie?" she asked.

"Not much. She was taken the day before yesterday. From her apartment building on her way to work, they said. These FBI guys know more than they are telling me, I'm sure of that. They've kept me here, in this room since I was moved from the Consulate. Apparently, I'm under arrest, but I don't know the charges. I get the sense they are not exactly following US laws here. I don't care though, being here I get the latest on the search. There is stuff happening. I can tell that."

"Neal be honest. I get the dead dog to scare you. But would these people actually hurt Charlie?"

Neal hung his head. Finally, he choked out, "I don't know. I honestly never thought we would be here. I'll kill myself if anything happens to her."

He was holding back a sob, Maggie could tell. She turned and left the room. Munoz and the other agents sheepishly removed headphones as she came outside. They had clearly been listening in to their conversation. "What exactly do you need from me?" Maggie asked suspiciously.

"You just did it. We wanted to hear his explanation to you, whether it tracked with what we already knew. It did."

"So, given you have my husband, where are you when it comes to finding my daughter?"

"Just about there, I think," he said, and pointed to a young man on a phone who was speaking Spanish. He nodded his head at Judge Munoz, smiled, and gave him the thumbs up. "Yes," Munoz said. "We have her. Safe and sound, I believe. They will bring her here directly. Should take about an hour."

Before he could say anything else, Maggie's knees gave way and she swooned. She marveled at the sensation as it was happening. A nearby agent deftly caught her and slid her into a chair as she went down. He got her a glass of water, and tears of relief came.

"Tell Neal," she croaked, knowing that despite her fury at him, no parent deserved the agony. An agent slipped into the room behind her.

Judge Munoz explained to Maggie that his team had been following Neal, and then Charlie too, after Neal had finally surfaced in Guatemala. They knew how the Russians like to operate; family was always a target. Ethan and Izzy had been safe, as the Russians generally avoided acting on US soil. Charlie was the logical target, but they had wanted to know Neal was nearby. Once they had spotted him, they had taken her.

The FBI had seen Charlie shoved into a van but had not been able to stop it. Fortunately, their local contacts had recognized the kidnappers as a local gang. They knew where they were likely to be holding Charlie, so things had moved very quickly.

When Charlie arrived forty minutes later. She fell into her mother's arms and burst into tears. She was fine, but still shaking and terrified. She embraced Neal when he came out of his room and they had a family moment, huddled together, tears flowing. The rest of the room fell quiet. When they finally pulled apart, it was as if Charlie was seeing the room for the first time. The agents, the guns. Her father, looking disheveled and disheartened. Maggie, looking exhausted but relieved.

Maggie, noticing how filthy Charlie was, asked Agent Munoz if she and Charlie could go back to her room. Charlie needed a shower and some time to herself. Her beautiful hair had been lobbed off in rough sections, Maggie did not want to think about how that had happened. A female agent moved in and asked gently if she could speak to Charlie first. She pulled her into a corner and spoke to her in a voice too soft to hear. Maggie saw Charlie shake her head and she hoped it was for the question she also wanted an answer to. The agent led her back to Maggie and said she was free to go and shower, for now.

As they left the room, Neal hugged her again but stayed behind as they left. Charlie seemed to finally get it. "Dad's in trouble, isn't he? Was that the reason I was kidnapped?"

Maggie told her, yes, that it was likely something to do with her father. She told her that the agents were from the FBI and that Dad was helping them. He was in trouble and it was going to take some time to work it out. She told Charlie that it was unlikely that he would be coming home with them.

Charlie was quiet and simply pulled her mother close. Tears fell silently.

While Charlie was showering, Maggie texted Brody and Olivia that Charlie was safe. The crisis had been less than twenty-four hours, yet it felt like a full lifetime for Maggie. She was grateful it had not been a long, drawn-out drama like so many movies made it out to be. She marveled at how efficient and effective the FBI had been. She was so grateful to them. Judge Munoz was now a hero to her.

She let Olivia and Brody know that she would advise them as soon as she worked out their travel arrangements. Brody called as soon as he got the text. She gave him a recap on what she knew, then begged off a long conversation, as Charlie was finishing her shower. She asked him to call the hospital for her and let Tammy know she was going to be out from work again for a bit. She would wait to tell the other kids what had happened until she was safely back in Boston with her baby.

Charlie came out of the bathroom in a towel and Maggie gave her some of her clothes. She saw a huge purple and yellow bruise across her upper back but did not say anything. They found the room service menu and ordered a large brunch, Charlie ordered for them in perfect Spanish. The food arrived and they realized they were both famished.

After an almost silent meal, they finally sat back with coffee cups in each of their hands. The hotel had sent up a large Thermos of spectacular café con leche. Maggie asked if Charlie wanted to talk about her experience, but she just shook her head as tears began to form. She was only willing to talk about the rescue.

As she told it, she was held in a small room, a closet really, blindfolded and tied up on the floor. There had been an explosion and then smoke under the door. She heard no gunfire, only yelling. The door had been flung open by a soldier. He spoke gently to her as he cut the ropes and took off her blindfold. He introduced himself as Sargent Jamal Baker and spoke English with an American accent. Then he led her through the house. She saw the angry men who had held her under guard, out front. She was in the countryside somewhere, but it was not familiar.

She was then hustled into a Jeep and had a rough ride back to the city with Baker and three other US soldiers. One was a paramedic who asked her some basic questions, examining her only superficially. He couldn't find anything obvious that needed fixing. They said Charlie would have to see a doctor later. She had then stayed pretty quiet and they brought her straight to the hotel room. They hadn't told her about Maggie or Neal.

Maggie finished her coffee. Charlie looked beyond exhausted. She knew she probably shouldn't, but she insisted Charlie take one of her anxiety pills and try to rest. She then tucked her in and sat with her until she fell into a deep sleep. She then went into the bathroom to call Agent Munoz to see when they could leave.

They were back in Boston within the week. Before they left, Charlie saw an army doctor who pronounced her fit to travel. She was *debriefed* which really meant answering some basic questions about the kidnapping. They had a military escort as they moved around the city, packing up her apartment, meeting friends to say goodbye and finally going to the school for a small party with the staff and children she had come to love.

During this time, Maggie noticed Charlie moved slowly and did not seem to register or care about everyday things. She claimed she was perpetually tired, yet to Maggie she seemed overly alert. She snapped whenever Maggie asked how she was feeling. The army doctor told Maggie that Charlie would need help processing the event.

Of course, Charlie's supervisor at work had been told what had happened. When she met him to say goodbye, he informed Charlie she was on medical leave until she wanted to return. The Corps understood these types of kidnappings, more than they cared to admit.

Maggie's emergency fund was exhausted by the end of the week, but she was grateful that it had been there to draw on in the first place. They had bought tickets to get back home on her old credit card.

Maggie had always thought that Charlie was the strongest, emotionally, of the three children. However, the kidnapping had shaken something in her. The violation was more than just physical; she seemed to have shifted in her world view. Her optimism was gone.

When they got back to Boston, Charlie moved into Maggie's little guest room. She was quiet and read and slept a lot. She said nothing about the old house or her things in storage. Maggie returned to work but came home immediately after she finished. She made Charlie's favorite meals, left her treats when she went to work, and took her through the boxes from her parents' house. It was hard work to catch her interest in anything for more than a few minutes.

Olivia stepped into the breech. She got Charlie to walk Buster, help her with meals and then taught her how to use the DVD player. They then spent hours together in front of the screen with Buster at their feet or in their laps. Charlie finally had a grandmother.

Shockingly, the stock market recovered in big leaps the week after Maggie got home, although she had not paid much attention. The US military plane's flight recorder had been found and then the crash was determined to have been a software glitch on a newly installed navigation system. The pilot's body was recovered. The Chinese were vindicated, and the US looked silly. The news cycle moved on.

It was all good, as far as the stock market was concerned. The bull market, where stocks just kept heading up, was reestablished, the pundits said. Everyone bemoaned not having bought when the market had crashed, forgetting that back then the world had supposedly been on the brink of war. Maggie learned most people find it hard to buy stocks if they think the world is about to end. But boldness does pay. Quite a few professional traders on CNBC apparently bought and did exceptionally well in just a week or so.

Maggie learned, unintentionally, that sitting tight during market corrections, not panicking, was the way to go. Corrections could be, and usually were, relatively short term. If she had sold shares like she had thought about doing, she would have missed the recovery. Her losses would be permanent. In an odd way, being pulled away to Guatemala was an act of grace, as far as her trading went. If she had been paying close attention, she was not sure she would have resisted the urge to sell into the falling market. She remembered that her favorite investment advisor Jim Cramer always said, "*Nobody makes a dime panicking.*"

She wondered about the impact of a bear market, a true twenty percent correction. Would she have been alright if the market had not reversed so quickly. If it had been a typical bear market, how long would she have had to wait until things got better? She turned to her computer and found that on average, a bear market occurred once every three and a half years and lasted about a year. Eventually, though, they do pass which was why having a long-term investment horizon was so important. *Keep calm and carry on* applied to the stock market as well as it did to life.

Maggie called Kate at Schwab after she had been home a few days. Kate immediately apologized about not answering Maggie's phone call or e-mail personally. "You have to understand, Maggie, when the market falls like it did, it's crazy here. A lot of people have never lived through something like that. So many people just want to sell, sell, sell. Or they want someone to stay on the line and just reassure them. Often systems get overloaded and slowdown, which makes matters even worse. In fact, I don't know if you saw it, but the market circuit breakers were triggered that first Tuesday. When the S&P 500 fell 7%, trading was halted for fifteen minutes. It would have been halted again if it had reached the 13% mark and if it had dropped 20%, the market would have closed for the day. Given a lot of trading is machine-based, they set the circuit breakers up to stop a complete breakdown in the market. The NYSE and the Nasdaq want people to catch their breath and not panic – maybe halt the machine trading for a bit."

Maggie said, "If think if I had gotten through to you, I would have been one of those people. I was in a complete panic. It was like the crash in The Big Short. Is there any way I can protect myself if this happens again?"

Kate sighed, "Look, Maggie, it will happen again. That is a big part of the risk of being in the market. As I tell everyone, there is no perfect way to protect a stock portfolio. You can mitigate losses by choosing more conservative stocks that are unlikely to fall as much as high-flyers like Tesla. You can diversify, try and have more fixed income."

"Yes, I saw that." Maggie replied, "My mother's Trust fund did much better than my account in terms of losses. She has more of the blue chip, dividend payors."

Kate continued, "You can also use 'stop-loss' orders. These are sell orders that are triggered if the stock price reaches a price you set. Better still, you can use '*trailing* stop-loss orders' that are slightly more sophisticated. These are orders that take into consideration the fact that most stocks generally rise in value. With a *trailing* stop-loss the price you chose is entered as a percent off the current price. As the stock rises in value, the stop-loss target price rises as well."

Kate paused to catch her breath, "And before you ask, Maggie, there is no perfect percentage for trailing stop-loss orders. I usually see them set at ten percent below where a stocks is currently trading. If you decide to use a stop-loss orders, use the GTC, or good till cancelled option, when the order asks for duration. A GTC order is in effect for sixty days here at Schwab. It saves you having to re-enter the orders all the time. Of course, you can enter and cancel these orders at any time, no cost to you."

Kate cautioned, "Remember, Maggie, stop-loss orders are great, but if they are triggered due to a minor hiccup in the stock, you could end selling the stock well below where you wanted. If the stock or the market rebounds quickly, like it just did, you may find yourself buying it back at a higher price than when you sold it."

Maggie hesitated, "Then I shouldn't use stop-loss orders?"

"Well," Kate said, "Hiccups happen, but they are not common. You could be caught out by one. But if there is another large, severe drop caused by what people call a *black swan* event, like the China episode, and it doesn't come back quickly, you may be glad you have stop-loss orders. It could help you raise cash to purchase other stocks on sale. And if the black swan event is severe enough, or takes a long time to right itself, companies might suspend dividends anyway so selling them wouldn't cost you income. You have to decide how much risk you want to take. The critical thing you have to remember is that if you get out of the market in a downturn, you run the risk of not getting back in in time to catch a recovery. I always tell people to ride it out if they have a long enough time horizon and don't need the money. Remember, planning to get either in or out of the market at the right time, especially in the middle of a sell-off is a fool's errand. Even professionals admit it's *impossible to time the market*. So, if you do decide to use stop-loss orders, remember you don't have to write them on all your positions. Maybe just use them on stocks where you have large gains you want to protect."

Kate paused and then added, "And, Maggie, one more thing. You have been doing really well on your option trading, but you can't write covered calls on a stock you have a stop-loss order on. You will lose the potential extra income you might earn selling those calls."

Kate could tell that Maggie was frustrated to hear this. She complained, "I can't be protected and still sell calls?"

"No, Maggie. Think about it. If the stock were suddenly sold because of a triggered stop-loss, you would have what is called a *naked* call contact, which is an agreement to sell stock you no longer own. You'll need to buy the stock if you are called when the contract expires. A lot can happen between the time when the stock is sold until the option expires. If the stock rises above the call price plus the premium you've been paid, you'll lose money. Possibly a lot of money. It's risky. You simply don't have the authority to trade options like this, you would need a higher level of option trading approval."

Maggie was disappointed to hear this but after she thought about it, she said, "You're right, Kate, probably for the best. Sounds like trading *naked* calls is like using margin to trade, too risky for me."

Kate then said, "You know, now that you are option trading, another way you could go is to consider buying some puts for protection, rather than selling them. It will cost you a little, but you can extend the duration and you don't have to watch so closely. Market volatility is falling, so the premiums are dropping. It may not cost you very much to protect your positions."

Maggie thanked Kate for the advice and in the week that followed, after she had done a bit more research, she put in a few trailing stop-loss orders on shares she had large gains in. She worried a little that a routine market hiccup might trigger these stop-loss orders but decided she was watching closely enough that she could probably get back into the stock quickly if that happened. She thought of the stop-loss orders as free insurance for her gain

She also realized that if she had more money, she *would* consider buying puts, rather than selling them as she usually did. That was another way to potentially insure her holdings against a violent market downturn. She told herself that if she started making more money trading, she would look into selling puts to protect her holdings. She could write these protective puts far into the future so she would not have to keep re-entering them every couple months like the trailing stop orders.

She had learned to watch that market volatility, which was measured by an index called the VIX. When the VIX was low, twelve or less, option premiums tended to fall, so she could buy option put contract for protection relatively cheaply. Maggie put an alert on her phone and decided buying puts would be worth a look if the VIX dropped that low.

In the process of thinking about how to protect her portfolio, Maggie also resolved to sell shares that had appreciated to lock in gains. She decided that she would set a *target* price for selling her stocks. Given that she was so disciplined about only buying a stock when it was down, she decided that she would consider selling some or even all of a position if the stock had a gain of 25% *after tax*. This was assuming that it had reached or exceeded the analysts projected target. She set alerts, which came to her as texts, to let her know when her stocks reached her target. She made a note to herself to check how long she held the stock too, to try and make sure she sold it after she had held the stock for at least a year so she was taxed at the lower, long-term gain rate.

If she ended up selling the stock with a 25% after tax gain, and still liked the stock, she reasoned she could always buy it back using puts at the price she originally bought the stock at. Maybe she would get lucky and be able to buy it again. She knew she did not want to run the risk of losing all the gains she had in another market correction.

Maggie also started to watch her portfolio to make sure no one stock became too large a percentage of the total portfolio. Since she had about twenty stocks, she set a target of five percent as the size of each holding. If any of her stocks appreciated in value enough to exceed five percent of the portfolio, she would trim it back. This *re-balancing* of her portfolio would help keep her portfolio well diversified and be another way to force her harvest her gains.

While her stock portfolios recovered, Maggie continued to worry about Charlie. Surprisingly, Olivia seemed to rally as she made Charlie her project. Maggie and Olivia brainstormed about what to do on the nights Charlie went off to bed early. They tried everything but neither of them felt they were seeing any marked improvement. For no clear reason, Charlie refused to see anyone professionally. Maggie wondered if the independence she had encouraged in her daughter was now a liability, not an asset.

One day, Olivia unexpectedly brought home a tiny Cavalier puppy. Charlie was suddenly like a child at Christmas again, Neal had always vetoed a dog. The puppy adored Charlie, but it seemed to really enjoy bedeviling Buster. The older dog growled and snapped initially, but by the end of the first week, if Buster didn't see the puppy in the same room, he went looking. The entire house laughed at the adventures of their newest addition.

Olivia let Charlie choose a name for the puppy. She chose Bella. Together, Olivia and Charlie arranged a christening party for the newest family member which involved a dress that looked like one of the royal christening gowns and a full in-house ceremony. There were piles of toys and treats, some for the people too. Libby, and her daughter's family, as well as Izzy, Ethan and Hannah came. Charlie laughed freely and often. It was the first time she looked relaxed since she had gotten home, and Maggie knew it was because she was surrounded by family and friends. Charlie used her phone to take photos of everything and had Bella perform the tricks she had already taught her. Charlie's laughter was a gift to Maggie. It was a beginning, and it meant more to her than any silly option contract ever could.

CHAPTER 21:
WHY MONEY MATTERS

Neal was suddenly back in America, Boston even, but in the Suffolk County House of Corrections in South Bay. He had returned with the FBI team and was facing a variety of charges. He was in Boston because he was slated to be a corroborating witness in an extensive Russian money laundering and influence case that extended from Boston to New York City.

After he testified, his lawyer had negotiated he would serve *light time* in a minimum-security prison in Concord. Both Izzy and Ethan had been to see him, individually, after having learned about Charlie's ordeal. Charlie was refusing to go at all. Maggie was not sure how the other children's visits had gone. They both seemed angry with Neal.

Maggie had gone to South Bay to visit only once. After some basic pleasantries, she slid over a copy of their divorce papers. Neal only glanced at them and shrugged. It was sad, but neither of them felt strongly about the dissolution of their twenty-six years together.

She also had the difficult conversation regarding Ethan's biological paternity. She told him that while it was not confirmed, Ethan was probably not his biological son. Neal was surprised, angry, and then, finally, devastated.

"For me, he will always be my son," Neal insisted. Then he added bitterly, "I suppose he'll think it's Christmas. He's always hated me." Maggie objected but he immediately switched the topic and asked about the girls. Maggie reassured him that they were his. He shifted from being bitter about the news to back to being angry with her. He said unkindly, "I always thought you were too high-minded to *cheat*." She patiently told him that she had slept with Ethan's biological father only once while she had been dating Neal. "I am really sorry, Neal. It happened just before we became engaged." Neal did not take any comfort in this, "You are just splitting hairs, Maggie. Cheating is cheating."

Maggie sighed, knowing he was right, "Look, Ethan doesn't know about his paternity yet, but I plan on telling him sometime soon, I just wanted to tell you first. He'll want a DNA test to confirm it I'm sure. I think we'd all like that. There is a possibility that I'm wrong, it was only that once, but the physical resemblance is very strong. His biological father's name is Brody Kavanaugh."

"That pilot your Dad hated?" Neal asked.

Maggie ignored the comment and said, "Yes, the pilot. Brody didn't know. He guessed when he saw the resemblance in some online photos Charlie posted this past Christmas. He came forward right away. I hadn't seen him since we got married but," Maggie paused uncomfortably, "Brody is back in my life now."

"'Back in your life?' Is that what you're calling it? I guess I should not beat myself up about Natasha then?" he said testily. "At least about that," he muttered under his breath.

Maggie got up to leave at that point, and Neal suddenly reached out for her hand. He looked contrite. "Hey Mags, I'm sorry. I didn't mean to sound so bitter. The news just took me by surprise and I'm angry at myself, about everything, I think. Don't go yet." Maggie sat back down.

Neal continued thoughtfully, "I've learned a lot about myself in the last year, and I'm not sure I like the conclusions. I feel terrible for the messes I left for you to clean up. Going silent. It wasn't fair and I know that you all must have worried. I understand about the divorce and we both know it wasn't just your being angry about my disappearance. It was time. There wasn't much there beyond companionship. But I do still love you, Mags. And the kids too, of course. I had a pretty good family thing going. Now, I think that I should have told you when things started going off the rails, it might have kept things from getting so bad. Plus, I should have been there more for the kids, participating in, rather than just being a spectator of their lives. I had the wrong priorities. Now it feels like it's too late."

Maggie paused, "You know Neal, I have learned a lot in the last year too. It hasn't been all bad. I've been really lucky in many ways. Mind you, I was pretty shocked at how little I understood about money when you left. Everything being in your name, the things I had signed without looking at and then how I had let you handle everything from the taxes to my mother's Trust. When you disappeared, I felt pretty powerless. When the house went, scared too."

Neal hung his head.

Maggie continued, "Now I feel like I have been, well, *reawakened*. Things are different. I feel in control financially and personally. I have a job I feel good about. I invest, I even trade stock options, can you believe that? What I have learned in the past year has more than just empowered me financially. My relationships with the kids, and the people around me, have never been better. I'm happy with my life."

Neal smiled wanly, "So you're saying I did you a favor, screwing up like I did?"

Maggie stood and smiled. She then leaned over and kissed him on the forehead, "You did indeed. And it is never too late for anything, especially when it comes to your relationship with the kids. They love you, just give them time. See you when you're out, if not before. Take care of yourself, Neal."

As she walked out, Neal shut his eyes and fought back the regret that weighed him down every day now. He got up and the guard opened the door for him and they headed back to his cell. Neal knew that Maggie and the kids had always been the *score* he had been looking for. How had he ever missed that. Why had he had traded them for *money* and *Natasha* of all things?

What Neal had not told Maggie, something she would only learn from the trial itself, was that Natasha was a professional Russian mob *honey trap*. She had been sent to ensnare Neal when his company's financial distress hit their radar. Russians thugs actively looked for smaller American businessmen with major loans coming due, especially those who had exhausted all other access to capital. A perfect set-up for laundering money.

Natasha, who was really Annika Yahontov, had been arrested almost immediately after Charlie was taken. The FBI's well-constructed case against her, which Neal had fleshed out in those first few hours with them, persuaded her to assist the FBI. She had kept meticulous encrypted records and was able to provide information that quickly confirmed to the FBI the name and location of the gang members holding Charlie. Together with what the local officials in Guatemala knew, she had made Charlie's imprisonment much shorter and less traumatic than it might have been otherwise.

She was also responsible for, to Neal's horror, taking the missing money that Neal had been accused of stealing. Neal had been devastated at her dishonesty, betrayal and her willingness to incriminate him to her partners.

The FBI agents searching their apartment with dogs were flabbergasted to find two enormous stashes of cash. There were bills in large denominations in a memory foam-encapsulated compartment within the mattress on their bed. Without the dogs, the cache would have gone undetected.

When they asked her how she had accumulated so much in cash, she had just laughed and said in her thick Russian accent, "Men are so stupid when it comes to money. They never think the girls, especially pretty ones, are good with it. Morons. I just take some every day, change a number here and there, maybe transpose a little. Never the same amount. Best when I find way to take a little of their Bitcoin which I sell and turn into cash. I give the hard dollars every week to woman who comes to do cleaning. The people who watch me, never check on her. Just a cleaning girl they think. She deposits it for me, so I give her little bit. Of course," Annika paused, "I could not tell you where she goes. Or where money is. She is very clever girl and when you arrest me, *she and money is gone*! So, I think, she has money. All these years I work with these men and they think I just a foolish girl who like to spend, spend money and buy pretty things. They *miscalculate* me."

Annika was going to be the prosecution's star witness; Neal was just a bit player. What no one knew was that when Annika completed her brief, negotiated sentence she would quickly disappear into the Brazilian Amazon. There, she would be happily reunited with her female partner, a former housecleaner and the quiet mastermind behind the successful theft of millions of untraceable Russian mob money.

For Maggie, one positive thing that came out of the FBI investigation was the return of stacks of personal documents out of the trove Neal had hidden. Annika had directed the FBI where to find it. The children's birth certificates, insurance forms, healthcare records, and other family documents were all returned by Judge Munoz. He thanked Maggie for her help and wished her well. Maggie cheekily told him that she liked the tan he had sported in Guatemala, "You ought to vacation more often." She then quietly thanked him again for rescuing Charlie so quickly. He smiled tightly, and politely left. Probably for good, Maggie realized.

Charlie announced suddenly that she was going to move out of Olivia's and in with Izzy. One of her roommates was leaving and had paid out the month, so Charlie could stay free for a bit. She wanted her own space and to be around people her own age, until she decided whether to get a job or go back to the Corps. She spent her days volunteering with a local land trust that often sent her out with a small team for trail remediation. She liked working outdoors with only a few people around. Olivia's suggestion that she see a local psychologist she knew finally took, and Charlie started weekly sessions. She was mending.

Brody had met the whole family now and spent some time with them at dinners at Olivia's. Izzy had once mentioned to Maggie that there was a resemblance between Brody and Ethan, but her tone suggested it was coincidental. Maggie was worried Izzy would say something to Ethan as well, but nothing happened. She knew she was being a bit paranoid, but something had to be said soon. Ethan seemed oblivious.

Olivia had once again bonded with a dog she had not originally wanted, and Bella followed her faithfully. Buster seemed fine with being upstaged. He had Maggie. Olivia's brother was in remission and they were planning an extended Italian vacation to celebrate. Maggie's sense was that he was still not that well, but he was rallying for his sister's sake. She was glad they still had each other, bickering aside.

Maggie's option trading rhythm was back after her bear market scare. She was again trading daily and maintaining her five hundred dollars per week average. She was careful to avoid needing any margin funds. Both accounts she oversaw were recovering from the market dive but were still slightly below where they had started. Surprisingly, hers and her mother's portfolios had recovered better than the market overall. She put that down to the conservative, *value* stocks she had chosen. She was glad now that she had generally shied away from the more volatile *growth* and *momentum* stocks.

She might have panicked about the market drop if it were not for the scare with Charlie. That had put the market gyrations into better perspective for her. Cash may be king, and stocks fun to trade, but in the long run her *family trumped everything*. That was her new motto. She talked to all the kids now, about their friends, their worries, and their ambitions. She finally felt close to them. And to Brody.

Maggie had a real surprise at work. Emma had taken a new job outside the hospital, a junior finance position, at a start-up company. The day before she left, she had invited herself into the CFO's office and had offered a very frank exit interview. He was startled. He was not even sure who she was, but he invited her in and listened.

Emma informed him that the coding errors Mr. Grimes had identified and taken credit for were in fact the work of a coder named Maggie Mueller in the Medical Records Department. "Mrs. Mueller also identified subsequent coding issues as well. I think she should get the credit."

The CFO was nodding his head and taking notes. Emma felt emboldened. "Furthermore," she continued, "*Mr. Grimes is a creep*. He is sexist, crude, and makes slimy innuendos. He tried to give me back rubs and said it was an 'accident' when he grabbed my behind. From what I understand, I'm not the first person he has done this type of thing to. Quite a few female staff members have similar complaints but were afraid to say anything. I was going to go to Human Resources before I left, but I wanted you to know too." The CFO looked grim and asked her a few additional questions.

"And you need to do something in the office about salaries." Emma continued. "At least the women's salaries in the office. We all got talking about Grime's behavior and then salaries came up. He pays the women in the office a lot less. We checked and compared them to the men. Same work, less pay."

Now, the CFO looked angry. Emma worried about what that meant and quickly finished the interview with a few kind comments about how much she had learned at her job and her respect for the work the hospital did. She exited quickly; very glad she had a new position waiting.

Emma came down on her last day to say a final goodbye. She had small tokens of appreciation for both Tammy and Maggie. She told them she would never have gotten the new job without her stint in the Finance Office. She was also proud that she had spoken up about Grime's inappropriate behavior.

"But, Maggie," she continued, "It was you that inspired me to take it further and to get the staff talking about salaries. The guy I was working with tipped me off to it, that the women might be earning less. You have been so open talking about money, you know budgets and my 401k. You are so practical about it. It has changed the way I see money matters entirely. It was odd, though, we all found harder to talk about our *salaries* than Grime's behavior. But now that all the salary information is out in the open, they are better positioned to do something about it. It was empowering."

"And guess what the best news is? Ed Grimes was fired this very morning! Dirty old pervert, deserved it," she said. "I felt bad though that I waited to say anything until I had my new job lined-up. He had been doing this stuff for years. Turns out he also failed to follow through on some of the additional coding issues, there might have been kick-backs involved. So, a crook too. I hope all these old fat sexist dinosaurs just die out soon."

The Grime's departure paid additional bonuses. First, women in the office found they had all gotten unexpected pay rises, their pay now equaled the men. Second, Maggie was called to see the CFO. That conversation had turned into an unexpected job interview, which in turn led to her being offered a position in Risk Management in the Finance Department.

The position would have a strong liaison role with the insurance companies, and her coding experience would be invaluable. There would also be a pay raise, to $75,000 a year. It would mean a change to a salaried position rather than an hourly wage role. Maggie, surprised by the offer, asked to be given time to consider it. The CFO said she could have two weeks.

Changing jobs was a big decision. In the Finance Department there would be a clear career path. The salary, more than she could make with overtime, was enough that Maggie would be able to relax. There was probably a chance to earn even more in the future. Maggie, however, liked her flexible hours and working with Tammy. They laughed a lot. She would also probably lose her ability to watch the market open. Nine to five hours would also make being home for the market close impossible. There was a lot to consider.

Before Maggie had a chance to discuss the job offer with anyone, she had a call from the Residences about her mother. She had gone on a respirator only a few weeks before, after a breathing issue had developed. Maggie had hoped the call might be to say they had taken her off it. Instead, it was the Director with sad news.

Her mother had passed in her sleep.

Maggie had visited her only two weeks ago to check how she was doing, speak to her doctor, and better understand the decision to put her on the machine. Carmen had come in to change her nutritional IV and had expressed disdain for the breathing machines. Maggie had told her then that her mother's lack of written instructions had made it hard for her to do anything about it. Maggie suspected that her mother would be appalled by all the extraordinary measures. She would have wanted to go with her husband, years ago.

Carmen, who was working a double shift—and the night nurse, who had arrived just as Maggie was leaving—both agreed. "Warehousing people," the older nurse sniffed. "These poor people are not going to wake up and start living again. Let them rest."

Only Maggie, her children, Brody, and the retired family lawyer were at her mother's funeral. If her mother had friends still living, and she probably did, who they were and how to contact them had been lost with her mind and the years. It made Maggie sad to see how weathered her father's stone was. She had never really understood cemeteries, but she vowed to try to get down to visit at least once a year. Seeing her parents' tombstones next to one another seemed fitting but it ended an era for Maggie.

Brody insisted on driving home. Maggie felt melancholy, not just from the loss of her mother, who she had mourned for years, but for the loss of her childhood. There were very few people who even remembered her as being part of another family. Her mother's condition had closed off Maggie's ability to reclaim much of her own history. No one had thought to capture the past when they could have.

Her major regret looking back was that she had not appreciated her parents more when she had them. Her brother's death had put a distance between them that she had never worked to overcome. She had let them drift away from her just as she had let her own life drift. She resolved now to make the most of the time she had with all the people she loved.

The children were riding back in Ethan's car. Both cars held the remainder of her mother's things. There was a chair and a writing desk from her grandmother's house, a lamp, three boxes of personal effects, and some framed photos and paintings from the walls. All of it came from her childhood home. Most of her mother's other things had been sold from the foreclosed house last year. Maggie realized it was nice to have mementos from her childhood again.

The real treasure though had been a set of well-labeled photo albums that had probably been used at one time as part of her mother's *memory therapy*. There were photos of long-lost relatives with names and little histories of their lives written in a bold hand. She realized she would be able to decipher much of what was in the boxes she already had. There were also photos of her brother and herself that she had never seen, and, sweetly, of her mom and dad in their youth with their parents. Maggie had suddenly recognized the handwriting as her father's, so the albums became even more precious. They had been a sweet and unexpected legacy.

Brody had said little as they drove back to Olivia's. Finally, glancing over he said, "I think it is time, Maggie. Today. I think we tell Ethan today."

Maggie could not find an argument against it. None of them were particularly overwhelmed by her mother's death, it had been a long goodbye. The finality of it was difficult, but more for her than the children. They had not had a grandmother now for most of their lives. Neal was back and had been told. Her new life had settled into a comfortable routine.

Olivia had planned a late luncheon when they arrived back, and had invited Libby, her daughter, her husband, and their infant daughter. Brody explained that having family around would give Ethan a counterbalance. Ethan could then decide if, and when, he wanted to tell the rest of the family. Since he had his car with him, Brody reminded Maggie that he could leave if he needed to. There was never going to be a perfect time, Brody argued. The company would give Maggie an excuse to keep the conversation short for the time being. Give it a chance to be absorbed. Maggie realized Brody was right.

After lunch, as the desserts were being served, Maggie asked Ethan to come up to her room to help with a computer issue. He followed unsuspectingly. When they got there, she asked him to sit next to her on her bed and she pulled his hand into her lap, holding it tightly with both of hers. She could not meet his eyes. She started the speech she had prepared in her mind for months.

"Ethan, baby, I didn't ask you up here for a computer problem. I have something very hard to tell you and I wanted to us to be alone. It's something that I have only learned about this winter, but that you need to know." Ethan stiffened, but she continued. "There really isn't any other way to say this. It's about Brody. Before I got engaged to your father, I was seeing him; he was my first serious boyfriend. He was at school but also in the Air Force. When he graduated, we broke up because he had to return to Colorado. We weren't ready to take the next step. I met your dad around the same time, and we had a whirlwind courtship. I only saw Brody once during that time, when he flew in from Colorado. The night I accepted you Dad's proposal I was already pregnant with you but didn't know it. We got married quickly because we thought you were your Dad's biological child."

As she turned to look at him, she saw he was having trouble with this. Tears were forming in his eyes. He was like an animal that wanted to bolt but did not see a clear exit.

Maggie continued, "Your dad is your father in all the ways that dads are important, but I think Brody is your biological father."

Ethan held his breath and then said, "Does Dad know?" There was panic in his voice.

"Yes, I told him when I saw him at the prison. After your visit. He was devastated, Ethan, honey. Devastated."

"I would've thought it was like Christmas for him. He never liked me." Ethan said bitterly. Maggie almost smiled at the clear reflection of Neal this phrase represented. Ethan had perfectly parroted his father, right down to the inflection. Maggie knew that the two men were connected for life, even if Ethan didn't see it at the moment.

Ethan then asked some logistical questions, like whether she was sure, who knew, and what Brody wanted. Maggie said she thought Olivia had guessed, and the girls may be suspicious. Ethan seemed angry, "Why? Because we are both tall and blond? Is it *that* obvious? How come I didn't see it, if you all do?"

Maggie emphasized that she and Brody were just going on appearances. Similar height, build, facial features, and some mannerisms. It was not guaranteed but likely. She said, "We, that is Brody and I, will do whatever you want. You can decide if you want a test to confirm it. Or you can let it be. You are in charge and you can decide who and when to tell, if you even want to tell." Maggie inhaled, paused and then said, "But Brody wants a relationship with you, if you do. He has two daughters he would like you to get to know."

"And if I don't want to?"

"He will be very disappointed but again he'll take your lead. He was as shocked as I was, so please don't blame him. He only found out this year. Just be aware though, honey, Brody and I are going to be a couple for a while. Maybe a lot longer. It is not like you can pretend he doesn't exist."

Ethan considered this. He didn't ask any more questions. He finally said, "I want to keep this quiet, until we're tested. See where things stand. Is he expecting us to come down and make a big announcement or something?"

"No, I think he just wanted to be accessible to you when I told you, in case you wanted to talk to him. I don't think he is expecting anything today. You don't have to talk to him if you don't want to."

Ethan was subdued. Maggie was relieved he was not angry at her, at least not yet. It was a lot to take in. He got up and offered his hand to pull her up. He kissed her unexpectedly on the cheek.

"Thanks for telling me, Mom." He turned quickly then and went back downstairs alone.

Brody caught Ethan's eye as he came back down into the kitchen, and Ethan acknowledged him with a curt nod. Brody was anxious to talk to Maggie and debated going upstairs to her but decided against it. She came down a few minutes later and was dry-eyed. She did not seek him out. It was not until everyone left that she had a chance to tell him how things had gone.

"He wants testing done."

"Easy," he said. Brody explained he had done a genetic test with an online DNA database, and all Ethan had to do was submit his as well. If they were matched in the database, it should be proof enough. Maggie was not surprised Brody had already taken this step.

"Did he say anything else?"

Maggie told him she had also explained to Ethan that they were a couple. One way or another, he would have to deal with Brody. She thought the fact they were together would have been an issue along the lines of, "Why is Mom dating so soon after a divorce?" but that issue seemed to be lost in the bigger *Dad is not my Dad* thing.

The two of them talked a little longer about Ethan and what Brody might do next. They decided to leave the ball in his court.

Maggie paused and said, "Come to think of it, the girls seem okay with us as a couple. They haven't said a word, one way or another. Is it odd? Do you think it is because they are angry at Neal's role in Charlie's kidnapping? Or are they just being polite?"

"Hard to say. I think the bigger issue was that Neal was more out of your lives than in it," Brody offered. "He allowed himself to be *just the paycheck*, that is a pretty empty life for a guy. I can tell you from experience. He missed out on a lot that was all there for the taking, right in front of him, every night he came home.

He made the choice, perhaps unconsciously, to make his own life smaller and less satisfying in the process."

Maggie suddenly realized that she had allowed, even encouraged, Neal to be *just the paycheck*. She had not shared the financial responsibilities of their lives. Her passivity had probably been a burden to Neal, may have even contributed to him making the poor financial decisions that had led to his disappearance. His inability to share his financial mistakes probably contributed to the cascade that followed.

Would things have been different if they had shared more about their finances? Could they have stemmed the early bleeding and become closer as a couple—and as a family—as a result? At this stage, it was too late to tell, but Maggie knew she would never make that mistake again. Money should not be a mystery or a power play between partners. Financial literacy was just another form of intimacy for couples to share.

Brody left that evening with a quick kiss on her cheek. They had still not slept together. The divorce coming through had ended up being a minor event because of Charlie. Maggie had focused on helping her, and Brody had to satisfy himself with being on the back burner. It was odd though—his kisses were almost becoming polite. Maggie worried she had missed a fundamental shift in their relationship. Had their moment passed?

As Maggie was executor and beneficiary of her mother's will, she was able to consolidate her account with her mother's fairly quickly. She paid no estate taxes as her mother's holdings were below the estate tax thresholds, both Federal and State. She was also finally able to write calls again on her McDonald's shares. Fortunately, the shares had been valued on the day her mother died, which had been an up day in the market. The price they traded that day was considered Maggie's cost basis. Since then, the shares had fallen in value a bit. If she sold them now, there would be no capital gains, so no tax due. Maggie was in the clear.

Her mother's Trust was dissolved and the remainder of it also came to her. Suddenly she was able to increase her option trading four- to five-fold, and the income from her option trading followed. She could see that with her expanded holdings she might earn close to two thousand dollars per week—over one hundred thousand dollars per year—just trading options. This was more than she was earning coding, and even more than the $75,000 per year the Finance Department had offered. But, of course, Maggie knew that trading meant risk. She might lose a lot any given year too. Working at the hospital meant steady paychecks, health insurance and a 401k. Being a *day trader* might pay more, but then again, it might not.

More importantly, inheriting her mother's Trust, meant her retirement target had been reached. She was now fully funded. She really did not have to work any longer. The dividend income alone would easily provide enough to live on, as long as she stayed with Olivia. Her emergency fund had been topped up to cover six months' salary and her budget had been generously reworked with plenty now allocated for *fun*. Maggie was again free from money worries, but this time she truly appreciated what a gift it was. She would never take money for granted again.

Brody surprised her the weekend after the funeral. He had told her they were going to have a Friday night flying date, to pack an overnight bag. He then drove them to Hanscom Airport. She was surprised that the Excel jet was waiting for them again. She had expected a small plane with him at the controls. As she stepped on, she smelled that this time, he had dinner catered. After they were aloft, he served her on real china plates and the food was superb. They drank chilled vintage champagne. It was incredibly decadent. It re-set Maggie's memories of the plane.

They landed three hours later in Fernandina Beach in northern Florida. They thanked the pilots, who grinned at them both. Brody produced a large overnight bag out of the luggage compartment. He went out to a Jeep that was waiting on the tarmac and opened the door for her. Maggie suddenly realized this was going to be *the* night. She was now single, Ethan had been told, and they were alone. Clearly, Brody *was* interested in more than a polite goodnight kiss. She felt nervous and a little shy.

He pulled in at a private lodge, an old Florida-style resort. It had a weathered, shingled exterior, crisp white paint, and a large wraparound porch with rockers overlooking a lovely, long, deserted beach. They picked up their key and were directed to a private cottage with its own secluded deck facing the ocean. It was late in the season but warm, and very quiet.

Their room was like a movie set: the lights were dimmed, and candles burned throughout the room. A small table was set with linen and china. There were crystal champagne flutes and a full champagne bucket. At the center of the table sat a small, glistening carrot cake. Her favorite dessert, with small plates and dessert folks set out. Brazilian jazz played softly. Deeply scented roses filled the room with perfume, there were even petals on the bed and table.

Outside, on their deck, a fire pit burned invitingly. Beyond that, the rising moon reflected on the calm ocean water. It was superb. Perfect. Maggie just gasped softly.

Brody grinned. That was clearly the effect he was going for. He stowed the bag and came up to her from behind, entwining her in his arms. He reached around and she met his lips, sharing a long, deep kiss.

"Dessert?" he asked nodding at the table.

She realized her nervousness had evaporated. She could not wait any longer. "Not done with the main course," she said huskily, and she pushed him onto the bed. They were both more than ready and any shyness faded as the intensity rose. Clothes melted away. Finally, they smiled at each other as Brodie slid gently on top of her. Neither was surprised when they found that they moved together perfectly, matched in both passion and a deep, primal satisfaction.

Afterwards, they found thick robes which had been laid out in the bathroom. While the candles on the table had burned out, the fire pit on the deck still beckoned. They took their cake and the champagne outside into the still warm evening. Brody filled their champagne glasses. The moon had risen completely, and its reflection was playing on the water.

"Worked for you then?" Brody asked, grinning.

She sighed with a smile and stretched her arms, "Honestly. The disservice people do themselves, denying a build-up like ours! You never get a second first time, but I really think it felt so much better. No comparison. I believe I can even say," Maggie saluted him with her glass, "It was a life-defining event for me. Your age and accumulated experience is impressive, sir. You have done your younger self a great disservice in comparison. Congratulations. Of course, *I do remember some youthful enthusiasm back then*. Can't beat young men in their twenties for enthusiasm. And staying power. Wonderful thing, staying power."

"Hmm, is that a challenge then? Accepted. Looking forward to accepting it already."

They sat companionably in front of the fire in the deck chairs, balancing drinks and cake on the chair arms. He leaned over to stroke her thigh which peeked out of her robe. "Remember when we talked about the future, the night that Graham died? It seems like since then it has been one life changing event after another. First Charlie, then your mother, and Ethan of course. I just wanted you to know that this weekend it is all about us. As I said before, I want to marry you, Maggie. I want you to say yes, tonight. I want to tell people, especially the nice hotel staff who think we're on our honeymoon, that we're at the very least engaged. I want to be able to eventually retire and spend the rest of my life with you."

"Well. Retirement. Not a word that comes up in many marriage proposals." She was quiet for a while before she continued. "It's funny, though, that you say that. Last year, I was living a life most people would envy. I had all the things a person could want, and then some. All powered by plastic cards I never gave a thought to. Yet I felt empty back then and I didn't even know why. And then it fell apart." Maggie smiled at the memory of the failed card swipes at the coffee shop so long ago.

"When I found out I would lose my house; I just went into overdrive. I had to deal with it, fix it, and just make my life work. I didn't ask myself if I could do it, I just did it. I didn't know then that I was pulling myself out of a decades-long stupor. Back then it was all about cash and how I was going to *retire*. Not a thought as to how I was living in the moment. I focused on that future point and fixated on the dollars. Money mattered so much; it almost took over my life."

Brody looked a little confused.

Maggie smiled at him, "But things shifted again when Charlie was taken, money suddenly went back to being a means to an end. A fuel, but not a goal. I have been living in the moment since then. My advice to everyone is to get control of your finances, better earlier in life than later. Life *does* come at you fast, and you never know what it will throw at you. If you start young, you almost *can't* fail. Once you have control, and you've ensured the fuel will be there, you can concentrate on more important things, like family and friends, purpose, even passion," she looked playfully at Brody and arched her eyebrow.

He rolled his eyes, and Maggie laughed. "What has surprised me most, though, is how much I have learned in the last year. Not just the personal finance stuff—though that is as *phenomenally* useful—but the life stuff. I feel closer and more connected to my kids. I have good friends now. I get up every day with a sense of purpose, to go to a job where I am needed and even get a paycheck. And, of course, there's you. I couldn't have even *imagined* having someone I connect with like I do with you. Both emotionally and, thank God, physically. Who knew *intimacy* could be so satisfying? My life is just so much richer, and I don't mean in terms of money."

"Sound like it has been a real journey for you, Maggie. I am happy that I'm part of it," Brody said softly.

"The single most important thing I have learned," Maggie continued "Is that money *matters* because it means freedom. Now that I have it, I will never take it for granted again. I am so lucky that I don't have to worry about money. I don't even have to work for someone else. I could just take the risk and simply work for myself, trading full-time just because I *enjoy* it. I could live anywhere in the world with an internet connection. Now I know how to get and manage money, I don't have to depend on or defer to anyone. I don't have to stress. My finances don't control me anymore, I control my finances. I get to choose. Money matters mainly for the choices and freedom it gives you."

Brody leaned over pulling back her robe to kiss her shoulder. He then dipped his finger into the cake's cream cheese frosting and ran it over her lips. Maggie grinned and responded by running her tongue over his finger lasciviously.

Breathing heavily, he said, "And when you are considering these choices of yours, where exactly do I fit in?"

Maggie leaned over and kissed him with her frosted lips and said, huskily, "Excellent question, sir." She then stood up and let her robe slip to the deck. She said, "Let's just go inside, and *discuss*."

Maggie's Financial Journal

KEY TAKEAWAYS FROM EACH CHAPTER

Prelude: Powerless

Any bank accounts that support your life should have your name on them. If a spouse or partner become incapacitated, or go missing, without signing authority on the account, you have no legal access! *Deferring to a spouse or partner when it comes to managing your money leaves you needlessly vulnerable*.

Set-up overdraft protection on bank accounts in case of unintentional overdrafts.

Chapter 1: Credit is not Just About Cards

It is useful to have some actual cash on hand, in your home, in case of emergencies. One hundred is a good start. Two to three hundred would be terrific.

Always have a **printed** backup of useful contacts for every family member. These should include last names, telephone numbers and addresses. In case of emergencies, you may not be able to access a family member's phone for these critical contacts.

Scan or create duplicates of critical family paperwork. Original paperwork can be destroyed or go missing. Make sure family members know where originals and copies are kept. Use the Cloud!

Start building your credit score as soon as possible. You must be at least 18 years old to get a credit card in your own name. Use it sparingly, and always pay it in full, and on time (late payments reduce your credit score).

The primary user on a credit card, usually someone with a good credit history, can **authorize** additional users on their card (usually children or spouses). These additional users are not responsible for the debts incurred on a card, and generally do not build credit in their own name. The primary user can cancel authorized users at any time, and if the primary user dies, authorized users will find their cards cancelled.

Joint credit cards build credit for both individuals, but also mean both parties are equally responsible for debts. Credit cards companies generally prefer to issue cards to a primary user, not joint.

If you can't get a credit card, prepaid credit cards are another way to start to build credit. These can be very useful for teenagers or young adults just starting out.

Know your credit score! You can find it online. It will range from 300 to 850. Having a good score, say above 740, will get you cheaper rates on car loans and mortgages.

A bad credit score can: stop you from getting a credit card, mortgage, or a bank or car loan. It may also keep a landlord from renting to you or stop an employer from hiring you. Good credit scores are a result of having credit and using it responsibly. (That is, paying bills in full and on time.)

About Bank Accounts:

- Make sure you have signing authority on all bank accounts you share with a partner or spouse.

- Consider separate, individual accounts for discretionary spending for each partner or spouse. Agree how these will be funded, that is how much goes in and how frequently. Doing this allows each person to spend freely on things important to him/her and eliminates arguments over individual choices.

- Have one account devoted to emergency savings and don't touch it except in true emergencies. Emergency savings should equal approximately six months of salary.

A trust is a legal entity which can own assets for the benefit of specific beneficiaries. If you, or anyone you co-own property with, creates a trust for that property, make sure you know who the trustees are. Trustees have *full* control. But if you co-signed on any debt that trust holds, you are *personally* liable.

YOU ARE NOT POWERLESS WHEN IT COMES TO UNDERSTANDING YOUR FINANCES! Get with it.

Chapter 2: Facing Foreclosure

Do not sign any documents without understanding what you are signing!!! Pay attention to any document related to financial commitments like mortgages or credit cards. Once you sign, you are responsible for the debt even if the other party does not pay.

Keep on top of your mortgage: Know the payment schedule, the approximate balance and how much you are paying in interest versus principle (the loan amount). If you find yourself unable to pay your mortgage for any reason:

1. Contact the bank as soon as you can and explain your problem. Ask what they can do to help until you are able to resume payments. ASSUME THEY WANT TO HELP.

2. Options banks can offer include suspending or reducing payments or paying interest only. They are unlikely to reduce the loan – you will have to pay it all back eventually!

3. Ask the bank if they are aware of any government programs that you could access to help you meet your obligations.

4. If you look like you will be unable to keep your house, consider a 'short sale.' This means the bank agrees that you can sell the house on your own and you arrange to pay the bank back what you owe. This way you can keep the money that your raise that is in excess of the mortgage balance.

5. Avoid foreclosure if possible. If the property does go to foreclosure, make sure you clear your personal effects out before the bank takes possession. Also, check what the property is sold for to see whether you are due money (if it was sold for more than the mortgage owed and the banks expenses related to the foreclosure sale.) Foreclosure will negatively impact your credit score for 7 years!!

To avoid having to pay mortgage insurance, target at least a 20% down payment when buying a home. A down payment of 20%, and a good credit score, will also mean a lower interest rate on your mortgage. You can get a mortgage with a smaller down payment but it is likely that will mean a higher interest rate and having to pay mortgage insurance, adding **substantially** to the total cost of the loan. TARGET 20%.

In the first few years of a mortgage, most of the payment is simply interest to the bank, not principle. Prepay whenever possible to reduce the principle, this will mean that every monthly payment will be less interest and more money being directed to reducing principle.

A house's furnishings can have value. It is useful to keep a full inventory on hand, with an estimated value. This is useful for insurance purposes and to help with resale of items if and when it comes to that. Do not accumulate junk, if you don't need it, sell it or donate it. Less things means less to take care of, less stress overall.

Having hobbies are wonderful but making a living from one is unlikely. They can, however, be a useful source of extra cash. Side 'gigs' can help raise cash for emergency savings or just fun money.

Chapter 3: Cash is King

CASH IS KING! At the end of the day, you need cash to survive.

Even in a world where credit cards and electronic payments are everywhere, you still need cash. It is especially important, if you lose the ability to have or use your credit cards or your electric payment systems. Power does fail occasionally. Keep a cash 'kitty' in your home – if possible a couple hundred dollars would be terrific.

If you need to raise cash in an emergency, do not overlook things that may have unexpected value. Online sites will give you an idea of what things might be worth. Many sites charge the buyer shipping and shipping companies will pack items for a fee. Clearing clutter can be profitable!

Selling online is easy but take precautions. Do not fall for scammers asking to wire money to you or visa-versa. Well known sites like E-Bay and Amazon rank buyers and sellers. Always choose the well-rated buyers.

Best option: ask for cash to be paid in person. Selling locally will often yield the best price. Do not let strangers into your home (unless other household members are there). Wherever possible, take small items you can carry to a public destination to sell them. Be prepared to have someone offer less in person than they did online (a common occurrence. Know if you are willing to accept it.)

A leased car has no residual value to the person who leases it. It is better to own a less expensive car outright than lease a luxury car.

Housing costs should only be about 1/3 of your take-home pay.

Know what you can afford. ***If you can't afford something, do not buy or live in it!***

Living below your means, will give you the ability to save money.

Chapter 4: Liquidity is Not about Water

Assets like furniture and furnishings may be worth significantly less when selling them – it's not the value to the seller that matters. It is the value to the buyer that determines the price.

If you have a lot to sell, consider hiring a professional like an estate agent or re-seller. They will take a commission but may identify things for resale you missed.

There are ways to turn spare change into cash. Some banks may take rolled coins for free or use Coinstar Machines (which take a percentage). Save those pennies!

Online banks are a good alternative for people looking for lower fees and higher interest on savings accounts. Since they do not have storefronts, their costs to operate are less and they can be more generous with depositors when it comes to fees and interest paid on accounts. Just make sure they offer all the things you need: a way to pay people, a way to deposit money, online and ATM access. Check to see what other services they offer as well.

Whenever using an online financial institution, make sure it is FDIC insured so your money is safe if there is an issue with the company.

There are a variety of ways to pay people using online services like Venmo. Learn about them as they are increasingly used by individuals and companies. Not everyone accepts online payments, but many do, and it eliminates the need for checks. Banking is evolving and it is best to pay attention and understand new innovations.

Money Orders and Cashier's checks are ways to turn physical cash into something that can be deposited or sent electronically or physically. Beware though, if lost they are like cash and can be converted back into dollars by anyone.

Getting online access to accounts gives you an ability to monitor what is going on. It is critical to have access to all your financial information online. Learn to use the sites, click on tabs and see where they take you. Make sure you use **secure** passwords to these accounts and do not use the same one for each account. These accounts should be the hardest for anyone to get into. Check accounts at least once a month.

Chapter 5: Net Worth is Only a Number

Net worth can be a mirage. Expensive looking houses can be mortgaged to the point the bank actually owns them, expensive cars can be leased, jewelry and other luxury items may have been bought on credit. "Rich" people may really just be people that owe other people a lot a money.

Credit card debt is the **WORST** type of debt. You are probably paying well over 20% per year in interest. Pay off any credit card debt ASAP. Do not let it accumulate. If you need cash to live, try and find some way to borrow money for less than the 20% or more the credit card companies charge. Avoid running up credit card debt at all cost.

Jewelry is not as valuable as people think – often it is worth little more than the actual value of the metal or stones. If you have a written appraisal for piece, hang onto it! Helps with resale. If something is not in fashion, it may just be melted down.

Designer clothes and purses hold value better than jewelry.

Vintage electronics, particularly gaming systems, can be valuable.

Do not overestimate the value of personal items or antiques – just because you paid a lot does not mean they are worth a lot. Having receipts and a 'story' for an item can make it more valuable in the eyes of a buyer. Use online sites to get a sense what something is worth – look for what people are asking for similar items.

Garage and estate sales can raise substantial sums of money (and clear a lot of clutter).

Chapter 6: A Budget that Fits

Prepare a Budget! It helps organize finances and clarifies what you can afford. Make sure you put aside money for savings, healthcare, retirement and fun. It does not have to be complicated, keep it simple. The main benefit is that a budget will force you look at your expenses and allocate them realistically. Keeping to a budget can be a great first step to financial security.

If you don't budget something for fun, you are likely to break your budget.

Do not forget health insurance! A health crisis can bankrupt you *or the people who love you*. Even if you have insurance, a co-pay can be very large. **Again, having an emergency fund is critical.**

In your early years, lower your living costs to help fund savings – consider living at home (but offer rent to your parents or help with their expenses!), take a room in someone's house or look into house sitting options. The more you save when you are young the less you will need to when you are older.

Look on secondhand internet sites or consignment shops for things you need – better prices and better for the environment!

Be prepared to supplement your income with overtime or even a second job. Remember, salaries tend to grow over time. Your starting salary is not what you will be earning 10 years later.

Chapter 7: The Government's Cut

There are lots of online resources to help to prepare a resume.

While applying for jobs online has become the norm, it can be impersonal and depressing. There is a lot to be said for going in person to apply wherever possible.

Dress professionally whenever you are interviewing - including informational interviews - or even dropping off a resume! Always try to be the best dressed person there.

Building a network of people to find about openings is also key. Talk to friends, family, friends-of-friends, parents of friends, etc. You never know where a job lead may come from. Let **everyone** know you are looking for work and follow-up on **any** lead.

Hiring a career coach, if you can afford it, may help you focus. There are also free online career assessments which could help narrow your search.

Always be honest in job interviews. You can put a positive spin on things but do not lie. Recruiters like to see energy, curiosity and the ability to learn quickly – have examples ready! It is illegal to ask about things like race, religion, pregnancy status, age, disability, citizenship, marital status or number of children. Salary, however, **should** be discussed. It is usually presented as a range. **Do not be afraid** to talk about money, it's a big part of why you are there!

When going to interviews, **DO RESEARCH.** Know about the company and what it does. If possible, check out the person you might be interviewing with. It is not stalking to check out someone's resume on LinkedIn. Practice interviewing online if you have not done it before. Have a set of questions you want to ask memorized. Get someone with experience to do practice interviews with you. You will be judged about how prepared you are, how much effort you made. It tells an interviewer a lot about how willing you are to go the extra mile and do the work necessary to get the job done.

Arrange references! Most jobs will want to call either former employers or people you have worked with before, even on a volunteer basis. Make sure you have spoken to people and they are willing to act as your reference before they are called out of the blue. If possible, let them know what you have said during the interview and why you think you would be a good fit for the job. Giving a reference some background will make them more relaxed when speaking to a potential employer.

A first job is not likely to be your best job. You may not be in the industry you want or being paid what you think you are worth. Be grateful for it and show enthusiasm, remember, it is only the first step on a lifelong ladder.

Keep your phone off during interviews! Use it minimally while at work.

Taxes are part of life. A big chunk of your income will go to paying Federal, State and even local taxes. On top of taxes, you will also have to pay FICA, which is another government payment you make to fund your future Social Security and Medicare payments. **UGH. Take advantage of any tax deferred accounts you can.**

A W-2 is a statement of the money you have earned for the year, and what you have paid in taxes. It is how the government (the Internal Revenue

Service or IRS) knows what you have earned and how much you have already paid in taxes.

SAVE MONEY by making food at home and taking it to work. Eating out for breakfast and lunch drains away money that could be saved. And it can be healthier.

Plan for healthcare needs! Ironically, the longer you live (the healthier you are) the more you may end up paying for healthcare. More years equals more cost.

Healthcare costs, *excluding* long-term care, are generally *at least* 10 to 20% of a retiree's expenses, often more. This includes cost for supplemental health insurance, co-pays and out of pocket expenses, prescription co-pays, dental and hearing costs. These costs often blindside retirees. **Medicare only pays 80% of medical expenses, at best.**

Long-term care costs can range from $50,000 a years to over $100,000 depending on the facility – and these costs continue to rise. **Most people fail to prepare for this possibility despite the fact well over 40% of people will need it.**

A health savings account (an HSA) lets an individual put up to $3500 in a fund that grows tax deferred. The amount you put in is also tax deductible. You will receive a debit card to pay for healthcare expenses not covered by insurance, like co-pays. Ideally, use *your after-tax cash* to pay for healthcare expenses while you can and let the HSA grow, undisturbed and tax deferred, until you absolutely need it. **CHECK IF YOU ARE ELIGIBLE!** These under-utilized accounts are a great tax savings.

It is possible to do your own taxes! At least once in your life, everyone should get a copy of the 1040 or a 1040EZ form. These are the forms used to file your federal income taxes. You can get them from either the post office or online. You do not need a tax preparer for a simple return. To fill it out will require an hour or two and basic math – fourth grade or less. You can even file online. Remember to also do your state tax return as well!

If you sign a joint return, you are responsible for what is on it. At minimum, review the front and back page of the 1040 form to understand how much money you and your partner made for the year. **Ignorance is not a defense!** You will be held responsible for any irregularities on your tax return, even if it was your partner, not you, that made false representations.

Chapter 8: Taking Stock

Paper stock certificates are not in general use anymore. If you find old ones, contact the company, or its parent, to see if they are viable.

A stock or a share of a company represents a percentage share in a company. You buy stocks to share in the success of that company through either an appreciation in the share price and/or by receiving a share of the profits in the form of dividends.

Stocks trade on 'exchanges'. There are many, across most countries, but the biggest is the NY Stock Exchange (NYSE) where over 6,000 companies trade. The NASDAQ, London and Tokyo stock exchanges are the next three biggest but together they are not as big as the NYSE.

There are many indexes that measure the performance of the US stock market. The most important are the DOW, the S&P 500 and the Nasdaq indexes. When these indexes are going up, the market is 'up.' Falling, and the market is 'down.'

Again, stocks generate wealth in two ways; 1) they appreciate in value and/or 2) they pay dividends.

♥**Over the past 100 years, annual stock returns (adding both appreciation and dividends) have averaged over 10% per year!!** Recently, however, this has fallen to more like 6 to 8%. Better than interest on a savings account.

It takes money to make money!

Chapter 9: Compounding is a Girl's Best Friend

There are many ways to learn about stocks. The best way is by doing, buy a few stocks and learn how to follow them. Learn in little bits as you go along. Financial professionals can make it seem more complicated than it is. Do not let yourself get overwhelmed. Investing in the stock market requires knowledge. You also need to learn about the business world. Reading the Wall Street Journal, paying attention to economic news and taking advantage of online resources can make a huge difference. Improve your financial literacy!

To trade stocks, you will need a brokerage account. A broker is middleman that facilitates you selling shares on the stock exchanges. Some banks have brokerage arms, some brokers can act like a bank. Easiest way to trade is to see if your bank has a brokerage arm. Or open an account with one of the many online brokerages.

Always check on what it costs to trade. Normally there is a commission on each trade. Fees, however, can be negotiated or even waived when opening a new account, especially a large one. And there are usually 'new account' promotions that offer a set number of free trades. Be wary of firms offering 'free trades,' ask how they get paid. Free trades can mean less customer service – which can be frustrating for people new to investing.

Investopia is a great online site which explains and defines investment terminology in simple language.

DRIP stands for Dividend Re-Investment Plans. You can designate all dividends you receive from a company to be automatically re-invested rather than accumulate as cash in your account – makes it easy to build a position in a particular company over time.

An **investor** buys stock to hold and appreciate over time. A **trader** is someone who buys and sells in short periods to make a quick profit.

Do the homework – watch videos and take advantage of investor education offerings of your brokerage house. Read books. Good starts are simple ones like <u>The Little Blue Book that Beats the Market </u>by Joel Greenblatt. Or try <u>Get Rich Carefully</u> by Jim Cramer and watch his show CNBC's Mad Money. He tries to make investing accessible for everyone.

AGAIN, DO NOT BE OVERWHELMED BY NEW TERMS! Forget the Greek alphabet for the time being. Keep it Simple Stupid – the KISS principle.

Trusts are a legal entities generally used to house substantial financial assets for the benefit of specific people or causes (the beneficiaries). Trusts can simplify probate when someone dies. Trustees are designated when a trust is set up and they have legal control over the assets held by the trust – not the beneficiaries. They have a legal obligation to carry out the purpose of the trust – but may not execute their role effectively.

♥**Compounding is critical to long term investment success.** Interest and dividends should be allowed to stay in an account and grow overtime. Money should always earn some type of return to take advantage of compounding. The longer compounding has to work, the better.

START SAVINGS WHEN YOU ARE YOUNG. It is a lot harder to make up for lost time later. The younger you are when you start savings, the more compounding will do the work for you. It is never too early to start.

Chapter 10: Fixed Income and the Problem with Fees

Fixed income refers to investments which are specifically selected to provide an income stream over time. Traditionally, fixed income accounts relied primarily on bonds that paid a quarterly coupon. With today's low interest rates, fixed income tends to involve dividend stocks in a well-established companies that historically keep and increase their dividend. Ideally for companies that have reliably paid a dividend over a long period of time (often called a Dividend Aristocrat) and/or dividend stock funds that may include mixes of bonds and dividend stocks.

Principle is the original sum committed to the purchase of any assets—independent of any earnings or interest.

When you purchase a **bond**, you are loaning money to an entity, company or government agency, which agrees to pay you a set interest, usually on a quarterly basis, until an agreed upon date of repayment of the principle (that is, the money you loaned them).

- **Bond Terms to Know**: Principle, coupon, maturity date, face value

- **Bond Principle**: is the initial size of a loan or a bond (the amount the bond issuer must repay).

- **Coupon:** interest payments on a bond, usually paid quarterly or twice a year

- **Maturity date:** The date the principle is to be paid back, in full, to the investor

- **Face Value:** Also called *par value* is the amount that is to be paid back to investor on the maturity date. Bonds can be traded before maturity dates! If bought or sold they may cost more or less than face (par) value because the interest rate they pay is higher or lower than the current interest rate.

TAX ALERT! Interest on Bonds issued by government entities (Municipal or *Muni*) may be **tax free** to the investor! Normally interest on bonds are taxed at your ordinary income rate.

BEWARE OF CHURN in managed accounts. If someone else is managing your investments and there seems to be a lot of buying and selling - find out why. There may be commissions on trading that make it lucrative for managers to buy and sell a lot. They may be costing you money!!

BE WARY OF FINANCIAL ADVISORS! Unless an advisor is a designated fiduciary (a legal term) he or she may not be putting your interests ahead of theirs when managing your money. If you use an advisor, make sure they are a fiduciary!

UNDERSTAND FEES. In a world where interest rates are low (below 3%), a manager's fees may significantly eat away at returns. Look for low or no-fee funds and always ask about fees and *expense ratios* so you understand them. It is possible to trade for little or no cost on your own. *Active* managers have not done very well when compared to plain vanilla index funds. **Do not be intimidated, ask about fees!**

Beware of *alternative investments* or any investment that you do not understand. Know what you own. If you don't understand it, and it can't be explained to you in simple English, it is not worth investing in.

Chapter 11: Understanding Limits

Compare fees at brokerage firms and compare promotions for opening accounts they offer. Getting free trades is a common incentive many firms offer when opening an account.

When placing a stock order online, always choose the *limit* order, not *market*. Set a price you want to pay for a stock and then wait for the price to come to you. BE PATIENT! If you don't get an order filled immediately, wait. You can always enter it the next day. Getting a stock at the lower end of the range it trades in, means you are more likely to show a profit on the stock right away.

Avoid GTC (Good Till Cancelled) orders when buying a stock. If the market makes a sudden shift, you could get caught paying more than you have to. Better to re-enter an order each day until you are *filled* (that means you get all the stocks you wanted to buy).

Always **REVIEW** an order before making it final. It is easy to misplace a digit or add an extra zero.

Money market funds can be used help generate cash on money you are waiting to invest. A money market fund is a kind of mutual fund that invests in cash, cash equivalent securities, and high-credit-rating, debt-based securities with short-term maturities (like U.S. Treasuries). Money market funds are intended to offer investors high liquidity with a very low level of risk.

Sweeping is a term used by banks and brokerage firms to describe taking excess cash from an investment account and putting it into a money market account until you are ready to invest. You can also sweep for yourself by investing in money market funds offered by companies such as Vanguard, Fidelity, etc. These funds usually pay more than a typical savings account with very little risk.

Chapter 12: Unexpected Benefits

There are many retirement saving vehicles available. Employers often offer retirement plans as a benefit, frequently matching contributions by employees in some way.

Individuals can also open retirement accounts in addition to their employers plans. These are called IRAs or Individual-funded Retirement Accounts and can be self-managed.

For profit companies offer retirement plans called 401k's. Non-profits organizations, like hospitals, can offer 403(b) or 457(b) plans, which are similar to 401ks. All of these plans are tax advantaged. Some allow contributions to be made pre-tax. The key is that these plans let the investments in them grow and earn dividends tax-free. This allows any income earned in these accounts to compound, helping retirement savings grow. There will be taxes owed when funds are withdrawn in retirement, but the expectation is that a retiree's tax rate may be lower then.

If an employer *matches* 401k contributions in some form, it is effectively **FREE MONEY.** Two key lessons: 1) start retirement saving as early as possible to give the maximum time for returns in the account to compound, and 2) contribute the maximum you are able to, so you get the greatest match possible because **Free money is free money.** Most firms will give you up to 6% of your salary for free in a retirement match – that is like a 6% raise.

Most employer retirement plans deduct money from each paycheck. This is then invested no matter what the market is doing. If the market is up, you pay more for a stock. If it is down, you pay less. This steady contribution system means you are investing using a system called ***dollar-cost averaging.***

You can access your 401k online. **LEARN HOW TO DO THIS**. (Ask your HR department.) Once online, learn two key things: how to change the percentage of your salary going into your 401K and how to change what you are invested in. **IT IS EASY.**

Once you know how to change the percentage of your salary going into your 401K (see above), if the market falls, consider increasing the percentage of your salary you are contributing to take advantage of stocks being on sale!

Talk with your benefit officer or human resources department to understand your retirement plan. Know what funds you have in it and how they are performing. Try and understand what funds your plan offers and check regularly what their returns are compared to the other funds on offer. Be prepared to change allocations if you have poorly performing funds. **PAY ATTENTION TO YOUR MONEY.**

Passive funds generally have lower fees and better returns than actively managed funds. Simple index funds, those that mimic a stock index like the S&P 500, usually perform better than the majority of actively managed funds. They can be the best choice for a retirement fund. Passive fund fees (expense ratios) are generally below half a percent(<.5%)

Most retirement plans offer Target Date Funds, or something similar. These are funds that are intended to change the mix of investments they hold as you age, moving into more conservative holdings later in life. (And the expense ratios, aka fees, on these funds are generally higher than a passive fund.) These are fine if you are on track in terms of your retirement savings. If you are behind, you may want to be more aggressive with your selections to try and make up for lost time. This, however, is a riskier approach.

Chapter 13: Making Choices

When investing, ask yourself: 1) what are my objectives, and 2) what is my timeframe.

- If you are trying to grow money, be prepared to assume some risk. The more growth you want, the more risk you generally have to assume.

- If you are trying to preserve money, focus on safer investments that generate income like stocks that pay dividends. Be prepared for lower returns, closer to three to five percent per year.

- Your time frame should be based on how long you have until you think you will need to live off your investments. The longer the better!

Keep it Simple! Do not complicate a stock portfolio. Know what you own. If you don't want to do the homework associated with owning a stock or if you have less than $10,000 to invest, **a simple S&P index fund is best.**

Understand the difference between **TRADING** and **INVESTING**. You 'trade' in and out of stocks in a short timeframe, even daily. You *invest* over a longer timeframe, usually a year or more. Investing is easier, trading requires commitment and paying a lot of attention to the stock market.

There are two major approaches to stock analysis. **FUNDAMENTAL** analysis involves researching the company itself, its finances, its products and markets. **TECHNICAL** analysis involves research the *price action* of a stock and looking for mathematical patterns and trends in the stock price itself. Fundamental analysis tends to be a better approach for investors who are just starting out.

To choose a good stock, look first for a good company. Then look at the stock price and decide what you are willing to pay for it. Sometimes the stock of a good company can be too expensive to buy, you may have to wait for the stock price to come down to a better level. Be patient. Stocks always go on sale at some point, especially during a market downturn or when there is a bump in the road for a company.

YOU WILL LEARN AS YOU GO. Analysts reports are a good place to start learning about a company and there are many places to access them for free. Do not expect to learn everything at once, good investors learn by starting small and then adding to their knowledge over time. You have plenty of time to learn - Investing is a lifelong activity.

Beware of advice – try and rely on analysis from **independent** sources like Morningstar, Reuters, etc. A lot of people recommend stocks because they benefit if they can convince people to buy them.

If looking to invest for dividends, there are four key things to consider:

- **Cash Flow** - Successful companies generate cash. When looking at a company, the annual income they report can be misleading due to a number of reasons. Always check *cashflow* as it is generally a better indicator of how well a company is doing.

- **Payout Ratio -** This statistic tells you whether the company can afford to pay its dividend. Payout ratios can vary by industry but greater than 100% is a red flag. This means the company is not making enough money to pay its dividend and may stop paying it (which is likely to cause the stock price to fall a lot!)

- **D/E or the Debt-to-Equity ratio -** This tells you how much debt a company has – always try and invest in companies with as little debt as possible.

- **P/E or the price to earnings ratio -** This ratio can tell you if a stock is *expensive* relative to peers. A value below 10 can indicate a stock is currently *undervalued*. A stock trading in a range of 10 to 20 can be considered a reasonable priced stock. **Remember P/Es can vary a lot between industries!** A very high P/E may be justified if the stock is a special case like a small company that is growing quickly.

Dividend Aristocrats are companies who have paid an increasing dividend continuously for over 25 years. They can be good companies to start with when creating a low-risk portfolio.

No one is going to care as much about your money as you will

Diversification helps protect a portfolio in case a given sector or industry hits a snag. It spreads risk. The stock market categorizes companies into eleven sectors with various industries segments in each of them. Try and select stocks from different sectors as you build a portfolio.

Use a *stock screener* to help identify potential companies to invest in. You can search by sector or industry.

PRICE MATTERS! Do not overpay for a stock. Look at the range of prices for a stock over the course of a year and try and decide what you are willing to pay. Select a price at the lower end of the stock's range. Remember, if the P/E is over 20, the stock is relatively expensive. Look at peers in the industry and compare P/Es, consider whether the company is growing. Beware a very low P/E, the stock could be cheap for a reason.

If a stock pays a dividend, the lower the price you pay, the higher the dividend yield to you will be. Remember: The dividend amount is fixed (unless the company changes it), so the yield (what percentage return you get for what you invest) will change depending on what you pay for the stock. Try and buy dividend stocks when they are *on-sale*, this often happens when the market sells off and good companies' stock prices go down as much as the bad.

Buy stocks in thirds! Buy a third first, and then wait to see what happens. If it goes lower, buy another third. Lower still, another third. This will lower the average price of your investment. Less *buyer's remorse* if it goes down. If the price does not go lower after your purchase, be happy with your gain.

Greed is not good. Patience works pretty well over the long run. You will almost always get a chance to buy more of a stock you like at a lower price as market and stock downturns are inevitable.

Chapter 14: Stocks and Bond Baskets

A college education is a major investment. **Question whether in today's digital economy you or your child truly <u>needs</u> to go to college**. A college degree is not for everyone and there are excellent career options outside of a traditional four-year degree. This is particularly true in healthcare and technology. Less than a third of parents can afford to pay in full for college – and many parents who do pay sacrifice their retirement.

College kids should do whatever then can to help pay their college bills. Live at home, take up part-time jobs, work at a paid job in the summer. **Work also helps job prospects after college and is an essential part of building both work experience and a job-search network.**

Try <u>**everything**</u> to graduate without debt. Having debt when you are young makes saving much more difficult.

CONSIDER THIS: Assume an 18 year old person, invested $25,000 a year for four years (instead of going to college) into a tax deferred retirement account. By the time she/he turns 60, the money will probably have grown to well over one million dollars.

A stock portfolio should be diversified to spread risk. Given the number of stocks available you can diversify many ways: across industries, by company size and even geographic location. If you only have a limited amount to invest initially, an easy way to diversify is to buy a stock or bond *basket*.

When looking for a dividend stock, do not 'reach' for yield. If a stock pays a high dividend, check why. Has the stock price dropped recently because the company is in trouble? Can it afford to pay its dividend? A company that pays a high dividend (more than a 5% yield) always needs checking out. If it suddenly reduces or stops paying its dividend, it may see a *significant* drop in its stock price.

In addition to looking at analysts' reports and company statistics (P/E, D/E, etc.), **check out senior management**. You can use Google to find videos of them talking about their company's performance and prospects. These can give you a good feel for what type of leaders they are. Interestingly, companies with women CEOs have performed better, on average, than those with male CEOs.

Bonds should be part of most portfolios. They generate income and have less risk. Buying a bond is different than buying a stock. It may require the assistance of a specialty 'bond broker.' A simpler alternative is to buy a bond fund, which is a basket of bonds. These funds can be researched like stocks. Ideally, look for a fund that holds high quality muni bonds (they should be AAA or AA) to limit tax on bond interest income.

The financial crisis of 2008 led to major changes in financial markets. It is also a great cautionary tale about the folly of "get rich quick" schemes and the impact of market crashes. Watch the movie The Big Short.

Mutual funds and ETFs are similar – both offer a basket of stocks. The major difference is liquidity. You have to wait until the end of day to sell a mutual fund. ETFs can be traded throughout the day on the stock market.

Check fees on funds. For two similar funds, select the one with the lower fee.

A simple index fund, which mimics the S&P 500, may be the best entry for a new investor with less than $10,000 to invest.

Active fund managers, i.e., stock pickers, generally underperform the market. **Passive** funds are generally a better investment as they have lower fees.

Chapter 15: Growth and Risk

In investing, stocks with higher growth prospects tend to be riskier investments. The stock price may appreciate faster, but it may also drop suddenly. These stocks may be called *momentum* or *growth* stocks.

Stocks that move up rapidly, with P/Es of 40 or more, and that have very little or no financial justification (i.e., no earnings) are the riskiest of all. These stocks, some of which are called "cult" stocks, are probably too risky for the regular investor. BEWARE.

Risk-adverse investors prefer to invest in established, financially strong companies with steady demand for their products or services. Returns, however, for lower risk portfolios are frequently less than 4%.

Risk-seekers look for newer companies with plans to grow. Risk-seekers accept that there will be volatility in their choices. They may enjoy returns, on average, of approximately 9% annually. (Although some years their returns can actually be negative.) Growth stocks generally do not pay dividends.

One way to assess growth is to use a PEG ratio, Price/Earnings to Growth. This ratio is a useful way to look at potential growth companies. It can be a trailing PEG based on historic growth rates or future PEG based on future earnings estimates. The ratio relies, however, on growth projections made by management or analysts. These estimates may not always be realistic. It is useful to look back over time and see how well management has met prior estimates to assess believability of growth projections. **A PEG of less than one is good!**

Portfolio planning involves accessing your 'risk profile.' It is normal to move into less risky holdings as one nears the age you will need to draw on the money. You do not want to lose money shortly before heading into retirement as you will not have the chance to earn enough to replace the money you lose.

Social Security is not enough for most people to retire on comfortably. It is intended to make up only about 40% of a retiree's income. Sadly, a third of Americans rely on it for 90% of their retirement income. Do not become one of these Americans!

A target of a 6% annual return on retirement investments is reasonable.

If any single holding in a stock portfolio becomes too large because it has appreciated in value, trim it (i.e., sell a bit) to keep the portfolio 'balanced.' As a rule of thumb, no one holding should be more than 10% of a portfolio.

Be prepared to buy if the stock market drops suddenly. When the market drops more than 10% it is called a *correction*. It will mean that stocks are effectively on 'sale' then. Have a list of what you want to buy and be disciplined, buying in thirds. It is unlikely you will catch the 'bottom' of any correction but buying a stock when it is down over 10% means it will be easier to make 10% on that stock when it eventually returns to its old trading range (which stocks generally do).

Try not to panic during a stock market correction!

Estimate your investment timeframe. This is the number of years from now until you are likely to stop working. You will have to rely on Social Security and your savings to live – calculate how long you have to invest. The longer the better.

If you have not been able to save for retirement, you may need to 'catch-up' and focus on investing in stocks with greater growth potential. Look at a company's PEG (Price to Earnings to Growth) ratio to help you understand its growth potential.

Identifying growth stocks may require more research than a beginner may be comfortable doing. Use stock funds focused on growth if you are uncertain which growth stocks to buy – there are many *growth* funds and ETFs. Chose those with low expense ratio and a good performance track record.

Remember the principle of *reversion to the mean*. With stocks, this principle means that while stocks trade in a range that trends upward, they will always be at the lower end of that range at various points over the year. Use this principle to help set a price for a stock at the lower end of that range and then be patient. Wait for the price to come to you. You do not have to buy a stock on the same day you add it to your shopping list. Sometimes it can take weeks or so to reach a price you are comfortable paying. The benefit is that when you buy at the lower end of the range, when your new *stock reverts to its mean*, you will have a profit.

If you have dividend paying stocks, check if the company has a DRIP (Dividend Re-Investment Plan). If you decide to participate, your dividends will be used to buy more stock in that company.

Again, if you have a *target date* or *age appropriate* allocation in your 401k, check whether this makes sense for your personal situation. If you are trying to catch up, you may need growth funds in your 401k! Most employee sponsored retirement plans have growth funds in them. Also, remember to check your 401k online every quarter – know how it is doing. **Do not set and forget your 401k.**

Chapter 16: Options are Not Stocks

Again, growth stocks are generally riskier. If you want growth stocks in a portfolio, a less risky alternative may be to buy a growth EFT or mutual fund. Risk will then be pooled over a basket of companies.

Blue chip stocks are generally large, well-established and well-known companies. Given their size, rapid growth is unlikely. You can add smaller companies - which may grow a lot faster – using a small or mid-cap ETF or mutual fund. There are also ETFs for international stocks and specific market segments. ETFs can help diversify a portfolio.

When thinking about your *portfolio* of assets, remember to consider your 401k holdings. You may be able to balance your investment risk overall by having an investment account with conservative holdings while using your 401k for growth stocks, or vis-a-versa.

There are three good ways to buy stocks:

1. **Legging or stepping-in –** As discussed, this is buying in thirds over a short period of time

2. **Dollar cost averaging**   Which Is what is done in 401ks and other retirement accounts. The plan manager buys every month regardless of price assuming there will be months you overpay, months you underpay, so you get a solid average over the course of the year

3. **Selling Option puts...**

Options are contracts. You are agreeing to buy or sell stocks on a set date. Each option contract represents 100 shares. **Option trading is not investing.** You need to keep track of it. You can use options to increase the money you earn off an existing portfolio.

You need special permission to trade options. You must fill out a separate form. There are many levels of option trading – beginners should start on Level One.

Never trade on the margin, especially when trading options.

If you want to buy 100 shares of a company, consider using a ***put*** option contract. You can sell a contract that says you will buy 100 shares of the company's stock at a set price (the *strike* price) on a certain day (the *expiry date*). You pick the price and the day. If the contract sells, you have *opened* a contract and will collect a *premium*, usually cents per share. The contract will *close* when it expires on the expiry date or when you buy it back.

The most basic option contracts are *cash-covered* or *cash-secured* puts and *covered* calls. Cash-covered puts means that the owner has either the cash or the securities she could liquidate to pay for the stock if she is *put*. Covered calls means that she owns the stock she has written a call on, and it will be sold at the agreed strike price if she is *called*.

Chapter 17: Enhancing Returns

The value of option contracts (the premiums) is derived from the underlying price of the stock they are written on. If the price of the underlying stock changes it will generally impact the premium value. Usually, a small change in a stock price, say 1%, can change the related option premium significantly.

Option premiums can swing dramatically over the course of the trading day, sometimes reversing course multiple times. In times of higher market volatility, premiums tend to be higher as there is more risk in predicting market direction. Also, individual stocks with higher volatility often command higher option premiums.

Stocks are traded both before and after the stock market officially opens. The pre-market and after-hours market, while open to retail investors, is where professionals trade large blocks of shares. While activity there can help predict market direction, it not generally recommended that beginners trade either before or after regular trading hours as prices can swing significantly.

How the stock market will *open* is generally predicted based on the trading that goes on after-hours, geopolitical or economic events or even the earnings of particular stocks. While the pre-market prediction of how the market will open can be a useful barometer, it can also be wrong. Or the stock market's direction can change quickly after the open due to any number of events.

The daily stock market is influenced by a wide range of events. Rumors, tweets, news stories, economic reports, or even stock specific information, can heavily influence the market. There is no set pattern, anything could happen at any time. This is why owning stocks is considered riskier than holding cash.

Watching the volume of shares traded on the market helps a trader understand whether there is conviction as to the direction of the market. High volumes of people selling stocks generally suggests people think the market is moving down. High volumes of buying means most people see the market moving up. Little or no volume means people are unsure of a market direction and are waiting on the side lines.

The first hour of trade frequently sets the tone for the day. Orders placed in the first hour of trade, particularly at the lower end of a range, are often filled. The last half hour of trade, 3:30 to 4:00 p.m., is frequently when you see the greatest volume of stock trades. A lot of machines trade then on automatic buy or sell orders. Day traders pay particular attention to the open and the close of the markets.

There are three ways stocks can make money for you: they can appreciate in value, they can pay dividends, or they can be used as collateral to write and then collect option premiums. Make your money work for you!!

'Cost basis' is the term used for the cost to purchase a stock. Once the stock is sold, the owner subtracts the cost basis from the sale price to work out the profit (or loss) that was made.

When an option contract is sold, it shows a negative *cost basis* despite the fact that the owner of the contract has been paid for the sale and cash has gone into her account. This is because, until the contract is *closed*, that is until it has expired or been bought back, the contract is a liability not an asset and it shows as a negative.

Stock gains are shown as either *realized* or *unrealized*. Realized gains result from the purchase and then the sale of a stock or option. 'Unrealized' gains or losses are *paper* gains/losses. They show up as positive or negatives in a brokerage account but until the stock is sold, there is no actual taxable gain or loss.

Since an option contract's price can vary over the course of a day, it can show a gain or a loss at any one time. In addition to daily fluctuations, as an option contract get closer to the day it expires, it tends to get closer to their actual underlying value. This is because there is 'time decay' built into an options contract. As it gets closer to its expiry an option contract varies less as the likely outcome becomes clearer.

Use the KISS principle (Keep it Simple, Stupid) when learning about the stock market. Do not over invest in specifics like alphas or betas or the wide range of ratios and financial data. Focus initially on understanding a company and what it does, how its industry works and what the general economic trends are. It takes years to learn all just the basics, there will be plenty of time later to learn about more sophisticated market analysis tools if you want to. It is not necessary, however, to understand everything to make money in the stock market.

Options can be used to supplement the income you earn off stocks. If the stock is not called or put before option expiration, you simply keep the premiums you were paid when you wrote the contract.

Stock or options held for less than a year are taxed at normal income rates. If held over a year, they are taxed differently, at long-term tax rates. Long-term capital gain tax is usually equal to or less than 20% (depends on the income level of the owner).

There are taxes on trading profits. Make sure you put-aside money from trading profits to pay taxes each year. Consult a tax professional if profits or dividends exceed ten thousand a year.

Publicly listed companies have to report earnings every quarter. These reports can cause a company's stock to swing wildly, particularly if the earnings do not match the estimates made by management or analysts who cover the stocks.

Make sure to include any investment income on your taxes!

Chapter 18: Death and Taxes

While it is possible to do your own taxes, investment activities (selling stock/earning dividends, etc.) can complicate your returns. Consider a hiring a tax professional if your investment activities generate multiple 1099s. (These will be sent to you by your banks and investment firms at year's end, just like a W-2s)

Pay attention to whether a stock sale will trigger a long-term (over a year) or short-term gain. If you can push the sale until after a year anniversary, the tax impact will be less.

Pay attention to tax liabilities and make provisions for payment as you go. Being surprised by a hefty tax bill at year end is not pleasant.

Your tax liability on investment income will vary based on your total income. The more income you have, the more you will pay in taxes on your investments.

Dividends are, currently, taxed at a lower rate than regular income. This may change so pay attention to tax rulings.

Always consider the after-tax yield of dividend income versus safer investment alternatives like bonds or money market funds. Again, do not reach for yield!

Some states have special taxes related to investment income. There can be extra tax surcharges beyond regular income tax, check what your state does!

Invest in tax deferred accounts wherever possible! IRAs, 401ks and other retirement funds are excellent ways to defer taxes. You can buy and sell stocks and options in these accounts and pay **no** taxes until you withdraw the funds. Ideally this will be after the age of 65.

Try and keep on top of your tax records throughout the year. One simple file to collect all tax paperwork as the year progresses means they are readily at hand when tax time arrives, which can be a great stress reliever.

Keep copies of all your tax returns. A digital copy (scanned) is generally the norm but a paper copy as back-up can be helpful.

The IRS has extensive powers. Keep clear records, file and pay on time and always be honest. If you respect the law, they will not bother you. Remember though, **ignorance is not an excuse.** Make sure you know, and review, what your tax returns say before you sign.

Chapter 19: Estate Planning

No one likes to talk about death but ignoring the realities can greatly complicate things for loved ones who survive you. Leaving them to scramble at a time when they are mourning has led to families being needlessly torn apart at a time when they really needed one another.

Wills can be simple or complex. They can be downloaded from online sites or worked through in great detail with an estate lawyer. They must be dated and signed by at least two witnesses. Either way, they are essential and should be a priority for everyone regardless of age. They should also be revisited after major life changes like marriage, divorce, birth of children or death of a spouse.

In death, marriage trumps most relationships unless a Will makes specific provisions. A new spouse can disenfranchise children, ignore charities and disavow spoken wishes. A written, witnessed Will ensures that your final wishes are respected.

Setting out what you would like for your own funeral is not morbid. It will probably limit arguments between family members. At minimum, specify cremation versus burial and where you might like to be interred. Remember if you would like obituaries written, specify by whom and which publications you would like them placed in. It may save family relationships that frequently fray over these types of decisions.

If you are the type, plan your funeral service! If possible, make sure there is cash available to pay for things like the funeral parlor, the venue where the service will be held, the food, etc. This can make things less stressful for those that survive you.

Consider leaving a letter or even a video for loved ones. These final missives are often priceless to family members. Remember a video or letter is not a substitute for a witnessed Will.

End of life planning should always include the following four documents:

1. <u>A witnessed Will.</u> This can be updated via witnessed *codicils* as needed

2. <u>A living Will</u> (often called an advance directive) that specifies what measures you would like taken if you are unable to communicate your wishes yourself. For example, do you want to have machines breath for you? How long should family members wait to disconnect machines if you are unlikely to regain consciousness? etc.

3. <u>Power of attorney </u>(POA) is a legal document that gives a person the power to act for another person in the event that person is unable to. The degree of authority granted by a POA can be limited to medical care, finances, property or it can be a broad authorization to act in all these areas. A healthcare proxy is another type of legal document that can grant someone power to make medical decisions for you.

4. <u>A revocable trust</u> – a trust allows beneficiaries to avoid probate court and guardian or conservatorship proceedings, all of which can be lengthy, time consuming and potentially costly (if third parties like lawyers are involved). While this trust has upfront costs to set up, avoiding court proceedings after death will simplify distributions to heirs. It is 'revocable' by the person who establishes the trust so changes can be made, for example beneficiaries changed, assets added, etc. <u>A trust does not eliminate the need for a will.</u>

Option contacts trade like stocks and can be bought or sold at any time. If a contract goes positive, consider closing it and re-writing it again.

Earnings season comes four times a year, generally about two weeks after each quarter ends. It extends for a two-to-three-week period during which the majority of publicly listed companies report their quarterly earnings and their estimates for future performance. Stocks can be very volatile during earnings season, offering chances to pick good companies on sale, or to sell a position, if the market overreacts one way of the other, which is common. Option contracts can swing even more wildly during this period. It can be a particularly fun time for traders, while attentive investors can sometimes pick-up stock bargains.

Chapter 20: Bull and Bear Markets

STOCK MARKET DROPS ARE INEVITABLE. When they are large and sudden is very hard not to panic. Hang on. Remember, they always pass eventually.

Bull markets do not last forever. Since investing is generally over a lifetime, average returns will prevail. A negative year or even two (bear markets) is not a reason to give up on investing.

Stock market corrections and crashes can be triggered by many things. Geopolitical crises, bad economic news, or simply a change in investor sentiment that snowballs into a major sell-off. Sometimes it is hard to pinpoint a single cause. You never know when it will happen, but it will. Try and stay calm through downswings. Focus on the simple fact that over a lifetime of investing, the trend is upwards.

Corrections (when the market drops about 10%) are generally short term. No one can time when it starts or when the market will turn and start to recover. It is better to simply stay in the market and not sell rather than to try and time getting out and then back in at the right time. Corrections appear to have gotten shorter in recent years; some have lasted only days.

Bear markets (when the market drops 20% or more) tend to last longer, an average of three years.

If you can't stand the stress of a market downturn, tune out. Do not keep checking your balance or turning on the news. As Elsa sings, "Let it go."

If you can stand the heat, consider buying when the market falls. Stocks are on sale. If you have a 401k, consider changing your percentage withdrawal to buy more in a downturn.

As Jim Cramer, the television host of CNBC's 'Mad Money' says, "No one makes a dime panicking."

There are a variety of ways to **help** protect your stock holdings (nothing is going to work completely, all the time, unless you hold only cash):

1. Select bread and butter, conservative stocks that are not considered *over-valued*. These generally drop less in a downturn.

2. Diversify, while in a correction or bear market, all stocks tend to drop, some industries or segments may do better, or even rise, in a falling market.

3. Use Stop-loss orders where appropriate. These *sell* orders are triggered only when a stock reaches a certain price. They are free to set up. The risk is if they are triggered by a routine slip of the stock market that quickly recovers, so you end up selling at a lower price than the stock normally trades at. If you want to re-purchase the stock you may have to pay more. Stop-loss orders have to be regularly re-entered (a GTC order generally lasts only 60 days). It can be time-consuming to manage stop losses across a range of holdings. They tend to be most useful on stocks that have a big gains that you want to protect.

4. A 'trailing' stop-loss works on a percentage basis, following the stock up as it gains in price. A common **Trailing** stop-loss order is set at 10% below where the stock is trading. Again, these orders have to be regularly re-entered. Trailing stop-loss orders are particularly helpful on stocks that have a lot of momentum and are rising quickly. These types of stocks are more likely to have sudden reversals where you may want protection.

5. Perhaps the best protection is to purchase a put option. This allows you to *put* your stock to someone at a set price. Put purchasers gen-erally buy put contracts at a strike price similar to where the stock is currently trading. Expiration dates are often well into the future. While they can cost a bit, you can choose the duration of a put contract, so it is easier to manage. Ideally set the expiration for a date that ensures you have held the stock for a year or more so that your capi-tal gain is long-term.

In times of higher stock market volatility, option premium prices tend to be higher. (Better for you when selling option contracts.) If buying options for pro-tection, it is cheaper to do so in times of low volatility when premiums are lower.

The most common measure of market volatility is an index called the VIX. It measures implied volatility of the S&P 500 based on the prices of its options. A value of below 12 is considered low, 10 to 20 normal and when it is above 20, it's considered high. The higher the VIX, the higher option premiums are as there is more uncertainty in the market.

If you enter stop-loss orders, you cannot write covered calls as a means to increase returns on your stock. If the stop-loss were triggered, you would have *naked* calls which can be problematic for inexperienced investors.

Just like setting a price you would like to buy a stock at, you should also set a target price to sell a stock at. A good price target is when a stock shows a gain of 25% or more after tax, especially if that gain is within a year of buying a stock. When it reaches that price, be prepared to sell some or even all of a position. It is important to have an exit strategy when you buy a stock. Remember, your profits on three stocks that gain 25% (assuming you re invest all your profits each time) is about equal to having one stock that gives you a 100% gain. And is generally easier to find stocks that gain 25% versus one that gains 100%.

Never let a single stock become too large a percentage of your holdings. While there is no hard and fast rule, if you own ten stocks, no one stock should be larger than 10% of your portfolio. If you own twenty stocks, no one should be more than 5%. Re-balance your portfolio every six months or so to make sure you are well diversified. A stock portfolio of over thirty stocks is difficult, even for professionals, to manage.

Chapter 21: Why Money Matters

Learning about personal finance, how money works in your life, and then handling it effectively, is a gift you give yourself. It can:

Empower you

Reduce stress

Build confidence

Enhance intimacy with your partner

Strengthen your children's life skills

Carry you through tough times

Ensure you can retire happily

Give you choices

Women can be, **and are**, very good at managing money and investing. While learning how to manage and invest is a process, a year of effort can make an *impressive* difference.

Financial transparency, talking about money is good for couples, good in the workplace and generally positive overall. Money is not something you should be are afraid to talk about. (Although bragging is always tacky.)

Fixating on a future date or financial target misses the point. Control of your finances frees you up to live in the moment and enjoy the important things in life like purpose, passion, friends and family.

Remember, Maggie's law:

Finances should not control your life; you should control your finances.

Money *matters* only as it is a means to an end: A happy life.